FEARFUL SYMMETRY

Book Two of the Fenaday and Shasti Chronicles

EDWARD MCKEOWN

Ad Astra Books

Fearful Symmetry By: Edward McKeown
Copyright © 2012 Edward McKeown
First Published by Hellfire Publishing, Inc 2012
First Ad Astra Edition Published 2013

For my mother, Catherine McKeown

Introduction

CLAUDIA CHRISTIAN, STAR OF BABYLON 5

Fearful Symmetry is well named. There is fear, as well as is hope in this fast-paced tale of action and thoughtful adventure. Edward McKeown has written a gripping story of espionage, assassination, and interstellar conspiracy. It's also the story of a woman coming back to life metaphorically, in a tale of resurrection and redemption. So the book operates seamlessly on two levels at the same time.

Edward told me that Robert Fenaday was the main character of the Fenaday trilogy, which began with **Was Once a Hero**, but it was Shasti Rainhell who captured my attention, especially in this second book where she is the focus of much of the story. Maybe I identified with her because, for all her genetically engineered strength and superiority, she is a woman, dealing with the issues that occur in so many women's lives: a hard and ungiving childhood, abusive spouse, the fight to find and retain one's integrity in world that won't extend recognition willingly. Her struggle spoke to me, as, if you have read my own book Babylon Confidential: A Memoir of Love, Sex, and Addiction then you know that I have dealt with more than my share of this.

For me, Shasti is the sort of character that I see too seldom in fiction. Many of the "woman warrior" characters do not seem to be actual women. As one writer I met complained, they just seem like "men with breasts." Shasti manages to retain her essential femininity while provoking fear, sometimes panic, in her enemies. She is powerful, independent, and intelligent, yet there is a longing in her for gentleness, for connection, and even for love. She is at once an uncertain girl and a confident professional fighter. Hey, maybe I can play her when Ed sells the movie rights! Seriously this is the type of character that appeals to me. Like Susan Ivanova from *Babylon 5*, Shasti has a rich interior life and emotional complexities that make her so appealing, I sometimes found myself thinking how I would play her... we'll have to wait for the movie...

In the midst of star-spanning battles and action, Edward makes sure his people, not characters but people, as they seem very real to me, are always aware of the beauty of existence and the fragility of their own lives. One feels at any moment that each of them, Robert Fenaday, Shasti Rainhell, Telisan and his fiancées, Mmok, are all at hazard, each could be taken from the reader as so many people are taken from us in real life, without warning, or without our being ready for it. So read but be ready. Don't look for stock characters who will effortlessly sail through adventures without being scarred, scared, or changed by them. And like those self-same characters, breathe deep when the action pauses, look around at the stars, the ice-ring overhead, or the friends that you are so lucky to have with you, protecting your back.

Be grateful for it all. Enjoy the read.

I did

Claudia Christian

Prologue

The war against the Conchirri irrevocably altered the Confederacy of Seven Species, as the Seven collided with and destroyed the eighth race in known space. The Conchirri, usually called the Xenophobes, possessed only one reaction to any other life form: genocidal fury. They could not be understood, reasoned with, or intimidated, only destroyed. It was a hard lesson for the Confederacy, but they learned it well. The Second Sector War ended the Conchirri and, with them, the old Confederacy, which had been little more than a trading association. The Seven now watched the stars warily, with weapons to hand and a grim promise of "never again." They had looked into an abyss, and it had looked into them. In that much, they'd become the thing they'd destroyed.

Much else disappeared in that war: lives, hopes, and loves, including Lt. Commander Lisa Fenaday and her scoutship the C.S.S. *Blackbird*. Her husband, Robert Fenaday, went nearly mad with grief. Flying a captured frigate renamed *Sidhe*, he roamed space, searching for his wife, and killing Conchirri mercilessly. Shasti Rainhell, a genetically engineered assassin rescued by him on one voyage, joined him in his search. They became a team, until the war ended and the market for privateers dried up.

In despair, Fenaday landed on Mars, only to find himself drafted by Lisa's former boss, a man identified only as Mandela. With Rain-hell and two new companions—ace-pilot Telisan and the ancient scholar, Duna—Fenaday voyaged to the devastated world of Enshar. They defeated the ancient evil that had scoured the planet clean of intelligent life. *Sidhe's* survivors and Fenaday, who finally laid the ghost of his wife to rest, began to pick up the pieces of their lives. But the past has a way of reaching out for you...

Chapter One

"Y ou drive a hard bargain," Gianni Martini said. His elegant face showed some of the strain of the marathon session.

Shasti Rainhell ignored the arms merchant's comment. She looked out from the balcony toward the skyline of Old London, her back to the buzz of the reception that the Martini-Henry Company had arranged in her honor. London's restored beauty made little impression on the colonist, though it was thousands of years older than any human city she'd visited before. Shasti had come to buy weapons for the re-established Shamrock Line of New Eire. The war with the Conchirri might be over, but space remained far from safe.

"I take it that we have a deal then," she said. "You'll send the contract over to my hotel, and I will have our solicitors review it."

Martini waved his arms in a grand gesture. "As you wish. Shall we have a drink to seal the bargain?" He gestured to a nearby waiter. The smartly dressed servant presented the platter of champagne with a flourish. Gianni plucked two tulip-shaped glasses. He presented one to her, looking up at her with a speculative gaze.

He wasn't the only one. Even in cosmopolitan London, Shasti attracted attention. At six foot-nine, she towered over the partygoers. She was marginally aware of men staring at her with interest, captivated by her flawless ivory skin and jade-green eyes. Women also stared, though some of the looks held a touch of envy. In Olympian society, where genetic perfection was social status, Shasti was an aristocrat of the highest order, for all that she had lived as a hunted fugitive for most of her life.

Shasti took the glass and drank. Champagne was new to her life, though she could easily afford such luxury now. The success of the starship *Sidhe*'s desperate voyage to Enshar had made her wealthy. Money meant only two things to Shasti: security and independence.

"I'm not used to looking up at a woman. Are all Olympian colonists so tall?"

"We're bred for size and strength," she replied, knowing where the conversation was leading. Business was over. Gianni Martini was handsome, wealthy, powerful, and he saw himself bedding her, adding to the long collection of women he'd doubtless had.

"And all so beautiful?" he asked.

Shasti controlled the stab of annoyance. *Predictable*, she thought. *How many times have I heard the like from men?* "Beauty is relative. Sometimes it's even a weapon." A gust of wind stirred her long black hair, and she closed the seal on the severe crimson jacket she wore.

"Thank you for the champagne," she said. "Please send for my security."

"What? You would deprive us of your company so soon?" Martini made a gesture of mock horror.

"Our business is concluded," she said. "I have other things to accomplish for the Shamrock."

"Ah, you mean for Robert Fenaday."

Shasti's jade-green eyes narrowed. She didn't like the sound of his name on Martini's lips.

Martini edged closer. "He is far away, and he doesn't own you."

"It is as well for you that he is a long way away," Shasti whispered. "And no one, no one owns me."

Martini saw his hopes of an exotic conquest fade, and the pleasant mien slipped. A retort died on his lips as he looked into her eyes.

Don't push me, little man, she thought. *I've killed more men than are in this building.*

"The contracts will be in your suite by morning," he said. "I'll have my assistant attend to it." He started to turn his back to her, but some instinct stopped him, and he backed away carefully. Shasti laid down her empty glass and strode from the room, people spilling out of her way. A limousine and her hired security awaited her at the entranceway. In minutes, she was back at the Dunhill Hotel.

Hours later, Shasti stalked out of the quaint, but expensive, Dunhill, wandering through the streets of London, confused and angry. She knew she should have stayed in her secure hotel room preparing for the next day's meetings. It would have been sensible, but after a few hours the room became oppressive, cage-like. Restlessness struck with full force and drove her into the streets.

Martini's comment had pulled off a scab. Robert did not own her, but once she had been property, a human not selectively bred—but made. Her creator, Jalgren Pard, headed the House of Denshi Assassins on Olympia. In the labs of the Order of Geneticists, Pard fashioned the template that gave rise to Shasti's existence. In designing her enhanced body, he endowed her with capabilities too near his own. The miscalculation nearly cost the master assassin his life when she escaped. She had lived free since, working on the wrong side of the law with the only talents she had.

Now, a Confederate pardon shielded her from all her past crimes, and the law sided with her. Still, life remained dangerous for an enemy of the Denshi order.

I wonder what Robert is doing now, she thought. She pictured Fenaday, sturdy, shorter than her, as most men were. He was nearly ten years older, with a pleasant, if not handsome, face, dark-brown hair, and green eyes.

They'd fought about their future the night before she left New Eire, a subject he usually raised. Shasti rarely thought beyond the day, turning aside his attempts to do so. In truth she could not even form a picture of her future life; it was so far out of her experience. She found the closeness of their relationship alternately exhilarating and frightening. Pard had designed and raised her to need no one.

Now she felt an absence. Letters and holo-messages from Fenaday helped, but they also emphasized the change in her. She felt incomplete and vulnerable in a way she couldn't understand and wasn't sure she could risk.

"No one owns me," she repeated to herself. "No one." She pushed thoughts of Robert and the disturbing complication of her feelings for him out of her mind. *I belong to myself.*

She passed the night as she had in her mercenary days, in darkened bars and clubs. Shasti drank excessively, seeking distraction, still moody and irritated, but she didn't experiment with other drugs. Alcohol, her body could shrug off by an act of will and manipulated chemistry.

A woman approached her in a club, her long blond hair spilling down her back. She was blue-eyed, lithe, with a well-toned body not much concealed by her dress.

"Hello," she said, looking Shasti over in a fashion she usually received from men. Women had expressed such interests before. Shasti had never responded to it. This time she welcomed any distraction from her thoughts.

"Hello," Shasti replied coolly.

"Ah," the woman said. "I thought your voice would be lower. I like it this way. It's musical." She moved close to Shasti, brushing against her. Shasti quelled the urge to knock her flying. People did not casually touch her. "Buy you a drink? My name is Sandara."

"I'll buy," Shasti replied. She wondered if the woman could be part of a trap, but Shasti was not known to be interested in women, making Sandara a poor choice for bait. It should be safe, perhaps even save her from her present mood.

A lot of drinks later, they ended up at Sandara's apartment. Shasti felt as drunk as she could remember being and willfully refused to use her body's defenses to shed it. Shasti threw her jacket on the floor and, with Sandara's eager help, quickly shed the rest of her clothes.

Sandara slipped out of what little she wore, then stepped back to look at Shasti. "My god, you have a fantastic body."

"Quiet," Shasti said. She leaned forward and swept the smaller woman to her, turning and pressing her to the wall. Her lips met Sandara's full, sensuous ones.

"Easy, big girl," Sandara said with a quick, nervous laugh. "Not so rough, please."

Shasti eased her grip on the smaller blonde, and Sandara's smooth, taut body slid down against her own. Shasti bent her head down, and Sandara's eager tongue darted into her mouth as her hands roamed over Shasti's body. Her legs came up to wrap around Shasti's waist.

After a minute, Shasti stopped, drawing a shaky breath. "Bedroom," she demanded.

"Second door on the right," Sandara gasped.

Shasti carried the slender woman toward the bedroom. Sandara laid her head on Shasti's shoulder. Her long, soft, blond hair mixed with Shasti's own night-black.

"You're so strong," Sandara whispered.

Shasti said nothing but tumbled them onto the huge bed she found inside the door, quieting Sandara with her mouth. She wanted neither to talk nor to think. She found her lips on the other woman's small, firm breasts, so soft compared to a man's. Fenaday's chest hairs always tickled her nose when she did this. She thrust the errant thought aside. No thinking. She tried to lose herself in the other woman's soft sighs of pleasure.

Her fingers explored Sandara's quivering body, followed by her tongue. She decided she must be doing it right as Sandara's breath began to come shorter and shorter. Finally, Sandara arched her back and cried out, her thighs clasping Shasti with startling strength.

Shasti rolled over and Sandara slid on top of her. "My turn," she said with a mischievous grin. She kissed Shasti passionately, starting with her lips and drifting to her nipples, then lower.

Shasti shifted, wishing for Sandara to find the right spot, the place where Robert would touch her without being asked. She stroked Sandara's head. If she didn't slip her fingers through the long hair, she could almost pretend it was him. *Stop*, she said to herself, *concentrate.*

It took some time, but fantasy and Sandara's flicking tongue brought her to a small climax. It satisfied Sandara, who moved up to play more. Shasti went with it.

Sandara told her vividly what she wanted. Shasti's hard body seemed to drive her wild. *Well*, thought Shasti, *if I decide to do something besides killing people, I'll have at least one other talent.*

Eventually Sandara collapsed, exhausted. Shasti felt vaguely frustrated, despite the other woman's enthusiasm. At least the experiment confirmed her belief that she preferred men. She wondered if it was her genetic programming or her own desires shaping this.

Shasti showered and dressed quietly, but Sandara woke as she put on her shoes.

"Won't you stay?" Sandara asked, blinking sleep out of her eyes.

"No," Shasti said. "I have work to do in the morning."

"Please take my number," Sandara asked, disappointment on her face. "Call me before you leave Earth. I'd love to see you again."

Shasti took it to avoid argument. Clearing the door of the apartment, she threw the number away, dismissing Sandara from her mind.

A hangover couldn't be as easily forgotten, even by her genetically engineered body. She'd allowed the alcohol in her blood too long. Still, she detoxed faster than a standard human. A growing depression waited beyond the physical misery. As she walked back toward her hotel, it occurred to her what she done with Sandara was callous, even brutal, a symptom of the emotional deadness with which she struggled.

A final revelation lay beyond that one. Fenaday would be hurt if he knew. With that realization, she came face to face with what she had been avoiding, the reason for her restlessness, for the trip away from the comforts of his home on New Eire. She no longer belonged entirely to herself. The realization brought a stab of an old fear. Fenaday cared for her, maybe loved her, whatever that meant. He was not like her ex-husband, Jalgren Pard. Yet, the thought of any man having a hold on her opened old wounds. She wanted, needed, the closeness he offered, but the reflexive habits of a lifetime bound her.

Suddenly, she felt a new emotion, shame. She should not have been with someone else. Created as property, Shasti would die before becoming chattel again, but standard humans made different claims on each other. They lost some freedoms, gaining new and different ones. The thought of the hurt Fenaday would feel gave her a strange, weak feeling. When she finally reached her own hotel, sleep eluded her. She sat by the window, watching the city lights, feeling more alien than ever. Hours later the sun came up, and she was no wiser for the vigil. *Well,* she thought, *I can at least do what he sent me here for.* Quickly, she dressed and summoned her security.

———

S hasti spent a long day negotiating the purchase of a five-thousand-ton Standard Assault Transport from the Confederacy. The vessel would be perfect for landings on unimproved fields on Colony worlds. She left the Confederate Embassy, deciding to walk back to the hotel alone. Her hired security protested, but the driver dropped her back in downtown London as she directed.

Again, she wandered about the old city, hoping that the crowds of humans would ease her aloneness. They didn't. She wandered deeper and deeper into her own thoughts.

As Shasti turned the corner by Harrods, something jarred her from her reverie. There was wrongness about the street. She drifted into the storefront and studied the area with a trained eye. It took a few minutes, but she spotted several overlarge and bulky men, positioned where she would have placed them. They were aware of her, trying to watch and not watch. Another minute revealed a woman of average build with a bag the right size to conceal an auto-pistol or laser. Shasti began to wonder about the wisdom of her unprotected venture.

A heavyset, middle-aged black man strolled up her side of the street. It attracted her attention, as he intended. His slow approach was meant to signal peaceful intent. As she studied the oncoming figure, it clicked. Fenaday had given her an exacting description of Mandela, the code name used by the spymaster who'd blackmailed them into the near-suicidal Enshar expedition. A standard human, strong in his youth, she assessed, but late middle age had begun to show. He met her eyes and smiled broadly, walking up to her.

"Fenaday described you well," she said. With the street so crowded and Harrods' front door at her back, she felt safe enough. She gazed over his head at the gunmen in the street, wishing she'd been able to smuggle a pistol into England.

"Hello, Miss Rainhell," Mandela said, his voice rich and pleasant. "I've seen images of you. They don't live up to the real thing."

Shasti ignored the comment and waited.

Mandela sighed. "I have a business proposal for you."

"Why would I consider working for you?" she asked, disinterested. "I almost died on your previous assignment."

"For the best of all possible reasons," he replied in good humor. "Like last time, I have something you want."

"What would that be?" she asked.

"How would Jalgren Pard's head on a silver platter suit you?" He smiled again.

Shasti faced him directly for the first time. Something terrible looked out of her beautiful eyes. Mandela froze; the gunmen in the street shifted nervously.

"Keep the platter," she said in a silky undertone known to very few still alive. Mandela offered her a chance for something she longed for, even dreamed of: Pard's death at her own hands. Only one thing could bring the spymaster to her, an assassination.

"I take it I have your interest," the spymaster said. He turned, waving a hand. The woman with the bag nodded and spoke into a concealed mike. A late-model aircar, its road wheels down, cut through traffic and pulled to the curb.

"May I offer you a lift?" Mandela asked.

She remained still and silent for a few seconds, evidently surprising Mandela. She was thinking of Fenaday. On Enshar, he'd impulsively promised to help her against Pard, if they lived. She didn't doubt that Robert would fight, even die, to protect her, but it was another thing to go into the lion's den. It suddenly came to her why she'd never reminded him of the promise. She'd feared Fenaday would follow her to almost certain death on Olympia. Unconsciously, she had put Pard as far from her thoughts as she could, delaying the crisis. Shasti stood, hovering between the life only recently opened for her and death—hers or Pard's.

"Yes," she said, choosing death. *I can't give up a chance at killing Pard,* she thought fiercely. *I can't forgive what he did to me, how he touched me, what he made of me. It's all I know,* she thought, in mixed relief and sorrow. *If I live,* she promised herself, *maybe I will be able to make it up to Robert. If not, maybe he will be better off anyway.*

Chapter Two

A month later, Shasti stood next to Captain Daniel Rigg, Confederate Air Space Assault Teams, on the small bridge of the Marine Raider, *Wraith*. Rigg had led the ASATs on the Enshar expedition. At six-foot-six and in perfect training, he could pass for one of the lower to middle orders of Olympia's genetically stratified society. Next to them, Captain Wargo, the *Wraith's* Skipper, stared intently at the images on her screens as the five-thousand-ton attack transport crept toward Olympia's orbit. The other four members of the bridge crew manipulated boards and controls in the low, red light of the horseshoe-shaped bridge. The world Shasti fled years ago loomed in the screens of the stealthy marine raider.

"Olympia," Shasti said, "an ideal gone mad."

"How's that?" Rigg asked.

Shasti shrugged.

"Come on, Rainhell," Rigg said, a smile playing over his dark, lean face. "Talk once in a while. I've read what there is to read. I need more. You're my native guide. Start guiding."

After a moment, she replied. "You've been to some of the separatist colonies."

"Yeah. They didn't always work out as well as New Eire. Think of Retief, Sappho, Lakota, and that disastrous Croat Colony."

"Olympia is unique," Shasti said. "It's a creed, not an ethnic group. Many of Earth's finest athletes followed Dr. Allessandro to this place. After minimal terraforming, they built a society based on ancient Greece's worship of human perfection. The healthiest mind, but only if in the healthiest body. It started with high ideals and beneficence. It degenerated to where the deformed, or ugly, need not apply. To where people became products. Olympians are supermen and superwomen; failing to measure up courts death.

"Most of humanity regards us as a bizarre cult. Only a few Olympians served in the Conchirri War and only under their own officers."

"Things are changing," Rigg observed. "When the Conchirri brought the roof down, going your own way seemed like less of a great idea. Even the Moroks and the Dua-Denlenn have stayed in the wartime alliance.

"We're here to make sure it stays that way," he added. "Pard and the Olympian government are buying surplus ships and weapons at a phenomenal rate. Part of the buildup is showing up in a much more robust Olympian military, much to the annoyance of Mr. Mandela. He wants to know where the rest of the stuff is going. Mandela tried getting sanctions passed, but the legislature wouldn't go for it. Too many individual planets are strapped for cash and want to sell their surplus military equipment."

Shasti shrugged. She didn't care about the government's motivations; she wanted Jalgren Pard.

"There's a nice ice ring looping around the planet," Wargo said. "Never saw a ringed Earth-type world before."

"An ice-comet shattered in Olympia's orbit sometime before the planet was colonized," Shasti said.

"Must be pretty at night," Rigg said. "Good for tourism."

Shasti eyed him.

"Joke," he said.

"Olympia is very mountainous," Shasti said, turning back to the screens, "with many volcanoes. The interiors are deserts, freezing at night, brutally hot in the day. Most of the settled areas of the planet are in the greener, more comfortable equatorial regions. That's where we will find Marathon, the planetary capital. It's on the coast, at the foot of a gigantic plateau."

"Not a lot of ocean," Rigg observed. "Well, we won't have to worry about parachuting into the sea then."

"There will be plenty to worry about without that," Shasti continued. "Our weapons will be enough to deal with the oscots, vendran, and other wildlife. My fear is running into a Denshi patrol, or a force of Olympian regulars. What is the latest from your ground contact?"

"We're still on for a HALO drop over the northern sector near Manki, at 0300," Rigg said. "Nothing new. I hate landing so far from the capital city, but we don't dare drop any closer. It will take at least a week to get from Manki to Marathon. Then we'll have to see what we can do about getting a shot at Pard."

"Pard," she said, her voice cold as February moonlight.

Rigg looked at her curiously. He knew she held a grudge against Pard, though he didn't know the nature of it. What he did know was that the woman was a consummate killing machine. It comforted him to think she was with them, until he remembered even she feared Pard.

"Yeah," he said. "The big trick is getting off planet again. *Wraith* will wait as long as she can. The *Intruder* will head for the rendezvous two days after the attack signal is sent. If we can't get back to the rendezvous point, then we'll have to try to break out using civilian transport. We have no other means of contacting the raider ship once the *Intruder* moves out of range."

"I remember the briefing," she said coolly. "As a last resort, we get to the Confed Embassy, and they try to get us out."

"Yep, they'll be just thrilled to see us too."

"Mr. Rigg," Wargo called, "ETA to the drop point is five hours and three minutes. From there you go in the *Intruder* and hope the brain boys are right about her invisibility to detectors. We've got two big space stations and a couple of patrol lines to cross. So far we've been lucky."

"Well, time to check equipment," Rigg said. "Thank you, Captain."

Shasti nodded and followed. They went down the narrow, green-painted gangway to the armory.

"So, Rainhell," Rigg said, ducking through a hatchway, "how did assassination become so respectable on Olympia?"

"Like everything else on Olympia," she replied, ducking even lower to follow him in, "with the best of intentions. Allessandro knew there would be conflict. He saw war as means by which the powerful fight each other using a couple million proxies, ordinary people fed to the God of War by leaders who stay behind in safety. Allessandro believed that the powerful should fight directly, leaving civilians out of it. Society would be less disrupted, and it supported his views on survival of the fittest. He sanctioned the Order of Assassins, House Denshi, led by his brother-in-law."

"Did it work?" Rigg asked, as they walked onto the armory deck.

"There've been no wars on Olympia."

"Can't say the idea doesn't have its appeal," Rigg added. "Nice to think of some REMFs stopping bullets or beams for a change."

"REMFs?" she asked.

"Rear echelon motherfu—" Rigg snorted a laugh. "Never mind."

They found the strike-team sitting on the deck, cleaning weapons. The four other team members were also over-large, excellent specimens, until they stood next to Shasti. No true aliens served in the team. Nonhumans were rare on Olympia and would attract attention. The decision provoked bitter complaints from Rigg's second-in-command and close friend, the Morok, Lt. Rask. Despite his best efforts, Rask could not wrangle his way onto the mission.

Other than Rigg, the team members remained almost strangers to her. Shasti hadn't trained with the team long enough for her own satisfaction. An air of urgency, almost desperation, surrounded Mandela's attempt to interfere in Olympian policy. Rigg, however, knew them well, which gave her some confidence. Randall, Zoski, and Kim looked tough and capable. Karen Minaravitch, the only other woman, rounded out the team.

The ASATs finished checking their armaments and equipment. Rigg, once a sergeant always a sergeant, checked it again. They began to apply blackface and hand camo. Shasti sat on the deck plates and concentrated.

After a minute, Rigg noted her lack of movement. "Rainhell," he said, annoyed, "time for camo."

Shasti's body shuddered slightly. In an instant, all of her visible skin turned a flat, non-reflective black.

"Christ almighty," Randall said. The others looked similarly stunned.

Shasti's eyes opened. They remained a cool jade color. The whites seemed even more pronounced. She met the stares of the standard humans. "This is what you are up against every second you are on Olympia," she stated. "Never forget it."

———

W*raith* avoided the Olympian out-system patrols and deployed her landing ship from well beyond the range of planetary detectors. The high-speed raider then fled for deep space as the landing shuttle headed for Olympia's night side. The *Intruder* was the latest design, horribly expensive but nearly invisible to radar or microwave. It lived up to its name, tip-toeing past Olympia's naval moon base and the lines of fighters and sloops patrolling the approaches to the planet. The *Intruder* slipped into Olympia's atmosphere. At ten thousand feet, the shuttle went into hover, its rear cargo ramp sliding down.

Shasti looked at Rigg and the other five members of the assault team, dressed in chameleon suits. They were low enough not to need the additional burden of oxygen, a blessing considering how much equipment they carried.

Rigg looked back at her and grinned. "It's your planet. After you."

Shasti nodded and strode out onto the ramp. The frigid, pitch-black night waited at the end of it. Above her the filigree of the ice-ring glimmered. Wind howled around her. Without hesitation, she threw herself off the ramp, spread-eagled. As she fell, she rolled onto her back. Above her, she could see the others dropping in a perfect file. Their helmet faceplates did not leak the eerie green of the interior HUD night sights through which they saw the world. They plunged earthward like black rocks. Shasti flipped over and concentrated on her descent.

At one thousand feet, Shasti's black airfoil deployed. The others formed up on her like geese as they made for a landing on the plateau. Shasti's boot slammed into the hard soil of her homeworld, but she kept her feet under her. The others dropped around her with less luck.

They buried their chutes with trained efficiency and moved out in a ranger file, each person following the phosphorescent tag on the helmet of the person ahead of them. The small force headed for the isolated farmhouse to meet their contact.

Shasti took point as the team trudged through the cold desert night. Early fall chilled Olympia's Northern continent; she was glad it wasn't winter. With barely a thought she raised her body temperature a full degree. Her usual 15-MM tri-auto rode on her hip, a strap across her chest holding some of the weight. The weapon, too heavy for most humans, was normally used by Humanform Combat Robots. She preferred its heavier killing power. She'd set it for projectile weapons, so the energy trace would be minimal. There were eyes in the sky.

They reached the contact point, a large farmhouse in an isolated valley. The team spent ten minutes in stillness. Every sense, artificial and natural, strained to detect a trap. Finally, Rigg stood, cautiously moving toward the door. In his hand he held a metal cricket. He gave a recognition signal, a series of metallic clacks. The door opened slowly. A woman of Rigg's size stood there, looking out. The two conversed. Rigg went inside for a second then came back out and gave the all-clear signal on the clacker. The others moved quickly into the house. Shasti, ever suspicious, brought up the rear.

Once inside, the woman turned on a lamp, then quickly drew curtains across all the windows to prevent the light from escaping. The light revealed a large, comfortably rustic room.

Shasti studied the woman. Early stock, she estimated, Selected not Engineered with abilities from good genetics, and none of the hallmarks of the gene-tampering technology responsible for Shasti's existence. She lacked the inhuman perfection and bilateral symmetry seen in the Engineered, the newest people. Shasti already knew that the older woman did not have dark-adapted eyes. She'd peered out of the door for a few seconds before spotting Rigg. Still handsome and lithe, the Olympian might well be close to sixty from the grayed hair and the existence of lines on her face. To the other team members, she probably appeared to be in her early forties.

Their contact looked over the members of the team then spotted Shasti. As she did, Shasti allowed her melanin levels to return to normal. Flat-black skin color vanished in a heartbeat.

The woman looked up at her in obvious fear and backed a step. "Aristo," she gasped, uttering the old slang for the Engineered.

"No," Shasti said. "I'm not an Aristo."

The other woman recovered her composure, but fear stayed in her eyes. "Obviously not in spirit, or you would not be here. But you are born Aristo—pardon, Engineered—for all the world to see. You may be the most perfectly made I've ever seen."

"Yeah, we've heard. She's perfect," Kim groused.

"Remember," Shasti said, ignoring Kim's comment, "on this world your social status is largely determined by your genetics. I'm a tailored life form, engineered from germ plasm. The amount of money put in my body would appall you. My size and general appearance mark me as an aristocrat."

The woman looked at the standard humans. "I had actual parents," she admitted, eyes downcast. "They were not sanctioned by the order of Geneticists. My creation was unassisted, done by their own bodies."

Shasti was surprised. The woman's appearance was better than her social status, given that she was entirely naturally conceived and far worse, unsanctioned. "I envy you those parents," she said.

The woman looked up, startled, then smiled sadly. "You are truly not Aristo to think so." She extended a hand hesitantly, "I'm Leda Jenner."

"Shasti Rainhell," she said, taking the hand. "Daniel Rigg, Kim, Randall, Zoski, and Minaravitch."

"Names you must not use after tonight," Jenner cautioned. "You have been briefed on your assumed names and identities?" They all nodded. "Good. You brought in clothes for tomorrow? Let me see them while you are getting out of that camouflage. Mr. Rigg, there is a safe in the basement for the heavy weapons."

"Not till morning," Rigg demurred.

"As you wish," Jenner said. "The bathroom is through there."

Jenner looked at their equipment, discarding a jacket of Kim's she ruled too ostentatious for his social status. Only Rigg, for all his size and lean strength, and Minaravitch, with her beautiful and symmetrical Russian face, could pretend to claim a status marginally exceeding Jenner's own. Jenner discarded a dress of Minaravitch's, pulling out something more suitable from her own closet.

"That dress," Jenner said, "isn't even close. It would be fine on a comedian. Who picked this material out for you? Was your briefing no better than this?"

Rigg shrugged. "Best guess I imagine. It's not a secret to you that we came with less preparation than these missions usually get."

Shasti chose a black, form-fitting body suit and a jade green jacket to match her eyes. "Am I all right?" she asked uncertainly. She had little experience of even Olympian civilian society.

"Aristos can wear anything," Jenner replied. "A woman of your breeding would display your physique with pride, so you are quite in fashion. That's good. You're far too big for anything of mine to be alterable. My jacket won't even cover your shoulders. I can take in this other for Minaravitch."

"Good," Rigg said. "Everybody else get some sack time. We have a lot of ground to cover in the morning."

———

Morning dawned over the desert. Shasti greeted it alone. She'd been suffering a mix of emotions since returning to her homeworld. Sleep eluded her, so she'd opted for guard duty. It gave her time to think, to remember things she usually blocked from her conscious mind.

Her life on Olympia had been hard, the training strict, but it had not been all bad. She remembered enjoying the animals in the K-9 Corp. She'd excelled with all weapons, including her hands. Even as a child, Shasti knew she was something special from Jalgren

Pard's interest in her. At fifteen, Pard introduced her to sex. Shasti did not question it and had taken to the physical pleasure eagerly. She'd felt honored when told of her impending marriage to Pard. It never occurred to her that she had a choice. All her life she'd obeyed orders without question.

Pard finished teaching her normal lovemaking. Then the trouble began. He enjoyed using force, inflicting pain. He'd taught her to enjoy sex but could not teach her to enjoy such games. With that, everything between them came undone. She no longer saw him as a god-like force of genetics and power, but as a degenerate.

She finally recognized their marriage for a mockery, his public claim of ownership. Worse still, she saw herself as an expensive, beautifully made toy, held for his exclusive use. Her training as an assassin and bodyguard had given her pride. Life with Pard denied her that pride. She began to learn of the world outside Pard's domain, enough to realize what she'd been cheated of.

Shasti waited her chance, enduring his abuse as best she could. Until one night, overconfident, he did not have her drugged or partially bound. Her hands tensed on her weapon as she remembered that night...

———

S hasti had secreted a kubaton in Pard's bedchamber, slipping it between the pillow and headboard. She hadn't struggled the last few times he had taken her, or rather had struggled feebly, letting him think that he had at last dominated her.

"On the bed," Pard said, his eyes roaming over her slender body. She feigned submission, stretching out on the bed and buying time to reach under the pillow for the small metal spike of the kubaton. She felt the bed sink under his weight as he positioned himself above her. Her hand seized on the kubaton and Shasti exploded into action. Pard, not anticipating a fight, missed his block, and the weapon slammed into his temple. Any other man would have died. It only knocked Pard on his side, though blood splattered on the sheets. He even managed a swing that knocked her off the bed. Like a tigress, she'd sprung back at him. He staggered upright just as she crashed into him.

Shasti was two hundred pounds of perfectly engineered, organic killing machine, the latest model. Her bones bent and gradually reshaped. Pard, for all his massive size and strength was First Generation Engineered. His bones broke. Her system pumped adrenaline and painkiller into her body. Cuts ceased bleeding almost instantly. Pard, powerful as he was, couldn't shake off the blow to the temple and he was too slow to catch the decades-younger Rainhell, powered by her frenzy of loathing.

Shasti feinted left and then drove low, catching his groin in her right hand and straining it through her fingers. Pard's agonized howl finally alerted the exterior guards. They began to yell through the door. Shasti abandoned piling killing blows on Pard, who still weakly warded her off, to leap to the doorway just as the door crashed open. The first guard plunged past her. Shasti landed a knife-edged palm on the second guard's neck, snatched his weapon out of the air and shot the first guard. Shasti whirled to finish Pard, only to see him disappearing behind a secret door. The weapon bucked in her hands on full auto. Blood splashed on the door as it sealed, but she couldn't tell if she had killed him.

Shuddering with reaction and loathing, Shasti pulled herself together. She had only minutes to make her escape. Shasti pulled a dead guard's jacket over the bedroom things Pard forced her to wear, grabbed both weapons, and fled. She killed everyone she encountered: guards, visitors, servants, a terrified maid. They were all apparatus of her rapist. All his things. Nothing in her life had introduced her to the concept of noncombatant, and the greater the confusion, the more chance of escape. Shasti started fires with her weapons, caused explosions. She hoped much of the encampment would react to the attack as if it were an exterior threat, never dreaming she was the cause. She shot a young valet in the garage, leapt into an aircar, and disappeared into the night.

Hours later Shasti had traded the use of her body to an offworld spacer and escaped Olympia. She killed that spacer at their next port of call and fled into Kandara's spaceport underworld, promising herself to remain free or die. More killing secured her a position with a local enforcer. Shasti was merciless, having never learned mercy, but she did not enjoy killing as an end in itself. Gradually, she came to prefer bodyguard duties and acquired a reputation. Offworld contracts followed. Every chance she got, she worked her way farther away from her homeworld.

Now she was back, and there would be hell to pay.

Chapter Three

R igg roused the others shortly before dawn. After securing the heavy weapons and equipment, they dressed in street clothes and grabbed a hasty breakfast.

"I have two vehicles outside," Jenner said. "That will make our party appear smaller and we can travel separately. Rainhell, I want you to ride in the coupe, posing as an insurance consultant for the Trakia Mutual Combine. I'll be your secretary. Rigg, you're our bodyguard. Olympia is a semi-lawless world. An Aristo like Rainhell would have a bodyguard, even several."

"You others will ride in the light truck. Your cover is that you are agricultural workers on a trip to the capital."

"Good," Kim said, slapping his hands together. "Rubes heading for the big city. It may explain any lapses we make."

"Just so," Jenner replied, as she packed her suitcase. "Rainhell and I can cover Rigg. As bodyguard he won't do much talking anyway."

"Strong and silent, that's me," Rigg said.

Shasti looked at him with an arched eyebrow.

"Okay," he growled, "it's you."

Jenner looked a little perplexed at their by-play.

"Let's go," Rigg said, grabbing Jenner's case off the bed. They loaded the red sport coupe and the larger green truck-van, quickly leaving the farmhouse behind.

The team drove out of the mountains and high desert districts, making good time heading for the capital and the seacoast. When they stopped in towns and restaurants, sometimes they pretended to know each other, sometimes to meet for the first time. Other times, they didn't communicate at all. Olympia, difficult to land on for offworlders, was not difficult to travel in. Society was factioned between the selectively bred and the genetically engineered, then between different groups of the Engineered.

In the late afternoon of the sixth day, their vehicles crested a highway and pulled into a scenic overlook. Shasti stepped out of the car and stretched, glad to be free of its confines. The others piled out too, also glad of the break from the long drive. Shasti walked over to the cliff edge and looked out. The air was humid and smelled faintly of the sea; they had outrun fall for the time being.

"Marathon," Jenner said from behind her.

The capital city gleamed in whites, blues, and silver, stretching for miles.

"I can see the coastline beyond," Minaravitch said as she shaded her eyes from the strong sun.

"Not bad," Rigg added. "It's got a fair skyline. You folks like to build up. Good. I had enough of underground cities on Enshar."

"It's grown," Shasti said with the faint surprise of the returned traveler.

"Population two point one million." Jenner smiled. A hint of colonial pride sounded in her voice.

"You can see how it was all planned," Rigg said, "all very orderly."

"Olympians hate random chance," Shasti said. "We like it all mapped and pre-planned whether it's a city or a strand of DNA."

"Has kind of a Mediterranean look to it," Minaravitch added. "Like somebody grabbed a tour book of Greece and decided to update the ruins."

"Enough sightseeing," Jenner said. "Let's get going. We want to make it before evening."

On reaching Marathon, they moved into one of two safe houses

Jenner's cell set up. Shasti chose the larger, so they could be housed together. They took several apartments in the structure, connected by interior doors. The neighborhood was transitional, frequented by business travelers and Aristos either at the beginning of the way up in life, or on the skids down. People minded their business. Shasti switched their cover. Now they posed as a team of disaster consultants looking for work.

Jenner contacted the other members of her cell, seeking information on Pard's movements and the purchases of armaments. "It's safer for both teams if we don't meet face to face," she answered when Rigg asked about the cell members. Rigg didn't like it, but he couldn't argue with the logic.

Shasti began checking the places Pard had frequented during their brief marriage. She found all the changes in Marathon a bit bewildering. The population had doubled. Many of Pard's old haunts, including his city home, were gone. Denshi's downtown offices had not moved, though it seemed most of their operations had been transferred to the old desert training facilities outside Marathon. That facility had grown into a huge installation, nearly a fortress.

They split up and began to follow leads, seeking contact with their target. Pard remained elusive. The head of the Denshi order kept his movements secret and had not been seen in person for some weeks. Shasti began to fear they would have to take him at the Denshi's public offices in Marathon. This made the mission far more difficult. Chances of success and survival dropped to minimal. They continued to search.

———

Weeks passed and they were no closer to accomplishing the sanction on Pard. Shasti, Jenner, and Rigg headed back to the apartment after a day's fruitless search. They stopped at a market for groceries and necessities, which Jenner and Rigg carried. It would appear strange for an Aristo like Shasti to carry anything. The oppressive stickiness of Marathon's tropical fall was breaking. It would be winter soon. As they turned onto the street, the same sense of wrongness Shasti had felt in London struck her again. Nothing showed in her face as she turned to the others. "Tara, I want to take a look at that electronics store."

Jenner, addressed by her assumed name, nodded and followed. Rigg trailed her. Shasti triggered a portable music com, hoping it would defeat any sound-detecting equipment aimed at them. They stepped into the storefront. Shasti pretended to be looking at a computer monitor.

"Something's wrong," she said to her companions over the music. "It's rush hour and there are too few people on the street. Those here don't look right."

Rigg cursed and looked up at the apartment. "The towel is out on the window."

Shasti looked at him, annoyed. "I'm aware of that. Don't look again. The team may not be aware of any problem and have hung out the all clear. Or they are dead and someone else has hung it."

"What do we do?" Jenner asked. Shasti looked into the older woman's drawn and frightened face and felt a moment's pity for her. Jenner was not cut from the same merciless cloth as she and Rigg. It hardly seemed fair.

Shasti used her excellent peripheral vision, looking beyond the others. She could see several men lounging in doorways behind them, with no obvious reason for doing so. *Denshi or police,* she thought. They must have trailed them onto the block. So the gate was shut behind them. There were too many people who looked like police or troops on the street, surely more snipers and others laired out of sight.

It's sad, she thought, *to die, leaving Pard to pollute the universe.* She regretted not lingering on that last kiss with Robert Fenaday, lingering enough to taste it now.

"We need to run," she said, with no hint of her interior death-song. "There are too many hostiles on the street and that's just the ones we can see."

"I'm not leaving my people without trying to warn them," Rigg snapped.

Shasti looked at him as if at a child. "They can't get out," she said patiently. "They will be blocked on all four sides, above and below. If you use your com, they'll know we spotted the ambush."

"I've got to try," he said, eyes locking on hers.

She thought a second. "We'll go into the store and you try to com them. We can fight our way out the back and hope they overlooked it."

"Hah," Jenner said.

Shasti turned off the music com. "I'm going to buy the Zuidai monitor," she said for any listeners. They had little chance; still even a few seconds of indecision would help. The others followed her as she pushed open the glass doors and stepped into the store. Shasti strode up to the counter with all the imperiousness of her class. She noted one man she suspected was police, then spotted the rear door. "I want the Zuidai holo-monitor in the window," she told the clerk.

The store clerk nodded, not meeting her eyes. His physique would be the source of much admiration offworld. On Olympia, his shortness and lack of facial symmetry marked him as a recessive and lower class. Shasti's engineered senses detected the sheen of sweat on his forehead and the smell of chemical fear on him. *So they're in here too,* she thought. "My man needs some privacy to make a call."

"Yes, madam," he muttered.

Before Rigg could reach his com, from outside came the sharp crack of a rifle shot, then a fusillade. Shasti's hand flashed out, driving the clerk to the ground. Her other hand snapped her autopistol from under her arm in a liquid move. Two Olympian police charged from the storeroom door. She shot both through their visors. Their visor armor was no match for the illegal, hyper-velocity, AP rounds the team's weapons fired. People screamed, and the smart ones dropped to the floor. Others ran. One man fled out the front. Police fire struck him, and he crashed into the show window.

Rigg shot the man Shasti had marked as a policeman. He didn't see a smaller woman Shasti would never have suspected of being Olympian police. The policewoman shot Rigg in the shoulder with one round. He spun to the ground. Shasti hit the policewoman in the left eye before she could fire again. Jenner fumbled her gun out but didn't get a shot off.

Shasti snatched up a weapon from the floor, flicked it to full auto, and emptied the weapon across the storefront, exploding the remaining glass, hopefully delaying reinforcements. Rigg, pale and white, climbed to his feet, stumbling toward the back. Jenner reached to help him, pegging shots out the front. Shasti hit the rear door and ran into two more plainclothes police. She shot the woman officer. The male officer fired and missed. Shasti and he collided. Shasti's engineered body slammed adrenaline into her blood. Almost quicker than sight, she hauled him off the ground, flinging him into the wall. He bounced off. Shasti shot him in mid-air.

They dove out the rear door of the store and into the street. An unmarked police aircar idled just outside the door. The two police they'd just killed must have come out of it.

"In," Shasti ordered. Rigg collapsed through the open front door. Jenner jumped in the rear. Shasti raced around to the driver's side as shots began to come down from the rooftop snipers. A laser whiffed over her but failed to stay on long enough to bite. It was like hot breath singeing her hair. Anti-personnel flechettes cracked the pavement and dented the roof of the aircar but could not penetrate it. She slid in, firewalling the throttle. There was the sound of a huge blast from the street of the apartment.

"The explosives," Rigg gasped. "They must have realized they were trapped."

"Yes." Shasti, steering frantically around traffic, climbed to the express air lane. "If pursuit is delayed, we have a chance. There's the other safe house." The aircar raced away at two hundred KPH, leaving the confusion and a towering cloud of smoke from the destroyed apartment in their wake.

"You'll never make it with me," Rigg said tightly. Jenner broke out the car's medical kit. She sprayed the wound with sealfoam, using a trauma tab to inject painkiller into him. "As soon as we get a distance away, you two get out. I'll take the aircar and draw the pursuit."

"No," Shasti said. She checked scanners and mirrors. Nothing close. She dropped out of the express lane, changed streets and levels, heading back for the ground where the car would be less conspicuous. *Rigg's tough,* she thought. *If he can manage a few blocks and some public transit, we'll make it.*

Rigg smiled through the pain. "Don't get sentimental now, Rainhell. Stay in character, willya?"

"No," she repeated, "you were right back there. We had to try."

"Rainhell."

"No. Fenaday wouldn't do it. What I've learned of being human, I learned from him."

———

J algren Pard looked up from his massive desk at the knock. He was working on contract negotiations for the sale of a former Dua-Denlenn merchant cruiser and had left word not to be disturbed. He didn't need to ask who it was. His personal aide would admit no one to his presence without checking with Pard first. The doors slid open, and Grigor Salmot, his head bowed apologetically, came in. The whipcord thin, dark-skinned man made no sound as he walked over the marble flooring and plush, red carpet. Stealth was second nature to Grigor.

"My Lord, there has been a development that Section Chief Vaughn believes you should be informed of," Salmot said.

"Yes?" responded Pard. Vaughn was an enemy of Antebei, Pard's current protégé and potential successor. The rivalry between the two young Fourth Generation Engineereds was intense and encouraged by Pard, who enjoyed it as other men might enjoy a horserace. His decision to put such young men in charge of Special Operations and Internal Security was controversial in Denshi. All the better, the assignments maneuvered rivals out of powerful positions. The two young men were loyal only to Pard and dependent on him for their survival against the earlier generations of Engineered. There was another reason. Denshi was devoted to the concept of genetic perfection. Vaughn and Antebei were the pinnacle of Engineering, especially Antebei. Leadership was thrust on them the way it had been on the young scions of royal families in the Middle Ages.

"You may recall, from Mr. Antebei's morning report of yesterday, about the infiltrators in Sector Five. Evidently, according to Mr. Vaughn, they were not Unionists or Neo-Reformists, but probably Confederate Special Forces. Unfortunately, the ambush set by Mr. Antebei's forces did not succeed. They did not catch them all in the apartment. Three outside detected the ambush. A rather spectacular firefight ensued, triggered when those inside spotted a sharpshooter, who then shot one of them. Either intentionally or accidentally, they set off a large explosion, which brought down a good part of the building, causing many civilian casualties. The others fought their way out of the ambush during the explosion, escaping in a police car. One may be wounded."

Pard sighed, pushing back from his desk. It seemed the world was filled with amateurs these days. "A stunningly poor performance, wouldn't you say, Grigor?"

"Not what one would hope or expect," Salmot replied diplomatically.

"I imagine there are no documents, or other proof, that these were Confederate troops?"

"No, sir," Salmot said. "These were standard humans, attempting to pass as lower-order genetic trash."

"Do not be so contemptuous of standard humans," Pard warned. "It is Antebei's chief weakness. He underestimates them, hence this failure."

"Yes, Excellency, I shall remember. There were some Olympians with them. That's what Mr. Vaughn wanted you to see. There is a surveillance datum in your in-basket."

Pard turned to a computer screen, activating it. The surveillance video image was barely adequate. It showed three people turning into a storefront. Then the image sharpened.

She had grown her hair long, in defiance of his preference. Clearly, she had filled out in figure and muscle mass, as he had envisioned.

Nothing appeared on Pard's heavy, immobile face, though his belly muscles tensed, as if in remembrance of pain, as he stared at the image of Shasti Rainhell.

"Mr. Vaughn thought it important you know," Salmot said, eyes carefully on the floor.

"Of course," Pard said mildly.

Salmot shuddered slightly; the kindly, gentle voice was a warning. Pard used it when he was at his most furious, a measure of his self-control. Actions of the most unpleasant sort often followed.

"They fled across the river into either Neo-Reformist, or neutral Quest, territory. We could call in any outstanding favors, possibly even with the Neos."

"No," Pard interrupted. "The female is not so important we should go to such expense. It might also give our enemies, particularly in the Army, the thought she could be useful to them. The greatest danger is our appearing worried about this in Parliament or among the Council. Others would seek to pry into our affairs, looking for advantage. Now is a very bad time for such inquiries and attention.

"No, this has been too public as it is. Rainhell is famous on other worlds. If she dies in the public eye, we may face action by offworld governments. Have the police back off. Assign Vaughn the task of finishing this. Tell him to use his best people, but to keep this quiet, even in Denshi. If at all possible, I want Rainhell alive.

"Have all sections dealing with Project Overman double security and minimize activity. It is unfortunate this occurred at this time. We must be careful.

"Finally," Pard said, turning back to his desk, "send Antebei to me. At once."

"Yes, Excellency," Salmot replied, not envying Antebei that meeting at all.

———

S hasti could scarcely believe their luck so far. They escaped the area of the police attack by cutting across several of the informal borders of Marathon to an area controlled by a party unfriendly to Pard's Denshi/ Military alliance. A few seconds work had disabled the unmarked police car's IFF and transponder, so they could not be tracked. They were now in territory loyal to the Neo-Reformist party. Definitions meant nothing. What mattered was that the Neos hated Denshi. Cooperation in anything Denshi wanted, including searching for them, would be minimal and grudging. Their best protection lay in the incessant, internecine political rivalry of the hotpot that was Marathon. Thin armor, but all they had for now.

After nightfall, Shasti ditched the unmarked in the Ithacan River near an industrial complex. Most of the workers had gone home hours ago. There was little traffic in the commercial area after dark.

Jenner had tended Rigg with the supplies from the police car's medkit. The vehicle proved a lifesaver in more than one respect. In addition to the medkit, Shasti found a riot gun and some off-duty clothes from the male officer, which more or less fit Rigg. They ditched Rigg's blood-soaked clothes in a trash can. No point in gifting the authorities with any DNA. Shasti broke the riot gun down and stashed parts of it on them.

"Can you walk?" she asked.

He nodded grimly.

They headed for a bus station. Mercifully, the hoverbus came soon, and they boarded it, heading for the poorer section of town. Jenner and Rainhell sat on either side of Rigg, keeping him upright. They changed vehicles several times under Jenner's guidance. When no one was around to see, Shasti used her extra-human strength to carry the big ASAT. She had always respected Rigg; that regard increased dramatically as they struggled toward their goal. Standard humans were fragile, even large ones like Rigg. All he had going for him was nature's haphazard design. Shasti's body, exceptional even on Olympia, would already be well on its way to repairing the damage done by the bullet. Her endocrine system would have locally anesthetized it and pumped in anti-inflammatories. She'd be feeling an endorphin high.

Near midnight, they reached the area of the safe house. Rigg's endurance finally gave out. They hid him in a darkened alley, propped up with a pistol in one hand. Shasti flicked to her night-black mode and accompanied Jenner the rest of the distance. With Jenner watching from a safe vantage, Shasti scaled the side of the building. Her fingers found purchase where a standard human's would not. She entered the fourth story apartment from the roof after crawling over much of the building like a spider.

———

L eda Jenner looked around the alley, hoping for Shasti's quick return. It took all of her self-control not to imagine Denshi assassins looking at her from every shadow. Minutes dragged on. "Hurry, Shasti," she whispered to herself.

The door to the old apartment building swung open. Leda snapped her pistol up, then relaxed as Shasti, her skin now restored to its normal ivory white, exited the front door. The big woman made her way over to Jenner's position, almost disappearing from sight despite Leda's efforts to track her. *God, she's part shadow herself,* Leda thought.

"Get into the apartment," Shasti ordered.

Jenner, relieved to get off the street and behind walls, sped up the street and into the building. A neighbor passed her on the way but paid no attention to her. Jenner could have sworn the pounding of her heart was audible to anyone in the area. She raced up the back stairs and entered the apartment but didn't turn on the light. The living room windows faced the street Rainhell and Rigg would have to come up. She could cover them from here with her pistol.

After a few anxious moments, Shasti appeared, her arms intertwined with Rigg's, looking like lovers on a stroll. They disappeared from view as they reached the building. Jenner hurried to the doorway, holding it open a fraction. The elevator opened. They were there, Rigg's head resting on Shasti's shoulder. Shasti had what she probably thought was a pleasant smile frozen on her face for anyone who might glance at them. The effect was perfectly horrible and mercifully short. With no apparent effort, Shasti scooped up Rigg and darted inside. Jenner sealed the door behind them.

Shasti carried Rigg into one of the two bedrooms, gently laying the unconscious man on the bed. She quickly checked the wound, breaking open the medkit. Jenner stood in the doorway, ignored, shaking. Now that they had reached some temporary safety, her nerves gave out. She leaned against the wall, slid down, and started crying softly. For years, she'd opposed the Olympian government. Tiny, inconsequential defiances, even after the Confederacy recruited her. Now, it was all too real. A dozen people had died in front of her today. The other members of their team were either dead, or already in interrogation, with all its horrors. She hadn't time to know the others well, but they were people, not numbers, to her. From the floor, through a haze of tears, she looked out the window. A few stars shone already, dotting the delicate arch of the ice crystal ring overhead. Around some of those stars were families now lacking sons, a daughter, perhaps a wife. It was horrible.

Shasti finished checking Rigg. Her cold green eyes swept over the older woman. "Stop that," she ordered in a frozen, lifeless voice, brooking no argument, backed by eyes that seemed to feel nothing.

Suddenly afraid of Shasti, Jenner choked off her crying. It occurred to her, if she wasn't able to pull her weight, Shasti might deal with the problem in a final manner. Jenner stood, eyeing the bigger woman warily.

"Be useful," Shasti said. "Is there food here?"

"There should be," Jenner replied.

"Hot soups, teas, would be good," Shasti said, standing. "He is deeply asleep, but I judge, in no danger of dying. The bullet went through. If a lung or vital organ were hit, he would already be dead. I shot him full of trank and antibiotics. When he wakes, he should be hungry. After that, pack some food. I doubt any of the team survived to be interrogated, but we cannot be certain. Denshi does not know about this location or they'd be here. Still, we may have to run. I'll watch the street from here. You go make something."

Jenner nodded and scurried for the kitchen.

Shasti Rainhell moved to the window, began assembling the riot gun, and wondered how much longer they would live.

Chapter Four

R obert Fenaday slammed open the door to the Shamrock
Line's general counsel's office. Secretaries and clerks scattered as he marched in.

Oswin Dewey looked up from his desk in surprise as his CEO
bore down on him. He started to stand. "Mr. Fenaday, what a
surp—"

"Silence," Fenaday said. "Sit."

Dewey looked as if he might protest for a second but thought
better of it.

"I've just found out," Fenaday began, "that Ursane Duna has
been trying to see me for months. Concentrate on that last name,
Duna. Does that mean anything to you?"

"Yes, sir," Dewey replied, "of course. Your friend who was killed
on the Enshar expedition."

Fenaday leaned forward, his hands on Dewey's desk. "He wasn't
killed, Mr. Dewey. He gave his life to save his world, his people and,
as an incidental, my unworthy ass. He died alone, in a hole, with a
monster that would have broken your sanity to behold. Because he
chose to."

"Most admirable," Dewey said, "of course—"

"And you did not see fit," Fenaday said, his voice strained, "to let me know that his only surviving relative needed to talk to me? Needed my help?"

"Well, sir, it was not a social call. He came seeking relief from the contract his uncle negotiated with you to give the Shamrock line exclusive rights to Enshar. I explained to him that a contract is a contract. There seemed no need to bother you with it."

Fenaday's right hand made a convulsive gesture at his right thigh. Then he stood up, his face cold and remote. "Mr. Dewey, it's as well for you that I'm no longer a privateer and do not carry a pistol.

"The Enshari are trying to rebuild a world and a race from the brink of extinction and you talk to me of contracts. Ursane would never default on Belwin Duna's sacred word. He only wanted some help, some latitude from the stricter provisions of the contract. I found this out an hour ago, by chance, when I ran into him at the park.

"And," Fenaday suddenly roared, "you turned my friend's family from my door like beggars!" Fenaday grabbed one end of the desk and threw it over. Dewey, wide-eyed, scrambled from his chair to a corner. Dewey's assistant, Lury, ran into the room and froze when Fenaday rounded on him.

Fenaday, chest heaving and red-faced, turned back to Dewey. "Belwin Duna was the finest being I ever met. I'm not even fit to walk in his shadow, yet his people worship me as a hero. I'm not a hero. Duna was the hero.

"Yes, Mr. Dewey, it is a good thing I'm a civilized businessman these days and not a privateer or I'd wring your miserable neck. You're fired. Get out of this building while you still can."

Dewey opened his mouth and Fenaday took a step toward him. The solicitor broke and ran for the door.

"Lury," Fenaday growled.

"Ye-ye-yes, sir?" said the younger man.

"You're now general counsel to the Shamrock line. You will immediately drop every and anything else you are doing and meet directly with Ursane Duna. You will arrange that all his requests be granted. You will ensure that he can reach me at any time of the day or night. You will have all this done by day's end or you'll be joining Mr. Dewey on the street. Is there anything unclear in these orders?"

"No, sir."

"Then why am I still looking at you?"

Lury ran out.

Fenaday looked out of the office at the staffers. People stood around, staring at him.

"Back to work, people," he said. "Today's performance is ended."

People moved back to their desks, watching him carefully.

Well, he thought, *I guess I have that coming. Probably looked and sounded like a maniac. But God, to think of Ursane being treated like an insurance salesman, it's enough to drive a man half-mad.*

To the Enshari, Fenaday rated second only to Belwin Duna himself. For Fenaday, all too aware it was Mandela's blackmail and not Duna's quest that landed him on Enshar, it left a bitter feeling of inadequacy. He'd been forced to go to Enshar and would have fled if the opportunity presented itself. Fenaday always felt like a fraud when near Duna's people, avoiding them when he decently could.

His mission accomplished, he headed back to his own office in the corporate tower. Fury ebbed, to be replaced by his usual grim mood. He hadn't heard from Shasti in over a month, since she'd taken a "job" on Earth. Temporary, she said in the holo-message, but she'd be unreachable during the job. With luck, she would see him in six months. The message was Shasti at her most impenetrable, beautiful, statue-like, unknowable. It hurt very badly when it came. Shasti had never lied to him before, so he had no choice but to believe her. He wondered if she wasn't lying to herself about coming back. Perhaps Shasti no longer wished to compete with a ghost.

For his part, he was unsure if he should wish her back. Maybe he'd made a mistake buying back his old home on New Eire. Everywhere he looked in it, he saw his lost wife, Lisa. Grief, which relented briefly after Enshar, reasserted itself, in part, after he moved back in. *Missing in action,* three words that left a gap so difficult to close. Every time he thought the wound healed, something opened it.

Shasti took and gave different things than did Lisa. In some ways much less, in some, maybe more. They were friends and, since Enshar, lovers in the physical sense. He knew he was closer to Shasti than any living person, but there were silences, gaps across which they had not reached. More puzzling was the sense that Shasti simply did not know the gaps were there.

An insistent buzzing intruded on his brooding. Fenaday reached wearily for the intercom. "Yes."

"Mr. Fenaday, there is a Mr. Mandela here to see you. He does not have an appointment."

Fenaday sat bolt upright, stilling the curse on his lips. *The spymaster, here?*

"Send him in. I don't want to be interrupted during this."

Mandela walked into the office, looking much the same as when Fenaday first saw him almost two years ago. Fenaday glared at him narrow-eyed, leaning back in his chair. He did not offer to shake hands. Mandela helped himself to a chair, not discomfited.

"We have a problem, Fenaday," he said.

"What problem could we possibly have in common?" Fenaday asked coldly.

"I think you once described her as six foot nine with eyes like green ice."

Fenaday snapped out of the chair, "What's happened to Shasti?"

"Got your attention now?" asked the spymaster. "Sit down."

In a moment of cold self-knowledge, Fenaday realized Mandela had played him like a trout.

I can't let the spymaster see the inner workings of my mind again. Fenaday sat back, trying not to shake. *It's always like this,* he thought. *Someone always comes to tell me they're gone. I'm never where I need to be.*

"What happened?" he asked when he could trust himself to speak.

"We don't know," Mandela said. "Rainhell took a job with us. I offered her a crack at something she wanted very badly, Jalgren Pard."

"Assassination?" Fenaday said in disbelief.

"Times are changing, Fenaday. You remember the beginning of the Second Sector War? The Conchirri slaughtered millions, rolled over the military of the Seven Species. Why? Because we were a joke. The Confederacy was powerless, a trading house for the member planets. The member planets' forces were small and poorly led. That's how the Conchirri got as far as they did. Once we organized, we wiped them out.

"That's not going to happen again, Fenaday. The day of every planet going its own way is over. The Confederacy is evolving. Next time something comes charging out of the night, and there will be a next time, it won't slaughter millions of civilians before we can fight. No more free lunch.

"Jalgren Pard is the leader of the Engineered, the genetically enhanced who are taking over the planet. They regard all other humans as inferior, not without some justification, as you know from being around Rainhell. We fear Pard plans to take Olympia out of the Confederacy. We don't need an empire of superhumans in that area of space. Hyperspace is thin there; the currents make transit from Olympia to Socha, New Eire, and Retief unusually fast. Olympian forces could strike those colonies before anything could be done about it.

"We have an interest in retiring Pard and his separatists," Mandela said, leaning back in the chair. "Rainhell has her own interest. I don't know what it is, but she wants him dead. She went in with a team of five others, including Daniel Rigg. We lost contact with them ten days after they landed, nineteen standard days ago. We don't know if Pard got them, or if someone local just got lucky."

"Is she dead?" Fenaday asked softly. It burned on his soul that she'd gone after Pard without him. He'd sworn to her, that day on Enshar, he would help her against her old enemy.

Shasti's sadness came back to him in a rush. *"I was an expensive toy, Robert, built to spec and just for him to play with. One day I decided I didn't want to be a toy anymore. I escaped. Sometimes, when he finds out where I am, he tries to have me killed. Pride, I suppose."*

In the months since their return, Fenaday hadn't acted on his promise. Now, it might be too late. If the answer was yes, Mandela would not leave the room alive. Pard would be next.

"We don't know," Mandela said, unaware of his nearness to death. "We don't have good contacts on Olympia. Right now, our embassy staff is bottled up in the capital. We can't even get at the few field agents we have. That's where you come in."

"What do you want?" Fenaday growled.

"The Olympian government can restrict our movements, prevent Confederate military people from even landing on the planet. What they can't do, is turn down a visit of state from the captain of the *Sidhe*, savior of Enshar."

Fenaday looked at Mandela. "It won't work. We'd be under observation all the time, surrounded by their security, for our own protection. We'd have no freedom of movement."

"You're refusing?" said a visibly surprised Mandela.

One for me, Fenaday thought. "No, you bastard. It's no more impossible than the Enshar Expedition. I'll take *Sidhe* and as many of the old crew as I can persuade to come or would trust. I'll also need as many of your people as I can get back to make this visit look at all probable."

"Mourner and her medics said they would serve with you," Mandela said. "Rask is raring to go after his friend Rigg. Mmok hates your and Rainhell's guts, but then he hates everybody. He'll go."

"Mmok," Fenaday said, surprised to hear the half cyborg's name. "I thought he was dead."

Mandela snorted. "He was never so alive that you could kill him. We rewired him, patched up the human parts. He's back and meaner than ever."

"Great," Fenaday said, without enthusiasm. Mmok was Mandela's watchdog. He controlled four Humanform Combat Robots and a platoon of other mechs through equipment planted in his shattered body. The HCR controller was a considerable asset, but a difficult companion. He and Mmok had almost drawn on each other in Barjan Deep. He knew Shasti and Mmok disliked each other on sight.

"What I'll need most," Fenaday said, "is Telisan. I don't think I can pull this off without him."

Mandela shrugged. "I can reactivate his reserve commission."

"The hell you will," Fenaday said. "He's engaged now. I'll send him a personal request. You'll take it by courier. If he's crazy enough to come, the courier can bring him back. I won't have him forced."

"As you wish."

"Is the stealth protocol you built into *Sidhe* current?" Fenaday asked.

"Nope, we will update it and more. There's some additional holographic equipment we'll add. You'll get something completely new, an *Intruder* shuttle. They cost as much as your frigate and are nearly invisible to microwave emitters and radar. We can't do anything with those crappy old *Dakota* shuttles of yours. The checkbook is open, Fenaday."

"Not enough. You want Pard dead. He's one of the unofficial leaders of a planet, head of an order of assassins. I'm going to have to go through a lot of people to get to Shasti, if she's still alive. I want a written authorization for any killing occurring in the course of this mission. It will be signed in my new lawyer's office."

Mandela smiled. "I can't do that. It's not legal anyway. There would be no force of law to it."

"I don't need force of law. I have you and you are the law. I want to know that if I go under, sacrifice everything I've gained back, you go with me."

"No," Mandela said flatly.

"Oh, don't take it so hard, old boy," Fenaday said, with a dangerous cheerfulness. "I've left detailed descriptions, computer-generated artist renderings of you, along with every detail of your blackmailing us during the Enshar Expedition in lots of places. It's all very secure. Ready to go, if I croak unexpectedly. Bet you haven't found even half of them. So if I go, you go anyway."

Mandela cocked a head at him quizzically. "I'll just deny everything—call them phonies, put up jobs, simulation, etc."

"Ah," Fenaday said, "very true. I'll never get you put away. I don't need to. You can't survive in the spotlight, spymaster. Your career as what you are will be over. Maybe you can get a nice slot in the Department of Agriculture."

Mandela sighed. "It's the personal touch, you know, very foolish of me. I should never have met you myself that day on Mars. It was stupid."

"Yes," Fenaday said, suddenly curious. "Why did you do it?"

"I knew your wife. Recruited her for Intelligence myself. She was one of the best, ambitious as hell, which I guess caught up with her. I even liked her, and I don't let myself do that. I was sure you were going to die on Enshar. The least I could do, if I was going to get her husband killed, was do it face to face. Like I said, stupid, an amateur's error."

"True," Fenaday said, "but it's the only human thing I've ever known you to do."

"No good deed goes unpunished," Mandela replied easily. "Say I agree to this idiocy, so you get my ass posthumously, if you lose yours."

"Then I and the crew go, so long as we're on the right side of the law. Those of us who survive won't live under your shadow for the rest of our days."

Fenaday leaned forward, his face expressionless. "I had better find her alive. I truly had better. I was nothing when you hired me for Enshar, but I'm getting bigger all the time. Maybe one day I'll come for you."

Mandela grinned broadly and stood. "Dream on, Rookie." He walked toward the door, stopped, and turned back. "Of course, if you ever do get that big, Fenaday, you'll be me. Then you won't have any choices at all. My people will be in touch tomorrow. Good night, Fenaday."

Fenaday sat in his office after Mandela left, holding his head in his hands. Reaction sank in. Shasti might be gone. It was a replay of that nightmare moment when the young officer came to the estate to tell him his wife was missing, presumed lost. It was happening again. He fought the clenching of his stomach, shaking in every limb.

He didn't know where he and Shasti fit into each other's lives. After long agonizing years, he'd finally accepted Lisa's loss, yet had not been able to go on from there. Shasti offered little help, insisting on living in the present. Only now did he realize it might be because she had difficulty imagining any future for herself. In many respects, she was an emotional newborn, inexperienced with anything more complex than the simple physical need for sex. They sheltered each other, brought together by circumstances and desire. It had sufficed for Shasti.

He didn't know if he loved her. It was not as it had been with Lisa. He'd felt no doubts then. Their lives fitted with near perfect symmetry. He did know that Shasti was the most important person in his life now. If she still lived.

Chapter Five

T elisan, former Confederation fighter pilot and first officer of the *Sidhe*, sat on the cliff top listening to the sound of the ocean, a sound he loved. Denla's yellow-white sun threw long, crisp shadows on the lavender seas below the cliffs. The white cliffs cast back the sunlight defiantly.

Behind him sat the ancient monastery of the Selen warrior-monks, an immense pile of white stone quarried from those same cliffs. Telisan was not a monk. Far from it, as the two young ladies he was engaged to would cheerfully attest. Of course, only one was a true female. The other was a demi-female. All three Denlenn genders were necessary to have a child.

He'd enrolled in the monastery to learn the traditional empty-hand fighting arts of the warrior-monks. Telisan had become interested in it through his friend, Fenaday, a master in a similar ancient human art. A fight on Mars, with thugs employed to stop the Enshar expedition, had taught Telisan that his skills in space were not mirrored on the ground.

After returning to Denla a year ago, rich beyond ordinary measure, he found himself sick of war, of so-called adventure. He maintained his reserve commission to do the flying he loved. Otherwise, Telisan withdrew from the world. For the most part, beyond Selen training, he looked forward to long periods of idleness.

Telisan had spent several hours in training. Now he meditated under the open sky, loving the beauty of sea and surf. Evening breezes riffled through his long, mane-like hair. Suddenly, his head came up. He thought he heard a voice. Telisan listened intently. Denlenn hearing was not as acute as their eyesight. This time he heard his name. Standing, he looked down the beach to see a lithe form running by the waterline. He recognized Sharla, his demi-female fiancée.

"Sharla," he called and waved as she spotted him. As he started down for the beach, worry struck him, a not uncommon experience now that he was engaged. He'd never worried back during the war.

Sharla caught up to him at the foot of the cliff, vibrant despite the long run from their dwelling. The demi-female was very athletic, if not beautiful. They'd met on the *Empress Aran*, where she served as a computer-tech in the weapons section. Her sense of humor and intelligence drew him to her; physical attraction came later. In his eyes she became more desirable every day. To a human, they would look much alike: tall with bronze, leathery-looking skin, rough mane-like hair, cat-eyes, thin almost lipless mouths. Sharla was slightly smaller than he, though tall for a demi-female. She was flat-chested but with a feminine curve to her hip. There were other details that would have been lost on an outworlder.

"Yes, darling?" he said. "Has something happened?"

"Arel," Sharla replied, addressing him by his first name, some-thing only a family member or lover might do, even then only when they were alone. To all others, no matter how close, he would always be Telisan. "There is a naval officer at the apartment. He bears an urgent message for you."

"Where is Arpen?" he asked.

"Entertaining the young man," Sharla laughed. "I believe she is in the process of making yet another conquest. The ensign will doubtless tell her anything she wants to know by the time we get there." They set off for the apartment at an easy jog. After a few hundred yards, Sharla gave him a wicked grin and lengthened her stride. He smiled back and matched his lover step for step. Together they raced around the headland.

Set into the cliffside above them was a Reika, a traditional country inn. The inn's dark wooden beams and tiny gardens had stood there for several hundred years. The monks disapproved of such luxury, tolerating it only for the sake of visitors. Sharla and Arpen had taken rooms there to be close to him after he enrolled at the monastery. Beyond the quaint structure, he could see part of a Confederate naval shuttle. Its fins reached over the waxy green of the nearby trees.

When they reached the Reika, Sharla's prediction proved to be true. Arpen was entertaining the young human in the common room. The ensign, chatting eagerly with her, didn't notice their arrival.

Arpen smiled warmly as they entered. Like all true females, Arpen was an empath. She couldn't read minds but sensed emotional and physical states. True females comprised only a fourth of the Denlenn species, and the males and demi-females were their traditional protectors, though since the war this too was changing. Twenty years ago, it would have been unheard of for an alien to meet a Denlenn female in person. The Confederacy and the two Sector Wars had altered much.

Arpen's huge, dark-brown eyes drew one in. She was beautiful, small, and curvaceous. Her physical attractiveness probably did not cross the gulf of species between her and the ensign. Her warmth and empathy did. Arpen could make anyone feel like the center of the universe merely by talking to them. Telisan had met her on the hospital ship *Solace* where he convalesced after the Battle of the Rings.

Despite her breaking of traditional barriers, it was Arpen who asked to formalize their triad, to avoid scandalizing their conservative families, she claimed.

Arpen stood gracefully. "Welcome back, Telisan. This is Ensign Horowitz from the naval courier *Cheetah*."

The young man snapped to attention and saluted. "Captain Telisan, I have a 'for your eyes only' communication." He extended a hand with a data crystal.

Telisan took it, looking warily at the small crystal, "Excuse me, dears."

He went into the other room. Despite the antique trappings, the inn held a modern computer system decorously hidden within an old chest. He activated the house computer then ran a military encryption program. A holographic image appeared. It bore the face he expected: Robert Fenaday.

"Hello, Telisan," said the image. "I hope this message doesn't beat my congratulations on your engagement and the gifts I sent. Those are coming slower. Even I can't afford to rent a naval courier.

"My friend, I have a terrible problem. Mandela offered Shasti a shot at assassinating Jalgren Pard, head of the House of Denshi on her homeworld. You don't know much of her history with Pard. If my word means anything to you, then I'll tell you he has it coming. Mandela claims Pard is a threat to the Confederacy. That's his story anyway.

"She dropped on Olympia with a team, including Dan Rigg. She's overdue…she may be dead. I'm going in after her, and if she is dead, to deal with Pard. Mandela says they cannot turn down a visit from the *Sidhe*.

"Telisan, this is my problem. It isn't right and it isn't fair to involve you. You're engaged to be married. You would be a fool to come. But come anyway, I need you." The image faded.

Telisan sat, deeply troubled, mulling over Fenaday's message. Assassination by the Confederacy? He found it hard to believe. The war machine created when the member planets organized under the Confederacy had outlived the Conchirri. As the old planetary militaries reverted to local governments, the cream of the military and the most modern equipment stayed with the Confederacy. Some advocated a stronger central government in the aftermath of the war. Perhaps, as many suspected, there was no way back to the old system. Still, the idea of assassination shocked him.

He knew of the Olympians. Since he'd met Shasti, he'd paid more attention to their activities. A delegation from Olympia had been on Denla months ago, buying war surplus shipping and equipment as the Denlenn military demobilized.

Such issues were irrelevant. His friends needed him. He owed debts to Shasti and particularly to Fenaday. They'd struggled together in the great quest to save the entire Enshari species. No matter that Fenaday and Shasti were forced into the venture by the government. Without them, Belwin Duna's mission would have failed. Telisan owed his life and honor to both the humans.

He returned to the parlor. "Ensign Horowitz, would you wait outside the door please?" The ensign nodded and left, giving Arpen a broad smile as he departed.

Telisan turned to his fiancées, explaining the situation. They'd never met Fenaday but knew every detail of that desperate voyage. "I do not know how to explain. I have only lied once in my life, caught between my oaths to Robert and to Duna. I failed to tell Fenaday about Duna's knowledge of what we would face on Enshar. A lie of omission, yet no less a lie. He forgave me. I do not think that, being human, he realized how great a sin this was to forgive. He handed me back his trust as if I never breached it, as if I had not sent him blind into a monster's den. This has never lain easy in my mind, as you know. To deceive an enemy is one thing. Falseness to one's own is an alien taint I wish I had never encountered.

"Now he needs my help. The venture is desperate. I wish, my dears, that I felt I could turn this down."

Arpen looked at him with sympathy. "Of course we must help your friend."

It took a second to sink in. "It is only I who need go," Telisan hastened.

Arpen now studied him with mild amusement. "I am sure your friend will appreciate the services of a fine surgeon."

"Arpen," Sharla protested, "it will be much too dangerous."

"Weren't you planning on going?" asked Arpen.

"Of course," Sharla said in surprise. "That's different. I'm demi-female."

"Now just a moment," Telisan, who had no intention of taking either, said, "I think this is too dangerous for you as well."

"More dangerous than the hospital ship *Solace* over Conchirri?" Arpen asked sweetly.

"Or the *Empress Aran* in a fleet action?" Sharla demanded, with more heat.

"This will be more like Enshar I think," Telisan said. "In any event, Arpen, it is far too dangerous to take you."

"I told you when we pledged that I was not willing to live within narrower horizons," Arpen replied. "I meant that. I'm the first Denla female to travel offworld, the first to become a surgeon, certainly the first in combat. Just because I love you both and want to be married does not mean I am willing to be less than I am. If you go, Telisan, I am going as well."

"As am I," Sharla stated.

Telisan tried one last tack. "Arpen, whatever will we say to your mother?"

"We'll tell her when we get back," Arpen replied.

It occurred to him that a human husband-to-be might have one advantage, not being outnumbered. He turned to the door and opened it. "Ensign Horowitz, the three of us will be returning with you. We will leave as soon as we pack and take care of some affairs."

Horowitz nodded. "My orders say you're the boss, sir."

"I'm glad someone thinks so," Telisan sighed.

49

Chapter Six

Hours later, the Denlenn triad boarded *Cheetah*, and the small vessel lifted off. Arpen and Sharla went into special liquid-filled chambers under sedation, to protect them from the savage acceleration of the courier. Telisan, citing his reserve commission, rode in the padded observer's seat on the bridge. As *Cheetah* raced toward Denla's orbiting military mass-driver to boost to a higher percentage of light speed, he began to wonder about the wisdom of his choice. Fighter pilot that he was, Telisan was used to quick, hard burns. But the scout was accelerating hard and steadily. The constant drag of acceleration began to make his face hurt after a few hours.

Cheetah's artificial singularity drive usually canceled the many gravities of thrust, but at this level of acceleration, gravity forces began to overcome the effect. Her crew had to endure as best they could.

Ensign Horowitz noticed his discomfort. "Quite a ride, sir."

Telisan turned his head slowly. "No worse than turning and burning in a *Spacefire* with a Conchirri on your tail. We didn't have singularity drives for AG in the fighters."

"True, but you fighter jocks didn't pull it for hours." Horowitz grinned, gravity making it sardonic. "*Cheetah* has the same artificial gravity as your *Sidhe*, but we're exceeding the tolerances of the singularity by two percent. As we say in the scout service, '*everybody eats our dust.*'"

For as long as you last, Telisan thought. Courier crews usually rotate out after a year. The wear and tear on the body adds up. *This time it can't be helped. Time is fleeting. At least there will be no thrust once we hit hyperspace.* Telisan settled back in his flight seat and tried to relax.

F ifty light-years lay between Denla and New Eire, but hyperspace was thin, with favorable currents. *Cheetah* entered New Eire system only two weeks after Fenaday's meeting with Mandela. The courier braked brutally coming into the system. As she neared the orbit of New Eire, she slowed to a tolerable gee for her passengers and hove into shuttle distance of the *Sidhe*. Telisan got his first sight of the blood-red, winged hull of the ten-thousand ton, four-hundred-meter-long frigate. She lay nestled up against a gray Confederation repair and supply ship, connected by umbilicals and gangways. Shipwrights and artisans crawled over the frigate. Even from *Cheetah*, he could see the actinic lights of welders. *Sidhe* was being militarized again with a full war load, the best Mandela could give them. It was appallingly familiar.

Ensign Horowitz offered many apologies about the lack of comfort on the *Cheetah*, mostly to Arpen. Now he insisted on flying the Denleni over to the *Sidhe* himself. The trip in the tiny cutter was flawless, something a trained pilot like Telisan could appreciate. Still, he had hoped to handle the controls himself.

"*Sidhe*, this is *Cheetah* cutter," Horowitz said, "on approach vector, Alpha, for your midship shuttle bay."

"*Sidhe* acknowledging," replied an unfamiliar voice. "Proceed to land." Ahead of them, battle-doors opened. They landed smoothly on the gray, metal deck as the doors cycled closed behind them.

"Thank you, Mr. Horowitz," Telisan said as they disembarked the shuttle.

"Yes," Arpen added, "an excellent flight."

Horowitz beamed a smile at her. "Thank you, ma'am. I have to return immediately. *Cheetah* isn't going to remain idle. We are off to Olympia to announce *Sidhe*'s visit. Good luck to you all."

The Denlenn trio exited the cramped hatchway into a cavernous bay containing the familiar shapes of *Dakota* shuttles. As Telisan walked down the shuttle ramp, he looked for the names. One was *Pooka*, the command shuttle. The other was a newer model; its name was rendered in standard and in Enshari: *Belwin Duna*. Denlenn did not express emotion by tears, yet for a second Telisan fought off the equivalent as memories of his dead mentor surfaced. He nodded to himself in satisfaction. The familiar acrid tang of ozone and lubricant bit at his sensitive nose. Telisan smiled. He did not realize until that moment how much he missed the ship.

"Telisan," called an excited voice. He turned to see Robert Fenaday running up to the shuttle. They gripped arms in Denlenn fashion, then pounded each other on the back like humans. Despite his excitement, Fenaday looked as if he had not slept much in the last few days.

"Thank God you're here," Fenaday said, "even if you are mad to come."

"More than you know," Telisan replied ruefully. "May I introduce you to my fiancées, Sharla and Arpen."

Fenaday looked behind him, obviously startled. The other two Denlenns stood there. He recovered almost instantly, walking up to greet them. "Ladies," he said, bowing. "This is an unexpected honor. I had hoped to receive you properly, at my home."

"Please do not worry, Captain," Arpen said, "both Sharla and I were naval personnel during the War. We are used to shipboard life. I'm sure our quarters will be quite satisfactory."

"Uh," Fenaday said. "Umm."

"We expect to work for our passage," Sharla added, with a devilish smile. "I'm a Grade One-Alpha computer technician, rank of Chief Petty Officer. I served on the Main Battle Carrier *Empress Aran* during the Battle of the Rings."

"I am trained as a neurosurgeon with a specialty in cybernetics," Arpen said. "I held the rank of captain and served on a hospital ship."

"She was decorated too," Sharla said.

"Sharla," Arpen protested.

Fenaday looked at Telisan. "My friend, this is too much to ask of you. Not only to drag you in to danger, but your loved ones? No."

"You need me," Telisan stated. "I am your friend and I am Shasti's. Even if you had not called me, I would have come once I knew. I own my place on this ship."

"Yes, yes," Fenaday said, looking pained, "never doubt that. I just can't see you risking so much."

"This is our matter, Captain," Arpen reproved, "and we have resolved it."

After a moment, Fenaday smiled at her. "Yes, ma'am."

"Then it is settled," she said, seeing his smile and raising it by a mega-watt.

Telisan looked at Fenaday. "You lasted all of five seconds against her."

"I have a feeling that might be a record," the human replied.

"It is," Sharla assured.

Fenaday and Telisan looked at each other and laughed.

"Mr. Dobera," Fenaday called. The Frokossi quartermaster came over, his big gem-like eyes blinking slowly, independent of each other. Dobera had never left *Sidhe*; the Frokossi princeling had nowhere to go. A death sentence awaited him on his homeworld, where he was deposed royalty.

"See the ladies and their luggage to Mr. Telisan's quarters," ordered Fenaday.

Dobera nodded. The iridescent scales of the lizard-like being shifted color in the harsh light. "Good to see you again, Commander," he said in a breathy, whistling voice. Telisan nodded a polite reply. Dobera's opaline eyes focused on the lady's luggage as he pulled out a pocket com to call for stevedores. Once royalty—always royalty.

"Sharla, when you are settled, please report to the bridge," Fenaday said. "I need a lead systems tech. Arpen, if you would be so kind as to report to Sickbay, we have medical personnel inbound. You could get a leg up on inventory and prep."

"Yes, Captain," they replied simultaneously, snapping off crisp military salutes as old habits reestablished themselves.

"As for you, my friend," he said, turning to Telisan, "there is no rest for the wicked. We're eight hours from launch. I have two hundred Navy techs running around prepping the ship. There's a lot to do. The shuttle with Mandela's troops is due just before launch."

"Then let us get to it," Telisan said.

The *Intruder* shuttle came into dock smoothly. Within seconds, pressure doors closed and atmosphere began to fill the shuttle bay. On the bridge, Fenaday did not wait. "Mr. Perez, stand by for initial burn in sixty seconds." *At least,* he thought, *it gets us moving.* "Mr. Wardell, you have the conn. I'm going to greet our new arrivals. Telisan, come with me."

The turbovator deposited them at the shuttle bay in the center of the *Sidhe's* delta-winged hull. In less than a minute, they were walking across the metal plates and tie downs toward the flat-black *Intruder. Sidhe's* two *Wildcat* fighters were attached outboard of the starship's wings for rapid launch, leaving room in the bay for the big *Intruder.* Crab assault robots covered its belly, ready for an atmospheric drop. Now they popped off like fleas, marching to a formation by the prow. One machine, different from the rest, caught Fenaday's eye, a saucer-shaped disk two meters wide: an airbot.

From the back ramp, a reinforced platoon of Air Space Assault Team troops spilled out. Unconsciously mimicking the robots, they formed up on the deck. Side hatches opened and more figures emerged. Humanform Combat Robots, the deadliest of the machines designed for the Conchirri war.

An unwelcome silhouette, tall, spare, and angular, followed the HCRs out. Kyle Mmok, Mandela's watchdog. The robot controller orchestrated the movements of the company of crab robots, airbot, and HCRs by subvocalized commands transmitted through machinery in his body. Most of Mmok's body had been cybernetically replaced. Unlike most of the maimed who received such transplants, Mmok made no attempt to make his cosmetically pleasing. The effect was half man, half machine and all intended, right down to the glassy obsidian square replacing his left eye.

When Fenaday last saw Mmok, he lay comatose after their final battle on Enshar, "shorted" out by an electrical discharge from a Shellycoat. Until Mandela had told him otherwise, Fenaday thought Mmok had died after being taken on the Marine troop carrier *Io*.

Mmok spotted Fenaday. His one good eye narrowed, and his normal grim expression turned sardonic. He walked toward them, trailed by six black-uniformed HCRs, distinguished only by different colored sashes.

"Fenaday," he said curtly. "Reporting aboard."

Fenaday nodded, equally cool. "Mmok, I see you're not dead."

"Not hardly. Disappointed?"

"No," Fenaday replied, almost surprising himself with the truth of it. "I'm glad you made it. We're going to need all the help we can get."

"Mandela sent me," Mmok said, stressing the word *sent*. "He wants his team back and the mission finished."

"Understand this clearly, Mister," Fenaday said, "you're on my ship. I have complete command this trip out. You work for me. The mission objective is to get the survivors. Pard is secondary."

"You're just after Rainhell's ass," Mmok said contemptuously. "I thought with all your money, you wouldn't be so hard up for a new girlfriend."

Telisan started forward, and Fenaday seized his arm. Fenaday moved past Telisan until he stood nose to nose with Mmok. Rage raced through him at Mmok's disrespectful mention of Shasti. Fenaday knew the cyborg was pushing his emotional buttons, trying to anger him. *I'll teach him to be careful what he wishes for,* he thought.

"Okay, you son of a bitch," Fenaday said, keeping his voice level and cold. "You want it rough. I'll give it to you rough. Effective immediately, you address me as Captain. We are going to get Shasti and the team back. You better be prepared to do whatever it takes to do that. If I say frog, you eat flies. You don't and I have a warrant from Mandela to kill anyone I need to, in order to get the mission accomplished. You cross me on this flight and you're going to be the first casualty.

"If you can't deal with that, take your goddamn robots and get back into the *Pooka*. We'll launch you in ten minutes. You can explain to Mandela how you managed to screw up this mission and get kicked off my ship so quickly."

Mmok glared at him, nostrils flared.

"Answer me, Mmok. Do it now. Be prepared to live or die by it."

Long seconds ticked by as they glared at each other. Finally Mmok choked out, "Agreed."

"Agreed, *Captain*," Fenaday hissed, holding onto his temper by his fingernails.

"Agreed, Captain," Mmok said, equally strained.

Taking a page from his old friend Belwin Duna, Telisan looked past the two antagonists and spoke to the slender, feminine-looking robot with the vivid blue sash on its uniform. "Hello, Cobalt. Good to see you are still operational."

"Operating nominally," replied the robot in flat, metallic tones. It was the sole survivor of the original four-unit contingent of HCRs used on Enshar. "Presence of command personnel Telisan and Fenaday noted and logged."

"It means hello," Fenaday said, appreciating the de-escalation. "I see they issued you new robots and more of them."

Mmok also seemed to appreciate the distraction. "Allow me to introduce the new members of my team. Cobalt, you know. This is Indigo, Azure, Cerulean, Midnight, and Sapphire. I am the first controller to manage a sextet of HCRs," he said with evident pride, gesturing to the machines.

They looked like slim girls, an impression given chiefly by the monofilament hair they used both for cooling and antennae. Each bowed as he introduced it, a Mmok touch, hinting faintly of both apology and mockery.

Mmok looked over at Fenaday with a chilly smile. "I'm entering my 'blue period.'"

"Of course you are," Fenaday returned, equally droll.

"Come along, Mmok," Telisan said, seeking to separate the two. "You know the way to your old quarters. Dobera will get you fixed up." The Denlenn waved at the spindly Frokossi quartermaster, who came over to take Mmok and his machines in tow.

More pleasant reunions awaited Fenaday. Rask, Dr. Shizuyo Mourner, and Dr. Yamata came over to greet him. He saw other familiar faces, many he could put names to, among the Confederate personnel. Fenaday had asked for as many Enshar veterans as could be found and persuaded to come. Most of the ASATs were new to him. Casualties in that force had not been light.

Shizuyo Mourner greeted him first. "Well, if it isn't Mr. '*I can't keep my ass out of trouble.*'" A tiny woman of mixed English and Japanese ancestry, Mourner was an exceptional surgeon and an expert on the Enshari. What hold Mandela had on her, Fenaday had no idea, but here she was. He was glad to see her quick, predatory face.

"I gather you've been briefed," he said cautiously. For security's sake, most of the crew did not know the real purpose of the mission. He suspected all of Mandela's operatives were fully informed.

"Yes, of course," she said, as if the idea that anyone would keep her in the dark was patently absurd. Yamata, who actually was from Japan, smiled and nodded. He seldom spoke. Mourner apparently talked enough for both of them.

Lt. Rask commanded the ASATs. He was a blue-skinned, goblin-like Morok, for all that he'd been born on Mars. The Morok strode over and shook hands, human fashion. Shorter than Fenaday, powerfully built, he wore the usual black hair of his species cropped short in a military haircut. The eyes that looked out at Fenaday were red with yellow sclera.

"Congratulations on the new brass on your collar, not to mention the decorations," Fenaday said, pointing.

"It's just more worries and headache." Rask grimaced, his pronounced canines evident. "Life was easier when I was enlisted and Dan did the worrying. Still, it's good to be sailing with you again, Skipper."

"I'm pleased to have all of you," Fenaday said. "This could get dicey."

"Do you ever do anything that isn't dicey?" Mourner asked. Yamata looked nervous at her familiarity with Fenaday.

He just laughed in response. "Doctor, if I live through this, I am never leaving home again, except to ride my horse or visit the winery. I promise."

"What's our status?" Rask asked.

"We did an initial burn as soon as your landing jacks were down. We're on our way to the main accelerator. From there, it's maximum speed to the earliest point we can use the stardrive. Hyperspace is thin between New Eire and Olympia, so the transit will be quick for the distance. Then we enter the system heading for Olympia's orbit after a hard-braking approach to the gas giant. We should be there in fifteen days."

"Over a month and half since contact was lost." Mourner shook her head.

"Yes," Fenaday said, turning grim. The passage of time was a goad, urging him to desperate efforts to launch. It had occurred to him after his meeting with Mandela that the spymaster must have been in New Eire system, awaiting word of the mission. He probably had already dreamt up the present scheme. What else explained the presence of a naval tender and the ease with which Mandela had gathered many of the Enshar veterans?

"I've been less successful at gathering the old crew than has Mandela," Fenaday said, trying to take his mind off Shasti's fate. "Many went on to comfortable postings and didn't want to risk another adventure. I found Li and Morgan from the LEAF troops broke in the offport. Carlos Perez and Dobera never left *Sidhe*; they served under her sailing master these last few months. I never gave up my captaincy, but *Sidhe* needed a commander when I was not aboard.

"The Tok brothers are back. Both turned up on New Eire, living the high life. They balked at the idea of the voyage until I broke security and told them that Shasti was in trouble on Olympia. There's been no holding them after that. Shasti saved both their lives in some fight on Morokat long before she joined the *Sidhe*. They've worked around the clock to get the ship ready, raging at anyone and anything slowing the process.

"Moshe Karass is back too. That fills out the old officer roster," Fenaday said. "He also knows." Karass had never forgotten how Fenaday hired him as *Sidhe's* chief pilot when no one else would. More, Fenaday had believed in him as a good flyer, not the incompetent his former company's lawyers made him out to be. Even though Karass had cleared his record with the funds from Enshar, he'd appeared on the ship the morning after Mandela's visit, working tirelessly on the shuttles since then.

Even with all the returns, Fenaday thought, *Mandela's people will again outnumber mine.* As usual, the spymaster was far ahead and gaining ground. Despite Mourner and Rask's friendliness and their shared time under fire, they were Mandela's and could not be trusted. *Thank God Telisan's come, even bringing help.*

Rask looked at Fenaday. "I'm sure she's alive, Skipper. Dan's there to look after her. I don't think there's much around that can kill her anyway."

"Yeah," Fenaday said. *But what there is that can lives on Olympia,* he thought.

Rask sighed. "They shouldn't have left without us, Skipper. It could only lead to trouble. I told Dan that."

Fenaday nodded, tight-lipped. He put a hand on Rask's shoulder. "Let's remedy that mistake."

Sidhe headed for the New Eire accelerator. All over the ship, the various detachments began the difficult process of shaking down into a crew. There would be little time before they reached Olympia. Activity continued at a furious rate. People began to settle in their slots.

———

T he sickbay surprised Arpen. *Sidhe* was a rebuilt prize-ship from the Conchirri War. Before the Enshar Expedition the frigate had run on a shoestring budget. Arpen feared the worst, but the facilities proved excellent. Fenaday had always shipped a doctor, even in the bad old days when the doctors were of questionable character. Sickbay had also been overhauled by Dr. Mourner during the Enshar expedition and added to since the Shamrock Line restarted. Now Dr. Mourner reappeared with a medical team worthy of a heavy cruiser. The implications were chilling.

The first day went by in a blur. They sorted out duties, shifts, and unloaded the tons of supplies left by the crew of the tender. Arpen rarely saw Sharla and Telisan. They were occupied on the bridge readying the ship for jump.

"Dr. Arpen," called a voice. She turned to see Shizuyo Mourner at the door to the small office. A tall, gaunt figure stood behind her, a human male in his thirties, half his face covered in cyber-prosthetics. She knew him to be Kyle Mmok, robot controller and Mandela's watchdog.

"Yes," Arpen said, "please come in."

"Thank you. I would like to introduce you to a patient, Mr. Mmok. He's having a number of interface difficulties. His visual interface is causing him particular physical pain. Since you are a specialist..."

"And since she'd like to get rid of me anyway," Mmok added dryly.

"Not at all," Mourner said, with her best professional manner. The strain between them was quite visible despite this.

"I would be delighted to work with you, Mr. Mmok," Arpen said.

"You mean on me," replied the half-cyborg, bitterness evident in his tone.

Arpen smiled. "Captain Fournier said the same thing to me when I met him on the *Solace*."

Mmok looked at her intently. "The *Solace*? At Conchir?"

"Yes," Arpen said, "during the Battle of the Rings. I met Captain Fournier after the first day of the assault."

"Yeah, Henri was with the 101st Robot Assault Force in the initial LZ. It was a bad landing," Mmok said.

"Dr. Arpen was on the *Solace*," Mourner said, "when it was hit by a Conchirri fighter. She was awarded the Silver Star for her actions in rescuing patients from a decompressing compartment."

"So," Mmok said with a grudging respect, "you got a medal."

Arpen looked into Mmok's one human eye. "What I got were seven lives saved before the emergency seals gave way. I wasn't about to have all my fine work blown up by lousy Xenos."

Mmok laughed a short bark. Mourner gave Mmok a curious look, as if she had never heard him laugh before.

"We settled their account though, didn't we?" Mmok said.

"Paid in full," Arpen said, giving the standard response of combat troops from the War.

Shizuyo Mourner, who had some reservations about the Confederacy's genocidal extermination of the Xenophobes, looked a bit askance at Arpen. It did not bother Arpen. She had seen the enemy and their works firsthand. They valued no life, even their own. She had no use for such creatures.

"Well, I'll leave you to it," Mourner said.

Arpen gestured to Mmok to come in and sit on the table. As he moved into the room, she immediately assessed him as a three-quarter cyborg, two legs, one arm.

She began running preliminary tests on him and called up his history on the computer screen. "I see that you were in the initial complement of cybernetic replacements. Is that where you met Captain Fournier?"

"Yeah," he replied. "Fournier recruited what was left of me after the Red Star campaign. I'd been a tanker with the 42nd."

"That explains some of this old code I'm seeing in your CPU. Why didn't you have any upgrades?"

Mmok shrugged. "Been busy, always on some assignment. Don't like being fooled with anyway. I had enough of that when I got mostly killed the first time."

"But that has changed now," Arpen said. "Was it the injury on Enshar?"

"You know?" asked Mmok.

"I'm engaged to Telisan," Arpen said. "He told me of carrying you out after the fight at the pit."

"I thought the other Denla female was engaged to him," Mmok said.

"We both are, and Sharla is a demi-female, incidentally. Denlenn have three genders. She'd be embarrassed at being referred to as female."

"Oh, sorry," Mmok said. "I guess I owe your fiancé. He's okay. Hell of a combat record at eighty-three kills."

"Captain Fenaday was glad to have him back, enough so to put up with getting us as well."

"Fenaday," Mmok spat. "Damn pirate, that's all he is."

Arpen glanced at him while adjusting a control. "You do not like our captain?"

Mmok twisted a lip into a sneer. "Mr. Silver Spoon?"

Arpen looked at him, confused.

"Fenaday is from a first landing family," Mmok explained, "on one of the ethnic enclaves separatists set up when they ran out on Earth. First in on the planet. They rape everything in sight, set themselves up as aristocrats, and lord it over everyone. I've seen it all over the Confederacy from Lakota to Retief. He's always had more money than he knew what to do with.

"You'll notice he didn't serve in the War—till after he lost something. I'm sure he would have been out there helping us earlier, except he had his foot caught in all that money."

"My fiancé says he fought well for the Confederacy after he joined," Arpen said with a faint hint of reproof.

"He's got guts enough," Mmok granted, "but he's in things for himself and his own reasons."

Arpen completed an adjustment, uploading a program into Mmok's CPU. "Let us see how this works."

"Hey," Mmok said, pleased. "That's better. The burning in my visual cortex just let up."

"Partially or completely?" asked Arpen.

"I don't feel it at all."

"Mr. Mmok," Arpen said, "I think that there are a significant number of improvements that I can make in your interfaces. I do not want to try them all at once. Even small changes in a cybernetic interface can be disorienting. Cybernetic integration is one of my subspecialties. Can you make time to see me, once a day, so we may phase these in?"

"Okay," Mmok said, almost shyly. "What time?"

"Say, end of first watch," Arpen said, Navy-style.

Mmok stood up. "Aye, aye, Skipper." He threw a sloppy salute and walked out of the office. A careful observer might have noted a lighter mood with the cyborg. Arpen was such an observer. Her empathic instincts had already opened up more of Mmok than he would have been happy realizing. Her diagnosis for Mmok was a common one in her experience with cyborgs. Depression, isolation, and the emotional problems from the mutilation, troubled Mmok far more than the interface difficulties, significant though those were. Her prescription was friendship and contact. What a human doctor would have to struggle with was second nature to Arpen. Befriending Mmok was an instinctual response. It was how a Denla healer worked.

———

On the bridge of the *Sidhe*, Robert Fenaday called battle stations. The klaxon slammed out its demand. Crew raced to stations. Fighter pilots hopped in the small cars that ran them and their launch crews out through tunnels to the fighter stations in the *Sidhe's* wings. Missile ports opened as warheads slid onto launch rails. Laser turrets began to search for computer-generated targets. Chain guns, firing a mixture of explosive and depleted uranium ammunition, came online.

Fenaday tried to contain his frustration. "Damn it, Wardell, where is that main gun?" Fenaday's board still showed red on the ship's main weapon, the mass driver running the length of her hull.

Wardell cursed and leaned into his speaker. "Mass Driver Control, where is your green light?"

Telisan rushed to the station. "Mass Driver Control, you have the second level safety lock still engaged. This is a Conchirri weapon with Confed fire control; it has double safeties because of the interface."

"Mass Driver Control, roger that," came the sheepish reply. "Safeties off, main gun up."

"Main gun, locked," Wardell said. The old former Navy gunner's face was a picture of exasperation.

"Fire," Fenaday said.

"A hit," Sharla called. She was running the computer simulation from the other side as the imaginary enemy. "I'm in range and returning fire. Be afraid, puny humans."

"Enemy 5CM mass driver has struck the tail, significant structural damage," Lt. Hafel said, relaying simulated damage control calls.

"Missiles inbound," Wardell added. "Counter missiles have stopped five. One inbound, chain guns have it. Missile destroyed."

"Main gun, recycled," Telisan said.

"Fire main gun and follow with a spread of missiles. Come hard to port and open the range."

"Damn," Sharla swore, retargeting her weapons. "Your main gun got one of my lasers and a ball gun. A missile is coming in through the hole. You got me."

"Wonderful," Fenaday said. "What a pity we were just hit by a Conchirri escort, which we should have blown up from well outside their range. We are now non-atmospheric due to damage."

"We need more work." Telisan shook his head. "A lot more."

Wardell stood up. "Permission to go kick some ass in Mass Driver Control."

"Affirmative," Fenaday said. "Secure from General Quarters. We don't have time for another simulation. We are coming up on the accelerator. That will be tricky enough maneuvering, so I'll take the helm myself on that approach. I don't lack confidence in you, Mr. Graglia," he said, addressing the young Navy officer who had come in on Mmok's shuttle, "but your last helm slot was on a battle-cruiser. *Sidhe* is a lot friskier."

"Yes, sir," Graglia said. He wore the rank of senior lieutenant. Mandela had hijacked him in transit to a carrier group for Fenaday's flight crew. Despite his impressive flight record, Fenaday didn't want him taking the unfamiliar Conchirri vessel down the throat of a mass accelerator at their current speed.

"When we come out the other side," Telisan said, "I want to re-run the exercise, only this time with an enemy light cruiser."

Fenaday spared his friend a grin. "Ambitious, huh."

"Hoo-rah," replied the Denlenn. They both laughed.

"The station is calling, sir," Hafel said. "We are entering the control area for the accelerator."

Fenaday slid into the helmsman's slot and checked his instruments. "Put him through to my station." He made slight adjustments on course and speed. Fenaday knew *Sidhe* as a man knew his own hands. Each ship possessed its own peculiarities. *Sidhe* would pick up a harmonic vibration at exactly two hundred km per sec. This could transmit to the controls under certain circumstances. In the close approach to the three thousand-meter aperture of the accelerator, the vibration could mean disaster. Fenaday kicked *Sidhe's* speed over the harmonic and recalculated the approach, humming, "Oh Danny Boy," as they lined up.

"This is New Eire Accelerator Station Control to *Sidhe*. Are you prepared for Accelerator Pattern Entry?"

"This is Captain Fenaday. I have the helm and am in preliminary line up."

Fenaday and the Accelerator began exchanging numbers, fine-tuning the vessel's heading. With his military transit pass, he could determine how far he wanted to push the vessel's entry speed.

"Ah, sir," Graglia said, "you are fifty KPS over the recommended entry speed."

"Yes, Mr. Graglia," Fenaday replied, "I am. Is that all right with you, or would you like to distract me some more?"

Graglia found Telisan at his elbow, looking daggers at him. "No sir. Sorry, sir."

"Don't worry, Mr. Graglia," Fenaday added, "if I screw this up, you'll never even know it. Mr. Telisan, sound the collision alert and secure for high-speed maneuvers."

"Yes, sir."

The klaxon sounded a tattoo. All space-tight compartments sealed. The ship readied for the acceleration.

Sidhe plunged into the electromagnetic net of the accelerator. Caressed by Saint Elmo's fire, her crimson hull raced toward the immense skeletal tunnel. The mass accelerator drew the ship into its embrace and, in a flash, flung her ahead at .90C, heading for the edge of New Eire's solar system, where field densities would drop to allowable levels for the stardrive to engage.

———

I n his office in the expanded Denshi compound, overlooking the foothills of the Eska Range, Antebei, Head of Section Seven, Internal Security, fumed in silence. None dared enter the office of the mercurial but brilliant Fourth-Generation Engineered. Word of the botched operation and Pard's displeasure with him raced like wildfire around the compound, half fortress, half office complex.

Antebei, so advanced he was considered by some as the first of the Fifth-Generation, had been bested by a mere Third-Generation female. Pard's old bed toy, Rainhell, had escaped him. His rival, that pedestrian genetic effort, Vaughn, now had the assignment.

Failure might upset his meteoritic rise in Denshi, already opposed by many of the Obsolete who feared his youth and ability. Antebei's rise was unprecedented, but so was he. His strength and endurance exceeded that of anyone created to date. He was the optimum balance of power and speed. Antebei ground his teeth in frustration; he must not allow it to happen. Somehow he must win back Pard's favor and soon. Already the old guard favored Vaughn, plodding Vaughn, for his traditional approach and attitude. Genius could not be so confined. Still, without Pard's favor, Antebei's own partisans would defect to Vaughn. For now though, all he could do was wait for some mistake by Rainhell or Vaughn to deliver either of them into his hands. Frustration built in him, interfering with his concentration.

He pressed a button slowly, reluctantly, as if under some compulsion. His secretary, Paula Kallian, entered, eyes downcast, looking as if she wished she dared bolt. But she did not dare. Paula was not Engineered; they did not fill such menial positions. She was not even Selected but came from the lowest class, the Unsanctioned. Her genetics were far too poor for the position she held. Few Olympians would find her attractive, with her imperfectly formed body. She was short, with breasts too large for symmetry. Her lack of perfection both repelled and aroused Antebei. What others saw as charity to the less gifted was to him a secret perversion.

Paula knew what the summons meant, another down payment on a position and wealth she could not otherwise hold in Olympia's increasingly stratified society. Antebei's beautiful face, modeled on that of Michelangelo's creation, was cold and foreboding. She came up to the desk. Before she could speak, he seized her, throwing her down on the desktop. His mouth found hers. His hands grasped her large breasts ungently. *Let it be quick this time,* she prayed. Against Pard's favorite, she had no other recourse.

Chapter Seven

L eda Jenner, as she had every day for four weeks, checked the street for a full five minutes before turning onto the block of their safe house. It was mid-morning and Olympia's primary hung in a brilliant cerulean sky, decorated with wisps of cirrus clouds. Sunlight reflected off the blues and whites of the buildings, making Leda glad for her sunglasses. She could see a tiny trace of the ice ring, visible in daylight when the sun struck it at the right angle. She took it for a good omen and started down the block, pushing a small frictionless cart loaded with groceries and those medical supplies she could buy without drawing attention. Fortune had put a market only a few blocks away.

Jenner zipped the light jacket that covered her auto-pistol. Mornings remained cool, so it did not look strange. Their apartment building, like most in this industrial area, dated from the original settlement of the capital. It sat back from the broad streets and their noisy commercial traffic.

So far, the alternate safe house set up by her cell had lived up to its name. Jenner suspected this was because the other members of her cell had been killed instead of captured. No one could have held out under interrogation this long. Still, the memory of the death of the rest of the team at the first safe house kept her from getting sloppy.

She carefully avoided eye contact with the few people on the sidewalk. Odds of running into someone she knew were small. She'd lived in Marathon for a few years after graduation, before giving up and moving back to Manki. Jenner avoided the sections of town where her old apartment and job had been. These were the first places Denshi would search. Though she had many friends in the uplands, she had no close relations and none of her friends lived in the capital. Her conscience twinged as she thought of those friends facing Denshi interrogation. They didn't know of her work against the Olympian Government, so they could not hurt her. She wanted to call and warn them, but Rainhell had vetoed it. Her icy-green eyes bored into Jenner when she protested, silently promising death if Jenner threatened their security.

Jenner found herself longing for home, the quiet farming community of Helios outside of Manki. Opportunities for the Selected were hard to come by in the rural county of Pleonaisse. For the Unsanctioned like herself, it was worse. Not only did the Aristos treat the Unsanctioned like dirt; they made the Selected crueler to her kind. Perhaps the Selected needed something to look down on, to reassure themselves that they were not obsolete.

She had been ripe for picking by Confed security when they contacted her. Jenner played the game, enjoying both the money and the small revenge it gave her on Olympia. Now, in the desperate straits they were in, Helios seemed like a warm, safe place.

At least, she thought, *I can get out of the house during the day.* Shasti's Engineered appearance was too great a danger. She grimaced as she remembered working on Shasti with all the cosmetic feminine arts, trying to make her look less like a high-level Aristo. Shasti found the process both distasteful and unusual, having never used such artifices before. Fortunately, Shasti's face was not well known on Olympia. She'd never allowed her photo to be taken and had changed considerably since fleeing Olympia at age sixteen. Unlike most of the Enshar survivors, Shasti shunned publicity after the expedition, hiding out on the Fenaday estate till other news overtook the media.

Now that they were actively sought, danger outweighed vanity. Jenner had dyed Shasti's blue-black hair to an undistinguished brown; a foot of it went to the scissors. Contact lenses made her eyes an ordinary hazel. Nothing could be done about her height, but clothes disguised her perfect symmetry and hid her obvious strength.

Jenner knew Shasti was still working on the mission. She haunted libraries, computer stores and public netways, tracking police movements and Denshi activities. The chaotic nature of the Olympian government prevailed even on the computer net. Olympians battled hackers constantly. Their privacy firewalls and viral protections were second to none. It made net tracing almost impossible.

Their attempts to reach the embassy failed. The Confederation Embassy was a secured point, ringed by Denshi and Navy troops. Even Shasti could find no discreet means of establishing contact or getting aid.

Tomorrow night Shasti would again slip into the offport, the mix of bars, warehouses, dives, and flophouses that surrounded every spaceport. They needed weapons, information, and a way off world. Security in the offport was far easier to circumvent than it was at the port itself. Yet, her efforts had come to nothing.

So they lived—hurt, alert, always afraid—for more than a month.

Jenner finally reached the safety of the door. To her surprise, Daniel Rigg opened it. Deprived of proper medical care, he'd battled infections and complications that would be child's play to a physician.

"Hi honey, I'm home," Jenner quipped. She liked the big ASAT, both for his sense of humor and his quiet strength.

The big man smiled, lighting up his usually solemn face. "Good, dear, you're just in time. Baby has been very sulky today."

Jenner laughed.

From the other room, Shasti called out, "I heard that."

Jenner put the groceries on the kitchen table as Shasti walked into the room wearing a sports bra and stretch pants. Her skin glowed with fine perspiration. Smooth muscle flexed on her arms and stretched the thighs of the pants. Shasti practiced martial arts several hours a day. It took the edge off her nerves, restoring her good humor, to the extent she had one.

The older woman looked at Shasti, admiring the perfection of face and figure, powerful, yet feminine. "Ah," she sighed, "what I would have given to have had your genetics when I was young."

Shasti looked back at her grimly. "My genetics came with quite a price tag. More than you would be willing to pay."

"Yes, of course," Jenner said. There seemed to be a pleasant, upbeat mood in the room tonight that she didn't want to dispel. Turning to Rigg, she said, "It's so good to see you on your feet again. Don't overdo it."

"Yeah. I feel more like my old self."

Shasti surprised them both by gently poking a finger in Rigg's ribs. Physical intimacy was unusual with her. "There is a lot less of your old self. Maybe tonight you'll have a bit more appetite."

"Who's cooking?" Rigg asked hopefully. Shasti and Jenner shared cooking duties while Rigg was bedridden. Cooking proved not to be one of Shasti's talents.

Jenner laughed again. "I'll cook for tonight. I think you might be up to a turn in the kitchen before long." Rigg looked comically crestfallen, and even Shasti laughed this time. Jenner looked at her quizzically. She had never heard the big woman laugh before.

The next hour was spent in an almost domestic fashion with Jenner preparing dinner. Despite the older woman's protestations about not overtiring himself, Rigg insisted on helping her, considerably slowing the process. Shasti retired to the living room to watch the video monitor, as always scanning the news for useful information.

Jenner looked at Rigg, as he stirred the sauce. "She is quite beautiful, isn't she?"

"I suppose," Rigg replied, his eyebrows rising in surprise.

"Have you and her...?" Jenner asked, her feminine curiosity getting the better of her.

"Good God, no," Rigg said. "She's a bit on the large, muscular size for my taste."

"Don't you like fit women?" Jenner teased.

"Of course," Rigg returned, the bright grin again splitting his too thin face. "But, well, she seems just too perfect. Doesn't need anyone. Sort of intimidating, I guess. Besides, she was pretty much involved with Robert Fenaday by the time I met her."

"Really," Jenner said. "The reporters missed that. What a shame—a romance and an exciting adventure."

Rigg chopped the onions with a chef's knife. "It was exciting enough, all right. As for Shasti and him, they kept it low key. They didn't much care for being talked about."

———

Shasti, in the other room, listened to them with a curious mixture of sadness and amusement. Her hearing was enhanced far more than even Jenner suspected. Their conversation spoke volumes to her about a life she'd never had. About ways of being with people, a human subtext she shared in only a limited fashion. She'd wondered if returning to her homeworld would ease her isolation. It had not. Perhaps the growing gap between the Engineered and standard humans could not be bridged.

Jenner was an example of selective breeding, even if she was unsanctioned, but she was not engineered. She lived on Daniel Rigg's side of the gap. When the ASAT looked at her, he saw only a woman of exceptional looks and vitality for her age. When he looked at Shasti, he saw an alien. Pard's movement in the Olympian government was based on the Engineered. While it had some general support, Pard drew the hard core of his power from the products of Dr. Hagen's labs. Maybe it was this alienation, the fear they inspired, that bound the Engineered together.

Pard, she thought, with a familiar reflexive chill. *I'll get you.* She knew the others could think only of escape. But she hadn't come so far to give up, at least not yet. Escape seemed no less impossible than destroying the monster haunting her dreams, dreams that came more frequently and vividly now. She no longer hoped for escape, just to put an end to the dreams. It seemed the wildest fantasy to believe any of them would survive. Denshi would close on them eventually. All she wished for was a clean shot at Pard before the end came. He must know she was here. He could not turn down the challenge of her presence on Olympia. She shared none of this with the others.

"Shasti," Jenner leaned into the room, "come to the table. Dinner is ready."

"Hey," Rigg said, "it's really good. I helped."

Shasti stood, looking at the two of them, appearing for all the world like impatient parents at the dinner table. "Thank you." Then moved by a sudden impulse, she added, "Tonight, I'll do the dishes."

The voyage out to jumpspace was a fast transit even by military standards. Fenaday pushed the star-frigate mercilessly. *Sidhe* needed to enter hyperspace from a particular point at the edge of New Eire for the fastest transit to Olympia. Any other entry point could add weeks, even months, to the journey. For many on *Sidhe*, only informed they were bound on a visit-of-state to repair failing relations with a member world, time seemed to fly. For others, knowing the true and desperate nature of the voyage, seconds dragged.

Keyed up after their efforts, Telisan and Fenaday sometimes unwound by sparring in the ship's small gymnasium. The younger Denlenn, with his fighter pilot reflexes, had come a long way quickly. Fenaday soon learned standard kagis were useless on the Denlenn, with his extra arm joints. It was like trying to tie up spaghetti. Though they battled each other, in their mind's eyes, each saw a huge shadowy figure, an image of fear, with a face seen only in holos—Pard.

Fenaday and Telisan plotted, planned, and argued over every detail of the mission to come, drilling the ship's crew constantly. In these sessions, with Mmok and Rask, tensions between Fenaday and the cyborg often flared. Mmok was bound to respect Fenaday's authority as captain, but cold formality did not prevent his sarcastic wit from biting. The cyborg avoided the two subjects that would turn the strain between them violent: Lisa Fenaday and

Shasti Rainhell. Otherwise, he needled where he could, despite Rask's disapproval and Telisan's yellow cat-eyed glare. It was not his job to make them happy, just to get the Confederacy's business done.

Mmok was provoked beyond his usual dyspepsia because they were bound for Olympia, the planet of perfect people. He could already see them looking down their perfect noses at him, the cobbled together remnants of something once human. Shasti Rainhell had looked at him that way. She would have died before living on as he had. The thought of her also disturbed him; beautiful, strong, unattainable for someone like him, unattemptable even. He hated her. He hated Fenaday even more for having her, for his wealth, privilege, and for his damned luck. Enshar did not make Mmok wealthy, as it had the spoiled landing family heir. He was regular military, worked for a paycheck, not a commission. No one called a press conference for him who'd fought as hard as any. Fenaday and Rainhell hadn't even bothered to see if he survived his wounds.

Fuck them, he thought, *fuck them all, but Fenaday particularly.* He and his kind, the separatists and ethnicists, would be swept away by the coming wave of Federalism. The playing field would be re-leveled. People would be judged on the content of their character, rather than from where their ancestors hailed.

Mmok spent most of his time alone in his cabin when he was not forced to work with others. He found the company of the HCRs, with their literal machine minds, more palatable to him than people. There was one exception. Each day since the voyage started, he spent several hours with Arpen. She improved his interfaces remarkably. His vision no longer troubled him, hearing was better, even the sense of "touch" he received through his prosthetics had improved. He walked less stiffly.

Mmok had never had much use for aliens. They were rare in the northern areas of what used to be Canada before the World Government took over. The Xenophobe war gave him little reason to change his opinion. He served reluctantly with Dua-Denlenn, regarding them with contempt. Enshari and Frokossi rarely fought outside of their respective systems. Their contributions to the

Conchirri war had been limited. He tolerated Moroks as good fight-ers, though he did not care for the smell of them.

He'd imagined Denlenn to be similar to their disreputable and mercenary cousins, the Dua-Denlenn. In this, he found himself wrong. He admired Telisan but could not abide his friendship with Fenaday. Sharla proved to be as efficient a comp tech as anyone could want, but Arpen shaped his attitude the most. He began to look forward to his daily work-ups with the Denlenn doctor. This surprised him. After his initial rehab as a cyborg, he'd never wanted to see another doctor again. Still, cyborgs required maintenance. He tolerated only minimal levels of it beyond what he could do for himself. Now, he found himself counting the hours until he could see Arpen again. He assumed that since there were no casualties among the warship's young and healthy crew, she was bored. Yet, it did not come across that way. She seemed interested, amused by his stories, even enjoying his company.

It took him back to a time before a Conchirri laser cannon sheared into his *Greyhound* light tank, severing him from limbs and a normal life. In a way, it hurt talking to her, so light and free. Some-times, he felt the presence of the man he had been, a man he thought long gone.

Too many deep thoughts, he said to himself, turning into the sickbay corridor. He resolved to keep today's session more professional and detached.

Arpen looked up from the desk, and her expression lit up space for at least several astronomical units. *How does she do that?* he wondered, even as he felt his own face muscles stretch into an unac-customed smile. *She isn't of my species, not even good-looking; still, she has a face like sunrise.*

Mmok's reticent promise to himself failed under Arpen's cheerful assault. They spent more time talking today, though she did some work on his tactile sensation buffer. Feeling foolish, but oddly lighter, he found himself blithering away on any subject she raised. All the while he fought the sensation he was giving himself away, unlocking things he wanted secret or buried. Around Arpen, he had no more chance of remaining frozen than did ice in spring.

"So," he asked, "when are you getting hitched?"

"When we return to Denla," Arpen replied absently, working on his cybernetic wrist joint.

"You mean if." He regretted the words instantly. "Sorry."

She shrugged. "The universe will go as it will go, not as I would have it. If I worried about such things, I would never have become engaged to a pilot and a warship comp-tech. Still, I will be glad when this is over. Telisan is so busy with the ship I hardly ever see him. Sharla is barely less so. You do me a favor by keeping a lonely Denlenn company."

"It's me who's lucky." He surprised himself with his sincerity. "I don't have much use for people, nor they for me."

Arpen stopped and stood. He was sitting on the examination table; even so, she had to look up at him. "Many, if not all, are uncomfortable around a cyborg. Some, in time, get past the issue and see you are the same person you were before."

"Arpen," he said quietly, "even I don't see that person."

"I do."

"You didn't even know me before," he protested with a slight heat.

"Nonetheless." Her eyes drew him in. "I see him."

Mmok looked at Arpen and shivered. Like most humans, he anthropomorphized aliens. He could forget Arpen was anything but a doctor, even if she was the most compassionate he'd ever met. She did not look human now. Her face was all strange planes and angles, huge reflective cat's eyes, leathery skin, lipless mouth. Alien. He felt as if she were pulling his soul out for them both to see.

The moment passed. Arpen looked away, seeming a little saddened. "I would like to see you take the chance to find these people who can look beyond. You must start with yourself. If you cannot see that person, how can they?"

Mmok was strangely bothered by her look of sadness, perhaps even of disappointment. *Why do I care?* he wondered, bewildered. *I've known this alien three lousy weeks. Why do I care?* But he did care.

"I'll try," he blurted out. A second before, he'd no intention of speaking, now the words hung before his face, unrecallable.

"Good." Arpen smiled. It almost physically warmed up the room.

"Well, I should get going," Mmok said, suddenly tired. They'd talked for well over an hour. Arpen was nothing if not intense.

"Same time tomorrow?" she asked brightly.

Mmok felt the same foolish smile spread over his face. "Of course. After that, we hit jumpspace."

"We will have time on the inbound leg," she said, as if the sessions were something she too did not want to see end.

"Sure, Doc."

"Remember what you said to me," she added.

"I will," Mmok replied. "I promise."

He exited Sickbay heading toward the galley. As he hit the ship's "Broadway," he saw Fenaday walking in the opposite direction. The Irishman's eyes flicked over him without expression. As they passed, Mmok grunted out, "Morning."

Fenaday looked surprised for a second. "Morning, Mr. Mmok."

Now why the hell did I do that? Mmok wondered. *I hate the son-of-a-bitch.*

Mmok entered the wardroom, grabbing a sandwich and some coffee. There were some people about. None spoke to him. He saw Rask sitting in front of a chessboard, methodically munching his food. His red eyes made the stare particularly vacant. Feeling almost as if his feet were moving of their own volition, Mmok walked over.

Rask looked up. His blue-tinged, goblin-like face was too alien to tell if he was curious, or merely noting Mmok's presence.

"You play?" Mmok gestured at the board.

"Yeah. I'm good too. Don't get much chance for a decent game."

"Maybe I can give you one."

Rask grinned, showing fearsome canines. "You're on. Have a seat."

Mmok folded awkwardly into a chair.

"You a betting man?" Rask asked.

"Say five credits." Mmok sipped his coffee.

"Black or white?" Rask grinned even more broadly.

———

B ack in Sickbay, Arpen looked up to see Shizuyo Mourner walking into her small office.

"So how is it going with Mmok?" asked Mourner.

"He progresses," Arpen said, "very slowly."

"I thought you would have those interfaces humming by now," Mourner said, surprise on her face.

"Oh, those could have been done in three days. They require considerable adjustment, but that was mere technical work. The true work is the healing of the soul; there, progress is by inches. His isolation is very complete. He populates his world with simulacrums of people, his robots, and does without the real kind. I hope daily contact with me will open up some interest in other people."

"Ah," Mourner said, "I wasn't aware you were a psychologist as well."

"It is not considered a separate skill among Denlenn," Arpen said. "Many of an individual's health problems start with the life they lead."

"Mind a piece of advice?" Mourner sat on the exam chair.

"Of course not. Please go on."

"You have been spending a great deal of time with this patient. I don't know how it is with Denlenn, but human patients can dump responsibility for their whole life on a doctor. Sometimes, it's better to retain some professional distance."

Arpen looked at her, puzzled. "How can you heal from a distance? Denlenn healers treat the whole person. In a sense, I do expect to take responsibility for the patient's life for a time. Healing Mmok's inadequate interfaces does not help his greatest illness, the alienation he feels from others of his kind. That is the source of most of the physical ailments he suffers."

"If he is depressed," Mourner said, "I can prescribe an anti-depressant."

Arpen checked herself. Mourner was a human healer. It was a different species, a different life. She could not assume her own way was right. Still, it shocked her to hear a doctor rely on a temporary change of blood chemistry as a solution.

"I do not believe," she said, "that drugs are an answer to loneliness and isolation. People are."

Mourner stood. "It appears, Doctor, that we practice medicine differently."

"So it would seem," Arpen replied. "We may have something to learn from each other. I shall bear your advice in mind."

"Perhaps." Mourner turned to leave. Arpen could not read human tone, or facial expressions well, but it did not take an expert to detect a lack of enthusiasm in Mourner's answer.

Arpen returned to her work, troubled. Human medicine differed from the holistic approach taken by Denlenn healers. She knew this from the war. Humans made superb surgeons. They raised pharmacology to a high art, even for other species. It was the distance between healer and healed among them that seemed so alien. Humans concentrated on "fixing" the problem, with a perception that people were like the machinery that skilled technicians repaired. Though more efficient than the Denlenn way, which required many more physicians and healers for a smaller population, it seemed cold and mechanistic to Arpen.

She was responsible for Mmok now, having taken his case. His physical ailments she'd resolved; now she sought to help him to a life more worth living. The medical relationship that was difficult for a human healer was very natural for a Denlenn female. Empathic skill was something prized above all else in her kind. It occurred to her that there was less innate psychological difference between human males and females than between Denlenn genders. What differences that did exist were minimized by a culture that insisted on equality between genders. Empathy became more a question of individual ability than gender characteristic. It explained much. *I must remember,* she thought, *they are alien.*

———

F enaday relieved Telisan on the bridge. The Denlenn stood and stretched, limbs going off in impossible angles, his unlined, yet leathery-looking face split by a very human-looking yawn.

"Everything okay?" Fenaday asked.

"Quiet and peaceful, Robert."

"I had something weird happen," the human complained.

"What?"

"Ran into Mmok, he said good morning to me."

"Hmm," Telisan said with the Denlenn equivalent of raised eyebrows. "Was he coming from Sickbay?"

"Arpen," they both said and laughed.

"Don't tell me she can find a heart for the Tin Woodsman?" Fenaday said.

Telisan hesitated.

Fenaday knew that Telisan felt that not all the bad blood between his friend and Mmok was the cyborg's fault. Mandela had put Mmok onboard during the Enshar expedition as a watchdog, certainly a necessary precaution at the time. Fenaday made no effort then, or now, to become friends with the cyborg. Nor had Shasti, who kept everyone but Fenaday at a distance. It was not surprising that she, Olympian and aloof, did not befriend Mmok or that Mmok attributed it to her planet's obsession with physical perfection. On the other hand, Fenaday passionately disliked Mmok, the HCRs, and their master, Mandela.

Fenaday gave in to his friend's discomfort with the insult to the cyborg. "Sorry. Not too sensitive I guess."

"He does what he must, as do we."

"Yeah, maybe."

"One should not forget he got his wounds in the Great War," Telisan reminded him. Mmok was, after all, a fellow veteran.

"Okay," Fenaday conceded, "you're right." He sighed. "I suppose I should have tried to find out if he was dead or alive after Enshar. I was occupied with Shasti and getting my old home back. Worse still, I would have had to go to his bastard boss Mandela to find out anything. I wasn't willing to do that."

"In truth," Telisan said, "I am at fault here as well. I made no more effort than you. I was in mourning for Duna and in love with Sharla and Arpen. I wonder if many of our troubles with Mmok do not come from our treating him like one of his machines."

Fenaday sighed again. "I'll make an effort. I doubt if it will work, and I will not be provoked by the son of a...by him. God help him if he mentions Lisa, or Shasti's, names with disrespect again. Otherwise, I'm willing to try and get along."

"Hey, wait a minute," Fenaday said. "It occurs to a suspicious mind that there's a greater force at work in this sudden concern about Mmok's morale: a controlling intelligence in the background, insidious and with its own agenda. Who could that be, I wonder?"

Fenaday looked at his friend, who appeared embarrassed and pretended to be studying the star field on the main screen. The human turned to cast a mock glare at Sharla, who suddenly found something interesting on her instruments. Fenaday leaned closer to the Denlenn. "Don't worry. I was married too. My wife could always talk me into things when she wanted to."

Telisan gave him a quick grin and headed for the exit. Fenaday sank into the cushioned command chair. It dawned on him that it was the first time he had mentioned his wife without the familiar knife-like pain in his chest, without the dimming of colors, the sudden heaviness of the air, crushing any joy out of life. It was good to be able to think of her without pain. His mind sometimes skittered away from remembrance because of that pain. *I mustn't let that happen,* he thought fiercely. *That is my past. I want to keep every second of it. I don't live there anymore, but I want, I need, to remember it, all of it.*

Balance still eluded Fenaday. He felt disloyal to the past when he thought of the present, and felt he cheated the present when he dreamed of the past. *Maybe there is no right way to do this. Maybe everything I do is wrong,* he thought. *Right now, all I can do is concentrate on saving the one I can reach.*

Sharla rescued him from spinning down further in such thoughts, bringing a transmission from Mandela. More useless information, all of it weeks out of date to what was happening on Olympia. He'd made a policy of not responding, hoping it annoyed the puppet-master. Sharla smiled Denlenn fashion. "You look lost in thought, Captain."

Fenaday hesitated. He'd known Sharla only a few weeks, but they shared watches daily on the bridge. Lately he'd spent more time with her than with Telisan. While Arpen captivated the crew, Fenaday had come to appreciate the demi-female, with her quiet competency, all the more. He looked about. The bridge was on fourth watch and fully manned. Graglia sat at the helm. Perez and his engineers were working on the large bridge monitors. The ambient noise from people and machinery would cover a soft conversation. He swiveled his chair away from the flight stations of helm and gunnery to face Sharla.

"Balancing the past and the present, I suppose. I feel uncomfortable with trying to start a new life without having found all the answers from the old one. I feel suspended, caught in the middle."

"You refer," Sharla said, keeping her voice low, "to your wife and to Shasti Rainhell."

He nodded slowly.

"Telisan told me much of your story. I may understand better than you realize. You balance between a lost love and a present one."

"Well, I don't... I don't know," he stammered, wishing he hadn't started the conversation, "that I love Shasti or that she loves me. I know she's important to me. I owe her my life."

Sharla looked at him skeptically. "So you say, but if it is not love, it appears much the same."

Not for the first time, Fenaday wondered what it must be like to be on a regular Navy vessel where the distances between ranks forbade such conversations. *Well, I did start this.* "As you say," he replied, waving a hand in surrender.

Sharla gave a little laugh, then turned serious again. "My life is always that way. I am demi-female, not one nor the other. I am the middle. My loves are the poles. They meet in me. As the demi, I am charged with finding the balance. I must favor neither one at the expense of the other. I soak up the shocks from both, so they do not pass through me. I am no more or less Arpen's than I am Telisan's. It is the role of my kind.

"You seek a balance between two loves, as do I. So I have a piece of advice to offer you. Only Shasti is here to be warmed by that love. One is not balanced with a gold bar in one hand and the memory of a gold bar in the other."

"I hear you." He nodded.

"Now that you have put up with my dreadful impertinence," she added, "you must let me make amends. I suggest we all have dinner in our cabin tonight. Tomorrow is jump. Once we are on the other side, in Apollo system, who knows what we may face? Please say you will come."

Fenaday could not help smiling at the earnest Denlenn, though a sudden foreboding lay on his heart. "Telisan is a lucky man," he said. "I should never have sent for him, and I should never have let any of you come. If something happens, I will regret it for as long as I live."

Sharla shook her head, her tawny hair rippling slightly. "You could not stop my fiancé, being who and what he is. He would have learned eventually and set off alone if you denied him a place. As Arpen said, this was our decision. We've made it, and there is no more to say on it. Now, will you promise to come to dinner?"

"Yes," he said, his throat tight, "I would be honored."

"Excellent. At eight bells then."

Fenaday nodded, turning in his seat so Sharla could no longer see his eyes. They stung with pent tears. *Our Father,* he prayed silently, *who art in heaven, keep my friends safe. If someone must fall, let it be me. Just leave me standing long enough to help Shasti, just that long. It is all I ask.*

As ever, there was only silence.

———

Shasti stepped off the hoverbus, having finally reached the area around the spaceport in the early evening hours. She'd left Rigg and Jenner in the safe house before taking public transit into the port area. After a careful look around the busy street, she started toward the seedier section closer to the fenced area of the port. The buildings were a mix of old and new. Most contained shops full of exotic offworld goods.

She found herself wishing she were on foggy Apeldorn or Kubota with its constantly swirling rainstorms. Unfortunately, Marathon's skies remained clear and cloudless, depriving her of any comforting cloak of haze or rain. She made do with the pools of shadow between streetlights. Olympia's small distant moon and the ice ring did little to dispel that darkness. Despite her size, Shasti had the ability to be unobtrusive at need. As she had painfully learned in training, people simply did not see unmoving objects. Be one with the dark, be one with the earth, be still and live. It was easier on her homeworld. Here, she was neither so much taller, nor so much more beautifully perfect, than other humans.

Jenner had helped her with cosmetic changes, but there was more. Shasti employed other subtleties, posing as a trader from the house of Bremard and adopting the mannerisms and bearing of a merchant. The Bremardi had fallen on hard times since Denshi operatives assassinated the last Duke. The killing had been professional, licensed, and legal, but many viewed it as advancing Denshi's interest more than those of the ostensible client. It gave one grounds for a grudge, even on Olympia.

Her fake identity would allow her cover to haunt the spaceport, finding some way for the rest of the team to escape Olympia. She'd long since discarded her original identity papers. Using them again courted instant capture. All members of the team had backup sets. They were quite genuine. Jenner's cell arranged the alternate identities and histories long before the Confed team started out for Olympia. They were for different missions. The first set, meant for closing in on the target, came from databases friendly to the guild of assassins. The second set, drawn from enemies of Denshi, was for after the sanction, or as a hedge against the situation they were in now.

Denshi and the government continued to hunt them quietly. The news contained no mention of the team. Reporters blamed the explosion at the apartment complex on Neo-Reformist extremists, trying to bring back the old ways of the Allessandro natural genetic programs. Shasti did not think the police had been brought in yet. In that much, her presence on the team provided an extra margin of safety. Pard did not want his laundry aired in public. He might even want her alive. She suppressed a shiver at the thought. *Never that*, she promised herself, *never that*.

Denshi lacked reliable access to the databases of the trade unions, the Neo-Reformists, or the merchant guilds. It was a system built for espionage, nourished by treachery and mistrust, and quintessentially Olympian. For Shasti and the others, the hollows in that interface were their only chance at survival.

Shasti stayed away from Denshi-controlled and influenced areas, which was most of the capital. A network of connections, safety lines and bridges existed among the neutrals and other enemies of Denshi. Shasti headed for one such bridge now, the *Space Witch*, a place for merchants to meet and barter cargoes. Though this section of town welcomed offworlders, there wouldn't be many. Olympians dominated the in-system trade. Aliens and offworlders remained restricted to the capital and the port area.

The big merchant vessels rarely landed. Most of their cargoes dropped planetward in shuttles. She sought some of the lesser operators, who sailed on smaller margins and landed mid-size vessels on the planet itself. They did most of the smuggling off and on-world. The government never entirely shut down the trade. Too many of the elite had become fond of illegal imports, a rot in the highest levels.

Shasti studied the *Witch* from the shadow of a nearby alley, decided it was safe, and sauntered over as if she had no fears or concerns in the world. Neon lights glared on its dark outside, promising erotic and sinful delights. The entrance was down three broad stairs. She slipped past a few spacers and locals who'd obviously started early and went inside. A long wooden bar backed by a mirror ran the length of one wall. Three bartenders served a large, noisy crowd. A band was setting up on the stage; meanwhile, recorded music kept the dance floor full.

A bartender caught her eye. "A beer," she said.

"What type?"

"Whatever's on tap."

The bartender slid a liter of golden, foamy liquid to her. She left a payment on the bar, edged into the darkest corner, and eyed the pickings. Several deep-spacers stood at the bar. A Dua-Denlenn, she dismissed out of hand, unable to bring herself to trust one. Several Moroks clustered in one private alcove. Not good. It would be difficult to get in and out unnoticed. A standard human stood at the end of the bar. He wore the uniform of the Trans-Nebula Combine, a possibility.

Shasti sipped her drink, enjoying the wheaty taste of it. Gradually, she drifted around the bar. Men came up to her and made conversation. She struggled with small talk, never an art of hers.

Most drifted off, disappointed, when she kept the conversation businesslike. Shasti started toward the man in the Trans-Nebula uniform when the front door to the bar swung open. Immediately, she faded back into an alcove. On stage, the house band cranked up, a momentary bit of distraction useful to her just then.

An Aristo stood in the doorway, surveying the room. At his side stood an attractive, slender Asian woman, not Engineered but Selected. She moved with an athletic muscular grace. Her hair, black as Shasti's own, was cut short to her head. Her stance said, Security, just as his said, Engineered. Shasti looked at him from the corner of her eye, about seven feet tall, young, stunningly handsome with piercing blue eyes under black hair. For a second, Shasti forgot the danger he posed to her, enjoying the look of him. Most of the Engineered were Denshi, or friendly to Denshi. Their presence in the bar could only be related to the hunt for her.

Noise, bodies, and light of the dance floor concealed her as she moved away from the entranceway, heading for the stage. The band's music quickly became uncomfortably loud for her ultra-sensitive hearing. Strobing dance-floor lights taxed her eyes as they tried constantly to adjust. It struck her that some improvements generated their own vulnerabilities. Too much specialization made for less flexibility.

Heretical thoughts for one of the Engineered and not to the point, she chided herself. *Escape now, philosophize later.*

She edged toward the area behind the stage. When no one was looking, she quickly gathered some equipment, a small amp and cables. Though she was overdressed to be a technician, it seemed the best chance. Several of the band support people looked up briefly then disregarded her, their concentration on the show. She made her way backstage in a maze of cables and amplifiers.

"Hey," called a voice. A bouncer had noticed her. "What are you doing back here?"

Shasti turned toward him with what she hoped was a seductive smile. Denshi taught feminine skills to some assassins, but she'd never had such training. Still, her natural beauty made up for what she lacked in art. She lifted the cables and amp with an expressive shrug. The guard looked at her curiously. Despite everything Jenner did to cover her inhuman beauty and symmetry, she was still remarkable. He might take her for slumming Engineered. He smiled back. "Okay, babe. Remember to hang on to your backstage pass next time." He watched her posterior as she headed toward the other side of the stage.

Once out of sight, she cut toward the dressing rooms. A couple of dancers were in the hallway, stretching out in the next to nothing they wore for costumes. One reached out and patted her on the rear as she went by. "Nice ass," she called out, as the others giggled. Shasti suppressed an urge to knock her the length of the hall. Two more turns left her in a deserted hallway. The music had faded to a tolerable level. She opened several doors to find an empty storeroom with an exterior window into an alley. Relieved, she ducked in. Ditching the amp and cables, she reached the window. Predictably, it had a security system. Shasti pulled out her intruder tools, disabling it in seconds.

Behind her in the corridor she heard running feet. She lunged out the window in an instant, into the alley. Shasti cursed silently. She'd had no time to conceal the amp or cables. She looked upward. The roof seemed safest. A drainpipe dropped down from the roofline. Shasti leapt three meters up it in one move. The pipe held her weight, and she shimmied up, pulling herself onto the roof. A lance of red light hissed by her shoulder. Her sensitive nose smelled the crisping of a stray hair, whiffed to gas by the weapon. In a convulsive move, she surged up and over, even as her brain coolly noted the weapon as a laser. Tri-autos used particle accelerators and pulsed an irregular blue. They had to be Denshi. Police would have called for her surrender.

Wasting no time, Shasti headed up the series of ascending roof levels, seeking a height from which she could leap across to an adjoining building. In the crowded off-port, buildings tended to be close together. She would never have been able to make the leap on any of the broad avenues outside the strictly zoned spaceport.

She reached the highest roof level, running flat out. The next roof was ten meters away. She hurdled the edge of the roofline, sailing across the gap. Her eyes were on the next roof, but she could still see the street below, a ground car running down it, lights and people on the sidewalk, all unaware of the life and death battle over their heads. *It's cold,* she thought, wondering why she even noticed. The roof came up and her feet slammed into it. She stayed on them, running and drawing the small slug-thrower Jenner had supplied her with. Not much of a weapon against lasers and tri-autos, at least it had a silencer. Fortunately, they wouldn't use mini-grenades in this built up area.

A rooftop door ahead and to the right slammed open. Two Denshi lunged out. Instantly, she went down in a shoulder roll and came up, firing first. The man took a bullet in the right eye and dropped bonelessly. The Asian woman was behind him. She dropped to a knee, firing a laser. It cut through Shasti's jacket. She jerked away from the beam, snap firing. The other woman stopped three rounds, center-of-mass, and fell backward down the stairwell. Shasti doubted the woman was seriously hurt. Body armor under the street clothes would stop the bullets. Still, squash-head rounds felt like being hit with sledgehammers; that and the fall would slow her down.

Shasti raced on, again leaping the distance to the next roof. Pulling up, she quickly checked where the laser bit her. Her genetically engineered body shrugged off cuts well, but this was a burn, and she'd never been hit with a laser before. The area already felt numb from endorphins and anesthetics. Bleeding had stopped. To her surprise, the wound had already closed. It looked like one several days healed on a standard human. She wondered what other abilities might be hidden in her body. Things she never learned, having escaped her training so young.

Recovered, Shasti sprinted on, leaping to a third rooftop. Shots cracked behind her. A bullet hit the roof's edge as she vaulted over. A second hit her a glancing blow across the shoulders of her light body armor. It knocked her sprawling for a second, slamming the wind out of her. She got to her feet in a low, crabbed run. No more shots came. She realized she must be below the sniper's sights. Shasti leaped to the fourth roof top and stopped. She faced an office tower across the next leap. It loomed over her level, and she could see no place to land on its sheer side. To her right lay the roof's edge as she now stood on the corner building. One glance at the nearby roof hatch told her that even her strength would be insufficient to force it without tools. On the left, the adjoining building stood four stories higher. With time she did not have, she could climb it.

Trapped.

She turned. The Engineered she recognized from the bar leapt from the second roof, where she had shot the two Denshi.

He's bigger than me, maybe as strong, but she thought grimly, *not as desperate.*

Shasti ran back toward the Denshi, firing the rest of her clip. It was too far for accuracy. She wanted the Denshi to take cover. Obligingly, the Engineered dropped behind an air-conditioner unit. Two other Denshi, firing from the second roof, also dropped. They thought she was running back toward their net. All they needed to do was wait. She dropped the empty clip, slamming in a new one.

Suddenly she doubled back, heading for the office tower, running faster than she ever had, running for her life. She heard the Engineered start from cover behind her, leaping to the rooftop she was on. The roof's edge came up. Shasti flung herself across a gap far wider than any of the others. Her body lofted toward the side of the office tower. Wind whipped by her. The Denshi behind her stopped his rush, probably thinking her suicidal.

It was not so. Shasti held her body in a diver's form as she dropped in an arc toward the building's glass side, her auto-pistol held in front of her in both hands. The pistol bucked as she fired 5mm squash heads as fast as her finger could move. Commercial glass exploded inward. She curled her body into a ball at the last instant. Hurtling through the shattered glass, she struck a desktop, wiping out computers and video screens as she careened into a cubicle wall. Shasti groaned, staggering to her feet, almost falling. Her body armor protected her somewhat, but she was cut on the face and hands, bruised all over. Only the thought of what capture would mean got her to her feet again. Alarms would be sounding, summoning police and private security. A mixed blessing, local police were Neo-Reformist or Quest. Denshi would not find them friendly.

Shasti hit a fire exit heading down. She needed to get out of the building before the authorities showed up. Not for the first time, she was grateful for the absence of security robots on Olympia. She hit the ground floor door and vanished into the night.

———

On the rooftop, Mikhail Vaughn, Head of Section Three, Denshi Special Operations, stood staring across the gap, shaken. He could scarcely believe his eyes. The leap was impossible, yet she had done it. For the first time in his existence, he, Fourth-Generation Engineered, was physically bested—and by a Third-Generation woman.

"But what a woman," he murmured, the details of her fleeing form still before his eyes. He looked at the street below and the distance between the buildings, then simply shook his head. He considered pursuit, but she would be long gone by the time even he could reach street level. His sensitive hearing already detected the sound of incoming sirens. Time to withdraw.

A door banged open behind him. Misa Tanaka and two others of her team ran onto the roof. They were Selected, not Engineered, and were breathing hard. "My Lord," Misa called, "are you all right?"

He nodded calmly as they ran over. Misa was quite beautiful, though considerably older than he, her Asian heritage stamped flawlessly on every feature. She looked battered and bruised at the moment.

"You are not," he stated.

"No matter," she said, shaking a headful of midnight-black hair. "She shot me. I fell down some stairs. Parmelan is dead. She hit him in the eye. Where is she?"

He turned and pointed at the window. For the first time he could recall, he saw astonishment on Misa's face. "Impossible," she said. Recollecting herself, she started to apologize. He cut her off.

"Don't bother," he said. "I saw her do it and I cannot believe it. She's special, that one.

"Now we must flee as well. The local police are en route. Come. We must recover Parmelan's body and get you to an infirmary."

"I'm fine," she protested.

"I smell blood," he replied, "and I see pain in your walk. I will somehow survive a day until you can rejoin me. Remember, you taught me well."

She sighed. "I was little enough use to you tonight."

Vaughn shrugged. "It is on my head. I said to try and take her alive. It was a mistake. Next time, we must shoot to kill on sight, even if we risk collateral damage. She's a tigress and we will never take her alive. Pity. She is magnificent."

Chapter Eight

Sidhe burst into Apollo System at ninety percent of the speed of light. The entry flare created by her materialization was a small fragment of hell dragged into the normal universe. As her scarlet hull coasted out of the flare, her weapons and scanners searched space around her, though the odds of encountering another ship so far out in the system were minimal.

Fenaday was desperate to get to Olympia, and the star frigate plunged into the system at a reckless speed. Still, he had to order *Sidhe* turned end for end. Riding her fusion torch, the starship began braking for entry into the inner system. Fenaday knew it would take the mass of the gas giant, Atropos, to slow her to tolerable speed for the next window to Olympia. She could slow on her own, but only by wasting her own fuel, a risk Fenaday saw no reason to take.

Sidhe's active sensors began to paint a picture of space around them as the disturbance of their entry dissipated.

"Contact," called Sharla and Sharon Hafel simultaneously. There was alarm in the human's voice, but Hafel was Navy trained. Her hands whipped over the deep radar controls deftly. Sharla's ECM board read a microwave emitter. They quickly compiled electronic hints and identified the contact.

"*Sword* Class destroyer," Hafel announced, "Eight-hundred

thousand kilometers distance, bearing one-seven-eight, mark two-seven-zero, relative."

"Heading and speed," Fenaday snapped.

"Heading is ninety degrees by ten. Speed estimate... Sharla, I have a low confidence reading of .05C?"

"I have a reading of .0425," Sharla said.

"No threat," Telisan said. "He cannot catch us."

"Still," Fenaday murmured, "a warship so far out."

"Contact ahead," Hafel said. "No ID yet. Extreme range. Thirty degrees by twenty, speed .30C. Heading, similar to ours, system inward. I estimate she's on the plane of the ecliptic."

Fenaday exchanged a worried glance with Telisan. "What did we blunder into, a fleet exercise?" Fenaday said.

"I have a very low confidence ID, auxiliary or small spacecraft carrier," Sharla advised.

"Poor acceleration, then," Telisan said, who had served on one. "She'll have a combat air patrol," he continued. "A CVE could have as many as fifteen fighters—*Crusaders*, possibly *Spacefires*."

"Scan?" Fenaday said.

"Nothing. The range is too great," Hafel responded. "We won't be in reliable radar range for at least three minutes."

"More for the microwave scanner," Sharla added. Telisan hurried over to their stations and began examining readouts and panels.

Mmok walked down to the place vacated by Telisan. Fenaday ignored him. "Best guess," Fenaday called, his gut tight with tension. On the voyage out, the idea that *Sidhe* might be in danger from the Olympian Self-Defense Forces seemed ridiculous. Now, barreling into their system at a high percentage of light-speed, with warships unexpectedly on their screens, it seemed much less improbable.

"An escort carrier," Telisan said. "Not a cracker-box by the look," he added, using the Navy slang for a converted civilian ship, "but a fleet escort."

"Intelligence reports Olympia bought two of them," Mmok announced unexpectedly. His face had an abstract look to it. Fenaday realized Mmok was accessing some internal database.

"One was *Yukikaze* class, with ten *Crusaders*, the other was a Denlenn model, *Lollor* class."

"Not good," Telisan said. The Denlenn's formal Standard slipped into the Navy style he learned in the Confederate Combined Fleet. "We sold several CVEs. One went to the Frokossi, but there were rumors it was a front for Olympia. I think I know this one, *Fleetfoot*. She was a special purpose carrier, carrying a flight of six ConAvro *Daggers* and brace of *Crusaders*."

"Damn," Fenaday said. "I'm beginning to understand how Mandela feels about member planet navies."

"Watch it, Fenaday." Mmok grinned mirthlessly. "You're starting to sound like a Federalist."

"God forbid," he replied, "and that's Captain Fenaday to you."

"Yes, sir," returned the cyborg, not discomfited.

"Confirming," Hafel snapped. "Her profile is still on file. CVE *Fleetfoot*, ahead and to starboard, twenty degrees relative. I am now reading two fighters."

"Two *Daggers*," Sharla chimed in. "I have confirmation; they just lit up with big burns."

"That's the CAP," Telisan said. "If that carrier has any sort of a captain, the ready reaction fighter will be coming off the catapult inside of two minutes."

"Are they heading toward us?" Mmok asked. For the first time Fenaday could recall, the cyborg looked nervous. *He's a grunt*, realized Fenaday. *He doesn't know what's going on.*

"Imagine a broad sloping well, Mr. Mmok," Fenaday said, "with a sun at the bottom. We're falling into that well at .90C, riding our fusion torch to slow down, on a very narrow window to a braking orbit with the gas giant Atropos. If we don't slow, we go to the bottom, up the other side of the well and off into deep space. So we have to go in ass backwards, our main gun unusable on targets inward of us.

"Those fighters aren't braking, and they aren't heading toward us. They are diving into the well head first, as fast as their torches will push them, adding to the speed of the launching carrier. We're still doing over three times that. *Sidhe* will plunge past them in a blur. Unfortunately, not so fast they can't get a shot at us as we pass.

"Normal fighters can't maneuver with us at near relativistic speeds," Fenaday continued. "They don't carry artificial gravity fields. Anything but the gentlest turn can make the pilot into jam at these speeds. Fighters are only a threat near planets or stations, where you move at orbital velocity.

"These aren't normal fighters. They're ConAvro *Daggers*, almost as big as a small ship. They carry a small singularity created by the carrier's drive. It will last four hours, as will the AG field it generates. In those four hours they can outmaneuver us. *Daggers* carry four anti-shipping missiles and a fighter mass accelerator."

"Enemy fighter launching," Hafel interrupted.

"Easy, Hafel," Fenaday said. "That's the Olympian Navy out there, a member planet, not the Conchirri."

Mmok snorted.

"That's the ready-reaction fighter," Telisan mused. "So he's at Defcon Four. He can get another fighter out in five minutes, but any launch after this point will be irrelevant. They won't get up enough speed to be a factor."

"Begin broadcasting a hail on all Confederate frequencies," Fenaday said. "Make it loud. I don't want anybody playing games about not knowing who we are. *Cheetah* must have told them of our approximate ETA and vector, but so far they aren't acknowledging our IFF transponder."

"I just picked up a maximum speed burn on that *Sword* destroyer," Sharla said, as she worked her instruments, "identifying as Bogie One."

"Stupid," Fenaday muttered, "waste of fuel. They couldn't close on us before we reach Olympia. Any reply to our hail?"

"No," Susan Bernard replied from the communication station.

"Captain," Sharla said, "there is a lot of ECM out there."

"Gunner," Telisan asked, "what IFF are you getting off the vessels ahead?"

Wardell turned back to him; there was worry in the old gunner's eye. "Non-standard, sir. They are not using Confed Identification Friend or Foe codes."

"Our own is broadcasting?" Fenaday asked.

"Affirmative," Sharla said. "Transponder is working."

There was a crackle of static, and a voice sounded from a speaker. Bernard adjusted the controls.

"This is Olympia Self-Defense Naval Vessel *Leonidas* to unknown vessel. Please cease your approach to our inner system. You have not been cleared for entry."

Fenaday looked at Telisan, then gestured to Bernard to put him through. "*Leonidas*, this is the Confederate Private Starship *Sidhe*, under command of Robert Fenaday. We are hardly unidentified. We are broadcasting Confed IFF, and our entry into Olympia was announced by the Navy courier *Cheetah* two weeks ago. My ship's silhouette is also the best known in explored space, unless you are aware of someone else flying a Conchirri frigate."

There was a pause, light-speed delay, and confusion. "This is *Leonidas* to unknown vessel. You are not cleared for entry. Please cease your approach. Please heave to for boarding."

"*Leonidas*, this is Fenaday of the *Sidhe*. Please cease the comedic welcome. I have announced myself. My IFF is working perfectly, as I assume your scanners are. Assuming the laws of physics are as well, I will not be slowing much this side of Atropos. You are welcome to accelerate and meet us there to escort us in.

"Let's add to that, *Leonidas*, that so far your welcome stinks. I have no intention of allowing an illegal deep space boarding of my ship. Your jurisdiction for boarding starts in the low orbit of Olympia, which I will not be entering. Who the hell am I speaking with anyway?"

"*Leonidas* to...to unknown vessel claiming to be CPSS *Sidhe*, stand by."

"*Sidhe* to *Leonidas*, I will not alter my course and speed at your request. Please advise your intentions."

There was no reply.

"Mr. Telisan," Fenaday said, almost reluctantly, "bring us to Defense Condition Four."

The ship's alarm whirred insistently. *Sidhe's* crew was already at stations from her exit from hyperspace, now all hatches and compartments were sealed. Non-essential systems went off-line. Susan Bernard switched all communications to her console to allow Sharla to concentrate on ECM.

"Captain," Sharla said, with an elaborate calm, "the fighters ahead have engaged active fire control. They are locking on to us."

"They wouldn't dare," Mmok sputtered.

"Break their locks," Fenaday ordered.

"Fenaday to *Leonidas*," he called, "what the hell are you doing, locking fire control on us? *Leonidas*, we formally protest this hostile act. There will be a complaint filed with the Confederate Planets Embassy. *Leonidas*, there will be repercussions."

Silence dragged on.

"Captain," Wardell said, "we are coming up on those fighters, fast. Firing range in one minute and forty seconds."

"I have broken their firing locks," Sharla announced in triumph. "All three are trying to reacquire us."

"*Leonidas*, this is Fenaday, requesting visual communication and demanding your fighters cease locking onto our vessel."

No reply. He looked at Bernard; she shook her head.

"Permission to launch fighters," Telisan said. "We still have time to get them into space."

Fenaday shook his head. "Hold *Wildcat* launch.

"*Leonidas*," Fenaday tried again, "if your fighters do not cease active fire control, I will be forced to assume you plan to attack."

"There has been another launch from enemy carrier," Hafel said. "Bandit is a *Crusader*."

This time Fenaday did not correct her.

"Mr. Telisan," Fenaday said, "have the fighters switch to internal power. I want them ready to drop in a second's notice. Mr. Wardell, return the favor, target those fighters, all fire control on the bridge. Energize main gun too. Sharla, stand by stealth mode."

Mmok looked incredulously at Fenaday. "I can't believe they'll fire on us."

"Maybe they seceded while we were in hyperdrive," he replied acidly. "Maybe they know why we're here. I've got ship-killers dropping into range. I'll be damned if I'll take the chance."

"Visual on fighters," Wardell called. *Sidhe's* main screen lit up and fragmented into several views. In the center was a small cluster of lights. Two were close to each other and dimmer. A third flared brighter, obviously far closer to *Sidhe*. They were the drive engines of the *Dagger* fighters, diving into the gravity well, seeking to match speed with the braking frigate. The images were subject to relativistic limits. The fighters themselves could be anywhere in a probability cone, depending on their maneuvers. The irony of the physics struck Fenaday. All vessels had their ass-ends pointed toward each other, yet they were closing rapidly.

"We are coming up on Bandit Three," Wardell said. "He launched last and is the slowest. Then we will pass Bandits One and Two. They have the best firing solution on us."

"We could minimize their firing window by a turn in any direction," Fenaday said, as if to himself. "It would blow our approach to Atropos and Olympia. We'd spend weeks braking just on the ship's nuclear torch. Might not even make planetfall. Could have to call for rescue."

"Well, Captain?" Mmok asked, emphasizing the title.

"It's a bluff," Telisan said. "It must be."

Fenaday straightened in his chair. "Launch fighters. Have them do a small burn to put them two thousand meters ahead and to either side. Gentlemen and ladies, we are going straight in."

The *Wildcat* fighters dropped, surging out to their assigned positions with only a quick thruster burn. Their speed matched *Sidhe's* own.

"*Leonidas*," Fenaday said, "I am coming up on your fighters, and they are still ranging on me. This is CPSS *Sidhe*, protesting an illegal attack by Olympian Self-Defense Forces."

"Nearest fighter has locked and fired two anti-shipping missiles," Sharla called.

"Shit," Mmok said.

"Weapons free," Fenaday called. "Get those missiles! Telisan, order our fighters to…"

A brilliant, silent flowering of light spread across the screen.

"Good work, Sharla," Telisan cried.

"Not me," she replied, "the carrier signaled a self-destruct on the weapons."

"Wardell, Telisan, hold fire," Fenaday ordered.

"*Sidhe*," announced a new voice over the speakers, "this is Commodore Aswa of the Olympian Self-Defense Force Navy. A most regrettable error has occurred. Your vessel defolded into normal space in the middle of a naval exercise. I am ordering all forces to stand down. Please stand by for visual communication."

Bernard brought up Aswa's picture on one of the panels of the main screen. He was a striking black man with a noble bearing and perfect features. Fenaday took an instant dislike to him.

"Confirming," Sharla said, relief in her voice. "All three fighters are taking a course well away from us, heading for their carrier."

"Captain Fenaday," continued the Olympian officer, "we are mortified at this stupidity. I was not on the bridge when you were detected, and our people foolishly imagined your vessel was a surprise part of the exercise."

"Can't they read a transponder?" Fenaday snapped. "We have been broadcasting Confed ID since we defolded, and our arrival was announced by courier and the embassy."

"Captain, that information was not shared with us. Clearly, there has been a mistake. We did not expect your vessel in this area. There have been a series of errors almost ending in tragedy. On behalf of all Olympia, I offer our most abject apologies. This is an inexcusable welcome to heroes of the Confederacy."

"What are a few rads between friends?" Fenaday said, in a cold rage. "Who ordered those missiles fired?"

"Captain," Telisan interrupted, "readings are in. The weapons were low yield and clean. Probably Mark Ones. We took no radiation inside the vessel. The fighters picked up a few rads, nothing significant."

"The weapons were launched without authorization," Aswa replied smoothly. "I personally ordered them detonated, as soon as I realized what had happened."

"I intend to prefer charges," Fenaday stated.

"As do I myself, Captain. I suspect a court will not administer a harsher sentence than has already been given. The weapons went off very near the launching fighter. Her pilot received a far greater dose than is healthful. She may not live, even with the best of care."

"We are clear of system traffic and active range finding," Sharla said.

"Secure weapons," Fenaday said slowly. "Cease active fire

control. Mr. Telisan, initiate fighter recovery. Set defense condition one."

"Captain Fenaday," Aswa said, "all Olympia welcomes your arrival and that of your ship and crew. You are cleared all the way to low orbit of Marathon on Olympia."

"Thank you, Commodore, but we will assume high orbit of Marathon till we are assured of a better welcome than what we have received to date. The conduct of your military has left us shaken. We have been fired on with nuclear weapons. Please see to it that there is no military traffic on our route. We do not want an escort. This matter is far from over, Commodore."

"I understand your anger, Captain, and I share it. We will honor all your requests in the hope of salvaging your good opinion. I will make a full and candid report, accepting all responsibility for the incident. We are transmitting all the necessary codes for your entry into Marathon's traffic pattern. Is there any other way we can serve you?"

"Only by keeping your distance. Fenaday out."

The screen returned to the star field.

"I have their code transmission in the virus buffer," Bernard said. "It's clean."

"Quite a welcome," Telisan grinned. His reflective golden eyes and leathery skin gave him a leonine look.

"Yeah," Mmok said. "Just like the ones the Conchirri used to throw."

"Well, we are still alive and inbound," Fenaday said. "It was pretty clever actually. They set up a live fire exercise, and we blunder into it. The Navy isn't warned of our arrival through some bureaucratic mix-up. Some hothead takes a shot, claiming he thought we were a holo-image-enhanced target drone. Either we're hit, or we take evasive action and lose our approach vector for months. Better yet, we get so mad we just jump out for home. The most they lose is some low-level operative."

"You forced their hand by refusing to alter course," Telisan added. "After we launched fighters, their chances for hitting us with one or two weapons were minimal. So they aborted."

Mmok crossed his arms. "I'll bet they weren't expecting us to be remilitarized. It must have been a nasty surprise when our fire control and ECM kicked in. Without them, we'd be toast."

"Let's press the advantage," Fenaday said. "We'll draft up a complaint to the embassy, broadcast it in the clear. If the public on Olympia doesn't know we are coming, they will now. Let's tell them about the reception we received."

"Good," Mmok grunted, "makes sense."

Sidhe plunged in, riding her fusion torch, heading for the gas giant Atropos. Chaos rippled out from her arrival.

———

I n the tallest tower of the uplands desert complex, Mikhail Vaughn stood very still before the master of the Denshi, reporting failure, something not well tolerated in the Guild of Assassins. Lord Jalgren Pard listened to the details of the battle with Rainhell with no visible signs of anger. He played idly with a small, black-lacquered box, one of a number of Asian curiosities dotting the office. It looked incredibly fragile in his bear-like hands.

"I take full responsibility for the outcome of the assignment," Vaughn concluded. "My team performed their best. It simply was not good enough."

Pard nodded his massive head. "At least you didn't blow up half an apartment complex on the evening news." He heaved a sigh. "The fault is not yours alone," continued Pard, to Vaughn's concealed surprise. "I did order you to take her alive, if possible. She has grown formidable since she left us."

"My Lord," said Vaughn, hesitantly, "we were told Rainhell was Third-Generation, among the last of that lot, to be sure, but..."

"You suspect she is more," Pard growled. He leaned back in his chair; the exotic woods and fine leathers creaked under his weight.

"Yes," he said. Gathering his nerve, he continued, "She shrugged off a laser hit. The speed of her reflex action is amazing. She was nearly a blur when in movement, even to my eyes, and I am optimized for reflex speed and coordination. Then there was the leap. I could not have made that distance. I do not think even Antebei, for all his athletic skills, could have."

Pard stood. Vaughn stiffened slightly, but the giant Denshi merely walked to the window overlooking his desert complex and the mountains beyond. The deep, rich, Persian carpet muffled his steps. Pard brushed a small wind-chime, a delicate tracery of ancient ivory and crystal. It yielded a few silvery notes. The sun was near to setting and painted the horizon with vivid oranges and yellows. Armored glass automatically cut the glare to acceptable levels. Still it caused the burnished gold and Chinese red of the walls to glow with inner life.

"You are right," he said, in a slow, heavy voice. "And it is past time you learned this information if you are to cope with Rainhell.

"I was working with Chief Geneticist Negola, back in '47. Many new technologies were coming out, some of which we later abandoned. We decided the time had come to push the envelope and work on a prototype. Not merely to advance incrementally, but to leap whole generations. Negola started a special laboratory. We used every technique, every wild theory, to create a prototype of an engineered human beyond anything previously envisioned." Pard's face grew rapt, as he discussed his dream, his driving force, the creation of the perfect human.

"It was all in vitro, of course, controlled labs, artificial wombs. There were disappointments, naturally, monsters, abortions in the hundreds. Then one day we came up with a perfect baby girl, the one offspring of the Special Lab. Even we did not know what we had. We put everything we could think of in her germ plasm: bio-controlled melanin, endorphin on demand, night sight, ultra-fast healing, and more. Apparently the resistance to burns took, from what you say. No, we don't know the upper limits of her abilities. I suspect Rainhell herself does not know them. She escaped this complex before her final training and experimentation could begin."

"Why raise her in the common crèche?" Vaughn asked, disturbed for reasons he did not understand by the story.

"Even then the Selected had begun to distrust our kind," Pard replied, "recognizing in us the seed of their obsolescence. Rainhell was an expensive product, possibly irreplaceable. We deemed it safer to raise her as a regular Third-Generation female. Our enemies in the Army, the Neo-Reformists, and others would have made her a target if we singled her out for too much special treatment. Also many years passed before we knew she had any real value, that she was actually an improvement."

"Finally, it is not unknown for jealousies among our own to result in premature deaths. Is it, Mikhail?"

Vaughn swallowed, remembering several prior rivals of his lost in "training accidents," and the near misses of the last several attempts Antebei doubtless arranged for him.

"So, how do you plan to kill Rainhell?" Pard asked, as he returned to his desk and dropped back into his reinforced chair.

"Do you still wish to keep the matter secret?" Vaughn asked. "It is what hinders us the most. If we went public, we would have her in hours."

"Idiot," Pard snapped. "Do not look for easy solutions. We are at a critical stage with the Outsiders. Our plans for a treaty are coming to fruition soon. Only now are our people reaching sufficient numbers to wield real power. Many are offworld with the Overman project. Most of our strength still rests in alliances. Revelation of the existence of the Outsiders will shatter these alliances and pull this planet out of our grasp.

"Rainhell is too public a figure to murder in the open. She is here illegally, doubtless to destroy me. She does not dare go public either. We could have her legitimately arrested. Once she was in prison, it would be simple to kill her. No, we are both in the shadows, and so it must stay. We have the advantage: we have time on our side."

"Then it will remain difficult and perhaps more so," Vaughn replied. "We are infiltrating Quest, Bremardi, and Neo-Reformist Territory, though slowly. I suspect the Army is aware something is up. Our agents, tracing associates of Leda Jenner, keep finding Army imposed dead ends. Our field people and theirs scuffled near Leda Jenner's 'safe' house in the Ionian Mountains, near Manki. Our people escaped without loss. They inflicted considerable casualties on the ambushers."

"I suspect General Dominici's hand in all these Army difficulties," Pard said. "She is no friend to our interests. I shall have Antebei's people double check on this. Army is his department. Perhaps he could double our watch on her."

"How is Antebei?" Vaughn asked coldly. "Has his ego recovered from killing fifty civilians on planet-wide media?"

Instantly, he regretted the comment. It was petty and would not serve him well with Pard. "Sorry, my Lord."

"He is probably still busy raping his secretary, though why he wants such low order trash is beyond me." Pard looked annoyed. He cast a sidelong glance at Vaughn. "This Paula creature distracts him too much; perhaps I should have her destroyed."

Vaughn was Denshi, a killer from his childhood years. Still, he had no taste for killing the helpless. What merit was there to stalking lambs? He saw himself as a killer of tigers. In one, lay honor and the glory of the hunt. The other was work for butchers, or worse, a killer like Antebei, for whom murder was a type of sex. He knew Pard was baiting him, but his own temper, usually carefully controlled, slipped. Vaughn felt his face grow hot and could not check his voice.

"Murder the woman for Antebei's flaws? Why?" he demanded. "The fault does not lie in her. Another will merely be forced to take her place."

"She could die too," Pard said. "What matter?"

"You would put Band-Aids on bullet wounds," Vaughn returned bitterly. "It is Antebei who is weak and unfit, though you refuse to see it."

"What of your own weakness?" Pard snapped. "Conscience, scruples, honors—these have no place in a life of power."

Vaughn looked him in the eye, greatly daring. "I'm a warrior, not a butcher. I lead by example, not fear. We do what we have to do to survive. You know I would cut down any threat to Denshi—male, female, old or young—but as with the ancient samurai, I do not draw my sword to gather watercress. This woman is no threat."

"Perhaps," Pard asked, with a faint look of amusement, "this secretary, positioned as she is with Antebei, is an agent of yours?"

"She is not," Vaughn replied stoutly.

"Why not?" Pard's voice whip-cracked. The question stopped the young man in his tracks.

"Fool. She is a weakness of your enemy. Much aggrieved. Ripe for the plucking, but you, blinded by your damn honor, do not deign to pick up this weapon. Must I do all your thinking for you?" Pard returned to his desk, sitting in front of his computer screen. "Get out."

Vaughn bowed carefully, recognizing the tone. He had over-stepped himself. *I've done it again,* he thought drearily, *failed in his eyes.* He was not thinking of the battle with Rainhell, but of the dozens of times Pard's face averted from him in response to some short-coming in him, or his work. *I will never please him,* he mourned inter-nally, unsure of why this should matter. Any human born of a woman could have told him of the trials of a father's approval, but Vaughn was Engineered, born from an artificial womb, raised in a crèche. He knew the word father, though its meaning eluded him. But such feelings as he had in that direction were centered on Pard, Lord and Master of The Engineered and, in the only sense available to him, his true father.

———

A rpen entered their small quarters on Deck Three with relief. She was tired. In addition to the usual somatic complaints of a small group of people confined to a starship, the fighter pilots needed treatment for minor radiation exposure. Then there were two men injured by a pipe burst in Engineering. She was also somewhat strained by dealing with the human healers, notably Mourner. The human method of "patch 'em and get 'em back to work" was distasteful to her. She knew they perceived her as slow and unfocused. She had faced the problem before during her wartime service in the Confederate Space Forces, dominated as it was in her sector by humans. She had forgotten how frustrating it could be.

In the far corner, lit only by a desk light, sat Telisan. Sharla, she knew was on the bridge on duty. It seemed she was not to have her two loves in one place anytime soon. Her bright smile dimmed when it was not returned by her fiancé. Telisan, normally so light and cheerful, looked as grim as death. Her empathic instincts engaged as she sensed waves of pain and upset from her lover. "Dearest, what is wrong?"

Telisan gave the Denlenn equivalent of a sigh. "We near the end of our voyage. Soon we will be engaged in the hunt for Rainhell and the others. A dangerous time is upon us, made worse by divisions among ourselves. Mmok's orders are to destroy Pard, if possible. Fenaday seeks Rainhell. I know him. He will kill Pard, if he can, or if he must, but Rainhell is his priority. Rask, despite Mmok's orders and against Fenaday's, will try to find his friend Rigg. We are a command divided again, just as we were at Enshar." Telisan sat back, looking directly at her for the first time.

"The human, Mmok, is the greatest danger," he said. "His HCRs and other robots have great firepower. We have no hope of besting them, even if we could count on Rask's company of ASATs. Few of the old privateer crew are with us, and they are questionable in reliability, save for a handful.

"I fear a time may come when Mmok will become a threat to Fenaday. They nearly killed each other at least once before. You know he has no love for Fenaday, or Rainhell."

"I am aware of it," she said. "It is one of the things I have been trying to break down in him, this poisonous envy and hate."

"Just so. You have access to Mmok in your treatment of him. Would it be possible to implant a device, or instruction in his cybernetics, to sever his ties with the robots? Not to harm him, just to disable his ability to control the machines."

Arpen looked at him stunned then turned coldly furious. "You ask me to sabotage a patient's body? To take advantage of a trust? You, who call yourself of the line of Selen?"

"It is because I am Selen," Telisan said, not looking up. "I have no excuse to hold back in my duty to our captain. I failed in this manner once before, at Enshar. Never again. Mmok is not our friend and may well be our captain's worst enemy."

"You appear to think rather less of my honor than your own. I am a healer of body and soul," Arpen retorted. "Mmok's sickness is born as much of betrayal by family and friends as anything physical. I have gained his trust to a small degree, as much as he is capable of. You ask me to destroy my patient, my oath as a healer, my soul."

"I ask you," he replied heavily, "to defend the captain and the ship. I thought I could count on your help in this difficult matter."

"It appears," she said, "we may both have misjudged the other. Never ask this again. Never mention it to anyone, even Sharla. I will see if I can forgive and forget you asked it of me." Arpen swept out of the room, before the emotion she felt welling in her could burst forth. The hatch sealed behind her. There was something irrevocable in its sound.

Chapter Nine

S tartled by a tapping sound at the window, Leda Jenner
snapped off the light and drew her auto-pistol. For a second,
she considered waking Rigg, then decided against it. Too
often in their first few days of hiding out, she'd been the source of
false alarms. The wounded ASAT needed his rest. Edging up to the
window, she twitched back the curtain. Outside Rainhell clung to
the window casement, her skin the night-black of melanin camouflage. Jenner threw open the window.

"Shasti! What's happened?"

"Help me in," Shasti said, sounding exhausted. "It's starting to
rain."

Jenner put the pistol down and reached for Shasti, struggling to
get the big Engineered woman inside the window. Her hand came
away slick and dark with blood.

"Shasti, you're hurt."

"Not badly," Shasti replied. "A laser hit, assorted cuts and
bruises from leaping between buildings and crashing through glass
windows."

"Oh, is that all?" Jenner muttered.

"What's going on?" Rigg walked into the room blinking sleep
from his eyes. Then he saw Rainhell. "Christ!" They helped Shasti

to the bathroom and stripped her out of her jacket. As they did, her skin reverted to its normal ivory color, highlighting the blood. For once, even Shasti seemed fatigued, but the real surprise was her wounds. The laser hit looked days old and half healed. As they washed dried blood off her, they found the glass cuts and bruises similarly closed.

"Jesus," Rigg said. "Anybody else would have bled to death."

"I wasn't designed to bleed to death," Shasti said, her voice dull and slow. "My body heals fast. It takes a lot of energy. I could use something to drink and some food."

"I'll finish with the first aid," Jenner said, applying waterproof dressings. "Fix something in the kitchen."

"I dunno, me… in a kitchen," Rigg said dubiously.

"Well, I am going to get her out of the rest of her clothes," Jenner continued.

"She doesn't have anything I haven't seen before," Rigg said.

Jenner gave him a withering look. "Man, scat."

Rigg grumbled but left.

Jenner helped Shasti out of her remaining clothes and into a shower. Shasti leaned against the stall and let the warm water beat down on her head, simply grateful to still be alive. She was cold to the touch and visibly thinner than she'd been hours ago, as her body drained its reserves for repairs. *Times like this,* she thought, *it might be nice to be fatter,* to have more fuel for her accelerated healing. Whoever designed her body with such low body fat gave priority to her sexual attractiveness over such practical matters. Eventually, she roused herself to come out of the shower. Jenner greeted her with a heavy robe. Shasti wanted nothing more than to drop into sleep. She felt too tired to eat.

A new scent brought her head up and fixed her attention. Rigg knocked and walked into the bathroom. He held a large mug full of steaming liquid. "I seem to recall that you liked—"

"Yes," she said, seizing the mug of hot chocolate.

"Sit," Jenner commanded. They helped her into the small living room.

Shasti lowered herself onto their threadbare taupe couch, carefully cradling the hot chocolate. When it was drinkable, she downed a healthy slug. Heat spread through her, and she began to feel alive again. Rigg returned with another cup and some sandwiches. Shasti destroyed the late dinner with silent efficiency. Afterward, she leaned back on the couch, a feeling of wellbeing stealing through her. Quickly, she sketched the night's disastrous events.

"Well, since they haven't crashed through the windows shooting, I guess you weren't followed," Rigg said. Leda Jenner missed a breath and looked at the windows.

"No," Shasti said, "I got away clean. We won't be able to try for the port any time soon. Denshi will cover the area like a fog now."

"So we're trapped again," Jenner said wearily.

"So it seems," Shasti shrugged.

"Maybe you made the evening news," Rigg said. Turning to the video set, he ordered it on and to the twenty-four-hour, planet-wide news. "It would be great to use the computer to scan, but Denshi might be looking for such scans. This is just the general broadcast."

A fine-featured Olympian woman was on the holo-screen. Shasti recognized her as another Engineered. They sat through the weather news till it cycled to the headlines.

"The President's office has released news of the arrival of the famous starship *Sidhe*, under command of Robert Xavier Fenaday of New Eire."

Warmth and the feeling of well-being fled Shasti.

"Tragedy was only barely averted, according to the OSDF Navy authorities, when the *Sidhe* arrived in the middle of a naval exercise. OSDFN units fired on the vessel before realizing *Sidhe* was not part of the exercise. Fortunately, the weapons were aborted before striking the ship. Captain Fenaday has filed an official complaint with the Confed Embassy here in Marathon. Confederate Ambassador Davis has apologized for Captain Fenaday's accusations against the Navy and High Denshi officials, including Lord Jalgren Pard, citing stress from the incident. Neo-Reformist leader, Jiri Bremard, has called for hearings in the Senate on the matter..."

"Shasti," Jenner cried, "he's here. He's come for you."

"Yeah," Rigg said, a note of rueful admiration in his voice. "He's done it now."

"Yes," Shasti said, "that which I feared the most has occurred. He's here, in range of Pard and his assassins."

———

Ambassador Davis of the Confederation Diplomatic Service looked down his long aristocratic nose at Fenaday and his command team. Davis sat in *Sidhe's* small wardroom, flanked by his aide-de-camp, a striking woman, and a marine officer straight off a recruiting poster. Fenaday felt sure the Confederacy considered personal appearance in making assignments to Olympia. It was beginning to really annoy him.

"Captain Fenaday," Davis said, after the initial pleasantries. "I must be frank. When the captain of the *Cheetah* handed me the diplomatic pouch with the details of the prior operation, I was horrified. I'm as concerned as anyone by the buildup in Olympia's armed forces. More so by the fact that we cannot even find all the forces we suspect they have. Still, I cannot see any justification for the actions taken. Assassination is clearly extra-legal. The members of the team are criminals, assuming any still survive.

"Now this...this, equally ill-thought out provocation, you and your vessel here to attempt a rescue—"

"Ambassador," Fenaday interrupted, "I am not interested in your assessment of the attack on Pard. I don't care if a piano lands on him tomorrow. I want what you should want: to get the survivors off Olympia. Mr. Mmok's mission is to destabilize Olympia and bring down Pard, and right now I don't give a damn about that either. I want those people. *Cheetah* brought you orders to cooperate with our mission. I assume you know who authored those orders and I will leave it to your imagination as to the career implications of failing to follow them."

Davis smiled without warmth. "I see you have a liking for plain speech. Well, here is some for you. I will obey the letter of my orders, not one step beyond them. If you are captured, I will of course deny any official sanction for your operations. You were a pirate once..."

"Privateer," Fenaday snapped.

"A distinction that I doubt will interest the Olympian courts," Davis said.

"No more than they will be interested in your denials," Telisan said pleasantly. "You must understand, Mr. Davis, if we are caught, your own position will be untenable."

Davis looked as if he smelled a dead cat.

Davis's aide waved a hand. "I'm sure the ambassador wishes for your discreet success," she said, "but we are uncertain of how to assist. We have brought briefing materials on all the major policy players, much of which you probably know already.

"Geneticist Hagen and Olympia's Cabinet have used the incident at the system's edge and your own unwisely broadcast complaint to refuse *Sidhe* landing rights, citing your disputes with the Navy and Denshi. If they cannot do a complete survey of the *Sidhe* and handle your ground security, they will not take responsibility for your safety. You dare not allow a customs party to see the cyborg, the reinforced platoon of combat robots, the *Intruder*, and all your other ground weapons."

"My name," Mmok said, coldly furious, "is Mmok."

"Of course," Davis raised his hands, "she meant nothing."

"I don't doubt that," Mmok sneered.

"In any event," Davis continued, "you are checked here, in orbit. Olympia does not approve of robots, cyborgs, or the alien members of the Confederacy. There is sufferance at least for the latter. I can get some of you downworld. A few. Perhaps Mr. Mmok. Certainly none of his robots. Nor could I get your ASAT force down with their weapons. What you could accomplish with a few people alone and unarmed on Olympia is beyond me. I suggest you leave the on-world search to us and not jeopardize our relations further."

Mmok fixed his one human eye on Davis. "The Olympians are up to something. They are destabilizing this corner of the Confederacy, not just with their Übermensch philosophy, but by arming to the teeth. We have a pocket separatist empire building here. The sort of thing that takes millions of lives to fix, because no one fixes the problem when it's small. We are going to fix this one while it is small. Major Vijaythilakan here," he gestured toward the silent officer, "can supply us with weapons from the embassy armory. As for what we can do, that is our problem."

There was silence in the room for a few seconds.

"So far," Davis said finally, "the best I have been able to manage is a dinner reception at 1800 hours tomorrow on the *Hermes' Shield* space port, orbiting below us. The president, the chief geneticist, their cabinet, and the combined military chiefs are quite prepared to meet you there. You'll have no cause to complain about the honors or dignitaries. You may be able to get on world under closely scrutinized conditions. I'm sorry, Captain. I see no hope for your mission."

"We will see," Fenaday replied. "The first thing we need is reprovisioning: food, water, fuel, some parts. It was a rugged trip out here, and we may have to run like hell at some point. So I want maximum stores on board. We'll provide you a ledger. Mr. Mandela pays the freight. Other than that, you get us down, that's all."

"If that is all," Davis stood, "then my staff and I will see you on *Hermes' Shield* at the reception tomorrow. We have a tremendous amount of work to do in the meanwhile. Good day, gentlemen."

Fenaday pressed a button on the table. Rask leaned in, immaculate in the black and dark-green of his dress Air Space Assault Team uniform. "Please escort the ambassador and his people back to their shuttle." The three Confed representatives followed the Morok out of the room.

Fenaday stood, followed by Telisan and Mmok. He wanted to get back to the bridge. Sharla was running as many sweeps and scans as she could, using the special sensors installed from the Enshar expedition, in the hope of finding some evidence of the team on Olympia's surface. As they left the conference room, Mmok's HCRs immediately surrounded them, much to Fenaday's annoyance. The machines were Mmok's power; he never missed an opportunity to flaunt them. The parade started down the ship's Broadway, heading toward the bridge.

"Well, here we are," Fenaday sighed, "orbiting the planet of the perfect people. Even the regular humans from the Confederacy seem to have been picked for their looks. I'll be hungry for the sight of a homely face before long."

"Look in the mirror," Mmok snapped.

Fenaday felt his temper flare in response. "Look who's talking. Shouldn't you be off in a field somewhere, scaring crows?"

Mmok snapped around. HCRs whirled, sudden and intent, into fighting stances, Fenaday and Telisan froze, their hands halfway to their sidearms. Mmok was breathing hard, almost shaking with rage, his human eye furious. Crew in the corridor fled into side passages. They faced off, humans and alien, surrounded by the best killing machinery in known space. No one moved.

No, Fenaday thought, *not like this, over a stupid damn insult. I can't afford to die. I just can't, not now. Shasti needs me.*

Mmok broke the spell, turning, angry and clumsy, away from them. The robots slid smoothly back into marching order. Fenaday let out a shaky breath and relaxed his gun arm, conscious of the hammering of his heart, the dryness in his mouth. He looked at Telisan. The Denlenn gave little back, though his mouth was a grim line. Which one of them Telisan was angrier with was hard to say.

Mmok half turned back and bit off a word. "Sorry."

Surprised, Fenaday found his voice again; it sounded thin. "Yeah, let's forget it, bad jokes both ways."

"If you are both done," Telisan said, sounding as angry as Fenaday had ever heard his friend, "there is much work ahead of us."

"Yeah." Mmok nodded, looking away. "We're on company time."

They continued to the bridge in wary silence.

―――――

Hours on the bridge revealed nothing. If Shasti and any of the team were down there, they couldn't signal the ship. Fenaday and the others studied everything in the briefing materials Davis supplied them with. They accessed the planet's global communication system only to find all traffic encrypted, something unheard of on a Confederate planet. They found themselves unable to hack into any system. There wasn't even one consistent encryption; every group seemed to use its own.

"This Pard," Telisan said, "is subtle."

"Yes." Fenaday rubbed his tired eyes. "We saw the trap at the system's edge and bluffed our way through. Then I overplayed right into his hands, filing protests, getting us banished to the high orbit, where I guess he wanted us. Worse yet. We can't really complain about Denshi. It's the Navy we've been knocking heads with. I may have been wrong, Mmok. Maybe the right thing to do was to drop the *Intruder* out by the gas giant's rings and let you make a stealth approach."

"No," Mmok said, "the outsystem patrols are better than reported. Despite your request, Aswa's fighters shadowed us all the way in. Then there are the Moonbase patrol sloops. We could get the robots down by launching the *Intruder* cold and starting her up later. Unlike the robots though, I need life support, even if it is less than a human normally needs. With me on board, there would be a power source operating. Without me, the robots are useless. Checkmate."

"We have to discredit Denshi." Fenaday slammed a hand down on his command chair in frustration. "If I can start something with Pard on the station, some dispute that causes him to lose face, maybe we can get our security turned over to someone else and get downworld. Then we can start working. Denshi and the Navy are still trying to get over the bad publicity for almost nuking us. Another mistake could get them out of our way. We've got money, bearer bonds, and gems for bribes, even some material for trade, but we have got to get to people."

"The best we may hope for," Telisan said, "is to get a few of us on Olympia. Then we must try to escape and find the others. It seems so hopeless."

Fenaday looked at his friend. For the last few days, it seemed some grief was acting on him. He appeared far from his usual optimistic, confident self. It suddenly occurred to him that Sharla also seemed very restrained. "Let's take a walk," he said to Telisan. "Mr. Wardell, you have the bridge."

They exited the bridge in silence, walking down to one of Fenaday's favorite spots, a small observation area over the hanger deck, with its window into space. A few crewmen lounged in the area.

They found reasons to drift away when Fenaday and Telisan walked in.

After they were out of earshot, he turned to Telisan. "What ails, my friend? You still sore at me about that little exchange with Mmok?"

"No," Telisan said grim-faced, "but my troubles center on him. You and he have different missions here. I fear at some point to find ourselves at odds with him and his killing machines."

"What else is new?" Fenaday said. "No, there is something more here. You and Sharla have been acting strange these last few days. Anything I can help with? I may not be Denlenn, but I'm a bit older, and I've been married."

"Perhaps you can help," Telisan said. The story of how he'd asked Arpen to sabotage Mmok spilled out of Telisan. When he finished, he leaned against the portal, yellow cat-irised eyes blinking in the equivalent of tears, exhausted.

"Oh my God," Fenaday said, numb with shock. The Denlenn's strict code of honor demanded the sacrifice of self. For his captain and his friend, Telisan had shattered his own happiness.

"I have owed you," Telisan said, "since you forgave me the lies on Enshar. Such forgiveness is a precious gift."

"Telisan," Fenaday said, anguished, "I'm not Denlenn, I'm human. Humans lie and forgive and forget all the time. I told you then that you owed me nothing. Even if you did, I would never have asked this of you, my friend. Never."

"I do not understand," Telisan said sadly.

They stared at each other without comprehension, trying desperately to reach across the gap of culture and species.

Fenaday put a hand on his friend's shoulder. "This is my fault," he said. "I should know by now that you don't know how to give by halves. I should never have sent for you."

"I would have come anyway," replied the Denlenn.

"Has Arpen broken off the engagement?" he asked, dreading the answer.

"No, but she has made me swear not to tell Sharla the cause of the distance between us, and she has moved into Sickbay."

"Maybe I could talk to her. I'll tell her I put you up to it. I made it an order and it's all my fault."

The Denlenn stared at him, obviously horrified. "No. Not a lie, not to Arpen. I love her too much for that."

"What can I do?" Fenaday demanded. "How can I help?"

"You have helped me by listening. I once told Duna that carrying a secret is a heavy burden to a Denlenn. I feel less alone now. Perhaps I may redeem myself to her by my conduct in the rest of the expedition."

"You are not to get yourself shot at just to look good," Fenaday demanded. "Telisan, I have very little advice for you, but here it is. Communication is the heart of a marriage. Keep talking to Arpen and don't let the distance grow. Don't forget Sharla in this either. She needs to know, or you'll tear her apart. If Arpen loves you—and I mean you, not the Selen war hero, but you—she'll forgive it. No one in a marriage is perfect."

"Interesting thoughts," Telisan said, smiling for the first time in days. He put his big long-fingered hand on the human's shoulder. Fenaday gripped his arm firmly.

"I am not going to let this expedition cost you either of those ladies or your life, do you hear me?"

"Yes," the Denlenn said softly, "I hear you, my friend."

"You are officially off duty from now till we head for *Hermes' Shield*. Go see Arpen. I'm going to relieve Sharla too."

"I must ask you, Robert, not to speak of this with anyone."

"Not if they use white-hot irons," Fenaday swore.

Telisan left, heading toward Sickbay. Fenaday walked slowly back to the bridge, deep in thought, his heart heavy with thoughts of his friend's troubles.

———

Unseen by the two, some sixty feet away, stood the HCR Cobalt, its mechanical senses an extension of Mmok's own. The half-cyborg sat in his cabin, two decks away and hung his head, the human parts of his face burning red. For the first time he could remember, he was ashamed of having spied on someone. Arpen had stood up for him against her fiancé. He wasn't angry with Telisan, knowing where the Denlenn's duty and honor lay. It was well played. What he hadn't counted on was Arpen.

"Dammit," he said to the room. Arpen loved Telisan; it was obvious to anyone who saw them together, or heard her speak of him. To his own shock, he realized he did not want to be the cause of Arpen's engagement failing, but he couldn't tell her anything, without being revealed as a spy.

I'd have been happier not knowing, he thought. *Well, maybe they can work it out. Fenaday gave him some decent advice.* Mmok returned to his briefing files, trying to banish the matter from his mind, without success.

———

Pooka carried them over to the immense disk shape of *Hermes' Shield*, entry port and principal defense of one hemisphere of the planet Olympia. Its sister station, *Diana*, orbited on the opposite side of the planet. An invader from deep space had to face one or the other. Conceived as civilian ports, they were converted to fortresses when interstellar war became a hard fact in the shape of the Conchirri Xenophobes. Over three thousand meters in diameter, each station boasted a squadron of near-space fighters and a sloop-of-war. Dozens of small merchant vessels could dock on their outer hulls.

Fenaday's ship orbited as far from the stations as possible. Trans-polar orbit allowed *Sidhe* to circle Olympia's globe in that gray space at the limit of each station's sensors. *Sidhe* orbited over ocean much of the time, relatively safe from prying eyes. The Olympians would have loved to park a ship or satellite near them, but did not dare press the matter after the shooting at the system's edge.

Angelica Fury, veteran of the Enshar expedition, sat at *Pooka's* helm. She'd left Mandela's shadowy service to work for Fenaday. He never entirely believed it and trusted her only so far. Still, she was an excellent pilot. He also figured if they needed a presentable person, Fury's dark red hair and video star looks would bring up the average. After Shasti, who dwarfed the petite Fury, she was easily the prettiest woman to ever set foot on the ship. Fenaday considered himself undistinguished in looks; he neither frightened children nor made women swoon. Mmok might excite an electrician. As for Telisan, he was handsome in a Denlenn fashion unlikely to be appreciated by the Olympians. Right now Fury's face was a mask of concentration as she lined up for an entry into *Hermes' Shield*. He could hear her speaking softly to ground control.

In addition to Fenaday, Telisan, and Mmok, the shuttle contained Rask and a squad of his ASATs in dress uniform with fully functional weapons. Fenaday convinced Olympia Security only grudgingly of the need for his own guards, softening the blow by billing them as an honor guard. He would have preferred to bring the robots, but wanted to keep their presence a secret for as long as he could.

Well, he thought, *at least they look good.* It had never occurred to him that *Sidhe* might have any use for dress uniforms. Privateers didn't get invited to state dinners. Only an hour before, he'd remembered that all he had on board were a few casual civilian clothes and the modified ASAT uniforms *Sidhe's* crew wore. The best he could manage was a set of crisp, new, fatigue green-blacks and his leather flight jacket, dressed up with several of the medals awarded him after Enshar. Fortunately he'd never bothered to take the medals off the ship and found the boxes while looking for his captain's cap. He ended up looking barely less scruffy than Mmok. In contrast, Telisan looked resplendent in his full Navy commander's whites, bedecked with jewel-like rank insignia and medals. He even wore a slender dress sword.

Pooka took an hour to match orbits with the station, giving them a fine view of the ice-ring. When they could see the *Hermes' Shield*, the reason for its name became clear. It looked like an immense, golden war shield, an effect enhanced by the dome in its center. It grew ominously in *Pooka's* canopy till it eclipsed all the stars. The station directed them to a military dock, and Fury touched down to a perfect landing on the pad. Clamshell doors began to close behind them. Fenaday and Telisan both gave approving nods to Fury. She responded with her usual wicked grin, clearly delighted to be along on the "trouble" as she called it. Fenaday suspected her sanity at times. He was not looking forward to the evening's work.

Exterior lights came on. *Pooka* rested in a tan and blue hanger on gray-painted, hull-metal decking. Lights on the clamshell doors that now formed the roof were too bright to look up at and triggered some of the polarization in the shuttle's canopy.

At the far end of the bay, large doors rolled back. Dark-blue uniformed troops filed onto the deck. Behind them came formally dressed civilians.

"Welcome wagon." Mmok frowned.

"All right, you savages," Rask barked to his ASATs, "the local Presidential Guard is outside. Let's show them what real fighting soldiers look like. Sergeant Kolla, lock, load, and lead them out."

Fenaday grinned to himself. Rask was so accustomed to Earth slang, one had to look twice to remember he was a blue-skinned, red-eyed creature from another world. Unlike Telisan, with his formal, sometimes archaic speech, Rask had no accent. He still sounded like a sergeant, despite the promotion. *Perhaps,* he thought, *all creatures holding the rank of sergeant come from the same place originally.*

The ASATs filed out the rear hatch. Half the soldiers surrounded the shuttle. The others marched to the forward hatch with Rask, forming up as an honor guard. Fenaday led his command staff out, with the petite Fury tagging along. *Hermes'* hangar deck smelled like hanger decks everywhere: cold, with an ozone bite to the air. In a corner, away from the doors, lay a burst can of lubricant, left behind by a sloppy technician. Deck crew squeezed past the dignitaries and honor guard, heading for the mess and trying to look inconspicuous. Someone would catch hell for that. Even the deck crew, he noted, looked like a college sports team. *Well,* Fenaday thought, *they may be pretty, but they still screw up.*

Rask's ASATs looked splendid, but the Olympians were a recruiting advertiser's dream. The smallest stood over two meters tall, powerful examples of every race from old Earth. They formed their own honor guard, a discreet distance from the ASATs.

The dignitaries behind them also looked like athletes, lithe and tall.

"Is short a crime around here?" Fury said.

"You'll be a novelty with the local boys," Fenaday murmured. "Good thing you're not fat."

"Good thing I have such a sensitive boss," she growled.

Fenaday half-turned to her. "Which one?"

Fury's face began to match her name.

"Lay off," Mmok whispered. "She quit, on the up and up."

Fenaday looked at Mmok for a second, then back to Fury. "Sorry."

"Yes, sir," she snapped back.

Fenaday sighed. The Olympians were approaching, and he had no more time for this. A man who looked like an Old Testament prophet led them. Bearded, stately, with dark eyes under shaggy brows and sun-weathered hands, an air of desert and stoicism hung about him. His black formal suit did not hide lines of mature strength in his frame. Next to him walked an ebony-skinned woman, dressed in a lighter hue of gray.

The prophet came up to Fenaday and introduced himself. "Delighted to meet you, Captain Fenaday. I am Enzi Pape, President of Olympia." He gestured to the woman next to him. "Allow me to introduce Vice President Alleti Narva."

Fenaday nodded. Narva was a woman of mature beauty. To the eyes she might have been forty, but Fenaday knew her to be twice this. For all the pomp and circumstance, both remained figureheads. Real power lay with Prime Minister Hagen, chief geneticist of Olympia, heir to the power of its founder, Dr. Allessandro, and with Pard, the enforcement arm of the government. They were not present.

Pape introduced some of the dignitaries with him. A bewildering barrage of names and titles Fenaday tried desperately to process. Admiral Dmitri Rissi, in charge of the Olympian Self-Defense Navy, looked genuinely young. Something about the inhuman regularity of his features, his huge perfect frame, told Fenaday this was another of the Engineered, like Shasti. He greeted Fenaday coolly, with a stilted apology for the missile launch.

The next person introduced was General Dominici, another attractive woman he thought might be much older than her appearance. Her face was unlined, though there was some gray in her close-cropped hair. Fenaday suspected plastic surgery was very common on Olympia. It seemed less a culture of youth than of beauty.

Dominici held his hand longer than usual, enough to make him look into her large dark eyes. She was, he recalled from the briefings, a holdover from the previous government. Rumor had it she was a Neo-Reformist. *This might be a friend,* he thought, as she moved down the reception line.

None of the other Neo-Reformist ministers, the houses of Bremardi, Nappi, or the Trade Unionists, were present. Fenaday stood in an Olympian military space station, surrounded by enemies. The hopelessness of his mission rose to choke him.

Fenaday introduced his command staff. After the initial pleasantries, they were taken to the station's main hall. A formal banquet room had been prepared with long tables set in a U shape. Fenaday and his people sat at the center of the table flanked by Olympians and near the president. Ambassador Davis and his entourage entered, rather pointedly, after Fenaday and his officers were seated. The Confederate ambassador was making no bones about keeping his distance from the famous crew of the *Sidhe.*

Speeches followed, the usual platitudes about having saved the Enshari. Fenaday squirmed, unhappy as always over the fuss.

At Pape's request, Fenaday told the story of the Enshar expedition. He had done it so often it rolled off his lips in a polished performance. He delighted his audience with the story, even surprising himself with how much he enjoyed reciting it. Like most of the Irish, Fenaday enjoyed a tall tale, whether in the telling or listening, and it was hard to improve on Enshar's desperate mission.

Pape looked at him with a curious expression. "It seems you have gathered many of the members of your expedition, but I do not see one who interests us a great deal. We do not see the Olympian, Shasti Rainhell. We, on her own home planet, know virtually nothing about her. She seems most intent on avoiding fame and the news media."

Fenaday was momentarily thrown by the open mention of Shasti's name, but quickly gathered his wits. "She is away on business of her own," he replied evenly. "I expect she will join us here in the near future."

"Ah," Pape said, "then you do expect to see her again."

Fenaday's expression changed, warmth and animation slipping from it, leaving the eyes cold and empty. "Oh, I shall see her again," he promised, "or there will be all manner of hell to pay."

Pape's smile faltered. "Of course."

Fenaday sat through the rest of the formal state dinner with little appetite, small talking with the president and his wife almost automatically. He blessed his father's memory for all the receptions he had forced the young Fenaday to attend. The rituals of the human formal dinner could be a grueling task to the uninitiated.

The dinner finally ended, and the party switched to a gaily decorated ballroom. Bars lined two of the walls. A band played softly on a dais. Above them hung a row of delicate chandeliers running down the ceiling's center. The spacers drifted toward one of the bars. Fenaday hoped no one would ask him to dance. Several of the local men eyed Fury. She treated them to smiles that indicated she was enjoying the attention.

Rask looked around the room. "Hey, these folks aren't as ugly as regular humans." He smiled a toothy Morok smile at Vice President Narva, who looked slightly faint at the sight.

There was a sudden stir at the far end of the room; people fell back from the huge brass-covered pressure doors. Fenaday, Telisan, Rask, and Mmok turned as one, sensing the disturbance as much as hearing it. Jalgren Pard strode into the room, wearing a dark gray suit and accompanied by his retinue of perfect people. But one did not notice them.

"Jesus Christ," Rask said, "he's big as a tank."

It wasn't far wrong, thought a dismayed Fenaday. He remembered Shasti's face when he promised his help against Pard. "You would look like a small child next to him," she said. It was true. Pard dwarfed Fenaday and all the other spacers, even most of the Olympians, not merely in height either. He massed twice Fenaday's weight and though he had thickened with age, it was a thickness of muscle. He wondered how Shasti, powerful as she was, had ever bested him.

"He'll take a lot of killing," Mmok whispered.

"Fool," Telisan hissed, "you, of all people, should beware of listening devices."

Fenaday put a hand on Telisan and Mmok's shoulders, giving them both a little shake. They stopped glaring at each other. With a moment's surprise, Fenaday realized they were scared. It probably sat ill with them, they who were seldom frightened by anything. Pard had that effect. Fenaday wondered if it was something subtle, designed into the genetic superman. Was it the face, with its large, somber features, like those of some ancient brooding king, provoking the fear? The image of Zeus, cannibal father and random slayer?

Next to him stood two handsome younger men, probably the aides Mandela speculated about in his briefing, Vaughn and Antebei. A woman, smaller and older than Shasti, but still devastating in her beauty and fitness, stood to his other side. He remembered the name Alexa, another high Denshi official.

Pard gave no sign of noticing them. Fenaday believed the assassin knew exactly where they were standing before he entered the room. Vice President Narva came toward them. She took Fenaday's arm. "Captain," she said, "there are some people you should meet."

Fenaday gestured at Fury and Rask to stay at the bar. "Telisan, Mmok, with me."

Flanked by his aides, Fenaday walked over to where Pard and a thin-faced man stood in conversation. Behind them stood the two young men. One was almost angelically handsome, but something cold and inhuman looked out of his eyes. It struck Fenaday suddenly, Michelangelo's David, life, imitating art, imitating life. The other man was lean and tall, with a strong Germanic face and brilliant blue eyes. Both looked like they could put down their drinks and run a marathon. *Oh for a Falstaff, a Fezziwig, or Jolly St. Nick,* thought Fenaday, *people with a broadness of spirit that could only come from some indulgence and the occasional human flaw.*

Fenaday stopped a pace away from Pard, surprising the vice president, whose arm slipped off his. The human took up a wide-legged stance. Pard turned to him, flanked by his aides, consciously or not, mirroring Telisan and Mmok. Tension rippled out from them into the room.

A fragment of an old poem surfaced unbidden in Fenaday's consciousness, as he looked up at the man he had come to destroy. Shasti's enemy and by his sworn word, his.

Tyger, tyger, burning bright,
in the forest of the night,
what immortal hand or eye,
could frame thy fearful symmetry?

Fearful it was. Pard's arms were bigger than Fenaday's legs. Just looking at him made Fenaday's guts feel like water. Suddenly the memory of Shasti's face, the pain and shame on it when she told him of the things Pard had done to her, lit a hot space in his chest. Fear slid away to be replaced with anger. *Provoke him,* he thought, *I've got to provoke him. Then duck,* he added mentally.

"May I present Prime Minister Hagen of the Order of Geneticists," Narva said, now showing some nervousness, perspiration beading on her silky, dark skin.

"Minister," Fenaday said with a dangerous softness. Several feet away, Hagen raised a glass in acknowledgment, saying nothing.

"I would also like to present—" Narva began.

"I know who he is," Fenaday's voice rose above the buzz of conversation. With deliberation he put both hands on his hips, ignoring Pard's outstretched hand. Pard let it drop easily, apparently unperturbed.

"As I know who you are," Pard said in a deep, pleasing voice.

"We share a common interest," Fenaday said. "She sends you greetings. Despite your best efforts to have her murdered, even after she was a member of my crew, she is in good health. The same cannot be said of the butchers you sent after her."

"Captain Fenaday," Narva said, shocked. In the distance, Fenaday could see Pape exchanging urgent words with Ambassador Davis.

"I'm afraid I do not know what you are talking about," Pard said dryly.

"Yes, you do. If you'd had any balls, you'd have gone after her yourself. But I understand she didn't leave you those in working order."

Michelangelo's David started a move and was instantly grabbed by his blue-eyed companion.

"Keep hold of pretty boy," Fenaday added, with a confidence he didn't feel, "or his designer face won't look so good." He gestured with his head. "That her replacement? You've traded downward, old boy, just as she traded upward."

Pard gave the young man struggling to break free of his companion a volcanic glance that stopped him cold. He shuttered the look before turning back to Fenaday, all bland. All around the tableau, people stared.

Damn it, Fenaday thought, *swing at me or something.*

"I'm sure there is some mistake," Narva said, clearly frightened now.

"No mistake," Fenaday said. He glared up at Pard, willing himself not to blink. *Hit me,* he thought, *lose your temper, damn you.*

"Who might this mysterious acquaintance be?" General Dominici asked. She edged into the scene, giving every indication of enjoying it. Pard's aides shifted from behind him, spreading out. In the background, several Army soldiers put down their drinks, starting a discreet approach.

"Pard knows," Fenaday said with a cutting smile, moving closer. Abruptly, he turned away from Pard and moved, managing to shoulder the young hotheaded aide. The man cursed and drew back an arm.

"Antebei," Pard growled.

One word. The tone froze the young man and made the hair on Fenaday's neck stand up. *Like being at a real zoo,* he thought, *and hearing a real tiger, not a recording.* Fenaday shivered, suppressing panic. Be mad, stay mad.

Fenaday looked up into the young man's rage-filled, perfect eyes, smiled, and barked a laugh.

"General," Pard said with an even tone. "Good evening." He turned slowly, gesturing to Hagen, who stared at Fenaday without expression. Fenaday returned a cold smile. Pard and Hagen moved away, screened by their aides and several naval officers. It cost Pard a retreat, but he ended the confrontation. *Not much victory,* thought Fenaday bitterly. *He retreats over ground he can afford to part with. I can't follow.*

Fenaday headed for the bar. *The natural refuge of the Irish,* he thought. He passed Ambassador Davis, busy placating an upset President Pape, without a glance. The band changed tunes and people began talking in a harsh buzz. The looks given Fenaday and his people were a mixture of fear, curiosity and, in some cases, outright hatred. Several faces held something different: respect, interest? Perhaps Denshi weren't completely popular even here.

They made the bar without being cut down. A nervous bartender took their orders and retreated to the far end of the bar as quickly as he could.

"When in doubt go for the balls, huh, Fenaday?" Mmok gave an evil grin.

"I've got to provoke him," Fenaday muttered. "What provokes a man more than thinking his woman is enjoying another man more?"

"Good thing it wasn't a question of size," Mmok returned.

"Well, they say it's not what you got, but how you use it," Fenaday said. "Not that you would measure up any better."

"That's what you think," the cyborg said. "Not all my enhancements are visible."

Fenaday snorted a laugh, some of the tension and fear leaving him.

Telisan looked at them, puzzled. Mmok and Fenaday rarely spoke, when they did, it was terse. It seemed Pard had joined them, at least temporarily, in a bond built of hate and fear. "What follows?" he asked of the humans.

Before Fenaday could answer, he saw General Dominici walking toward them. Several of her aides trailed her, out of earshot, but where they could watch her.

"Mr. Fenaday," she said, in a throaty but pleasing voice. "Gentlemen."

Telisan acknowledged the courtesy with a half bow. Mmok, as usual, grunted.

"You have a taste for dangerous games," Dominici said.

"As do you," Fenaday smiled, sipping his whiskey, "or why are you talking to me..."

"After," she interrupted, "you insulted the leading assassin of an order of assassins in public?"

"Exactly."

Dominici looked at Mmok and Telisan. "Don't you boys have somewhere to be?" she asked, smiling. They looked at Fenaday, confused.

"Mingle," Fenaday said. The two moved off into the crowd toward Fury and Rask. Fury, noted Fenaday, stood at the center of a group of young Olympian officers. Her diminutive good looks were making her a hit with the boys, as predicted.

Fenaday found himself alone with Dominici. Her aides took up station at the other end of the bar, causing the bartender to flee to the opposite end. Dominici snagged him long enough to secure a glass of champagne.

"Bartenders have excellent instincts," she observed.

"Apparently other people share his concerns," Fenaday said wryly. "Maybe they think I will spontaneously combust."

"Pard has been known to make such things happen. For far less insult than you just dealt him tonight."

"Maybe he will try," Fenaday said. "My death could come with a high price tag."

"You're hoping he'll try," Dominici stated.

Fenaday studied the Olympian. Her eyes, half hidden behind sooty thick lashes, betrayed nothing beyond an ironic sense of humor. She had the Mediterranean features her name suggested, olive skin, large brown eyes, full lips. Her body suffered little from the tailored military uniform.

"Why would I want that?" he asked, buying time to think.

"Oh please," she replied, smiling again. "Reconnaissance by fire is an old technique. As long as Pard doesn't strike at you, there is no way to press him. No way to force your way downworld, where you want to go, at least with freedom to move."

Fenaday looked out over the crowd. He caught a fell glare from the man Pard called Antebei. He stood near the entranceway, staring. Fenaday grinned broadly, and the perfect man's features spasmed in rage. He spun and stalked out.

"Pard's catamite?" he speculated.

Dominici smiled again. "Pard likes them young, but I never

heard of him liking boys. My information is that he likes girls. Young, tall, with green eyes and black hair on ivory skin."

He turned quickly, provoking a shift in her aides, quelled by a razor glance from her.

"You seem to know a great deal about his likes," he managed.

"Oh, yes, his and yours," she replied sweetly. "May I call you Robert?"

"Where is this going, General?"

"And you may call me Maria," she said. "I think you and I should talk, privately."

"Yes."

"But not here," she said. "I have already been greatly daring. I have secure quarters on the far side of the station, Army territory. I'll send an aide to find you a half hour after the reception ends. Denshi Security will not like it, but they dare not interfere." With that, Dominici gave him a dazzling smile, ran her hand over his upper arm suggestively, and slipped away. Her aides filed in behind her.

Fenaday was not alone at the bar long. Telisan and the others quickly drifted over.

"What happened?" Telisan asked.

"An invitation," Fenaday murmured.

———

P ard's retinue followed him down the corridor. Once they reached the secured Denshi area, Pard rounded on Antebei, who'd lagged behind.

"What idiocy was that?" he growled.

"Sir," Antebei said woodenly.

"You allowed a standard human to control you, to play on you like a musical instrument. Is this superiority?"

Antebei looked at the floor like a child. It tasked Pard's patience. "Return to the shuttle," Pard said. "Await us there."

"Yes, sir," Antebei said, his face and voice carefully neutral. Pard saw further and knew the young man was seething. Antebei's body-guard followed him out.

Pard looked at Vaughn, who looked back, his face expressionless, for all that he could only be happy with his chief rival's troubles.

"Take charge here," Pard ordered. "Admiral Rissi has already mishandled Fenaday once. Prevent him from doing so again. Minimize friction between Army and Navy security. Do not allow Dominici to gain further from the incident. You will not succeed in keeping her from Fenaday, but I doubt the dissolute slut's interest is much beyond adding another notch to her bedpost."

"Yes, sir." Vaughn exited smartly with Misa Tanaka following him.

"The rest of you have your assignments," Pard announced. The other Denshi operatives dispersed, leaving only Pard, his personal guard, Salmot and Hagen. A detail of Hagen's proctors stood a discreet distance away.

"What do we do about Fenaday?" Hagen demanded.

Pard gusted a sigh. "Ignore him. He can do nothing against us so long as we give him no opening. Shower him with awards and honors, surround him with dignitaries and vid-stars. Run out his time.

"We must keep control of his visit and his itinerary. That fool, Rissi, almost cost us that control by flinging a nuke at an interstellar hero. Those who saw the incident in there will forgive Fenaday's temper tantrum. Had Antebei or I struck him, regardless of the provocation, neither the public nor our enemies would ignore the outburst. Disgrace is dangerous in politics."

"But the accusation, the attack—" Hagen began.

"Mean nothing," Pard cut in. "We control both houses of Parliament, the Presidency, and you head the Eugenics Board. Our position cannot be assailed. Only our own mistakes can damage us."

"I admire your self-control," Hagen said, "after the things he said to you."

"Then emulate it," Pard snapped.

Hagen nodded, lips pursed.

Pard realized that he'd been too harsh. "Come, Minister, are we going to allow this near monkey to disturb our plans? He's probably off somewhere struggling with a banana right now."

Hagen barked a laugh. "As you say, Lord Pard. I shall see you back on the surface." He walked toward his escort of proctors.

Pard turned and headed for the shuttle. Salmot trailed him silently. It pleased Pard to think of Fenaday as a mere monkey. The thought that Fenaday would seek a physical confrontation became almost amusing. Pard could crush a standard human like Fenaday with a single blow. He flexed the powerful muscles of his forearms then calmed himself. *I've lived for over eighty years and no man has bested me,* he thought.

But one woman has, came the thought, unbidden and unwelcome. Shasti, his most precious possession, turned on him, injured him, and fled him. Now she disgraced herself by mating with this monkey. It filled him with disgust.

How could she? he wondered. Fenaday stood barely six feet tall. His asymmetrical face held neither beauty nor design. There existed no field of physical endeavor in which Fenaday could compete with him. *She must be mad,* he thought, *or else it is a deliberate attempt to get back at me by debasing herself with this random work of nature?*

True, he thought, *I put constraints on her, demands, but she lacked for no physical comfort. Her sexual naïveté, assuming that it was all pleasure and no pain, had been an obstacle. Perhaps I brought her along too far, too fast. But I created her for my needs, to my specifications, having no higher purpose. That might have been my mistake,* he mused. *I made her too strong and too fast.* In the end it was like adopting a tiger cub. As the creature grew, it became more and more dangerous, requiring more and more control. Yet controlling her made the pleasures all the sweeter. It proved his dominance and strength.

I am not to be ruled or controlled by women, he thought. *It's how the weak control the strong, with ties of deference and culture. There is only power. Dominate or be dominated.*

The guards and attendants saluted or stepped out of his path. Pard strode aboard his personal shuttle. Doors sealed behind him. The captain, an Engineered Denshi operative, stood at attention.

"Everything is ready, Lord," the young woman said. "We are awaiting your command."

"Excellent," he replied. "Take me back to Marathon, Captain."

Minutes later the shuttle kicked free of *Hermes' Shield,* leaving Pard's enemy stranded behind him, impotent.

Chapter Ten

The reception did not last long after the incident. The president coolly, but appropriately, congratulated Fenaday and his people on their service in the Enshar Expedition. Mercifully, Pape did not actually hang medals on them, simply handing them the boxes to desultory applause. He invited Fenaday and his senior officers to a tour of the Capital in the morning, under a heavy Navy/Denshi escort. A naval attaché offered them quarters, which they accepted for a few hours, announcing their intention to return to *Sidhe* for the night. The latter seemed to offend their Navy host, but Fenaday insisted on it. The attaché left to inform his superiors. Fenaday's party found themselves alone again in the large ballroom.

But not for long. Ambassador Davis stalked over, pushing past Telisan and Fury to seize Fenaday's arm. "What in hell were you doing?" he spat. "One diplomatic incident isn't enough for you? The president is incensed over that scene with Lord Pard."

Fenaday casually reached over, placing his thumb on a pressure point in the middle of the ambassador's forearm. Davis winced as his hand involuntarily opened and Fenaday pushed his arm away.

"I told you," Fenaday said, with an elaborate calm he did not feel, "that I needed to get free of Navy and Denshi security. The

Navy tried to nuke us coming in. If I could get Pard to lose his temper and pop me, we might have been able to embarrass the government into removing both Denshi and Navy security. You don't think I was chest-bumping with that monster for ego, do you? It was a slim chance, I'll grant, but it almost worked. Michelangelo was going to swing. Pard stopped him."

"That," Davis said, "is both insane and the stupidest thing I've ever heard."

Fenaday turned a cold look on Davis. "I'm a desperate man, Ambassador. You find me a way down onto that planet with freedom of movement, or I'll do it myself and you won't like the results."

Davis and Fenaday stood toe-to-toe, unblinking.

"Ambassador, shouldn't you be off somewhere, kissing the appropriate posteriors?" Mmok asked.

Davis shot him a murderous look, then spun on his heel, heading for the exit and his nervous staff.

It seemed to cheer Mmok immensely.

Fenaday gave the cyborg a sour look. "You're a lot of help."

Mmok shrugged. "He's never going to do anything for us anyway."

"Unfortunately true," Telisan said, "but we did not need another enemy."

"He won't cross Mandela," Mmok replied. "No one does."

Further conversation was forestalled as the naval officer returned and conducted them to a luxurious suite where they could rest for a few hours. He also offered to take them on a tour of the space station. Fenaday sent Telisan, with Rask and an ASAT for an escort. The others stayed with Fenaday and helped Mmok search the rooms for surveillance devices. They found and disabled six of them.

The Army aide-de-camp showed up at their quarters on schedule, which provoked a loud discussion with Denshi/Navy security in the lobby, before they were let in. Two hulking troopers the size of bears accompanied an Olympian Army lieutenant. The lieutenant wore a slate-gray dress-uniform complete with fine chain-mail epaulets, a blood-red sash, and an ornate holstered pistol. The soldiers with him wore city-camouflage uniforms, body armor, and carried riot guns.

"Sorry, sir," the officer said. "I'll have to search you. Just routine, sir."

"Of course," Fenaday replied. Expecting this, he had not tried to hide a weapon.

After the brief but professional frisk, they left the guest quarters, heading for the small lobby area under the unhappy eyes of blue-uniformed station security. Dominici's soldiers and the Navy/Denshi contingent stared stonily at each other as the lieutenant bent over the desk, signing some form. Fenaday, standing unarmed in their midst, felt vulnerable.

A large, open shuttle car rested on its magnetic rail in the ten-meter-wide tubeway. It bore OSDF Army markings and the same slate gray of the officer's uniform. They piled into the ten-person car with the guards facing outward in the front and rear. The lieutenant sat with his hand on his sidearm, eyes roaming over the corridor, other rail cars and the few station crew in sight. Noiselessly, the car pulled forward into the traffic. They changed levels and directions, seemingly at random. Fenaday looked about at the stations and shops that lined the tubeway but quickly lost his orientation. As they came to one industrial area, an Army soldier stepped out from the maze of tan and silver piping and waved them down. He leaned in, whispering urgently but quietly to the officer. Fenaday noticed a fresh burn mark on the man's armor. The air smelled faintly of smoke. In the distance Fenaday saw some more soldiers moving through the catwalks and piping.

The lieutenant gave the soldier a quick order, and the party backtracked, heading for another corridor.

"What's happening?" Fenaday asked, looking in all directions.

"Nothing to worry about sir," the officer replied. "Just routine."

Fenaday pressed his lips together, saying nothing.

The cart backed off, and they took an elevator to the next deck and drove on. Eventually, they reached a checkpoint area filled with soldiers. After they debarked, the lieutenant spoke to an officer at the desk. A squad of armored men trotted out to take the car they had just arrived in. There was a visible rise in tension. The officer and two troopers walked Fenaday past other guards and check-points, until they arrived at an ornate set of wood-covered doors bearing the insignia of the Army, a sword upright in the middle of a DNA strand.

"Have a good evening, sir," said the officer. "These men will be waiting for you when you leave. The sergeant at the last desk we passed will call for me." He put a card into a slot, and the doors whooshed open. Fenaday noted that the wood veneer masked the thick armor of the doors. They'd withstand explosive decompression or gunfire.

When they closed, Fenaday's guards remained on the other side. He walked into a space more like a hotel suite than the office he anticipated. A small table on a plush white rug was set with candles, a bottle of white wine, and two glasses.

Fenaday turned at a sound from the adjoining room to the left. Its door opened. Dominici stepped out from what was evidently her bedroom from the furniture he glimpsed. She wore a diaphanous robe, hiding only the details of her body. She smiled at his surprise. "Not used to female admirers, Captain? I would have thought you much in demand."

"Umm, not so I noticed," he replied, confused.

"Foolish women," she said, walking up to him. Her eyes, level with his, were a dark, intense brown. They seemed to draw him in. "Let's save the wine for after," she murmured, letting the robe fall. It slid over her breasts, dropping past her flat middle to the floor. She leaned forward, pressing her mouth to his. Fenaday's brain whirled as she leaned her body into his. He could feel her nipples against the front of his shirt. She moved to pull him down on her, onto the rug, but he pulled slowly, insistently, back.

Dominici looked at him with mock chagrin on her face. "Am I going too fast for you? I thought you liked assertive women."

"I like all types of women," he replied, his face and other places hot. Gently, he disengaged her arms from his neck. "This isn't the reason I came, or that I thought you invited me."

"Business first, pleasure later?" she said huskily.

Fenaday got himself under better control. After living with Shasti, he was again used to the warmth and excitement of making love. Distracted and exhausted by the desperate preparations for rescue, he hadn't realized how much he missed it until now. The thought that Dominici understood this, and was using it, angered him. More than ever, he hated being manipulated and he doubted a woman of Dominici's position was such an undisciplined alley cat. No, if she had such needs, she would attend to them discreetly. This was manipulation.

Dominici watched the by-play on his face with more understanding than he suspected was safe for him. "So," she said with a slight smile, "you're not quite as easy to handle as I thought. That's good. One hopes for sense in an ally." The seductive mien dropped off like the clothes she'd shed.

Fenaday stared at her; some of his bemusement must have shown through. Dominici's smile broadened. She bent down and picked up the filmy robe. Casually draping it over her body, she sat back on a couch arm, completely unselfconscious. The effect was more erotic than her initial invitation.

"Then you weren't interested," he said slowly, trying to figure out her game.

"Oh, I'm interested," Dominici replied. "But this is mostly business."

"Odd sort of business for a general," he muttered.

Dominici laughed. "Don't be prim with me, Robert. I believe in total war, and I use every weapon I have. If I could make you mine, it might be a worthwhile conquest, and I assume you would be worth having. I guarantee you would enjoy yourself. I'm very talented, one of the side benefits of a long and healthy life.

"Besides, Denshi has spies in the military, possibly on my staff. You were seen being delivered to me. Rumor will be I bedded you for curiosity or sport. They may buy curiosity, or they may figure out the real reason, but I will have sufficient cover to turn aside any inquiry. Sometimes a reputation is useful."

Fenaday found his eyes dropping to the curves of her body. Dominici looked like a woman in her late thirties or early forties, but her body appeared even younger. The briefing said she was in her sixties. It was almost impossible to believe. Beyond a few lines to the face and a touch of gray in the hair, there was little sign of age on her.

"Of course," Dominici continued, "I can see that I might not measure up to your standards. Shasti Rainhell would be a hard act to follow. She is one of the Engineered, Third or Fourth-Generation even. The new race, heir to Olympia, I could not hope to compete with her perfection."

"You are not Engineered, I take it?" he asked.

"No." Dominici frowned. "My parents were selected by the Order of Geneticists under the old Allessandro program. What you see," she said, rising in a mocking pirouette that caused her filmy robe to float around her, "is what God and Dr. Allessandro, if there is a difference, intended."

Fenaday found his breath a little tight and forced his eyes back to her face. Dominici was attractive. She lacked Shasti's height or symmetry, and the muscular build looked a bit chunky for Fenaday's taste. Still, she was well made and very fit.

She is not my friend, he reminded himself. *She is playing with me, trying to get a hold on me. This is business.* He reached for the wine bottle and poured two glasses. He moistened dry lips with a sip of cool, slightly sweet, white wine, offering the other glass to Dominici. "I sense a dislike of the new order, and I thought Pard was the reason for our meeting."

"I am sure whoever sent you gave you an extensive briefing on the divisions in Olympian society," she replied, walking over to him and accepting the other wineglass. "Possible friends, definite foes. Oh, please do not bother to deny it. You are here for Pard and the team that came before. Army Intelligence established that a Confederate strike force dropped on Olympia approximately sixty-three standard days ago, though I will grant we have no idea how."

Dominici returned to her perch on the couch arm, leaning back as if to display her superb body the better. "None of the members of the team," she began, "were taken alive. Your Rainhell was seen, but not taken or killed."

Fenaday controlled himself with an effort. *Shasti's alive. At least she was.* Relief washed over his senses. He snapped back to focus on what Dominici was saying.

"It was clear from the bodies," Dominici continued, "after genetic testing, that they were Confed. We know some survivors escaped, we don't know how many, since we don't know the original size of the force. Of course, you could remedy that?"

He said nothing.

Dominici sighed, appearing irritated. "Fenaday, the only reason your people are still alive and at large is that we have been running interference for them. We were the ones who captured the other members of Leda Jenner's cell, to keep them out of Denshi's hands."

"Then you would know where the alleged survivors are?" he asked.

"We did not get all of them alive," Dominici said, gently swirling her wineglass. "Unfortunately, the one who knew the location of the safe houses was killed."

"You're not holding the off-planet team?" he asked cautiously.

"No. To the extent we have a common enemy in Pard, I'm your friend."

"Well, you have been very friendly so far," he said, trying for lightness.

"Then return the favor," she purred, leaning forward.

Think about sports, food, cold showers, anything, he said to himself.

"Motivation," he said, unexpectedly, "why? What is your problem with Pard? Why don't you go to the government with what you know? Pard's been good to the military, buying up every weapon in sight. You could earn great favor with him."

"Pard loves the Navy, not the Army," Dominici raised the glass to her lips and sipped, watching him through the raised rim of the crystal.

"Not enough, General," Fenaday said. "You're asking me to trust you. You claim to know my motivations. I need to know yours."

She looked at him thoughtfully, then put down her glass on a table, "What am I?"

"What?"

"What am I?" she repeated.

"Olympia's senior Army general."

"No, that's who I am. What am I?"

"A woman." He shrugged.

"Thanks for noticing." She smiled. "A human woman, just so. I may be the product of selective breeding and special training, but I am all human. There is no real difference between us on a DNA level. Not to be immodest, I just have better codes.

"Pard is taking Olympia in a different direction than Allessandro intended. He and the Order of Geneticists are moving into creating people, making a new species of humanity. They are fucking with DNA, the ultimate tie that binds. Olympia is being divided, not by the usual squabbles, but by a growing gap between people like me, and people like your friend, Shasti the Engineered. She is not very far down that road. You could call her human plus. The newest people are not being born; they are coming out of labs, exclusively.

"How long before they discard the basic model? Nature's haphazard design, with all its flaws. How long until the newest people have horns, claws, extra organs, three eyeballs? How long till the freak show?" she asked, pacing around the room, arms folded across her firm breasts, the sheer robe trailing behind her.

"Allessandro believed in *human* perfection. The Geneticists and Pard are perverting that into a new alien race, right under every-one's nose." Dominici walked over to the table to refill her glass. Fenaday had to stop himself from looking at the supple way her body moved. He shook his head when she gestured with the bottle. She sipped some wine before speaking again.

"I have grandchildren, Fenaday—beautiful, near perfect, human grandchildren. But they are not Engineered. I don't want to see them in a new underclass lorded over by freaks from laboratories. That is what will happen, if Pard and the Geneticists are not stopped.

"You're suspicious of the armaments Pard's building. So am I. He's up to something big. Denshi manpower has been disappearing lately. Where to? Ships not on the Registry? Secret bases? If he isn't stopped soon, it may be too late. So I need you, Fenaday. Pard is the linchpin. I need him taken out, and I can't move openly against him.

"You need me. Rainhell is down there, and she can't last forever with Denshi after her, even with my help. Denshi are good. They will get her."

Fenaday stared into her dark eyes, trying to read something. Dominici revealed nothing. *What choice do I have?* he thought. *I can't stay in orbit forever.*

"I believe you," Fenaday said. "Maybe I'm a fool for doing so, but I do. I'm going to take the chance you are not setting me up. You're partially correct about my mission. You hit on why I was sent, dead on. They want me to take out Pard. I'll do it if I can, but I'm only interested in Shasti and the other members of her team. If it comes to it, I'll settle for just her.

"A wise being I once knew told me he would forgo revenge for a home. I failed to follow that advice once. I won't make that mistake again. I'll go through Pard, if I need to, but I would as soon go around. All I want is her."

"You'll have to go through him," Dominici assured him. "Never doubt it. Pard knows she is here, and he will kill her unless you kill him first. I assume you have the means to deal with Pard?"

"We didn't bring an army," Fenaday said. "We aren't here for a stand-up fight. We have to approach by stealth, overwhelm the local force, make the kill and run like hell. The problems are how to get down, find our people, and after the strike, how to get offworld again."

"We are looking for your people now," Dominici said. "I can provide you with schematics of Pard's complex, data on troops, operations, and most important, somewhere to run to after the strike. However, your forces get onto Olympia, I don't believe you would be able to get off without help. You'll get Army protection on a base until you can be extracted."

"If you can do all this, why haven't you taken care of Pard yourself?" Fenaday asked.

She grimaced. "Not so easy. The Army holds the ground; the Navy holds the sky. I told you, Pard has people in the Army as well. If I moved against him openly, I would find myself relieved by the President and probably in an accident soon after. I have one shot at him. Once I start, I am committed. Do or die. Understand this, I won't be able to do much until Pard is dead, or at least till Denshi is in disorder. Once he is down and we occupy Denshi offices, we will find enough to disgrace Pard with some plot. He has dozens, I am sure. Likely we won't even have to make anything up."

"Can you do anything about getting us downworld?" he asked.

"No, damn it, that's Navy jurisdiction. I have no influence in that area. You'll have to come up with something. Congratulations on having the smarts not to get boarded or docked to the station. Either would have been disaster. I know you got by our detectors the first time. Can you do it again?"

"Yes," Fenaday said, "I think so. This close to the planet, we assume the ship is under surveillance. We'll need a little luck, some diversion, but we can do it."

"Mind telling me how?" she asked sweetly.

Fenaday smiled back at her. After a moment, she laughed. "You're right about the surveillance, but you picked your orbit well. They can't park a ship or satellite close in such a high orbit without making a diplomatic scene they don't need. It makes it much more difficult. Still, I don't see how you could manage a drop without radar detection. However, that's your problem. You don't get my help till you attack Pard."

"Everything hinges on Pard," Fenaday said. "You're taking huge risks even talking to me. Betting your life on the efforts of a privateer you've never met, with forces you don't know. Ms. Dominici, a smart man might think you were pretty desperate."

"I suspect a lot about your forces," she returned dryly, "and you're right. I said you weren't a fool. My position weakens almost daily. I represent a waning power, the Non-Engineered in the high command. They've been trying to force me into retirement, or a transfer. Either is the functional equivalent of a death sentence for me and perhaps my kind. So I'm desperate, enough to take a wild chance with you and the Confederacy.

"Don't bother to talk to me about rogue operations or personal vendettas. The Confederacy is behind you and you've got more than you've shown. Or," she smiled, "I'm an idiot and you're dead."

"I would hate that," Fenaday said. He was not going to share the information on the *Intruder* or his cyber-force. He suspected Dominici guessed, just from what she knew about Enshar. The gap in her knowledge was the top-secret *Intruder*. With the information she could supply, they might actually have a chance.

"It's a deal," he said, "intelligence now, and after we strike Pard, protection."

"Excellent," Dominici smiled. She put down her glass then walked over to her desk, returning with a small metal box. "Here are the plans for Pard's complex; he changes things randomly, so it's not complete. The other files show a list of Pard's forces and the naval forces he can lay immediate command to. Denshi doesn't trust the Navy. They handle their own security, and nothing less than a battalion level attack is going to make much of a dent in that complex. In the city, there are police and Geneticist Proctors to contend with. Regular troops would make short work of them, but they are more than adequate against assassins. Denshi security is probably the best there is. Takes one to catch one."

"Like the Ninja of old," he said, taking the box.

"The what?"

"A force in ancient Japan on Earth, known as Ninja or the Shinobi, assassins and bodyguards like the Denshi, exerting power in the same fashion. But an assassin is just an overly expensive soldier in a real war. The Shogun government wiped them out when they became too influential."

"We have that chance here," she agreed. "Denshi has many more regular troops than we can account for. Many of them are gone. We don't know where. Navy troops have been filling in, but Denshi doesn't use them in their own facilities. Pard may be under-defended, more at the compound than in the city, where they can call on Denshi-friendly police and Hagen's Proctors. My information is that Pard is heading back to the complex for the next three days, lying low while you are here.

"Everything you need is in these files. There is a code for contacting me. Use it sparingly. It takes Denshi an average of two weeks to crack them. I won't need another. Since that's about as much time as I have left.

"Now, Captain," she added, "your last chance to mix business with pleasure?"

Fenaday felt lightheaded. Dominici stood right next to him, her scent more intoxicating than the wine. Her skin looked firm, smooth, and flawless. He shook his head to clear it, taking a step back at the same time. "It isn't that you are not attractive," he said ruefully. "You are. My thanks to God, or Dr. Allessandro, but I'm spoken for, at least I think so."

"How quaint," she replied, seeming unoffended. "Still, I'm glad saying no wasn't easy. A woman doesn't like to think she's losing her touch. Wait two hours, Captain, then walk out to the antechamber. My guards will take you back."

"Two hours?" he asked.

"I do have my reputation to consider," she said, walking out of the room with an intriguing sway to her hips.

Fenaday felt his stomach muscles tighten. *Baseball,* he thought, *Sunday Mass, icy-cold January breezes.*

Chapter Eleven

Guards escorted Fenaday back to the shuttle bay, where the others were preflighting *Pooka*. Seeing his own security, in the form of Rask's ASATs, brought a feeling of intense relief. A half-dozen of *Sidhe's* honor guard stood watch outside the shuttle when the doors to the bay cycled. The ASATs snapped to attention as he entered, leaving his Olympian escort behind. Telisan and Rask hurried over to greet him.

"I'm okay," Fenaday assured his anxious companions. "Let's get back to the ship. I don't know about you, but I've had enough for one evening." The others knew he had given standing orders that nothing was to be discussed until they were safely off the station and away from spying devices. Mmok would have used his time to make sure no one had slipped by their guards and bugged their vessel. They clambered into the old *Dakota* class shuttle. Fenaday walked onto the flight deck to find Angelica Fury already in the pilot seat.

"Glad you're back, Skipper." She seemed to have gotten over being mad at him.

"Thanks." He put a hand on her shoulder. "How soon can you get us out of here?"

"We've got an exit window set and ready to go. If you're ready, I'll get started on my checklist."

"Okay, Angie. Let's get going."

Fury popped her checklist on the screen and keyed her mike. "*Hermes*' control, this is *Pooka*. We are preparing to leave. Please confirm cleared exit vector."

Pooka sealed, and the bay began preparation for decompression. In the back of the shuttle, the ASATs stowed their weapons. Rask oversaw this, though he kept his own weapon handy. The bay lights went out, and the shuttle's cut in automatically. *Pooka* lifted. Back out under the stars, Fenaday sighed in relief, maneuvering room at last.

Telisan and Mmok waited impatiently until the shuttle cleared the near area of the space station. "Rask," Fenaday called. The Morok locked down his weapon and joined them on the flight deck.

"Course plotted and locked in," Fury announced. "ETA to *Sidhe* is one hour and ten minutes. No real flying to do till then. Want me to take a walk?"

"Thanks, Angie," he replied. "It's not you..."

"Forget it, Skipper." Fury smiled and waved her hand. "It's all just business." She sealed the lock behind her.

"At last," Telisan said.

"Yeah, give," Mmok added. "What happened?"

"We have an ally," Fenaday said. "General Dominici is going to help us. Pard is gunning for her. She thinks she has only a few weeks left. She wants to strike at Denshi, the Engineered, and particularly Pard." In a few minutes, he laid out the details of the meeting. The codes, contacts, her offers of help and the reasons why. He handed the data crystals and disks to Mmok.

"Christ, Fenaday." Mmok grimaced. "Some muscle queen throws her legs around you and we are supposed to believe this?"

"Oh, enough out of you," Fenaday said, too tired for the usual verbal battles. "What choice do we have? We're stalemated in orbit, getting nowhere. Time is against us. We have no way to find our people, no help from downworld, even from Davis.

"Do you want to storm Pard's fortress blind? With no better information than Mandela's—you know I wish I knew his real goddamn name—obsolete data? Besides, I didn't sleep with her."

"Why not?" Rask asked.

Fenaday glared at the Morok. "She wasn't after sex. The pass she made was pure manipulation; she wanted the extra hold on me. You know, I don't just sleep with everyone who asks."

The Morok seemed to consider this for a second. "How come?"

Fenaday looked exasperated. Mmok snorted a laugh. Telisan seemed confused. "I'll explain human mating rituals some other time," Fenaday said. "Meanwhile, we get back to *Sidhe* and start planning how to get downworld. That's the area Dominici can't help us with. She may not be our friend, but she isn't Pard's either. That will suffice for now.

"Somehow we have to locate Pard, then get our forces down outside of Marathon unobserved. At least we have somewhere to go after the sanction. Getting off was always the weak part of the plan."

"As it was with Rigg's mission," Mmok said. "They had three options. The shuttle was going to rendezvous at the landing site near Manki two days after the sanction. If the government fell and the Neos took over, no problem. If not, they were to break out as best they could, or as a last resort, head to the embassy. I don't think any of us want to rely on Davis."

"We agree on that," Fenaday said. "All right. Mmok, get that data processed for download so we can get to studying. Start updating our landing profiles. I'm going to sack out for an hour."

"Dreaming of beautiful women?" Rask grinned.

"Is there any other kind around here?" Fenaday said.

"One does see only the most handsome of your species," Telisan said.

"It's what this society was created for." Fenaday yawned, fatigue creeping into his voice. "Developing the perfect human. If you don't measure up, I guess you fall into some grunt underclass. I wonder where they keep the poor people?"

"Where did you keep them on New Eire?" Mmok asked bitterly.

"What?" Fenaday turned toward the cyborg.

"The poor, Fenaday, the non-Irish, those who weren't related to the First-In families."

"New Eire was settled by Irish refugees," Fenaday retorted, "for Irish refugees fleeing the New Troubles. It was to be our place, free from the burden of history."

"Yeah," Mmok said, looking him in the eye. "You, the Amerindians, the Palestinians, everyone with a historical grudge or slight. Look, a new world, where just your own kind live. The ultimate fence.

"But try being a white on Kwanzal, or black on New Eire, or anybody on Lakota who ain't one. Here all you have to be is pretty and talented. Maybe they are the most honest."

To everyone's surprise, the anger in Fenaday's eyes faded. "There's some truth to what you say," he replied. "I didn't know much about it until I became poor and had to survive in the spacer sections of the offport. I never saw those people till I ended up as one of those people.

"Telisan, we treat a full alien like yourself better than we treat others of our own kind who are of different ethnic groups. There's no quota on Denlenns or Moroks immigrating to New Eire. There is on other humans. So, Mr. Mmok, I guess you have a point."

Mmok seemed disconcerted, almost embarrassed by Fenaday's agreement. Telisan looked merely relieved, another Mmok-Fenaday donnybrook being the last thing they needed.

"Well," Mmok shrugged, "you were going to sack out. We'll wake you when we arrive."

"No info on human mating rituals?" Rask asked.

Fenaday rolled his eyes, unsealed the doors, and walked out. Mmok followed, looking dubiously at the data crystals.

Rask glanced at Telisan. "Actually, I'm not all that curious. Frankly, to me, it's amazing they reproduce at all. Nice guys, humans, but ugly. No decent fangs."

"To each his own," Telisan said diplomatically, thinking about goblin-like, blue-skinned women with an internal shudder.

Fenaday, hearing the by-play as he unlatched a bunk in the small cabin behind the flight deck, snorted a laugh. The others walked past him, trooping down to the cargo deck. Angelica winked at Fenaday as she headed for the pilot's chair, autopilot or no. Fenaday shut the thin panel to the room and lay down. Despite fatigue, his mind would not stop racing and planning. Would not stop worrying about the woman he'd crossed space to find. His eyes drifted to the tiny porthole and the world below.

Fifty miles below, Shasti Rainhell looked starward from her bedroom window, wondering if she could see the moving dot of light that was her ship. Even with her enhanced vision, the task remained impossible. So near, yet so out of reach. None of the group's special communication equipment escaped with them. They could make, buy, or steal equipment for standard radio transmission eventually, but Denshi would easily pick up such a broadcast. Assassins would arrive long before help. Still, she considered it. If they could run fast enough, they might stay ahead of the enemy long enough to arrange a rendezvous. Slim hope with a wounded man and an amateur.

The ruthless part of her soul considered and weighed the options, debating whether the time had come to sacrifice the others, to free herself to strike at Pard. They were a burden, tying her down. Every day spent with them increased the chances of capture. Pard was still the official mission. More than that, killing him was her own desperate need, running like blood through her body. It verged on being a waking dream.

Shasti shelved the thoughts for now. Normally she would have been out, prowling around, looking for information, weapons, and a means of contacting *Sidhe*. Those duties fell to Jenner tonight. Beyond a slight fatigue, Shasti had fully recovered from her injuries in the Denshi ambush, but she still judged it too dangerous to stir out of hiding. Rigg, still weak from his wounds, slept as usual.

She walked over to the small desk in the living room. From it, she drew a small pad and a box of pencils. She'd been almost too embarrassed to ask Jenner to buy them. When she finally did, the older woman only smiled, returning later with all the necessary items. Shasti went back to the window, sat in the moonlight, and opened the pad. She'd filled it with sketches: her dog, Risky, New Eire, and now a drawing of Fenaday. Even with her near eidetic memory, she found drawing from recollection difficult. The drawing of Fenaday wasn't very good. She wished she had kept some pictures, but of course such personal material could identify one on a mission. Even the pad was a mistake in that respect. She looked down at the image of Robert smiling back at her. Professionalism be damned.

She looked around the dingy room. *Quite a change from the Fenaday home on New Eire,* she thought. A sudden memory took her back there, to another window overlooking the rocky coast behind the estate. She remembered sitting in the bay window, the sun striking warmly across her shoulders.

Shasti and Robert had returned to New Eire only a few weeks before. Fenaday purchased back his old estate from the company that had bought it for a conference center. He intended to restore the home. Shasti had endured a variety of social ordeals as people came to call on "The Fenaday," restored both to power and wealth. There were formal parties at which the men watched her and the women couldn't figure out what to make of her. The huntsman of the local fox hunt, actually hunting for a more noxious reptilian pest called a malazard, wanted permission to restart the hunt across the estate grounds. He wanted Robert to serve as Master of the Hunt. It meant horses had to be bought and events planned.

Charities showed up with hands outstretched. People with griev-ances and debts from when Fenaday sold off the Shamrock Ship-ping Line also appeared.

Shasti took it on herself to act as gatekeeper, her formidable demeanor allowing her to dispose of the hordes expeditiously. Robert and she used the freed time to explore the towns around the estate. Days found them walking hand in hand through Duncannon or Horton. Nights flickered with firelight, brandy, and sensual delights in the estate's halls.

She'd seen the cloak of old sadness fall on him only once since they moved into the manor. Their second day at the house found them reopening the library. He'd picked up a dust-covered book left lying on a table. Someone had dog-eared the pages. His face fell when he saw that.

She'd come up to him, concerned.

He remained silent for a few seconds. "Lisa must have done that," he said finally in a soft voice. "I used to fuss at her about it." He stroked the book's binding for a second, his face closed in old pain.

She'd felt helpless. What would a standard human woman say? What would she know to do? Shasti could only stand mute. He replaced the book, leaving the pages folded. It took him several hours to shake off the melancholy.

On the morning of their third week, Fenaday surprised her. He'd found her sitting on the study's bay window, dressed in her usual practical ship clothing. Risky, the K-9 she'd rescued on Enshar, lay on a rug nearby, dozing in the sun. The window held a cushioned seat and had become Robert and Shasti's favorite spot in the house. They sometimes had an informal breakfast in the study, just the two of them.

She turned on hearing him approach to see him standing in boots, breeches, and a tweed coat.

"Today," he said, "is our day. I want to see no one but you. I've banished everyone else from the house." He reached for her hand. "Come with me, I've got a little surprise." His hand felt warm, firm with the extra muscle of a man who practiced martial arts, but not rough or callused. He led her through the grand hall of the ancestral home.

She found riding boots in her size by a hall tree. After she pulled the boots on, he led her out to the courtyard. There, stamping in the still cool morning air, stood two horses, saddled and bridled, held by a young groom.

"We're off for a ride, and Mrs. Ferguson packed us a picnic." Fenaday smiled and gestured toward the horses.

She looked at the animals. Horses had accompanied humans to almost every colony world as cheap self-replicating power for the early settlements. She hadn't ridden one since her childhood training on Olympia.

"Which one is mine?" she asked eagerly.

He laughed. "The big one of course." He walked over to the dark bay. "This is Chance," he said, stroking the horse's muzzle. "He's a Dutch Warmblood gelding. My trainer found him. He's very even tempered, good for a beginner."

He patted the gray horse. "This homely rascal here is Sydney. He's a half Arab, half who knows what. I found him in a hack stable scaring the hell out of tourists about ten years ago. They didn't know what they had. When I sold everything else, I lent him to a cousin. It's been a while. I'm a bit large for him, but he's a tough scout."

Sydney snorted and started to explore Fenaday's pockets, looking for carrots. Fenaday laughed again and pulled some out of an inner pocket. Sydney munched them quickly, eyeing Chance, who gave a jealous nicker.

"There's some in your coat over there." Fenaday pointed. She turned to see her leather ship coat on a fence post. Carrots stuck out of the right pocket. She picked up her jacket and pulled out some carrots for Chance. The bay crunched the offering and looked for more. She stood stroking the horse, enjoying the sight and smell of him.

"Shall we?" he asked.

"Leg up, Miss?" asked the groom, a teenage girl like most of the barn help. The place seemed full of them, in love with horses, dogs, and the outdoors.

Shasti felt a stab of envy looking at the groom's open, friendly face. *It would have been nice to grow up like that,* she thought. "No need," she said putting a foot in the stirrup and vaulting easily into the saddle.

"Nicely done," the groom said.

The comment amused Shasti; she gave the girl a small smile.

"Let's head up the coast," Fenaday said, wheeling his horse about. "I have a place in mind."

They took a dirt road down to the beach. The Connemara coast of New Eire possessed a rocky, storm-tossed coast with an austere beauty. They rode out onto the sand and gravel, pushing the horses into a canter. The art of riding came back to her quickly. She'd loved training with the horses; riding was one of her few pleasant memories of Olympia. *I wonder if they still have them at Denshi,* she thought. There'd been talk of phasing out the horses before she escaped.

They galloped along the waterline for a while, throwing up spray, which even the horses seemed to enjoy.

"How do you like New Eire so far?" Fenaday grinned when they slowed to ease the horses. The wind tugged at his brown hair.

"It is so different," she said. "I've lived my life in spaceports, ships, bases of one kind or another. It's a new experience to be in a real home."

"I suppose so. It didn't seem like much of a home when I was growing up in it, especially after my mother died. Maybe," he said shyly, "you and I will do better."

Shasti couldn't think of anything to say.

He let the awkward moment drop. "If I remember right, there's a good spot for a picnic on that bluff." They turned their horses toward the hill, taking a narrow, rough path winding up from the beach.

They dismounted, tying the horses off in a dell, safe from the wind, with plenty of grass to crop. Fenaday and Shasti pulled off the saddlebags and he untied a gray blanket as well. They walked farther toward the top of the bluff. Fenaday cast about a little before finding the spot.

"Here it is," he called, spreading some red-gold bushes apart. They entered a little natural hollow just back from the cliff, sheltered from the wind by the cliff face, allowing a view of the sea and its whitecaps.

He unrolled the thick blanket he'd brought, and she joined him on it. The saddlebags yielded a treasure of cold chicken, bread, white wine, apples, and cheese.

She looked at his face as he poured a glass for her. It seemed younger these days, less pinched and worn with worry and strain. He both laughed and smiled more.

"What are you thinking?" Fenaday asked, handing her a wineglass and breaking her reverie.

She took the glass and shifted closer. Their shoulders touched. "New worlds," she replied, "so many new worlds for me."

He didn't speak. His hand touched her face, brushing her night-black hair back.

Shasti felt something stir in her. She sipped the wine, then put the glass on a rock behind her. "That's a nice soft blanket you brought," she said.

"Thick too," he replied, setting down his glass.

"Big enough to wrap around us," she observed, "not that it's very cold."

"Want to work up an appetite?" he said mischievously.

Their lips met and they kissed, excitement building in them as they opened each other's clothes. They rolled on the blanket, encouraged by the cool air. His hands gently and firmly touched her body. She held him close, pleased by how quickly he became hard in her hands. She slid under him after a few minutes.

"I want you," she said. "I want you inside me now." She spread her legs and arched her back, taking him in. Their tongues met and danced, heat building in them. His motion quickened as they built toward climax. Every sensation seemed so clear to her. The taste, the feel of him, the texture of the blanket under her back, the arch of blue sky over his shoulder. She felt the muscles of his back under her hands; she slid them down to grasp his butt, hard from a lifetime of stances and kicks.

Ah, she thought, *I've never made love like this, so free, so simple. It feels like I am giving myself up to the sky.* Joy welled up in her; her eyes rolled up as her body took possession. Pleasure rippled out in waves. She cried out as he went rigid filling her with a sudden heat. They collapsed together, catching their breath then laughing from sheer happiness.

They lay together, he resting above her on his elbows. A habit, she realized with a hint of jealously, learned from smaller and more fragile women. She pulled him close, savoring the feel of his weight, not wanting him to withdraw from on and in her...

———

The pencil snapped in Shasti's hand. She looked at the drawing pad with her lover's face, then back up at the night sky where he circled the world she'd become stranded on. *I must be mad,* she thought, *to have cast all that to the wind only to come here and face torture and death. Fool,* she thought in sudden anguish. *Why?*

You know, whispered the dark, cold part of her soul. Even the happiest memories of Fenaday and his gentle lovemaking can't make the other ones disappear: the older ones of Pard, the rapes, the pain, and the degradation. *Have you forgotten being caged? Forgotten the sting of leather on your skin?* Sometimes a sight, sound, or smell would take her back to Pard. She'd freeze in the act of making love, her body becoming strange and foreign to her. It was why she'd rarely had sex. The memories had never intruded with Fenaday, but she feared that someday they might, marring things forever.

I cannot be free while Pard lives, she thought, *I can't. I am sorry, Robert, sorry. You've come for me, all this way, all this danger, for me. Love?* she wondered. Her mind skittered around the word like a frightened animal. Even her breathing grew rapid. *Is this what normals feel,* she wondered, *what all their poetry and songs mean? Why do I feel sick? Afraid?*

She realized the fear was mostly for him, so near Pard and his allies. There was fear for herself as well, for venturing out of the unseen, defended places of her soul and beginning to feel.

Chapter Twelve

P aula Kallian made her way from the elevator bank, slowly, painfully, desperate for her own door. She was one of the rare employees given an apartment in Denshi's high-desert complex. It was considered quite a perk. Most others had to take the shuttles down to the bridge over which passed the one road to the complex. From there, they took a Maglev into Marathon or its suburbs. Today she was paying for her privileges. Antebei had returned from the space station in a fury, the worst she had ever experienced. It meant he was out of favor with Pard again, seriously so.

Bitterness and regret welled up in her. She had jumped at the chance for a job in Denshi, hardly believing her luck when Antebei himself hired her out of a janitorial job after a chance meeting. It was better than anything the unsanctioned child of parents with defective genes could hope for. College was beyond her means. Her parents, laboring in jobs little better than her own, could not help her. Her father was often ill, making the family financial situation sometimes desperate. She remembered him sitting on the porch of their small home, bent double with coughing. Her mother making cup after cup of hot tea to ease the spasms.

Then came Antebei—tall, handsome, and interested in helping her. *How naïve*, she thought, *how utterly naïve.*

She came to Denshi as his secretary and personal assistant. Money, for the first time in her life, was plentiful. Decent medical care held her father's illness at bay, abating her mother's tears and worry. Paula's family was secure as never before.

Antebei's attentions flattered her at first, then frightened her as they grew in intensity. Eventually, he made no more pretense of seducing her, taking her when he felt like it. Each time grew more violent, though afterward he was often apologetic, showering her with gifts and attention. It was, he insisted, their secret. If she complained or told anyone, he warned, she would find herself out on the street, her family again condemned to poverty and neglect.

Who could she turn to anyway? Antebei headed Section Seven, Denshi Internal Security, a veritable prince among the Engineered. She was genetic garbage, barely an adult, in Denshi on sufferance. She might simply disappear, as did many inconvenient to Denshi. Worse, they might strike at her family. Torn between terrors of poverty, death, and Antebei's lust, she chose to suffer alone, in silence.

She reached the door of her sanctuary and passed through. Pain caught her as she reached her living room. She went down on one knee, with a soft moan, leaning against a couch, a wetness spread down the back of her thigh. *Oh god*, she thought, *I'm bleeding again.* She started to sob quietly. "I can't live like this anymore," she whispered.

"Maybe you won't have to," said a deep, resonant voice.

Her head snapped up in terror. On the other couch, so still she hadn't sensed him, sat Mikhail Vaughn, Head of Section Three, Special Operations. Abruptly, she realized he was not alone. A tautly built Asian woman, older than her, stood in the shadows behind him. Her eyes glittered in reflected streetlight.

"Don't be afraid and don't turn on the light," he said.

She nodded, carefully not moving.

"There is nothing to fear," Vaughn repeated softly. He leaned forward until his clear blue eyes were in the light. "You know if we had any ill intent, you would never have seen us or known anything. Please, sit."

She crept up onto the couch, wincing.

"Antebei is a brute," Vaughn said, distaste on his face.

"I have no complaints," she whispered back, looking down. *This is bad,* she thought. *Vaughn is Antebei's chief rival. He's signed my death warrant by his presence in my apartment.* Despair welled up in her soul. She knew Antebei had her watched, as he watched everything.

"Please go away," she whimpered. "He'll kill me."

"He *will* kill you," Vaughn replied. "As he has the others before you. You know that. It is only a matter of time."

She shook her head mutely.

"He will," Vaughn said with certainty. "But not because of our presence. Your watcher is busy with a healthy young man in an apartment several floors below. It seems the duty has become tedious for her. The electronic devices have been circumvented. No one detected us. We are quite adept at being invisible."

A spasm of pain crossed her face.

"You need medical attention," Vaughn said.

"It's nothing. I fell," she replied.

"It's torture, sexual torture," Vaughn said. "He's like that. It ends one way: a string of broken toys left by a sick child."

A spark lit in her, and she looked into the Denshi lord's eyes. "What? A flaw in the Engineered?"

The Asian woman shifted; Vaughn stilled her with a slight gesture.

"We are not perfect," Vaughn said stiffly, "just more capable. Our friend Antebei believes he is a law unto himself. Personally, I think he is insane."

"What do you want?" she asked.

"To help you."

She gave a small bitter laugh, astonished by her own daring.

To her surprise, Vaughn smiled. "So, you are not a fool. Clearly, I want you, your access to Antebei's files and plans."

She shook her head. "Just kill me. It will be easier than what he'll do to me."

"I'm offering you a way out," Vaughn said. "You know why

Antebei wants you, you know he hates wanting you. One day he will snap and you'll die. I've seen it before."

"I do what he wants," she replied, stubbornly.

"It's not a protection. It wasn't for his governess when he was fifteen."

"What do you want from me?" she cried. "What recourse do I have, genetic trash that you think me? I'm all my family has to keep them off the street, my father is ill..."

"What will happen to them when he kills you?" Vaughn shrugged.

She stared at the floor.

"Listen," he said. It brought her eyes off the floor to meet his, which in turn seemed to disconcert the big man. *He's probably never seen anyone with two different color eyes before,* she thought. *No recessives need apply.*

"I am Engineered and Assassin. There are more corpses in my past than even I care to remember, but I am offering you a way out. As I see it, you have no choice. My way may lead to death, but there is at least a chance.

"Antebei is a madman." Vaughn leaned forward, his eyes locked on hers. "I don't know why Pard cannot see it. He cannot be allowed to rise to the control of Denshi. We would go from being the scalpel of a surgeon to a butcher's cleaver. I am going to stop him, and if you want to live, you'll help me."

"Or you'll kill me," she said dully.

"No," Vaughn replied, "I won't have to do a thing. If you tell him that you turned me away, he will be so enraged by my touching on his weak spot that he'd kill you even if he believed you. If you don't tell him, then you play Russian Roulette every time you walk into his office.

"A time of crisis is coming. I feel it. A sword is hanging over Denshi and Pard. Its name is Fenaday. Another enemy is on our world already. Antebei has been provoked by Fenaday, as has Pard. Pard is smart enough to ignore it. Antebei is too vain to do so. He will strike back, seeking Pard's favor, or to salve his own ego. That would be a disaster for Denshi.

"You do not need to be a steady source of information. Such are always eventually found. I want you for one task, one mission. When and if Antebei moves to strike at Fenaday, you will inform me by contacting Tanaka here on a secured channel we will arrange. You dial the number she hands you and ask for Channel Z. It is untraceable in the complex and encrypted."

"What do I get out of this?" she asked.

"For starters, ownership of your body. I'll better that with two-hundred thousand Confederate standard credits, relocation offworld for you and your family, or to a position with my office, under our protection, at twice your salary."

"If Antebei comes out on top?" she asked.

"Then you and I will be discussing our foolhardiness in hell," he replied impatiently.

Paula thought of herself, bent over Antebei's desk. His body pounding hers with no thought or care, his hands pressing down hard on the back of her neck.

"Almost to the breaking point," she murmured to herself in sudden realization.

Vaughn's eyes bored into hers, as if he could read her thoughts.

"He is going to kill me," she said, as if in surprise, the barriers her unconscious had raised against the thought, finally falling.

"Yes." Vaughn nodded.

"I'll do it," she said, her mouth a hard, bitter line. "Not because I believe you or your promises, Denshi Lord. I've never seen any honesty or compassion in any of you, but because he is going to kill me, and none of you will do a damn thing about it. This way at least, maybe I'll finally hurt him back."

Her nerve broke and she looked away. "Get out," she whispered.

Vaughn stood, quelling his temper with effort. No one spoke so to him and lived, besides Pard and his masters. To be upbraided by this short, over-built piece of genetic trash, without even matching eyes, was almost more than he could take. How Antebei could desire her soft, almost fat, body eluded him. He nodded curtly to her and strode to the door.

Tanaka followed. She placed the paper with the contact number next to the woman and whispered something to her. Kallian did not look up.

They slipped into the hallway, then to the stairwell. On the floor below, they boarded a service elevator where the security systems were locked out, dropping to the sub-basement.

Misa Tanaka looked sidewise at him. "You'll do it, won't you? You are going to help her?"

Vaughn looked at her in surprise, then shrugged. "She did not believe me and threw my offer back in my face. Why do you care what happens to that pathetic creature?" he replied, still nettled by how she had spoken to him.

"We have much in common," she said.

Vaughn looked at her in puzzlement. "You? You have nothing in common with that woman."

"Really?" she replied. "What could I do, if you were to use me so?"

"I assume," Vaughn said, with a surprised laugh, "you'd kill me."

She looked at him flatly. "Me, alone, against a Fourth-Generation Engineered? I'd have little chance. Even if I won, I would be hunted by all of Denshi. My family would be slaughtered. No, for all my skill, I am no safer than she is. I have no more protection than your word."

Vaughn stared, at a loss for words.

"You will keep your promise?" she persisted.

"What did you say to her as we left?" he asked.

Her mouth drew into a grim line, but her voice remained toneless. "I said, trust Vaughn. That was my word of honor given, Lord. Is it worthless, too?"

Vaughn went hot with rage, then cold. Tanaka had been with him since he was fifteen. Next to Pard, she was the person he knew the longest. He valued her, and not just for her skill and the protection she provided his back. He had learned much from her. She was twenty years older than he, with a wider experience of the world. Standard humans and the Selected used the word friend; it came hard to him, even as a thought.

Vaughn knew he had crossed some invisible line, trespassed on those assumptions that normal people—people raised by families— real people, maintained with each other. It was a familiar feeling.

Raised in a crèche with only the disinterested benevolence of doctors and other professionals, he simply did not understand much of human relations.

Tanaka's face remained hard and closed to him. Disappointment and disapproval showed in her body and her downcast eyes.

They strode out of the elevator, he in the lead. He felt her, with that situational sense developed in the Fourth Generation, as a small, hot shadow at his back, an angry, silent presence. Suddenly, he stopped and rounded on her. For a second, he was surprised to see real fear in her eyes.

"All right," he snapped. "I will do all that I said. If I can save her, I will. Does that suffice for you?"

"Yes," she said, surprising him with a smile.

He turned away, still angry. "It is for this sort of foolishness that Lord Pard thinks me weak and unfit," he growled. "How he would laugh to see me so."

Tanaka reached and touched his arm. He glared down, offended.

"I was much sought after in Denshi," she said softly. "I could have served any lord, any of the Engineered. Many of them were more powerful and promising than you at the time. I chose you and serve only you. Because no matter how you came into the world or how you were raised, you kept a man's heart and soul."

Confusion warred in Vaughn's mind. Somehow, her words made him feel like he was inhaling champagne. He fought the feeling. It was just another symptom of his weakness. Pard always warned him of the danger of being ruled by women. He looked at Tanaka, beautiful for all that she was not Engineered. They had never been more than teammates, yet she held a special place with him. He wanted her approval, the look she gave him when she was pleased with him. A look he received so rarely and least of all from Pard. It was the look on her face now.

"Come," he said gruffly. "We stay too long here."

"Yes," she said, still smiling slightly. "As you say."

Chapter Thirteen

How absurdly easy, Paula Kallian thought. In an age of ultra technology, among professional spies and assassins, she could learn Antebei's plans because she could walk into his office and look at the flat screen holo monitor the head of Section Seven left on. She almost laughed. Antebei, head of Denshi Security, so sure of himself, did not take even basic precautions in his own lair. *Hubris,* she thought. The Engineered always likened themselves to the early Greeks: perhaps they even mirrored their ancient arrogance.

She wondered if the most effective spies were always secretaries. There was a bitterness to that thought, Kallian acknowledged. Antebei did not think enough of her to worry about it. No more than he thought of her needs or desires when he took her.

Quickly, she read the screen, recognizing the name Moussa. Yesterday Antebei had asked her for their files. The Moussa brothers served Oldark, but as head of Security, Antebei could requisition operatives from other sections at need. She had processed the memo to Oldark; that and the attached files, led her to believe this was the move Vaughn wanted her to watch for. Quickly, she scanned the text. She'd guessed correctly. Antebei had ordered the Moussas to board *Sidhe* and bomb the vessel. She studied the graphics of the starship. Ships were outside of her experience, but she recognized *Sidhe's* silhouette from the news. The flashing icon for the bomb blinked in an area she thought might be the engineering spaces. Kallian was too afraid to try to copy the file. Antebei couldn't be that lax; there would be some security protocol. She thought of paper and pen, but it would take too long. She had no sophisticated spy gear on her. It would never have gotten in through office security. No, this was enough risk for now. Her nerves stretched to the breaking point. With a gasp, she backed out of the office, heart pounding.

She got hold of herself, then walked out to the outer office, nodding to the guards on duty. It was lunchtime, and she often went home. It would give her time to do the book code. On the way back, she would stop at a public communicator and ask for Channel Z. It was as much as she dared.

M isa Tanaka hurried into Vaughn's inner office. "News," she said, excitement in her dark eyes. "Kallian called in. I have the recording. Antebei has an operative named Moussa, perhaps two with the same name, I can't tell, going up to the *Sidhe* with the supply shuttles. The plan is to bomb her engine room. That's all the information she sent."

Vaughn grinned savagely, his blue eyes lighting. "At last," he said. "At last, he has gone that one step over the edge. Antebei is trying to buy Pard's favor by killing his rival, for the insults he gave them both, as if Pard is as vain a peacock as he is. Ah, this is a rich feast, indeed. Fool, to imagine Pard would be pleased by the death of the most famous captain and ship in the Confederacy. Think of the scandal, the investigation by the Confederacy and our enemies. What a fool."

"Are you sure?" Tanaka asked, her look impenetrable. "Fenaday has his woman, flaunts it publicly, and faces him down in public. Something even the Army does not dare. He may be more pleased than you think. Engineered or not, he is a man."

"Have a care," Vaughn warned. "Pard is not like lesser men."

"No disrespect intended," she said, "but there is a danger in believing one's own propaganda. Pard may denounce Antebei in public, even punish him, but secretly, he will be pleased."

Vaughn grunted, unhappy but forced to consider the idea. "All the more reason to foul his plans. They bode ill for Denshi and my own plans, no matter how Pard might secretly feel. If the attempt miscarries and reveals incompetence, that will be the downfall of Antebei. He only just survived blasting an apartment of civilians into the evening news. Another such failure will seal his doom."

"Excellent." Tanaka nodded. "But how best to ensure it?"

"The simplest solution that fits the facts," he replied. "Did Kallian say how long after the supply shuttle leaves before the bomb goes off?"

"No, it would be at least five hours, long enough for the shuttle to get down and the crew dispersed. It will be obvious the shuttle delivered the bomb. They would be intercepted on landing if it exploded while they were still in the air. They may fail. Security will be almost impossibly heavy on the ship."

"Possibly," Vaughn said, "but give Antebei his due. The Moussas are the best infiltrators Denshi ever produced. They'll come up with something. We will give Fenaday a call when they start down. When he finds the weapon, the Moussas will be arrested on landing." Strong, perfectly even teeth showed in a broad grin. "How will poor Antebei escape his fate then?"

Sidhe refused the civilian contractor shuttles permission to land in her shuttle bay, claiming it was full from three *Dakotas*. Fenaday's *Wildcat* fighters picked up the small cargo vessels and tankers from well outside fighter gun range, escorting them until they split to dock at various cargo airlocks around the blood-red hull of the privateer. Fuel, water, food, oxygen, all manner of supplies were lofted to the star-frigate in the small tenders. The trip to Olympia had been hard on the vessel.

Mmok's security was not overwhelmed, but it was busy. He couldn't use the HCRs or lesser robots where they could be seen, so he fell back on Rask and *Sidhe's* remaining Landing Expedition Assault Force Troops under Li.

Contractors trooped on to the starship. Security checked them in. Boxes, crates, and cylinders came out of the shuttles. Hoses were attached for fluids and fuels. Each was monitored at the filter point by a ship's technician to protect the vessel from poisons or chemicals.

Dean Moussa stepped onto the deck of the *Sidhe* and found himself face to face with a Denlenn of indeterminate gender. The nametag said *Sharla*. He decided it looked more feminine than not. A brisk and effective security check was made of the people and cargo with him. Very professional, he thought approvingly, almost as good as Denshi. Not that it would work on the Moussas.

Sidhe crew checked each cargo unit as it came in. First came cylinders filled with synthetic meat for the ship's kitchens. One special cylinder concerned him. It looked like all the others, but the cylinder was double walled. A low-level EM field prevented *Sidhe's* scanners from detecting its hollow interior. That interior held meat of a sort. His identical twin brother, Aran, lay unconscious in it, held under by a REM sleep emitter. Denshi surgeons had improved on nature's almost perfect match. Both men were identical down to fingerprints. It would take a retinal scan or brain wave analysis to tell them apart. Even there, the differences were minimal.

Sidhe's crew ran a portable scanner over each cylinder as it came in. Many cargo boxes would be opened; the synth-meat, in its rather disagreeable liquid form, was unlikely to be. They had planned on its being scanned all the closer. This was the moment of danger. An apish Morok trooper waved a scanner over the two-meter long cylinder. Satisfied, he waved an overlong arm at Moussa.

Moussa's crew made their way under close escort of *Sidhe* security to one of the small holds. *Sidhe* was a warship, her holds compartmented to reduce the risk of explosive decompression. The series of small compartments made it harder for the starship's crew to keep a constant eye on them, though it was clearly impossible to escape the area of the ship they were confined to. Dean made several trips to and from the shuttle. He made it a point to speak to several of the security crew, assuring that they would remember him as being on the *Sidhe*. None answered him in anything but monosyllables, but that didn't matter. Moussa nodded at the foreman of the Olympian stevedore crew, a Denshi plant. The man nodded back casually. Dean joined a group headed for the Olympian shuttle. Once aboard, he slipped into a hidden compartment in the Olympian vessel. He knew none of *Sidhe's* crew would board the shuttle, but if they did become suspicious and check, he would still not be found.

Back in *Sidhe's* cargo compartment, in the back and out of sight, the Denshi foreman manipulated a control on the elder Moussa's cylinder. Quickly, it opened, automatically ceasing the REM sleep wave keeping Aran under. The foreman pulled him to his feet as he sorted himself and his equipment out. A lanyard attached the C-8 explosive charge to his body. The foreman left without a word. *Sidhe* security, believing the compartment empty, followed him back to the airlock.

Aran did not waste an instant, climbing up a pile of supplies to the electrical maintenance duct running toward Engineering. The passage was large enough to allow for repairs and doubled as a ventilation shaft. It was still a tight fit for a man in a hurry. His portable hand comp guided him as he wormed his way to a vulnerable coolant and fuel junction. *Sidhe* used a fusion torch for her main drive, but she carried a considerable supply of highly reactive rocket fuel for her thrusters. It was the work of a few seconds to plant the bomb. The resulting blast and secondary explosions would take out the frigate, well-built though she was.

With no excess motion, he made his way back to the cargo area. If the plan was working right, he should be in Hold Four, where the loading was still going on. He reached the compartment and looked down. Good, they were still working in there. He dropped a micro-periscope in. Looking around, he located the guards. A check of his pocket comp told him that the next screen would let him into the back section of the hold. Grunting slightly, he wormed his way to that screen, opening it with a micro-cutter when the screen balked. He checked again with the micro-periscope; the image on the portable computer screen remained clear.

Aran slid down onto some stores scaffolding, replaced the

screen, climbed down, and walked out to join the other stevedores. They ignored his appearance and filed past the *Sidhe* guards, trailing their servos and carts. On another world, such duties would have fallen on robots with only a few human supervisors. Fortunately for his mission, Olympia held such machines in disfavor. As they trooped into the airlock bay to the shuttle, a long Morok arm reached out and hooked Aran. "Hold it, you."

Obediently, Aran stopped, turning to face the red eyes and blue countenance of a goblin-like Morok. This one wore ASAT fatigues and officer pips.

The foreman of his team walked over. "Is there a problem?"

"I didn't see this guy go out to the hold," the Morok growled. "My tally sheet shows him as back on the shuttle already."

"Come on Lieutenant," the foreman said, "your guys checked us out as we came out of the ship the first time. We've been in and out a dozen times. You just missed him coming back out, that's all."

"Maybe," the Morok said. "Hey Li, bring a scanner." An oriental human came over, his scarred face betraying nothing as he ran a scanner over Moussa. The Denshi operative tried to look merely annoyed. Inside he was worried. The bomb had been sealed in an atmospheric pack, so C-8 particles would not cling to him. If even a tiny trace escaped...

"Nothing, sir," Li said.

"Fingerprint check?" the Morok asked.

"He's the same guy we checked in here before."

Rask walked onto the Olympian shuttle and did a quick head count. It tallied. No extra people. How had the Olympian gotten past them coming out? Still, he was clearly the same man. He walked back over to the guard station, still convinced something wasn't right.

"Happy?" Aran asked.

The Morok gave him a toothy grin of primarily canines. "Only when I'm eating human babies." Li smiled, for a split second then suppressed it. "Okay, get back on the shuttle. You can sit out the rest of this unloading. I don't want to see your face out here again."

Aran shrugged. "Hey, I get paid anyway."

The foreman grumbled about the additional workload as Aran

headed for the shuttle. Only when he was alone in the Navy shuttle did he allow himself a small smile of triumph. He settled into the comfortably padded chair. Poor Dean would enjoy a far less comfortable ride down in the secret compartment. Then he closed his eyes and went to sleep.

———

Kallian was just outside Antebei's office when the call came in on his most private and secure line. Antebei could have had it routed into his office. He preferred to have her as gatekeeper. Perhaps it made him feel more important. *It must be the bomber,* she thought. She picked up the tiny wireless headset. A holo flashed before her eyes. It said, "Incoming ultimate security message-for Lord Antebei's eyes only."

"Sir," she called, not wanting to venture into his office. He looked up annoyed, then his attitude changed when he saw the headset. "The call you have been expecting is holding on Channel R."

"Excellent," he replied. "Initiate transfer."

He made a motion over his desk. A Plasteel barrier slid between them, cutting off her sight of him. This suited her fine. Since her last experience of Antebei, she could barely hold her loathing in check. It was a simmering hysteria, lurking just beneath the surface. She pinned her hope on Tanaka, Prime Selected and Denshi, but Selected nonetheless. Kallian trusted no Engineered, male or female. In their two contacts Tanaka was brisk, yet under the hard exterior Kallian sensed sympathy. It was her only hope.

Chapter Fourteen

"C aptain," Susan Bernard called from her communications station, "I'm getting something here."

Fenaday snapped to attention. He and Telisan were just finishing another fruitless scan of Olympia from Sharla's station. "What is it? The team?"

Bernard frowned in concentration. "I don't know. It's not a communication. There is no call tag on it; it's a bit of out of place datum. A micro-squeak, compressed data."

"Bounce it over to Sharla's station," he commanded. Bernard nodded and hit the controls.

"The team?" Fenaday repeated.

"A moment, Captain," Sharla said gently.

Sharla spent a minute running her computer. "No ID. No route back to the sender. It got through the virus buffer, then signaled its arrival to Bernard's station. It's coming on screen. Captain, it's a message specifying a frequency. It says, stand-by for an incoming message in three minutes on this frequency, two-way video. There's a decode program attached. Somebody wants to talk to us, discreetly."

"Maybe it's Shasti?" he said, turning to Telisan, almost frightened with hope.

The Denlenn made a peculiar gesture, then realized Fenaday would not understand it and put a hand on his arm. "Think," he said. "Where would Shasti come by the equipment to do this? Please do not raise false hopes for yourself."

"Yes," Fenaday said, realizing the sense. "Yes."

It took years for the next three minutes to pass. Finally, the main bridge screen lit with the image of a man's silhouette, blocked out by a computer mask.

"Captain Fenaday?"

"That's me. Who are you?"

"A friend."

"Then show yourself."

The image on the screen laughed and shook its head. "I think not."

"Okay. What is it you want?"

"To help you. A very foolish man has placed a bomb in your engine room. I don't know exactly where, or when it is to go off. I suggest you get moving. Good luck and good bye." The image flicked off.

"Sound General Quarters," Fenaday snapped. "Bernard, get me Perez, then Mmok." The ship's siren began its syncopated whooping.

"Perez here."

"Carlos, get everyone but the emergency detail out of Engineering. Put what you can on automatic. There may be a bomb in the Engineering spaces."

"Dios mio," Perez swore. "We go."

"This is Mmok," snapped a new voice on the circuit. "What the hell is going on?"

"Mmok, get your HCRs. Get down to Engineering; there may be a bomb in there."

"Affirmative, on my way."

"Sharla, you have the bridge." He grabbed Telisan's arm. "Let's go."

"It's a bomb all right," Mmok said ten minutes later. "Cobalt detected it during one of her sweeps."

Fenaday looked at the innocuous box, hidden behind the electrical trunk. Behind and below him, Telisan directed the evacuation of the adjacent corridors and compartments. "They must have carried it in with the supplies we ordered up from the planet. Probably one of those cargo handlers put it here. I don't know how they got this close to the engineering spaces from the shuttle bay."

"I don't either," Mmok grunted. "I thought we had everyone under surveillance every second they were on board. Somebody got away, or it's an inside job."

"Christ," Fenaday said, remembering the mutiny in orbit of Enshar. "Not again."

Mmok shook his head. "I don't think it's an inside job. I'd have detected this much explosive on the ship before this. This is top professional. Look at this." He gestured. "The placement is superb. Everything in this area is vital. It's a small charge, but it is in the right place. This is how you bomb a warship," he said with professional satisfaction.

"Can you disarm it?" Fenaday asked.

Mmok gave his sardonic grin. "With a toothpick."

Fenaday smiled broadly.

"What are you so damn happy about?" Mmok asked.

"Victory goes to the side with the fewest fuckups," Fenaday replied. "This is their first. While they were ignoring us, we couldn't do a thing. Now they've struck, badly. It gives us an opening for a counter.

"This bomb is going to be our ticket onworld," Fenaday said, his mind clear and racing. "We'll move it into the ordnance handling room next to the shuttle bay. That space is outside the main armor belt, designed to blow out in case of accidental explosion. We detonate it ourselves, just after we launch a shuttle. *Sidhe* will declare an emergency. She'll demand immediate descent onto the capital's spaceport. They won't be able to turn it down. *Sidhe* will advise they have lost contact with the shuttle launching at the time of the explosion.

"The shuttle will be the *Intruder* with the assault force in it. We enter the atmosphere and do a HALO insertion into the target area. The shuttle will land in a remote area and wait for a call for extraction.

"Meanwhile, we'll have the *Sidhe* down in the capital raising hell," Fenaday concluded.

"Not bad," Mmok said. "They may believe the shuttle was destroyed, especially if we blow out a little radar/microwave chaff with the explosion.

"Now, will you get the hell out of here so Cobalt and I can tame this firecracker? The timer says there are two hours left. I don't trust it."

"With pleasure," Fenaday returned. "I'm on my way to the shuttle. Keep me informed."

Mmok grunted a response as he closed the clearplast visor of his body armor and headed toward the bomb.

Fenaday wormed his way back to the entrance then hit his throat mike. "Fenaday to Sharla; put me through on a discreet channel to Lieutenant Rask and then Corporal Schiller."

"Rask here."

"How fast can you get the assault team ready for insertion?"

"We're on fifteen-minute standby," Rask replied. "We've been practicing the drop for the last three days. All the equipment is pre-positioned and ready in the shuttle. We can go when you give the word."

"You have the word, Mr. Rask. I'm en route to the shuttle."

Mmok's voice came on the net next. "Fenaday, I popped the casing and I am working on the bomb. Indigo is bringing the robot team to the shuttle and will attend to the loading of the mech-force. She'll be at the shuttle."

"Affirmative," Fenaday said. "Fenaday to Corporal Schiller. Get Risky into a drop chute and report to the shuttle."

"Aye, sir."

Telisan waited for Fenaday in the corridor. He wore a headset; his command privileges allowed him to listen even on the discreet channel.

"Telisan," Fenaday began, "you'll take *Sidhe* in. Demand to be part of the search for us. Get the embassy involved, as well as the Confederate military liaison. Don't let them stop you.

"We'll try for Pard sometime within twelve hours of insertion, barring a problem. You'll have to monitor Mmok's channels. He'll fire off a micro-squeak on the prearranged frequency before we go in."

"As we planned," Telisan said. "Do not fear. I will not let you down."

Fenaday gripped Telisan's forearm Denlenn fashion. "They say a man who has found even one friend in life is rich. I have been lucky enough to have Lisa, Duna, Shasti, and you. It's been a rich life, no matter how the next few days go."

The Denlenn gripped back equally hard. "Bring yourself and Shasti back. There will be other days to deal with Pard."

Fenaday nodded with a shy smile. He headed for the shuttle bay, leaving Telisan to make his way to the bridge.

Fenaday ran into the organized chaos of shuttle bay. The skeleton shuttlebay crew, all of whom were in on the deception, raced to finish preparations on the high-tech vessel. No one else was allowed into the bay. The assault team surrounded the matte-black *Intruder*. HCRs marched into the shuttle; they would jump with the team. Crab robots and the airbot latched to the shuttle's belly. A flight crew put a drop-shield over the machines to protect them from the heat of reentry. They would then parachute from the exterior of the shuttle.

The live complement of the assault force was a mixture of ASAT Rangers under Rask, with some of *Sidhe*'s LEAFs, including Li, the Toks, Morgan, and Schiller with his charge, Risky. Risky snuffled and licked Fenaday's hand. The genetically enhanced German Shepherd's intelligence kept him quiet and tractable despite the frantic activity. Risky knew it was work time. If the dog got within several hundred yards of Shasti, he would home in on her like a missile.

Fenaday ruffled the dog's fur and hugged the shepherd. "Last time, it was she and I who found you. Now we have to go find her. Right boy?"

Risky whined an agreement. Fenaday released him to go back to Schiller.

Fury piloted the shuttle with Kieran McLoughlin in the second seat. Both worked furiously on the pre-launch checklist. They gave Fenaday a thumbs-up as he entered the shuttle, reaching for his jumpsuit and equipment. Detailed planning was paying dividends. In minutes, the shuttle would be loaded and ready to go.

Fury waved a hand at him. "Mmok on Channel One, sir. Putting him on speaker."

"Fenaday here," he said, struggling into his harness.

"Mmok. The timer was a trap, just as I expected. The bomb was actually set to go off in fifty-three minutes. I like this guy. He's devious. I've dismantled it, stabilized it, and put a reliable trigger on it. Cobalt's moving it into the handling storeroom. Sapphire's rearranging the stores to dampen the blast. I've added some nano-cutter bombs on the outer hull side to shape the charge so it will blow outward and minimize damage. We can set it off any time we want."

"Excellent, get down here as soon as you can."

"Is there anything in there that could cause damage to the ship?" Rask asked.

Fenaday controlled a stab of irritation. After all, Rask was a ground-pounder.

"No, there isn't. I didn't want to empty the storeroom. There might be port police and inspectors coming aboard. It would look suspicious if the store room was completely devoid of debris."

"Fenaday to Telisan."

"Telisan, here."

"It is T-minus ten and counting. Prepare to execute Plan 'Milton.'"

"Affirmative. We are ready to initiate a synchronized orbit over Marathon and can begin a descent at any time. All Operation 'Milton' communications are being encrypted. Only secure personnel are on the bridge. We are go.

"I must advise though, it is a very uncomfortable feeling waiting for a bomb to go off on one's own ship. My previous captain would have never approved."

"True," Fenaday said, "I derive some pleasure from imagining myself presenting the repair bill to Mandela. I'll see you if we live."

Fenaday turned to Angelica Fury as she moved to the copilot seat, displacing McLoughlin. He'd take out the shuttle, turning it over to Fury when they reached jump altitude. "Okay, Trouble, let's fly."

Fury grinned at the mention of her nickname and reached for the controls.

———

At midnight, *Sidhe* advised Marathon ground control of the launching of a shuttle. This was not unusual. Fenaday had been joyriding fighters and shuttles around *Sidhe* on one pretext or another since they arrived. He insisted on providing his own local security with the ship's *Wildcats* and *Dakotas*. Marathon ground control was unhappy about it, but they had no legal right to interfere with a captain in such a high parking orbit so long as he didn't drop into an active control zone. It was also rather impolitic to annoy a visiting dignitary, especially one whose ship had been fired on when he entered the system.

The *Intruder* hadn't left the shuttle bay since they reached Olympia. Fenaday had changed the names on the *Dakotas* to make it look like *Sidhe* had her regular complement of three *Dakotas* aboard. Since *Sidhe* had not come into atmosphere, there had been no customs search of the starship. An inspection would have quickly discovered the *Intruder*, despite Fenaday's best efforts at camouflage and concealment.

Fenaday piloted the *Intruder* out the port side of the starship, away from the planet, hoping to foil observation for a precious few seconds. *Sidhe's* engineers had altered her silhouette with plastic and metal panels so that, at first glance, she resembled a *Dakota*. These improvements would not stand any close examination and could be blown off by remote control. The *Intruder* moved a few meters away from the bay entrance.

Then all hell broke loose. The bomb exploded in the handling storeroom; its external hull bulkhead bay, weakened by Mmok's nano-cutter shaped charges, bulged and blew out. Explosive decompression quickly cut off as the warship's emergency systems activated. *Sidhe* had been designed to survive worse.

A cloud of *Dakota* parts, general debris, and chaff, pre-positioned in the shuttle bay, exploded outward, blown into space by compressed air from the main airlock. On radar and microwave scanners, *Sidhe* shattered into hundreds of targets, shooting off in mostly planetward vectors. The *Intruder* shed her camouflage, blown off by explosive bolts. It would add a convincing touch. Fenaday sent the matte-black *Intruder* flashing downward, screened by the thousand bits of wreckage and her nonreflecting surfaces. Above them, in a dramatic touch typical of Telisan, the frigate began to tumble.

On the bridge, Telisan hit the general quarters klaxon. "General quarters. General quarters," he called. "All hands man your stations. Explosion onboard amidships. Fire and rescue parties to the shuttle bay. Medical teams to the infirmary. Shuttlebay, report on shuttle status. We were in launch mode. Stand by for search and rescue. Damage control report to the bridge."

All this was in the clear, for the consumption of anyone, particularly news media, who might be listening. There was little danger of casualties. Telisan had rearranged work schedules so the area, usually unoccupied anyway, would have no one near it.

"Sir," Sharla called, in a panicked voice, "*Pooka's* signal has broken up. She must have been hit while launching." Sharla, a veteran of the Conchirri fleet battles at the end of the war, was also hamming it up for anyone listening in on the ship's intercom frequency. She wouldn't lose her cool had the Conchirri themselves suddenly appeared in orbit.

"Attitude control is off-line," Graglia said. "We are out of control and dropping from orbit."

More of Sharla's doing. From her computer station, she manipulated systems to make the damage look worse. It was convincing and would be undetectable afterward.

"*Sidhe* to Marathon Control," Telisan called. "We are declaring an emergency."

"Marathon Control to *Sidhe*." The voice was male, controlled and professional. "We acknowledge your distress call. Please state the nature of your emergency."

"We have an explosion amidships in the hanger bay area. We have lost attitude control and are dropping from orbit. The shuttle

Pooka was launching from the bay when the blast occurred. We have lost radio and radar contact. She may have been destroyed."

"*Sidhe*, this is Marathon. An emergency has been declared. All traffic below you is being re-routed. Are you able to restore sufficient control for an atmospheric entry? Do you have casualties?"

"Marathon," Telisan said, signaling Sharla and Graglia, "we are regaining control of our attitude. Thrusters remain off-line. We do not have sufficient speed to maintain orbit. With the thrusters possibly compromised, I do not want to risk a manual burn for higher orbit. If it fails, I could lose any useful landing window we have. We are lining up for the current window to Marathon."

"Damage control reports we are again spacetight," Sharla reported. "All shuttles have received damage. We have no power to the wing-mounted fighters. There is no chance of an SAR launch for the *Pooka*. We have no visual contact with the *Pooka* from any station."

"Marathon, did you copy?" Telisan demanded. "We are vectored for atmospheric entry on a glide path. We have lost contact with and cannot launch search and rescue for our shuttle. Captain Fenaday was aboard with twenty other people. Do you have a fix on them? Request immediate SAR for the shuttle."

"Marathon here. We are passing your SAR distress call to Space Guard. We have no vessel in an orbit compatible with immediate SAR at your altitude. You were above all other traffic. We will give you a Space Guard ETA as soon as we know. We have no lock on your shuttle. Radar and microwave show hundreds of targets. We have no visual on your shuttle.

"You're cleared to descend as best you can. Do not use any vector between two-one seven and two-two-zero. Those would put you on a course for the city. If you can vector two-two-five, that will set you up for a bay landing. Weather conditions are nominal for a water landing."

"Affirmative Marathon," Telisan said. He turned to the helmsman. "Down angle on the bow, seventeen degrees. Begin giving me heat readings as we hit atmosphere. Check computer generated approach vectors.

"Sharla, sound the atmosphere warning. We are going in."

Sidhe dropped planetward, pelted by questions.

———

A dozen kilometers below *Sidhe*, the *Intruder* shuttle entered the atmosphere of Olympia, heading for the outskirts of Marathon and Pard's desert complex. Its matte-black, incredibly expensive surfaces absorbed microwave and radar transmissions. Her hull vectored heat around so that to a heat detector she appeared as a much smaller object, a piece of debris little bigger than a baseball. It did make the interior of the shuttle damn hot, despite the air conditioning. Everyone inside who could shed heat by sweating did so.

The heat finally lessened as the shuttle reached the freezing dark of the upper atmosphere. Now cool and invisible, she would appear to have burnt up in reentry. Fifteen minutes later, Fenaday slowed the *Intruder*, not daring to approach Pard's high-tech complex any closer, even with all the shuttle's stealthy refinements. Quickly, he turned the flight controls over to Fury.

"Good luck, Skipper," she whispered, as if Pard might overhear.

"You too, Angie," he replied. "I'll see you at the pick-up point or in Marathon."

On the shuttle's underside the heat shield fragmented. Airbot and the crab gun robots dropped off like fleas into the night below. The *Intruder's* rear ramp ground down as her red interior lights cut back to minimum. Cold air blasted into the shuttle. Fenaday felt his stomach clench. He stood at the back of the company of troopers, a dense, dark mass of shuffling people, heading for the yawning black at the end of the ramp. All he could hear was the roaring of wind and muffled curses from the troops near him. Mmok and the HCRs jumped first. The others piled off right after. He spotted Risky an instant before the dog and his handler vanished off the ramp. Fenaday rushed toward the ramp's edge and into emptiness.

An icy wind slapped Fenaday's body as he flung himself into space. HUD data reflecting off the inside of his visor gave him an artificial horizon and a fall direction for their landing zone. For a few seconds, none of this helped. He fell through the dark, flailing wildly as if trying to swim. Everyone disappeared, and the world became a formless black pit. His last jump had been over a decade ago. He'd forgotten the sensations. After a few panic-stricken seconds, he managed to get himself spread-eagle, stabilized to the ground. He remembered how to steer and aimed himself in the direction of the HUD arrow, trying to head for the LZ. The HUD now painted tiny sparks on the visor, other members of the team in free fall.

Falling from ten thousand feet seemed to take forever. Fenaday fought a growing nausea and the feeling that the automatics had failed, leaving him to plunge into the ground. Suddenly the canopy deployed, jerking him upright with a groin-straining jolt.

The smallish Olympian moon was a quarter full, giving a pale light that did not seem to touch the ground. The ice-ring glittered all the brighter for the moon's weak competition. He didn't need either. His HUD painted the ground an eerie, glowing green. Feeling more confident, Fenaday steered the chute in the direction of the arrow. A jump computer in the canopy reformed it into the optimum shape for steering in the direction he wanted. The small sparks of the other team members disappeared into the glowing green ground like snowflakes. Below, details appeared all at once, rock, scrub, and small gnarly trees. At the last second, he remembered not to look to the ground, raising his eyes to the horizon. *Never pull your legs up*, he thought, *it just bangs your ass on the ground.* Fenaday kept his legs tight together. No sense in getting a tree limb in between either. He dropped his weapon bag on its lanyard. His parachute automatically flared into braking mode.

He hit hard and rolled on rough, rocky ground. A stiff wind at ground level battered him against a scrubby tree before the chute automatically collapsed itself, rolling into an easily buried ball. He stood shakily, clawing open his weapon bag to reach the carbine tri-auto. To his alarm, he saw no other Confed troops. Quickly he buried his chute and the empty weapons bag, then moved off in the direction of the LZ. He powered up the carbine and flicked off the safety. For good measure he loosed the tie-downs on his Martini laser pistol and Scottish dirk. He stared anxiously at the strange plant life, much of which looked like crosses between cacti and bare, twisted oak trees.

After a few minutes walking, he heard something coming down the draw toward him. Heart hammering, he dropped into cover behind a rock and brought up his carbine, trying to sight through the washed-out green of night vision. It gave the world an unreal, nightmarish feel. Dirt crunched under feet, ahead of him. He sighted on the sound.

"It's Indigo," the HCR called in Mmok's voice. "Lousy drop, Fenaday. You were a thousand meters off. Follow Indigo back to the main body." The HCR walked into sight, its doll's eyes fastened on him.

"Any landing you can walk away from," Fenaday quoted. "Everyone else make it down all right?"

"One ASAT landed badly; medic says he's not concussed. He'll make it. Crab 17 is too badly damaged to move. Had it bury itself."

The HCR set a good pace, and Fenaday huffed, keeping up over the rough ground.

In a few minutes, they rejoined the rest of the force. Fenaday felt naked, traveling without either Shasti or Telisan. He was relieved when Li, Morgan, and the Tok brothers came over, forming up around him of their own accord.

Risky was too well-trained to fuss or whine when he saw Fenaday. He came over and butted his head against the man, until Fenaday petted the K-9. Then the dog went back to work watching the area. Lance Corporal Schiller stayed close to his canine companion.

Fenaday looked over at him. "Remember, keep an eye to him. He has a special signal for Shasti. If he puts his right paw on his nose then goes on point in a direction, that's where Shasti is."

"Yes sir," replied the young K-9 handler, "I remember."

"Of course."

They set out for Pard's complex. Mmok's crab robots spread out about a hundred meters to act as a screen. The airbot hovered silently above them in the dark, occasionally darting off to check their route. The machine had another purpose. It broadcast a low-level EM-jamming field over them that interfered with optical and heat detection, just in case a satellite should look down. HCRs formed the inner screen. The rest walked in a ranger file behind Mmok and Rask.

With luck and speed, they could reach the area above the complex in a few hours, time enough to attack well before dawn. Dominici's maps laid out the best hope for a safe approach, with traps and sensors marked. Mmok's machines would see them around any unscheduled patrols or remote sensors. Fenaday prayed Dominici's information on Pard's whereabouts was accurate. To attack and miss spelled doom for everyone. Dominici claimed a Denshi deprived of Pard would be divided, slow to react, its alliances suddenly cast into doubt. He hoped to God that she knew what she was talking about.

———

"Come in, Paula," Antebei said. His eyes roamed over her body, making her feel unclean. He seemed in a good humor. The call must have brought pleasing news. "Now," he added as she hesitated.

No, she thought to herself, *he wants to celebrate. No.* Obedience was her only protection, but the thought of him on her, in her, filled her with nausea. What choice did she have? Her feet moved her into the room almost as if they belonged to someone else.

He pulled her to him, sweeping her off the ground as if she weighed nothing.

Something snapped in her brain. Suddenly, she began fighting, clawing, her face stretched tight over her skull, teeth showing, eyes mad. It only excited Antebei more. He slammed her down on his desk, tearing her clothes open, thrusting himself inside her. Paula screamed and bit. No help came. Those in Section Seven knew better than to interrupt their master's play. He pawed her large breasts, biting her again.

Reason banished, she pulled back as far as she could and spat. "You perverted lab-made freak," she screamed.

It drove Antebei further into a rage. He slammed a huge fist against her temple. Paula's senses faded. *Bastard,* she thought, unable to speak. *I'll get you, bastard. You murder me and I'll still get you.* He snapped her head to one side with one massive hand, pressing it against the desk. She felt pressure and heaviness and then nothing at all.

Antebei pushed himself off the body, rage and lust satisfied. He looked down at the canted neck, the blackening bruise, and staring eyes. Staggering like a drunk, he reached a wall, reveling in the dark afterglow of it. He moaned with the sensual, liquid tingle running over his nerves. It ebbed quickly. Like a man surfacing from a deep dive, he drew a breath, shook his head, and looked about the room, as if seeing it for the first time. His eyes came to rest on the body, with its torn clothes, flat on his desk.

"No," he said in horror. "No, not again, no." He lunged to her side. "No, no don't be dead. Paula, wake up." It was no use. She was gone, beyond remorse, beyond any apology.

"Why," he demanded, "why fight me? You know I have no control when I'm like that. I always make it good later. Why?" he demanded, shaking the corpse like a child's doll.

She slipped off the desk to the floor, falling as only the dead do. Antebei swore.

After a while, he collected himself, using the com on his desk to call his bodyguard, Chatelaine. "There's been an accident," he said numbly, "a terrible accident." The horror fled as if it had never been, leaving behind the usual grayness in which he lived, when not lit by rage.

"Yes, sir," replied Chatelaine in a professional tone. He'd grown familiar with Antebei's accidents. "Where did it happen?"

"The parking level garage. My secretary fell. Please come by my office and pick up the necessary materials. Use our private entrance."

"Yes, sir, on my way."

Antebei looked at Kallian once more. "I really thought I might feel something, this time," he said thickly. "I hoped I would. They made me too good, Paula. All I am is an assassin. It's all I can be."

He closed the door on the way out. It seemed respectful.

———

Vaughn's silver and black aircar settled to the pad, blowing up the usual desert grit. As soon as the ground wheels touched, he hopped out, slamming the door and striding for Tanaka's apartment. She lived in a small, unattached building near the edge of the complex. He'd ordered it built for her after he'd come to power. Now he moved up the sand and gravel path, past the garden plants she so carefully tended, fighting the desire to break into a run. Tanaka was inexplicably unavailable. Even her personal com-link didn't respond, a serious security violation. A frisson of fear shot through him. Had Antebei made some move against her? The thought of how bare his back would be without Tanaka quickened his steps. For a second, he debated calling for backup. To be wrong would be to look foolish. Ridicule could be as dangerous as weapon fire to a man in his position. He checked his pistol and strode boldly up the walkway.

His fears were for nothing. Tanaka opened the door at his ring.

"My Lord," she said dully. Her eyes looked puffy. Tanaka crying? Impossible.

Worry flared to anger. "What have you been doing? Why are you not at our office? Why this dereliction?"

"Yes," she said. "Dereliction. Failure in one's duties. Indeed, I am derelict today." She walked back into the apartment. Perforce, he followed.

He frowned at her, anger replaced by confusion. "I do not understand? What's going on?"

"I have been derelict," she replied, visibly pulling herself together. "I've failed. Paula Kallian's body was found in the sub-garage. A fall, they say. She lies in the morgue. The family has been sent for."

Vaughn crossed his arms. "Unfortunate, most unfortunate. Still, if Antebei discovered she was working for us, he would hardly have killed her. No, she would have been useful against us. This smacks of his sickness, a sudden rage perhaps."

"Perhaps she could no longer stand his touch," Tanaka said, looking out the window into the fading orange-reds of the desert. Sunset brought deep purples and blues that halted just beyond the sodium lights of the complex.

"Foolish," he said. "It was almost over."

Tanaka walked away from him suddenly. She opened the door to the porch and stepped out. The desert air hit him like the slap he sensed Tanaka wanted to deliver. He followed her out. Standing behind her, he searched for something to say. "Misa, you were crying, weren't you? Why?"

"We couldn't even save one abused kid," she said. "That's pretty poor, don't you think? A mother's pain, a father's dreams, now cold meat on a slab. I'm just glad that after forty-three years in Denshi, I still can cry over a murdered child. She'd have been nineteen next month."

"It is unfortunate," he repeated. "I would have honored my promise. You know that."

"Yes," she said, relenting a little. "That is all you feel though, isn't it? That the death of this poor young woman, escaped from the dregs of the underclass, abused by the powerful, murdered when she was so close to freedom is...unfortunate."

"What else?" Vaughn said, confused and annoyed. "What is it you want of me?"

"Tell me. Would you feel any more, if it was me dead?"

He did not answer, unable to find words.

"What would you have of me, Tanaka?" he said, finally.

"I have a favor to ask," she said, still looking out into the desert. "Ask."

"Go see Kallian's body. It's in the morgue. Watch the family when they come. Then come back and tell me what you feel."

"Enough with this foolishness," he snapped, pulling her around roughly. She did not resist his tremendous strength. "We have work to do."

She looked up, black, impenetrable eyes staring into his. "Not I, my Lord. If you will not grant me this favor, then I have no further work to do. I will be leaving your service. Even if my retirement is to be no different than hers."

"Don't be a fool," he said.

"I need to know," she said, looking at him, "if there is more to the Engineered, more to you than rage, anger, and the need to dominate others. I need to see something more."

"This is ridiculous," he replied. "What need do I have to feel more? How does it profit you? You are rendered weak and unfit by these soft emotions. Yet you demand them of me. Tanaka, see reason. I'll forgive this foolishness, but enough."

"No, my Lord. You may dismiss me, or I will leave. Or in this one last thing, do as I ask you. I will never again trouble you with these matters. Or is it that you are afraid of what you might feel?"

"I will go," he said coldly. "When I return, we will discuss if you have any place in Denshi." He spun on his heel and walked back out to the aircar. Anger darkened his gaze. He feared to stay even another second, lest there be another Kallian.

Vaughn's aircar zipped the short distance to the administration building. He parked in the secured parking area for VIPs, then made his way inside. It would not do for Antebei, if he had no suspicions, to learn of his interest in Kallian. He used a restricted accessway, moving through maintenance and utility passages. His electronic pass made him invisible to the security systems. There were other safeguards that did not answer to his pass. These he avoided. He was not Fourth-Generation for nothing.

Vaughn moved by secret ways to the morgue, entering through the upper gallery, a place normally reserved for students. For a big man, he could move quietly at need. Instinctively, he slipped into a shadowed section by a ceiling support. From there he peered down into the morgue and the table on which Paula Kallian lay. She lay modestly covered with a sheet. Her bruised, waxy face aroused a strange feeling in him. Pity? Regret? Mere words to him. Yet why did his stomach feel in knots? Why this unease at the sight of a body? He had seen enough before and been the cause of many. Today, somehow, it was different.

A commotion at the far end caught his attention. He faded further back into the shadows. Several handsome, efficient Denshi medical personnel escorted two smaller figures, older people, Selected, but low order. The woman, on whom age's hand lay heavily for an Olympian, staggered, held by a harried, sickly-looking man. *My God*, Vaughn thought, *he's balding*. Their genetics were obviously so terrible he wondered how they had ever been licensed to marry. They'd been denied children; Kallian had been Unsanctioned. Lowest of the low on Olympia. No wonder she had been so desperate for the job with Denshi.

The older woman threw herself at the body, harsh tearing sobs erupting from her. "Oh my baby, my baby, what have they done to you?"

"Madam," one of the techs said, "it was an accident, a most unfortunate fall..."

Kallian's mother ignored them. Her father knelt next to her trying to console her. The sobs turned into screams of accusation. "Bastards," she shrieked. "You killed her. Don't think we don't know." She sobbed like a lost soul.

Suddenly there was no air in the room, and the walls were closing in. Vaughn, who had never fled anything, fled the morgue and its well of grief. Once back in the hidden passage, he flashed up the stairs till he reached the wide, high gallery level over the ground floor. There he slipped into the public sections of the building. Out among people again, he schooled himself back under control with the biofeedback skills of the Fourth-Generation. He commanded his heart to slow, his adrenaline level to drop, and his breathing to return to normal. In a few paces, he was to all the outside world, Mikhail Vaughn, Head of Section Three.

Inside, something had changed. Kallian's mother's screams had cut themselves into his soul and a certain innocence was lost. *Damn you, Tanaka,* he thought. *You intended this. What good does it do an assassin to learn such things?* He reached for the car's com. "Tanaka," he called.

"Sir?"

"Meet me in the plaza, outside our office. I have done as you asked."

"I'm on my way."

———

Telisan used the secure line, at least he hoped it was secure, with the book encryption. Sue Bernard placed the call in the Olympian net. It went through quickly.

"Here," was the only reply, but he recognized General Dominici's voice.

"We are at the port; our forces will reach the objective at or around 0300."

"One day, you have to tell me how. We are ready at our end. As soon as satellite cameras pick up weapons fire on the objective, we will initiate blocking maneuvers and cut reinforcements off. Are you secure?"

"Barely. We are buttoned up and all hands are armed. Denshi and Navy Security tried to board us after the tugs moved us into dry-dock. So far I have been able to keep them off the ship by screaming assassination on every public channel. I'm demanding guards from the Confederate Embassy," Telisan said. "I've tried reaching the embassy; the ambassador is unavailable."

"Clever bastard," Dominici said. "All right, we will get Army troops down to you as soon as we can. You've got to keep Denshi off the ship."

"Denshi Security sent an ultimatum a few minutes ago advising that if we did not open the hatches, we would be boarded by force," Telisan said. "I told them I would consider it an act of piracy and respond in force if they did."

A fusillade of shots rang out behind Telisan. He looked up at the monitor to see a party of Denshi or Navy scattering back toward cover. *Sidhe's* crew fired from airlock loopholes made to pass tools in and out without cycling the big doors. Not ideal, still it allowed them to put fire down without exposing the ship to a rush. All the real troops were off with Fenaday and Mmok. He had over one hundred and fifty crewmen, but Telisan did not give much for their chances against regular military. Their only hope lay in staying buttoned up and keeping enemy ground forces at a distance.

"Hurry," he said to Dominici.

"Keep your pants on, flyboy, at least till I get there. Dominici out."

Sharla reached over and stabbed the off button, muttering in Denleni about those who mate out of season.

Tanaka met Vaughn outside, by his parked aircar. Vaughn hoped a walk in the desert wind might lift the tearing screams of Paula Kallian's mother out of his mind. They still ripped at his nerves in a way nothing else ever had, as if they'd left an echo of agony to reverberate in his skull.

The pair went barely a dozen feet before an aide ran up to Tanaka with a message. The young Denshi trooper handed it to her, bowed to Vaughn, and discreetly faded away.

Tanaka crumpled the paper and tossed it on the ground. "A bad day is bad to the end. The goddamn bomb went off. Fenaday was outside, in a shuttle. It's gone. *Sidhe's* wrecked and heading for the spaceport. They never reported the bombing, so the shuttle came down and the Moussas got away.

"We overestimated them. They must have blown up the bomb trying to disarm it. It's over," she continued. "Antebei has succeeded, and we will become an organization of butchers."

A leaden heaviness enveloped Vaughn, but he shook his head. "Still you misjudge. Pard will be angry with him. He is not as you think."

"He's not that different," Tanaka snapped. "He's had his own Kallians, a string of them. Rainhell was his mistake. She was Engineered and could fight back. We real humans seem to be toys to you Engineered."

Vaughn's face went dark with rage. "Enough," he roared. His hand snapped to her throat, smacking aside her parry. He lifted her into the air, blue eyes burning, grip locked on her trachea. She should have been fighting. There were techniques for this. Tanaka knew them; she'd taught them to him.

"Go ahead, Aristo," she hissed. "You're no different than the others. Go ahead."

Vaughn's mind whirled, shocked by his sudden rage and loss of control. Blue eyes locked into Tanaka's black ones, seeing many things there: fear, hate, love, depths, and nuances, other things too complicated to put names to. She was a true human; he was the product of labs. All his loyalties lay in tatters. Tanaka had guarded his back since his teens. She spoke ill of Pard and the Engineered. Yet, what had Pard been to him but a brutal taskmaster? Didn't the crimes she laid at the door of the Engineered belong there? Even Rainhell, one of his own kind, had been used as a toy, a piece of property, with no concern for her own needs.

Emotions boiled away. Gently, he lowered her, running a huge hand over her hair. Tanaka did not shy away. She simply stood, her eyes still holding his.

"I'm sorry," he whispered, feeling numb and exhausted. "Sorry," he repeated, stroking her hair, his voice rough and thick. "Did I hurt you? Are you all right?"

"Yes, sir," Tanaka rasped.

He shook his head. "No, don't call me sir. We are more than that, aren't we? You kept me alive when I was a child in training, already a target. You've watched my back every day since then. Have I used you so ill?"

Tanaka was still for a moment, then her hand, in an uncharacteristically uncertain gesture, fluttered to touch his face. "No," she whispered. "You have not, but I have not always been so lucky." She turned slightly away. "When I was young, I served in Pard's personal guard. I did things in his service I try not to remember, especially against House Bremardi. Sometimes, when I am walking, I suddenly see a face belonging to someone long dead. When I look a second time, I see it is not them, but for a second my blood chills and my heart stops. Nights are often worse.

"People died. Not because they threatened Denshi, or the Order of Geneticists, but because someone wanted their wife, husband, or lover. Trivial reasons: to advance careers, for money, for stupid slights and differences. They didn't just die, they died badly, to make a point. I grew disgusted and disillusioned. Pard judged me unsuitable for his SWAT team. Too many scruples.

"I went to security, hoping to outlast Pard, hoping to see Denshi turn back to the days when there were rules. When children and the helpless were not considered valid targets and the Engineered did not use assassins to quiet all opposition. Instead, I saw Antebei, only a teenager, but already on his way up in Security. They rush you Engineered into adulthood so soon. After he murdered his governess, I realized worse was to come unless I did something about it."

She looked up at him. "I looked for someone else to serve, to develop as an alternative to Antebei and those like him. Someone with a shred of conscience. You were the same age as Antebei, but you were different. I remember how books and videos of King Arthur's knights and the ancient samurai fascinated you. You dreamt of fighting dragons or other great warriors, not murdering old women and children. You wanted to be a hero and understood that meant there were things you could not do. There had to be some difference between you and the villain.

"You," she said, her eyes bright, "became my hope for something better in Denshi. Some return to what we had once been when Denshi served as an alternative to war. A way to keep conflicts between the powerful and leave common people to their lives. So, I left Security before Antebei rose high enough to stop me. I looked out for you until I could persuade Special Operations to take me on as your bodyguard."

"You never told me," he said, his face slack with astonishment.

"In the beginning it would not have made sense to you. Later, Pard became interested in your career. I did not want trouble between you on my account. It was the past. One learns to let things go with age."

They stood side by side, looking down. Overhead, the stars and rings grew visible, hard and white. In the distance, thunder rumbled. A storm was coming from the mountains.

"You should have told me sooner," Vaughn reached into his vest, pulling out a 12mm Ingerbretsen pistol. Only an Engineered could hold onto the monster when it fired. He popped the magazine and checked the rounds. "You know," he said absently, "I should get that laser pistol you are always talking about. I still don't like weapons that reveal where you are, but they are good for close range."

Tanaka stared at him, suddenly afraid. "What are you going to do?"

"Something I should have done long ago," he said. "I'm going to kill Antebei."

"I'll help you," she said. "We'll do it together."

"No," he said. "You were right the first time. You're my body-guard and can protect me even against another Engineered, but if you draw on him first, they'll hunt you and your family. Leave him to me."

"Promise me something," she demanded, her arm on his, her dark eyes intent. "See how the ground lies, watch for an opening. See if Pard is not a fool."

"As you wish," he gave a small smile, "my guardian angel."

Suddenly there were tears in her eyes, and in the biggest surprise of his life, she threw her arms around him and hugged him hard.

———

Shasti knew something was wrong as soon as she entered the apartment. Jenner greeted her at the door with a nervous expression. Behind her, Rigg sat in a chair, his head in his hands.

She put down the bag with her equipment in it and turned to Jenner. "What's happened?" she asked, foreknowing the worst.

"It...it was just on the news," Jenner stammered. "I am so sorry, Shasti. There's been an explosion on the *Sidhe* just as they launched a shuttle. Captain Fenaday was on board. Space Guard is going up. All they see on the screens is wreckage, nothing else so far. I am so sorry."

Rigg stood up and walked over. He knew better than to touch her, but there was sorrow in his deep voice. "I am, too. You know I liked Fenaday, even admired him."

Shasti felt a terrible remoteness wrap her. She had never wanted to sort out her feelings for Robert Fenaday. It was enough she felt happy with him, enjoyed his presence in a fashion she did not enjoy anyone else's. The why of it had never been resolved. It struck her suddenly that he was the only person who had ever asked her what *she* wanted. He thought about her. Not always in big gestures, as on Enshar when he refused to leave her trapped under a beam when they thought a Shellycoat was just behind them. It was in the little things, like taking a supply of chocolate down to Enshar, or asking for a painting of hers for his cabin. Now, dead? Not to be seen, touched again? It was unreal.

Jenner put a hand to her arm. Shasti focused on her, frightened that it took her a second to remember who the Olympian was.

"Please, sit down," Jenner said.

"No," Shasti said distantly. "I have to go now. I found Pard. I know exactly where he is. I have to go kill him."

"Shasti," Jenner pled, "think sensibly. You are in no state to do anything. We haven't planned—"

"No," Shasti repeated in the same flat, absent voice. "I have to go. I'm sorry. You will have to escape as best you can." Shasti turned back toward the door, picking up her pack. The rest of what she needed was in the cargo compartment of the cycle she had bought.

Rigg reached forward to stop her. Her head snapped around, sheer murder in her eyes stopping even the tough ASAT. Shasti seemed to focus on him for a moment. The maniacal stare faded. "You can't help me, Dan. You're not recovered enough.

"Leda, you're a good person and brave, but not much use in a fight. Dan needs you. I'm sorry to abandon you, but there is one thing left for me to do. Kill Pard. Not only for what he did to me, but for Robert. He was my friend. I only ever had one."

"Two," Rigg said.

"Three," Jenner added through tears.

"Maybe if there is a next life," Shasti said, "I'll be able to see and understand such things.

"Goodbye, my friends. Farewell." Shasti opened the door and slipped out.

Jenner broke into hopeless tears. Rigg put an arm around her.

Shasti sped down the stairs. She felt oddly light, no fear, no worry, no future. Thoughts of Fenaday hurt. She kept those at a distance. They could stay at that distance for a little while longer, till she finished her one remaining task. Pard had hurt her again. She would kill him, or die. Either way, he would never hurt her again.

She mounted the cycle and looked skyward. "Goodbye, Robert," she whispered to the night sky. "I should never have told you about Pard; and I should have told you if I ever loved anyone, it was you."

Shasti focused her mind on Pard. "For both of us," she said starting the bike.

Chapter Fifteen

Salmot roused Pard shortly after he had turned in. Pard always slept alone, even if he'd bedded one of his favorites earlier in the evening. Tonight he'd retired early.

"What's happened?" Pard asked, suspecting it could only be bad news.

"There's been an explosion on the *Sidhe*, ten minutes ago," Salmot said. "No details are available yet. Admiral Rissi says the ship is dropping. It looks like she's heading for a landing in Marathon."

"Interesting." Pard stretched muscles capable of bending steel bars; the joints cracked. Lately, he found himself stiff in the mornings. Today it seemed worse. *Age*, he thought, *even we can't engineer that away, at least, not yet.*

Pard dressed, armed himself, and followed his aide-de-camp to the oak-lined conference room in the center of his office tower. He'd ordered it done in a medieval style, like some ancient king's court, and proofed it against even heavy rifle fire. Heavy wooden chests and other antique furniture surrounded the fifteen-hundred-year-old table brought out from Old Earth itself. Original tapestries hung on the walls.

The others took longer to arrive: Oldark, crèche brother and former rival, also aged in the service of Denshi. Vaughn entered with his shadow Tanaka, followed by Alexa, Pourlos, and the others. The heart and mind of Denshi trooped into the room. Pard seated himself at the head of the immense table. Salmot stood behind him.

Antebei entered last, making his usual grand entrance, accompanied by his guard, Chatelaine. He looked well pleased with himself and nodded to the others, save his childhood rival, Vaughn, as he took his place at the table.

At a nod from Pard, Oldark began. "There's been an explosion on the Starship *Sidhe*. The vessel is damaged, apparently severely as she is dropping out of orbit. The Port Authority says she is back under control, making for a landing at Marathon."

"The big news," Antebei announced with a cold smile, "is that the stain on Denshi's honor has been removed. The explosion destroyed the shuttle *Pooka* with your enemy, Fenaday, aboard. They are screaming for Search and Rescue, but we deem there to be no chance."

Everyone turned to stare at Antebei. The triumph in every line of his body made it obvious. Pard closed his eyes, as if in some small pain. "You arranged this," he said, his voice calm and even.

"Yes, Lord. That animal insulted Denshi, and worse, you, in public. Unlike some," he glared at Vaughn, "I'm not prepared to let such attacks on our power go unchallenged."

"Attacks on your vanity, you mean," Vaughn said, his mouth a grim line.

"You value our Lord's dignity as lightly as your own," Antebei snapped. "He insulted Denshi publicly. He even brought up that creature Rainhell and her assault on our Lord."

"And so," Pard began in a deep voice, one that gathered strength as he spoke, "you took it on yourself to bomb the best-known starship in all of space. You murdered her famous captain, a man celebrated as the savior of an intelligent species. You did all this because you completely fell for what Fenaday wanted: to make us strike at him, to pull us into the light, just as we approach the fruition of our greatest plans. You handed Fenaday what he sought. He'll strike back at us from the grave. The Neos, the Bremardi, the Army, and the Confederacy itself will pursue his public accusations against

House Denshi. There will be investigations into places we could normally bar. We will be hounded. You have crafted a weapon and put it in our enemies' hands."

Antebei's beautiful face paled as Pard's voice rose to a bellow, something no one had ever heard before.

"I did it for you, sir," he stammered, "to avenge the insult."

"I am not vulnerable to words, boy," Pard growled, disgust in every line of his heavy face. "This is not a schoolyard. This is power. True power, which you are manifestly unfit to command.

"You've disappointed me for the last time. You are dismissed from our service. Go back to buggering your secretary. It's all you are fit for."

Antebei's face exploded in fury. The dismissal served as a death sentence for a man with so many enemies. He jerked upright, hand clawing for a weapon. With a curse, Vaughn reacted instantly. His left hand flashed under his jacket, emerging with the big-bore pistol. Vaughn's round slammed out an instant before Antebei's. His 12mm knocked Antebei backward. Antebei's shot went into the ceiling, causing an explosion of plaster fragments. Antebei flipped over backward, firing while in the air. The round smashed into Vaughn's right shoulder. Body armor under his silks stopped penetration. It still felt like a troll's hammer.

Tanaka's laser sliced through air into Chatelaine before the man could fire at Vaughn. Chatelaine toppled, lifeless.

Antebei landed on his feet, sprinting for the door, as everyone save Vaughn, Pard, and Salmot hit the floor. He pegged a shot at Tanaka, but she dove behind a massive antique wooden chest. The shot struck the chest, blowing one end into splinters.

"Antebei!" Vaughn roared as he leapt atop the massive table. His weapon bucked, armor piercing and squash-head rounds ripping alternately from its massive barrel. Two rounds hit. Antebei went down into a roll, again snap-firing on the move, seemingly unhurt even by the 12mm. Return fire burned by Vaughn's face. Antebei surged to his feet, his face demonic with hate.

Vaughn dropped prone on the table, his gun arm outstretched, firing. Antebei's return shot blazed over him. Vaughn's round caught Antebei between the eyes, slamming him back into a chair. Vaughn staggered to his feet, one arm dangling from his smashed shoulder. He walked across the huge oak table and looked down at the corpse.

"These are from Paula," he whispered, emptying his weapon into his rival's face till the slide clicked open. Dizziness assailed him, and he eased down from the table to find Tanaka already at his side. He smiled at her anxious face as she pulled open his jacket to look at his shoulder. He waved her off. "It didn't go through," he said, "or my arm would be off."

Vaughn spared Antebei a final glance. "Looks like I am better made after all," he muttered, "not so pretty, but faster."

"Of course," he said, turning back to Tanaka, "now he looks more like a Picasso than a Michelangelo."

She shuddered and turned away from the corpse.

Vaughn turned to face Pard.

Silence and the smell of Chatelaine's burnt flesh hung in the air. Pard had not reached for his own weapon. He sat with his right hand raised, forestalling Salmot, whose drawn pistol menaced the room.

Watching the game to the end, Vaughn thought, *the final test of your creations? Had to see how it came out? Damn you. Are we nothing more than racehorses? Would you care if I lay there and Antebei stood in triumph? Paula, you were right about us after all.*

He met Pard's eyes to see pride and approval in them. For the first time in Vaughn's life, he didn't give a damn.

The others regained their feet, eyes wary, hands on weapons, trying to figure out the new order and what options they had.

Pard waved. "Put up your weapon, Grigor." The slim, deadly assassin holstered, and tension dropped visibly in the room. Vaughn slowly put away his empty pistol, wincing at the move. Pain made his vision blur.

"Are you fit?" Pard demanded.

Vaughn swayed. Tanaka quickly butted her smaller frame against him, steadying the huge Engineered. "Yes," he said thickly. "What are your orders?"

Pard stared dispassionately at the body of Antebei. *How could I have failed to see his weakness?* he wondered. *Perhaps I have grown old after all.*

"Gentlemen and ladies," Pard began, "this fool has brought hard days to Denshi. With Fenaday's death we will live under a spotlight. We must restrict our activities severely. Most important, we must not be seen to be the force impeding the investigations the Neos and others will demand. It will be difficult to keep the Army from exploiting this. Dominici will seek to remove our security people from the Spaceport."

"Perhaps the Army can be made to believe some other faction responsible, the Navy or the Bremardi?" Oldark asked.

"No," Pard shook his head. "Only the Navy and our people have access to the starship. Any investigation will confirm the damage is from a bomb. Assassination is our trade. Everyone will know Denshi did this.

"I must apologize to our House for allowing such a fool to rise so high among us," Pard continued. Surprised faces turned back to him before resuming their carefully neutral expressions.

"Please retire to your various centers and take all steps necessary to keep Denshi's profile minimal for the foreseeable future. Move your forces around. Do not allow them to be pinned down by the Army or the Bremardi. Oldark, you will leave as soon as possible. Take Antebei's people as well as your own. Watch them. They are not to be trusted. I will keep only my personal guard here."

The others nodded and rose, ignoring Antebei's body, heading for the safety of their offices and troops. Each commanded a force of troops temporarily based at the compound. Pard rotated them through to provide additional strength and serve as quasi-hostages.

Even with them gone, I will have several hundred men available, with still more in the city. I'd normally keep more troops, but Project Overman consumes so much of our resources. It leaves me in a weaker position than I could hope.

Truth is, he thought, *I slipped badly relying on Antebei. I believed him the stronger, unburdened by Vaughn's archaic notions of honor. It calls my judgment into question for the first time in fifty years. Questioned once, it might be again. I may no longer seem invulnerable. I can count on little help in the days ahead. Time to work on that.*

He looked at Vaughn. He needed the victor to rally to his side. The younger man, with his Fourth-Generation genetics, seemed recovered from the gunshot and no longer needed Tanaka's aid to stand. His eyes, now clear from pain, showed nothing, though his arm still hung limp.

"You were right," Pard said. *Start with that much of a concession,* he thought.

"That realization has come late for some," Vaughn replied.

Pard checked his anger; he needed the younger man.

Tanaka nudged Vaughn. He looked down at her. Something passed between them.

"Your orders?" Vaughn said again. Pard saw relief wash over Tanaka's face and filed the fact for later consideration. He might need leverage on Vaughn.

"Go to our Marathon office. Assume control there. Do what you can to keep tabs on the *Sidhe*. If you can get our people onto the ship without causing major casualties, do so. Find a way to blame the explosion on something mechanical. Thin cover, as I said before, but we have few options. Rainhell will doubtless try to make it to the ship. Kill her if you can. Do it quietly. Exert what control you can over the investigation. Coordinate with Hagen. Keep ties with the Navy open; we may need their troops. I will be busy with Project Overman."

Vaughn nodded. "Yes, my Lord." He and Tanaka left.

Pard looked at Salmot and gestured toward Antebei's corpse. "Have him reduced to fertilizer and used in the garden. May he serve us better there than he did in life."

Salmot called the outside guards, then trailed Pard as he headed back to his room, deep in thought. Only an hour had passed, yet everything was different. Pard's brain worked furiously. The timing of this debacle could not have been worse. Several of the Others were onworld, hidden in the Denshi complex. If necessary they could be disposed of, but the risk to Overman was immense. He would order it only as a last resort if the investigations came too close.

He regained his rooms, leaving Salmot just outside. Pard walked over to the huge window with its view of the desert mountains beyond. He could see little. The compound's lights made the wilderness beyond their glow all the more impenetrable. Alone with his thoughts, he could no longer deny the truth.

Yes, Antebei, I am pleased by Fenaday's death. The idea of Rainhell, the very stuff of my dreams, preferring another man does gall me. A standard human, not even a superior specimen, has Rainhell and has her willing and eager. She's even conceived feelings for him, something I intended only to happen with me.

He remembered the surgeries to repair the damage she did to him. *I'll repay her,* he thought, *many times, in the same agonizing coin. If only I had known she was on the original team, I would have made her capture a priority. She's a ruined dream now, unworthy of my attention. If she's taken alive, I will hand her over to the interrogators for practice.*

Chapter Sixteen

Fenaday crawled through the predawn darkness to the hillcrest where Mmok and Rask lay observing Pard's complex. After hours of slow, tedious effort, they'd arrived at the hills west of the complex undetected, thanks to Mmok's cyber-sensors and robots. "What's the situation?" he asked.

"Curious," Mmok said, his usual antagonism to Fenaday buried by his professionalism. "The energy readings and movements that the HCRs and the airbot are detecting are far less than this complex should be showing, even allowing for the early hour."

"Which means," said a grim-faced Rask, "either they're expecting us or, for some reason, the complex is mostly empty."

"Well, well," Mmok said. "A pretty problem. You're the captain. What do you say?"

Fenaday looked out over the complex and shivered as the cold desert wind picked up. The complex contained an assortment of twenty solid, Empire-style buildings dotted by lights. The green of his night vision painted the ornate buildings, festooned with statues and columns, only in shades of brightness. He could true the device for daylight and see what they looked like in full sun, but it would ruin his night vision. Skybridges linked about half of the structures. He could see no movement.

Fenaday studied the near ground. A splatter of desert shrubs and short spiny trees covered the area. Draws and arroyos sculpted the broad slope of the hillside below them. Farther toward the complex lay a large flattened area of filled and graded dirt. He recognized it as a killing zone similar to the one he had used with deadly effect against the Shellycoats of Enshar.

"Best advice, gentlemen," he demanded, "empty or ambush?"

Mmok looked at him. "Can't tell. Fifty-fifty."

Rask met his eyes. "A smart man would not make an ambush look like an ambush. Pard is a smart man by all accounts."

"You call it." Mmok shrugged, as if the subject held no interest for him.

"Follow me," Fenaday said, his mouth suddenly dry. To his surprise, Mmok extended an arm to bar him.

"This ain't a bayonet charge," Mmok growled. "We got robots for the point and you have veteran ground fighters. I'll lead with the crab robots, then the live troops, then you. I'll hold the HCRs for reserve."

Rask grinned. "That's right, sir. Follow us in with your people. Our guys will hit the wall nearest the flak tower there and cut the fence. Then we spread out with half the robots to either side and take the main buildings. You take your trouble team and search for Pard."

Fenaday hesitated, then nodded, secretly glad to leave the attack to them. Mmok subvocalized to the machines, and the crab robots sidled over the top of the hill, starting down. Rask signaled his live troops with hand gestures. Fenaday waved to Morgan, who brought up the trouble team Shasti normally led. They assembled around Fenaday. The rest of the Landing Force troops attached themselves to Rask. Corporal Schiller and Risky stood near Fenaday. The K-9 trainer made a series of gestures to the dog then slipped his leash off. Risky's brain was genetically enhanced enough to understand both the gestures and the danger on the other side of the hill.

Rask went over the top. His ASAT Rangers followed, almost invisible in the pre-morning darkness. Fenaday's turn came at Mmok's signal. His boots crunched on the sand and rock as he stood. The breath of the trouble team fogged in the air. He waved his hand in a signal to spread out his people. They crept down the hillside, scurrying from cover to cover. Risky, with his natural advantages, got out in front quickly. The dog moved in small rushes from one safe spot to another. Fenaday envied the shepherd's closeness to the ground.

At best they might reach the edge of the killing ground undetected. Mercifully, Pard's complex was not a true fortification, or the approaches would be mined. Still, Dominici's information showed the defenses they faced as formidable.

Flashes and blasts lit the sky. *Looks like we don't get that close unmolested,* thought Fenaday. Crab robots became visible as they raced forward, firing. The compound's defenses opened up. Machine guns fired tracers and depleted uranium slugs. From the towers, lasers stabbed down.

The crab robots moved at maximum speed, skittering in and out of cover, particle beams strobing, launching grenades and shaped rocket charges. Fire poured from the complex. The Confederate cyber-forces quickly proved too much for the Denshi perimeter defenses. Bullets bounced off armored crabs. Lasers bit but did not easily penetrate. Rockets began to fly out of the compound and the ground erupted.

"Move up," Mmok said into their headphones. There was no further point to radio silence. "Rask, flank to the right. Enemy fire is moderate. I am concentrating four of the crabs on those bunkers to the left."

"Moderate, he says," Morgan spat, adding some choice Irish curses.

"Cobalt and Sapphire, hit that flak tower," continued Mmok's voice.

The HCR robots moved forward in a blur. A tower-mounted laser struck Sapphire a glancing blow. The slim robot's clothes flamed. It rolled instantly, dousing the fire, and sprang back to its feet. Cobalt joined Sapphire. They turned their heavy tri-autos on the chain guns and fired as they bounded over the security fence. Tower lasers could not cope with the speeding HCRs and targeted the slower crabs instead. One hit Crab 14. The robot staggered, badly damaged. Sensing its imminent electronic death, the crab used its remaining energy to catapult itself to the fence line.

"Fire in the hole," Mmok yelled on the net. Everyone hit the ground. The crab exploded in an ear-shattering roar, taking down ten yards of fence and a tower.

"This is Rask. Medic to the bottom of the hill. Two men down."

"Keep going," Fenaday called out, rising from the ground. "Don't return fire. Let the robots do it. Keep moving forward. Run, damn it, run."

They hit the floor of the valley, passing two of Rask's men with the medic. One was clearly dead, the first installment on the butcher's bill.

Tracer rounds bounced off the ground in front of him, looking deceptively lazy as they tumbled. Knowing that for every tracer they could see, seven non-tracers followed, Fenaday's team hit the dirt as machine gun fire swept over them. Fenaday landed so hard he skidded, ending up with dirt in his mouth. Morgan was a fatal split-second slower. A tracer bounced up and hit the human, cutting through his body armor. He spun, smoking from the force of the heavy machine gun bullet. More hit. Morgan's body dropped in their midst. Li screamed and rose to return fire.

"No," Fenaday shouted. "Leave it to the robots. Up and through the fence."

Rask's ASATs reached the wire and attacked the buildings. Denshi troops poured out in response, only to be cut to pieces. The fight was not one-sided. Two of the crab robots shattered under sustained rocket attacks before the Denshi rocket teams were wiped out. Fenaday watched with a grim joy as Pard's ground troops broke in retreat.

An armored car roared around the corner, its turret tracking toward the spacers. Suddenly the HCR Indigo appeared on its turret, tearing open the top hatch and flinging in a satchel charge. Indigo leapt diagonally to the nearest rooftop as the armored car erupted in flame.

Fenaday's people made it to the downed wire. As they zigzagged into the cover of the nearest building, its doors flew open. Two of Pard's troopers burst out. Everyone slid to a halt, facing each other in surprise across a distance of three meters. Guards and spacers blurred into a fast draw.

The genetically enhanced guards won. A bullet slammed into Fenaday's breastplate, throwing him flat on his back. Hanshi Tok screamed as a laser cut into his right arm.

Risky did not freeze when the humans did. He smelled the enemy just before they hit the doors. The shepherd piled into the nearest guard, teeth seizing a weapon strap. The one hundred-pound K-9 jerked the weapon clear of the guard's hand. Lokashti Tok shot one Denshi. Schiller hit the one fighting Risky.

Lokashti turned to tend his brother, who lay on the ground moaning, clutching an arm. Li helped Fenaday to his feet. The bullet hadn't gone through; still his chest felt as if a horse had kicked him.

"Good thing it wasn't a head shot," Schiller told him, as the spacer struggled for breath.

"Move everyone into the building," Fenaday ordered through clenched teeth. "Hanshi, stay with your brother till the medic gets here. The rest of you, with me." He looked out over the compound. Firefights raged everywhere. Indigo blurred into sight, heading for a bunker across the square. He couldn't tell if they were winning or losing. *Mmok's problem,* he thought. *I'm here for Shasti and Pard.*

"Down three men already," he muttered. "Schiller, you stick with me. Li, as soon as the medic gets here, you and Lokashti pair up and start searching. Find Shasti if she's here. Get Pard if you can, but find Shasti."

"Yes, sir," Li said, eyes darting everywhere.

———

S hasti had reached the area of the complex unobserved, just before midnight. She'd driven cross-country from the main highway. When the ground grew too rough for the bike, she ditched it in a draw and proceeded on foot. The climb out of the gorge dividing the complex from the outskirts of Marathon took her over an hour. She dared not try the bridge itself as Denshi guards manned it. Once out of the gorge, she traveled across the broken country faster than an ordinary human could, despite the weight of the heavy triple-auto weapon she'd stolen from a Bremardi armory. She did not need night vision equipment. Her engineered eyes pierced the dark like a tiger's.

Her black insulated jumpsuit kept the cold desert night at bay. With her melanin camouflage, she and the equipment blended into the night perfectly. Neither the feeble crescent moon, nor the ice ring, raised a highlight on her.

Topping one hill, she spotted a convoy of vehicles leaving the compound, heading toward the bridge and threw herself flat. Armored cars led troop transports and ordinary vehicles; over these hovered choppers and aircars. She crawled forward, careful not to be skylined. The insulated suit granted her another advantage: its chemical composition and structure diffused heat. Infrared scanners could not detect her except at close range.

What's this? she wondered. She used her binoculars to check the markings: Oldark, McPherson, and other high Denshi. None of the vehicles bore the insignia of Pard's personal guard. Clearly Pard had decided to shift some of his forces out of the compound, doubtless to complicate his enemies' plans to use the bomb blast against him. He would force his enemies to deal with more targets by moving Denshi forces toward his various political strongholds, a veiled threat against the Army and the Opposition parties.

It complicated Shasti's mission. Pard might be in the convoy moving out toward the capital, or he might be in the compound. A few seconds made the answer clear. She had no chance of doing anything against the alert and speeding convoy. While the compound might also be on alert, there she possessed an advantage. She knew the compound well. Much could have changed, but her odds of slipping into the base seemed immeasurably better, slim as they were. She gave the convoy a wide berth, moving carefully from cover to cover.

In the hours before dawn she worked her way to the lowland below and east of the Denshi compound. Electronic monitoring and patrols normally swept the area. Tonight, she could detect no sign of foot patrols. Had they been pulled farther in? Perhaps the compound was undermanned with Oldark's evacuation?

This area that supplied the base's water and sewage had always been the camp's Achilles' heel in one sense. An armored or large-scale assault would find the swamp a killing ground as they bogged down in it. For single infiltrators, it provided a good way to approach the area. Shasti reached the end of the bog, traveling paths known to her from when the compound had been a much smaller training facility. She went carefully, searching for the sensors. Her superhuman eyes and nose saved her from tripping them. She could practically smell metal and plastic. Perhaps the shock of Fenaday's death had unlocked something in her. Every sense seemed stronger, more acute than ever. She could see each leaf clearly; every sound reached her ears. Always a good stalker, now she moved so silently that a skoosh did not notice her till she put a foot near the small, rabbit-like creature. It bolted in terror.

At the edge of the swamp, she found the flattened, cleared zone, which surrounded the camp. The patrols she feared earlier could be seen in force on the other side of a chain-link fence. Her practiced eye found some cover in the field, but no way to reach any of it. Automatic sensors, only partially reliable in the swamp, would detect her the instant she moved from the bog's edge, despite her infrared and visual camouflage.

Shasti settled in to wait, hoping desperately for a break. The cold of the desert night finally began to penetrate her suit. Each minute closer to sunrise moved her closer to failure. After an hour of watching regular, perfect guard work, despair began to creep into her soul. Pard was no fool. She'd only penetrated the outermost shell of the security, accomplishing nothing.

She started as a flash lit the predawn sky. Heavy firing broke out instantly. Shasti flattened, thinking she'd been discovered. She quickly realized the sound originated on the other side of the compound, toward the hills. It grew immediately in intensity. She could see the actinic lights of lasers and the flash of more explosions. Clearly it was no mere raid by gunmen. *Army,* she thought. *Who else possessed such firepower?* From the sound, the attacking force exceeded company level, backed by light armor.

She could hear the troops talking on the other side of the fence. A distant voice called for the soldiers to keep an eye on their own front. Another flash and the top of the nearest flak tower exploded, hit by a wild round from the battle on the other side of the compound. Suddenly officers appeared, yelling orders. Soldiers began piling out of the bunkers and buildings, heading for the other side of the base. An armored personnel carrier, already firing shells at a high angle, joined the troops. It could only mean the attacking force had breached the compound and the defenders were in desperate straits.

Shasti surged out of the bog, running serpentine toward the compound. A robot gun stuttered, and she leaped sidewise. The machine, programmed to deal with lesser creations than Shasti, couldn't track her leap. Rounds spattered the ground beside her. Her tri-auto took out the perimeter gun mounted on a pylon. She snaked forward, hoping no other weapon covered the zone. None did. A pair of insulated clippers got her through the wire.

I made it, she thought triumphantly. *I'm back inside.* She raced toward the steps of the nearest building. From the top landing, she could see the other end of the complex. Intense fire filled the streets. Glass shattered off buildings and lights exploded, plunging sections into darkness. In the far distance, she caught glimpses of running soldiers. They moved forward professionally, in bounding formations, covering each other. Even with her vision, she could not make out uniforms, but there was no mistaking quality infantry. Shasti turned and dashed into the doorway. This building connected with Pard's apartments by a bridgeway higher up. Shasti let her skin revert to its normal color, relieved of the slight energy drain the melanin camouflage cost her. In the bright interiors of the compound it would just make her more conspicuous.

Hysterical office workers crowded the corridor she entered. Night shift, she realized; the complex ran all twenty-five hours of the Olympian day. They fled past Shasti, taking the Engineered woman for one of their own, as they headed for the basement and shelters. She saw guards in the red and black Denshi livery at the far end. They disappeared in another direction. Chaos ruled. Shasti shoved through people, heading upstairs. More clerks, technicians, and janitorial workers fled down the stairs. They also took her for one of their own and barely looked at her.

At the top of the stairway, an alert guard locked eyes with Rainhell, somehow recognizing an enemy in her. His weapon snapped up half a second too late. Her tri-auto crumpled him with a short burst. His own wild shot struck a middle-aged computer technician at the foot of the stairs. The woman crumpled with a scream. A young man, his hands empty of weapons, turned to aid her, saw Shasti, and froze. She stared down at him malevolently. He continued to edge toward the fallen woman. Shasti remembered the faces of the people she had killed out of hand when she fled this place, years ago. Armed, unarmed had not mattered then. She'd cut down young and old alike. They had all been Pard to her. Not now. She'd learned things in the years since.

When she didn't react, the man seized the sobbing woman, struggled to lift her, and fled as fast as he could. She turned her back on the pair and on a measure of her past, heading upward. She'd come for Pard. She would deal with any who stood in her way, but today there would be no random slaughter.

———

P ard frantically loaded his valuable documents, data crystals and disks into a carryall bag. His face remained calm though his mind was in turmoil. Somehow he had miscalculated, failing to foresee this attack. How was it possible that the compound's formidable defenses could be overwhelmed with such speed? Clearly, this was beyond the capabilities of the Neos or any other lesser Houses. It could only be the Army. Yet of all his opponents, he feared the Army least. He'd thoroughly infiltrated Army HQ, yet his spies gave no warning of Special Forces on the move. How had Dominici managed to get so powerful a force free of his spies?

No, Army did not make sense. So open a move was uncharacteristic of the Army, which paid at least nominal homage to the civilian law of the planet. Something else was going on.

It struck him suddenly. All the pieces fell into a pattern. It could only be the Confederacy. Interfering with a member planet's politics would be an unprecedented move by the usually passive multisystem government, but the pieces fit too well. Rainhell was not the author of the plot against him, merely an agent.

He bolted to the window, carefully looking down the street. He saw robots engaging his troops. Metallic, crab-like, they skittered forward. One fell under a missile fired by a Denshi assault helo, one of the few to get airborne before the hanger was overrun. A small, slender figure, blue-sashed, hair streaming banner-like behind it, sprinted out of cover on a nearby rooftop. For a brief second he thought it a woman. It lunged into the air as the helo swung around to engage it. Their shot missed the speeding machine. It landed on the helo's side, stove in the door, and fired into the cockpit, then leapt off the falling chopper, landing among some Denshi troops. It flashed among the troops, not bothering to fire, killing them by hand in seconds. Then it raced down the street, firing a laser at other retreating Denshi. A Humanform Combat Robot, it had to be the Confederacy then; no one else had such machines. Even the Confederacy possessed only a few hundred.

I can use this to my advantage, Pard thought, *if I can escape. A Confederate plot to intervene in Olympian affairs will put me back on top, insulating House Denshi from complicity in Fenaday's murder. I'll tar the Confederacy with Rainhell's acts and the present attack. It might even give me the opening to bring Operation Overman out into the open. First though, I must survive.*

Salmot opened the door, breathing hard, his sidearm out. "Excellency, the attack on us appears to be overwhelming. They have armored fighting robots, and our defenses cannot stop them."

"Did you signal Raque to eliminate the Others?"

"Yes, my Lord," he nodded, "as you directed, but that end of the complex is under attack. Communications through the complex are under physical and cybernetic assault. The net failed before he could report back."

"There is no help for that. We must flee, old friend, while we can. Unless our attackers are fools, they have allies onworld blocking reinforcements to us."

"Army," Salmot spat.

"Among others," he agreed. "Those are Confederate cyber-forces out there. We would need a Naval Landing Battalion to even hold them."

The two men hurried into the corridor, where four of Pard's personal guard covered the area.

Salmot checked his portable computer. "Your aircar on the roof has been destroyed, and the hanger area for the helos has fallen. As near as I can tell, the underground ways are still held."

"Then there's no way out but down," Pard said. Not trusting the elevators, they headed for the stairs. Three guards took point a few meters ahead. One brought up the rear.

"Grigor," Pard ordered, "commit the reserves to an attack out of the Broad Street surface entrance. That should bring them up behind the initial attackers and give us time to escape down to the bridge. If any of the air crews are still in the air, have them attack."

The lead guard reached the stairwell door and pulled it, while the others covered the swinging door with their weapons. A deafening bang and a flash lit up the corridor. Two guards went down in pieces as the corridor lights shorted. Flechettes from the mine struck Pard, slamming into his unprotected face and hands. The incredibly tough fibers of his suit protected his body, but the impacts hurt savagely. Pard lunged backward with astonishing speed, carrying Salmot with him. The third guard slammed into the wall, body spasming under the impacts of weapon fire.

A face loomed up in the dust and smoke of the stairwell, over the bucking barrel of a heavy tri-auto.

"Rainhell," Salmot screamed. They fired at the ghostly white face. It disappeared. Another mini grenade flashed, knocking Pard and Salmot to the floor. Fortunately for Pard, their last guard stopped most of the blast. Protected by the bulk of Pard's powerful body, Salmot came up clutching a bleeding arm. Salmot snatched his weapon up and emptied it into the corridor at Rainhell's last position. Fire came back out of the smoke, pulsed energy and hot lead.

"She's out of minifrags," Salmot shouted.

"Obviously," Pard gritted.

They fled for the exterior of the building. There was no other way to the underground from where they were. They would have to chance the streets.

"Use the com," Pard said. "Call for help."

"Can't," the smaller man said. "It's smashed."

Power failed and the corridor plunged into darkness for two long seconds before the emergency lights came on. Fifty meters behind them, Rainhell raced in the low, harsh, emergency light. Both men fired. Rainhell hit the floor, sliding into a shadow, firing back. Their handguns were no match for the big weapon. They fled, firing over their shoulders, ducking in and out of doorways, running for the turn of the corridor. Pard made it first. Rainhell's tri-auto stuttered on its machinegun feature. With a yelp, Salmot slid to the ground, his eyes wild.

"Grigor!" Pard shouted. He leaned back into the corridor, spotting Rainhell at the other end, running flat out. She saw him and dove toward an office door. Pard's shots slapped the wall and her right hip as she disappeared into the room. Pard reached for Salmot to drag him into the side corridor. The tri-auto stuttered again as Rainhell fired through the thin interior walls between them. Salmot's body jerked and his eyes emptied of life. Cursing, Pard snap-fired through the holes Rainhell's big weapon blew in the wall. Rainhell jerked under the impact, but did not go down. Ballistic-proof clothing, he realized. Proof against the big bore handgun's hollow-point anyway. *Damn*, he thought, *hollow-point when I needed an AP.* Rainhell's weapon came up, and he dodged back just as she blasted the wall he'd been using for cover.

Pard turned and ran with incredible speed for someone so large. His vitality remained undimmed by injuries that would have demanded immediate attention in a standard human. He hoped to find a heavier weapon, a tri-auto or laser, but right now what he needed most was distance from his former wife.

———

Vaughn looked up as Tanaka ran into his office in the downtown HQ of Denshi. The pair had flown there hours ago to check in at the command center before heading for the dock where *Sidhe* lay. A nervous Admiral Rissi demanded a consultation about the starship. Vaughn offered to meet Rissi's aide, wanting to work on the naval liaison in person. The aide should have arrived an hour ago.

That the usually imperturbable Tanaka felt the need to run, heralded disaster.

"Pard's under attack," she announced.

For a second his mind refused to process it. *The complex under assault?* "What strength?" he snapped.

"We don't know. Communications are being jammed, and the landlines are out. Last report indicates the complex's defenses were being overwhelmed by enemy armor."

"Not a nuisance raid," he growled. "But how? Our people have every Army base under observation. They've been unusually active, but we have no report of any forces moving out."

"We must have missed some special forces," she said.

"It would take a battalion at the least," he countered.

"Oldark called in," Tanaka continued. "Someone blew up the Maglev rails. He's trying to move forces back toward the complex. They've been stopped by Army troops with heavy tanks setting roadblocks in front of his force. It will take our people hours to break through them, if they can. Alexa's people are at the airport, but they report Army pursuit ships over the base. There are no Navy fighters in sight."

An aide ran in and handed Tanaka a paper.

"Our aircraft," she read, "are either grounded by red tape, or surrounded by Army troops. Our communications are under attack everywhere."

Vaughn strode out into the command center, similar to the Combat Information Center of a major warship. The main scanner map showed the distribution of Denshi forces worldwide. A glance told him many of the channels had failed.

"We underestimated the Army," he said, as if to himself. "Dominici's been planning this for a while. She must have moved her most loyal forces off the bases a fraction at a time. The less reliable ones are in the bases, and she is pulling them out now. Well, our people will raise some hell with them there.

"Contact Navy HQ for me," he said, with apparent calm, "I need to speak to Pourlos as well."

"He's on Channel D, sir," replied the tech. "Putting him through."

"Pourlos here."

"What's the situation?"

"We still have the *Sidhe* surrounded by our people and Navy troops. I don't know how long we can contain them. She began broadcasting in the clear again about fifteen minutes ago, claiming that Denshi or the Navy planted the bomb. They are demanding Army and Confed troops to protect them from the Navy and us. We intercepted a communication between Ambassador Davis and General Dominici. She's sending heavy armor, along with a contingent of embassy marines, to the ship.

"We are taking some small arms fire from the ship. I've pulled back. We can fight our way into her, but we will have the Army closing in from behind if we do."

"Do we oppose them?" Pourlos demanded. "We can hold them for a couple of hours at least. We can blow up the vessel if need be."

"Sir," Tanaka interrupted, "Geneticist Hagen is on the Black Channel. They have Army troops appearing around their offices."

"Hold on, Pourlos," Vaughn said. He pulled up the Black Channel on the main viewer. Hagen appeared, his face sweaty and frightened. "Vaughn, this is Hagen. I cannot reach Pard, and there is firing down at the Starship. It looks like the Army is making its move. I cannot reach Navy HQ. They tell me Admiral Rissi is unavailable."

"Damn," Vaughn said. Their biggest ally in the Navy, either incapacitated or waiting to see what developed.

"I've got Army troops approaching. Looks like military police and light armor. All I have here are uniformed security, proctors, and some police."

"Dominici wouldn't dare," said a stunned Vaughn. The geneticist's labs were the closest place to a holy site on Olympia, built by Allessandro himself.

"We dare not risk their entry," Hagen said. "If they seize our files, it will be prison or worse for all of us. If I have to destroy them, we lose much of our political power. Vaughn, I need Denshi or Navy troops fast."

Vaughn bit his lip in thought. Everything certain had turned insecure, with the Navy unreliable in the face of a suddenly aggressive Army. Dominici led them to believe she was ineffective, dissipate, and it worked. Pard might be dead or wounded. It all fell to Vaughn in the command center. He could not get troops to Pard for several hours at best. The battle there would be over one way or the other by then.

It dawned on him that with Antebei dead and Pard's fate unknown, he might need to consider a universe without the leader of the Engineered. None of the others would destabilize the counsel by supporting another member for Pard's position. They hated and distrusted each other too much for that. Their only common interest lay in him. He needed to consider the future. What could be saved? What would Pard do?

"Minister Hagen," he said firmly, "do not destroy the files. Denshi and Navy troops with armor will be arriving shortly."

"Excellent, excellent," Hagen said, visibly relieved. "This will not be forgotten, Vaughn." He switched off.

"Pourlos," he called. The man's face popped onto the screen. "You heard?"

"Yes, sir," Pourlos responded without hesitation. It seemed he felt the new wind blowing as well.

"Pull your people off the *Sidhe*. Leave a small rear guard to hold there. Arrange it so they do not know you have left. Take all your troops and equipment to Hagen's offices. If the Army tries to enter, fight." Pourlos nodded and disappeared.

Tanaka looked at him, incredulous. "Armor? Pourlos has a few small-arms proof police cars and four twenty-ton armored personnel carriers. All the real armor is with Oldark."

"It will have to do." Vaughn shrugged.

Vaughn turned to the communication staff, all of whom stared back at him with expressions varying from concern to outright fear. "Get word any way you can to our Army infiltrators," he snapped. "They are to sabotage anything they can reach and slow the Army down.

"Call Oldark, Alexa, and the others," he continued. "Have them break contact with the Army and move whatever forces they can to

Pard's complex as soon as possible. Evade and infiltrate. Do not fight if possible.

"Keep trying to reach the complex and to raise the Navy Command. We need Navy fighters and Navy troops and we need them fast."

A loud boom from the ground floor made the building shudder. Vaughn drew his pistol. "I will be downstairs. Tanaka, you are with me."

Chapter Seventeen

F enaday moved warily onto the skybridge. An exposed position, but he could see no other way across. Schiller brought up the rear, his carbine hunting for targets. Risky padded along between them, his weapon-resistant dog blanket scorched by a near miss. The K-9 showed no ill effect from the hit.

Several bridges in this section of the complex joined buildings at different heights. No trace of dawn could be seen in the east, and the warmly lit skyways contrasted with the deep blue-black of the sky. Even the crescent moon was hidden now, gone behind gathering storm clouds. He saw flashes, the flickering of flames as Mmok's forces battled the Denshi. The skyway insulation blocked the sound of battle.

Desert grit sifted off his boots as he stalked forward. Blood from small cuts he didn't remember getting slowly slid down his chin. *It feels unreal*, he thought. *We're figures of slaughter invading the quiet sanity of an office building.*

Risky barked suddenly. Fenaday half-turned to see the dog leaping and pushing against the glass to their right. On the skybridge above, fifty meters away, a huge man ran by. He moved so fast, he was gone almost before they saw him. Fenaday snapped his carbine up. "Pard," he snarled.

Another sight stopped him before he could get off a shot. A woman flashed into view, running hard. Tall, lithe, with an ivory-white face, her black hair trailed behind her.

"Shasti," Fenaday yelled. He ran, waving his arms. Risky barked furiously, almost somersaulting in his excitement. Fenaday yelled Shasti's name, banging his rifle on the glass, but she disappeared, intent on her quarry.

"Look out," Schiller screamed.

Fenaday snapped back to the here and now, throwing himself backward in a reverse roll. Glass exploded as the hall filled with weapon fire. Five Denshi blasted away from the far end of the skyway. They appeared suddenly, evidently not expecting to find anyone, or perhaps attracted by the barking, thinking it might be one of their own K-9s.

Schiller's carbine triggered on full auto as a particle weapon hit him. His body went over backward, but the burst of full auto fire struck several Denshi. One fell. Armor saved the other two, but the impacts knocked them into their fellows, fouling their aim. Fenaday rolled out flat in the prone position as Risky raced past him. The charging dog took a snap burst and fell, yelping.

Fenaday emptied his carbine into the packed guards at the end of the narrow skybridge. Two more fell, one clearly dead. The others dodged, firing back wildly and trying to drag the wounded into cover. Fenaday dropped the empty carbine, snatching for his heavy laser pistol as shots cracked around him. He drew it and fired. A wounded guard went down, his faceplate burned through. Another beat at flaming clothes.

Fenaday's laser touched off the sprinkler at the far end. Water flooded down. Laser light flashed the sprinkler water into steam, giving him some cover. The guards flinched from the laser's searching beam. Return fire came at him wild and high. A bullet creased his arm. Another glanced off his back armor. He played the laser like a fire hose, flashing it around at any face that showed. Meant for bursts, the Martini laser quickly grew hot in his hand, its charge depleting. Fenaday snatched up Schiller's weapon with his free hand, emptying both magazine and capacitor at the far end.

Inspiration struck. A frag grenade would kill him and Risky, but a smoke grenade... He pulled one and tossed. The guards ducked the thrown grenade, giving him precious seconds for the hissing device to emit dense black vapor.

"Come on, boys," he yelled in the smoke and vapor-filled skyway, hoping to fool the guards into thinking reinforcements had arrived.

"YAAHHHH," he screamed, crawling fast for the far end. *Let 'em think there's a bunch of us running upright,* he prayed. Risky barked encouragement, struggling forward on three good legs. Shots came out of the water and smoke. Again, too high. Then the guards broke, retreating from the end of the skyway into the left side corridor. They continued firing through the sprinkler water. It slicked the floor as they retreated.

Fenaday booted one of their dead men into the corridor. The corpse jerked under bullet strikes. He yanked a fragmentation grenade off his belt and lobbed it down the corridor, then pulled Risky back into the skyway with him. The blast blew out windows on the outside of the building, taking out the lights in the corridor. Under the cover of the dust and blast, he threw his last grenade, going for distance. The skyway rocked again. Fenaday reloaded his carbine and leaned into the hall. At the far end, under emergency lights, he saw one man running away, helping a wounded comrade.

"Keep after them," Fenaday yelled to his imaginary troops, firing short bursts from his carbine. The guards disappeared.

He ran back to Schiller. The young K-9 handler lay dead, eyes empty and accusing.

"Damn it," Fenaday sank to his knees. His ears rang from the explosions and shots, and weariness dragged at his limbs. "Damn it all." He turned to Risky next. The dog limped over to him, his armored blanket scorched and torn. At close range it couldn't stop all the weapon fire. Fenaday put field dressings on the worst wounds using trauma tabs from the dog's own aid kit. He took the shepherd's head in his hands. Brown eyes looked back at him, containing an intelligence not human, but more than animal.

"I have to go, Fella. You're hurt. Go find Rask. Understand? Find Rask and stay with him."

The dog whined in disagreement. Fenaday repeated his instructions, pointing back the way they had come. Risky limped back across the skyway.

Realizing he'd used up most of his ammunition, Fenaday pulled extra clips off Schiller's body. Re-armed, he ran out of the skyway and headed right. It took him away from the direction the guards had fled and toward where he last saw Shasti. Fenaday moved as quickly as he dared. His leather jacket shed most of the water, but his clothes under the body armor were soaked with water and sweat. The building's air-conditioning struck a chill into him.

Fenaday padded along, trying to look in all directions at once. As he passed one door, it opened. Snapping around, he loosed a shot. A young girl, not long out of her teens, screamed. The bullet from the carbine missed, but the particle beam nicked her side. She grabbed at the wound and froze. Her perfectly engineered features looking at him in sheer terror.

"Hide, damn it," he snarled at her

With a sob, the girl slammed the door.

Great, he thought, *now I'm shooting kids.* Fenaday started running. He reached the windows and looked out over the compound. A flash of movement caught his eye. Shasti, heading out of the burning main gate. He lost her as she left the pool of firelight. Fenaday sped down the stairs, throwing away caution. At the bottom, he kicked open the door. Sounds and smells from the battle awaited him on the other side. A blast pelted the area with debris. Dust and bits of paper debris swirled around him. He ducked back into the building, then dashed out, running low, bent almost double. When he reached the next bit of cover, he tried the mike. "Mmok," he rasped, "Mmok, come in." He got only splutter and crackle, a gabble of encrypted speech.

Hell, he thought, *either the frequency is overloaded, someone is jamming it, or both.* He wondered if they were unlucky enough to be using the same frequency as Pard's troops. In any event, he could get no help. Jamming would not affect Mmok's telemetric control of the robots, but he had no way to break into that secure circuit.

He got up, starting out low, and ran about a hundred meters. Then firing broke out in front of him. Fenaday hit the dirt and rolled. Nothing struck near him. *They're shooting at somebody else,* he realized, feeling momentarily weak with relief. He fast-crawled on his belly until he could see into the plaza ahead. The terrace he lay on extended over a broad building front, lined with columns. A squad of Pard's troops had caught some of Rask's troops on the street. The ASATs were in the open with only a burning aircar to hide behind. As he watched, one ASAT dropped and his teammates dragged him back into cover.

Damn, if he ran off after Shasti, they wouldn't last a minute. He battled with himself for a second, then Schiller's face came back to him. Fenaday cut right, until he reached a raised section of terrace behind Pard's troops. Return fire would sweep him away easily, but he had no other choice. He lay prone, switching the selector to full auto to alternate mini-grenades, particle beam, and depleted uranium slugs. Wishing for some more real grenades, he sighted in on the farthest man, squeezing off a burst. The Olympian dropped. His rear armor couldn't handle the hammering at close range. Mini-grenades sprayed the others with shrapnel, causing more panic than harm as fragments rattled off their armor. Fenaday dropped another man before the Denshi located him.

Pard's troops snapped around. Fenaday hit another man. This one did not go down, armor or luck. The carbine clicked empty: mini-frags gone, capacitor and magazine empty. *I'm dead*, he thought numbly. *I hope it doesn't hurt.*

Return fire blazed around the prone Fenaday. Shots spalled the marble he lay on and chips cut him through gaps in his armor. A mini-frag banged off over him. It felt like a gorilla bouncing off his back. With a scream, he rolled, frantically grabbing for his laser. Again he fired in a flashing, wasteful arc. Not deadly, but enough to make men flinch and spoil their aim. Below, the ASATs saw Pard's troops lit by the sweep of the laser. The ASATs poured fire up on the Denshi. Most fell, others fled into the interior of the building. The ASATs made the bottom of the stairway, continuing their duel with the Denshi in the building.

They can fend for themselves now, Fenaday thought, amazed at still being alive. *I'm after Shasti.* Fenaday ran back toward the gate, reaching for his last clip only to find it gone. He slung the empty carbine, running on armed with only a laser and his long Scottish dirk. The palm tingler in his laser pulsed, warning him of depletion. Maybe two or three short bursts left.

Reaching the gate, Fenaday quickly checked the bodies, civilians mostly. The few dead soldiers' weapons lay either empty or smashed. No help there.

Here I am, he thought, *running from an inferno, out of ammo, alone, in the dark, chasing a crazed superwoman and a deadly superman. This simply sucks.*

Loosening his Scottish dagger in its sheath, he settled into his best running pace. It wasn't very fast. He stayed on the main road, chugging along past scrubby brush and small twisted trees. His breath rasped, and his ribs grew sore. Ships' captains did not get much chance for marathons. He did not know if Pard and Shasti fled on the main road. If they went cross-country, he'd never find them. He was no tracker. Fenaday reasoned that Pard's best chance lay in getting over the bridge spanning the gorge. Reinforcements and escape lay that way.

After two miles he stopped, fighting the desire to retch. *More time in the gym,* he promised himself, *if I live.* Pushing forward into a trot, Fenaday dropped most of his equipment, including the empty carbine. He took a mouthful of water from the canteen, then left it by a large gray boulder.

The eastern sky ahead began to lighten. A winter storm filled the sky with clouds. Thunder rumbled. Fenaday threw away the heavy helmet with its night vision equipment. He kept only the short-range talker, his knife, laser, and aid kit. He struggled on for another two miles before realizing he needed to drop the body armor. Shasti ran like a gazelle. Pard was either no slower; or had quite a lead since Fenaday had not caught up to them. Fenaday shrugged off the heavy body armor, even his leather jacket. *A stern chase is a long chase,* he thought grimly, flogging himself back into a run.

I've got to find her, he prayed. *I've got to. If you're out there, if anyone is out there, I'll trade you anything just to find her alive.* He'd made the same desperate plea the night the young lieutenant arrived to tell him Lisa was lost. No one answered then either.

Fenaday thought about the aerial maps he'd studied. Mountains to the left confirmed he was still on the main road. The ravine ran north to south in a curve. Pard would not double back as Fenaday's force had attacked out of the mountains to the west. They had to be on this eastern road.

As if in answer to his thoughts, firing broke out ahead. Fatigue forgotten, his legs lengthened into a flat run.

———

P ard loped on. Even at his age, he could outrun the fittest standard human male. His pursuer was not such; she was Engineered, younger, fitter, closer to perfection. At some point, he needed to make a stand. With luck, he might make the bridge before she caught up with him. Most of the troops there would have raced back to the compound when the attack began. A few would remain on the bridge to defend it or, if needs be, explode it.

He knew she'd trailed him out of the camp. Her lithe body made her the better runner, but she hadn't overtaken him. He must have hit her. Pard alternated AP's and hollow points in his personal sidearm. The hollow point squash-heads would not penetrate her body armor. Still, the smash of one would disable most men. She was not a man; she was Unknown-Generation Engineered. Her body recovered amazingly fast. With luck, one of the APs might have cut through. Whichever struck her, clearly it had done some damage.

Cresting the last hill before the gorge, Pard stopped in dismay. The gate post was shot up, part of it burning. He could see bodies scattered at the bottom of the hillside. One of the robots must have cut them down as they raced back to defend the compound. Pard hurried on. The men were beyond help, chewed to pieces by medium-caliber weapons. One of the guard's weapons looked usable. He scooped it up gratefully, heading for the bridge.

A shot slapped the reddish soil next to him. In a trained response, he dropped like a man shot, then lunged under the cover of the smoke, diving into the burning structure before she could retarget him. *Stupid,* he thought. *Both of us. Me, for stopping beyond cover; you for a hasty long-range shot.* To the master assassin's trained mind, the shot spoke volumes. It expressed desperate rage. Had she waited, she could have caught him out on the bridge. Not the cool, killing skill of an assassin at all. She'd be no closer than the last hillcrest, five hundred meters away. Too far for laser or particle beams. She must be low on ammunition to fire only a single shot.

So, he thought, *wounded and alone, low on ammunition, you chase me. Ah, Rainhell, did I train you no better than this? Perhaps you were never more than a bed toy after all.*

Pard moved deeper into the damaged building. He could not chance the bridge with her above him. He'd have to run five hundred meters under her gun. She would not miss a steady, aimed shot over such a distance.

A sensible person would stay on the hill, under cover, keeping him in check, unable to go forward or backward. Make it a question of whose reinforcements arrived first, Denshi's or hers. She would not, he judged. She would come to him because she dared not take the risk Denshi would arrive first. She wanted to kill him herself, so she would close, sacrificing her advantage. *Fool,* he thought. *Assassins kill without passion and flee when they miss.*

Casting about in the wrecked building, he searched for a vantage on the hillside, hoping to hit her as she came on. The back of the guardhouse did not offer a good view. It did not face the hillside squarely. He could not use the burning section, and smoke hung heavily on the hillside, eroding his view further. At best he might get a deflection shot. He set up by a shattered window and checked his weapon. One mini-frag. Damn.

Even expecting her, he failed to anticipate the tigery rush she made from cover she'd somehow reached unseen. The tri-auto bucked in his hand, particles, the mini-grenade and bullets hit just behind her. Pard cursed as the weapon's battery pack hissed. The particle beam began to sputter. He ejected the magazine, six rounds of caseless 5mm left. He'd shot off the two clips for his sidearm earlier. Her long shot had done her some good. He lacked the time to either field strip the weapon or check other bodies for ammunition or power packs. *Bitch,* he thought, *she is going to make today one of those days.*

Warily, he moved back, leaning into the smoke-filled corridor, searching. She must be inside by now. A fearsome smile lit his face. It had been years since he faced a worthy opponent face-to-face. Suddenly she appeared at the far end. A beam snapped by his ear. He returned the favor from a diving roll. More fire broke out as their beams hit flammable material.

Pard dropped to his belly behind a metal desk at a T-intersection. There was less smoke and better air. He saw her booted leg in an eddy of clear air and cut loose with the particle beam, playing it like a hose. A cry rewarded him. The sputtering particle weapon cut out. Shasti did not fall, leaping instead to disappear into the smoke again.

One for me, he thought, *if only a hot foot. It must have hurt.* She didn't get a return shot off. He switched positions, starting to move down the corridor just as a burning drapery behind him flared up. It silhouetted him as he lunged toward the nearest office door. An AP round slammed into his side. Body armor and the angle diminished the blow but could not stop the round from penetrating. It dug a gouge an inch wide, six inches long on his ribs.

"One for you," he muttered, shrugging off the pain. Blood loss he could not dismiss so easily. It poured down his side. Unlike Rainhell, his generation of Engineered lacked built-in bio-medical self-repair. *We were built big and tough,* he thought, *and I am the biggest and toughest of all.* He tore strips from his jacket, then stomped through the wall into the adjacent room, gaining distance and time to bind his wound.

More smoke billowed as the fire spread. Pard opened a window and stepped out, rifle in front of him, intending to circle the building and flank her.

He came out on the bridge side. A breeze played here by the canyon. Immediately to his right, the road split to go around the white outpost building that looked directly across the bridge. *Sun must be up,* he thought, *light's still bad though.* He heard a rumble of thunder and spared a glance for the clouds.

Pard crept down the side of the building, crouching as he passed under the windows. A loud bang sounded behind him as something inside blew. Glass shattered over his head as Shasti Rainhell leapt out the window, choking on smoke, landing square on his back. It was the last thing either expected. She fell heavily on him, sending them both sprawling. His weapon flew out of his hand. She hit the ground on her back. Quick as a cat, she jumped up. Only slightly slower, Pard surged to his feet. With a roar he smashed the tri-auto out of her hands with a backfist. The weapon discharged, spalling the wall behind him. Chips cut them both. He lunged forward to grapple. Rainhell, her beautiful ivory face twisted, green eyes blazing, stomped a foot in his sternum, grabbed his jacket and, dropping backward, threw him over her head. He hit heavily. They both scrambled to their feet and lunged for each other. They flashed in and out, trading kicks and blows. Rainhell drew a long-bladed knife and waded in. He blocked, took a cut to the arm, but got a grip on her wrist. Her knife spun away into the canyon.

They squared off a pace apart. Shasti, so big among regular humans, looked slender and fragile next to him.

"Bastard," she spat. "You low-life *bastard.*"

"All this way to tell me that," he taunted. "My little Shasti, have you never grown up?"

She screamed and plunged in, hands flashing. Pard smiled and leaned into her. Mass still counted. He had twice hers.

Rainhell spotted the bandage on his ribs and slammed a roundhouse kick in. He feigned a stagger and caught her in the face with a fist. The blow rocked her. He followed up, putting her on the defensive. His huge foot booted her midsection and doubled her over. With one hand he reached under, lifted her, and flung her into the bridge abutment.

———

Fenaday raced through the smoke and around the building. He saw Shasti. Pard stood over her, slamming her head against the bridge.

"Paaaaaarrd," Fenaday screamed, rushing down on him. The giant ceased battering Shasti's head against the railing, whirling to face him. Fenaday snapped off two shots. The first hit Pard's shoulder, making him drop Shasti. She sprawled face down on the gravel road, unconscious or dead. Pard dodged the second shot. Fenaday's laser sputtered on the third shot. The beam, too weak to cut through Pard's vest, still caught it on fire. The big man backed against the railing, batting at the flames. Fenaday flung the pistol at Pard's head, tucked into a forward roll, and lunged into Pard's belly, dirk in hand. The impact rocked Pard back against the bridge railing. He lost his balance. Fenaday slashed wildly with the knife, connecting in Pard's gut. He shoved until he felt like his back was breaking.

As Pard toppled over the rail, his hand snapped down on Fenaday's neck, pulling him up and over.

Fenaday desperately grappled with Pard as the genetic superman's hands found purchase in a girder. They stopped with a neck-breaking jerk. The dagger came out of Fenaday's hands as he clawed for handfuls of Pard's clothes. He pulled himself upward on the giant's back, wrapping his legs around the barrel of Pard's chest. The huge Engineered's head snapped backward. Fenaday leaned aside. Pard's fist crashed down on Fenaday's thigh, and the feeling left his leg. Fenaday reached around with both hands, gouging both of Pard's eyes. Pard screamed.

Fenaday grinned in savage satisfaction. But victory was short-lived. From inside his vest, Pard produced a small knife. He reached behind him, the blade pointed downward in his huge hand, and slammed the small blade into Fenaday's back. Fenaday's breath left in an agonized gasp. Pard still hung by his right arm, his face a gory mask. He pulled the blade out for another stab. Fenaday reared back, the wild smile of the Irish, seen in many a losing battle, on his face. He slammed blows into Pard's right elbow. The joint gave a wooden crack, and Pard howled. The Olympian dropped the knife, gripping the girder with his left hand, as Fenaday, shrieking like a madman, struck the right elbow again, snapping it.

Pard turned his head. "Fenaday," he spat out. "Wait. We can work out a deal."

Fenaday felt the strength draining from his legs as icy agony spread from the stab wound. In seconds he would fall, and Pard would be free.

Fenaday laughed wildly. "Work this out, you genetic freak." He slammed at Pard's remaining elbow as Pard bucked furiously, trying to unseat him.

"Shasti," he screamed, crying out her name with each blow to Pard's elbow. His legs failed him. He clung to Pard's neck, hoisting himself higher to hit the elbow. Pard cried out as the elbow broke and his weight tore at the fractured joint. Fenaday felt something seize his hair. Instinctively, he reached up, loosening his grip on Pard. The Olympian's hold failed. With a deep shout of despair, Pard plunged to the bottom of the gorge a hundred meters below.

His eyes blinded by tears, Fenaday felt himself hauled upward. Reaching the top railing, he grasped it like a lover. Shasti still had hold of him, but her strength failed her. She fell to the pavement, her back sliding down the metal side of the bridge. With the last of his own strength, Fenaday pulled himself over the railing, dropping onto the ground near her. Darkness rushed in on him.

Sometime later, Fenaday's eyes opened. Breath came in ragged gasps. It felt as if the knife was still in his back, ice cold and deep. Tears flowing down his face, he reached for his aid kit. Numb fingers struggled with the catches. The universe narrowed to his battle with the latch. Finally, it sprang open, and he fumbled out a combat trauma tab. He reached behind his back, almost passing out again from the pain. He got the tab as close as he could to the wound, triggering it. He hoped the plastic bandage would cover the knife wound. In seconds, the unutterable relief of painkiller spread through him. He fought the lassitude brought on by the relief. *Shasti,* he thought. He raised his head. She lay against the railing like a rag doll. He could not feel his legs or get them under him. He crawled. Blood covered her face. Her eyes were unfocused, but she smiled. She turned her face to him as he called her name. "Pard's dead," she said happily. "He's dead."

"Are you badly hurt?" he gasped, crawling toward her.

"Pard's dead," she repeated, as if he'd missed something terribly important. Fenaday reached her and pressed a trauma tab on a fractured rib. The device hissed open, its bandage covering where splintered bone showed through.

"We have to get up," he said. "My radio's gone. No one knows we're here. We've got to get to our feet."

She shook her head slowly, as the drugs took over. "Can't," she whispered, "can't see. Doesn't matter, Pard's dead."

"You be the feet," he insisted. "I'm your eyes."

She smiled through the blood. "Can't," she repeated, as her fingers fumbled up to touch his face. "I'm sorry, Robert, sorry."

"Up," he insisted. Shasti sighed and blindly reached hands toward him. They struggled to rise for a few seconds, then slumped back to the ground.

"Sorry," she said, tears leaking down her blood-covered face.

"It's okay," he choked out. "We'll rest here for a few minutes. Then we'll try again."

"I think," she said, her voice soft, but clear, "we will rest here for longer than that."

The will drained out of Fenaday, replaced with a desperate fatigue. "Yes," he replied softly.

"Kiss me goodbye, Robert," she said.

Fenaday raised his head and kissed her softly on the lips. His head fell forward on her chest and his eyes closed. Shasti put an arm around him, as if to hold him close, then her head slumped to her chest.

A cold rain began to fall.

Chapter Eighteen

Telisan stared anxiously from the cockpit of the *Pooka*. He'd fought his way out of the net around the star-frigate after most of the Denshi troops pulled out. Now *Sidhe's* two shuttles flew just over the treetops, drawing occasional small-arms fire, steering an erratic course from the seacoast to the plateau holding Pard's base.

"Look," Karass demanded. Telisan's head snapped up as the *Dakota* class shuttle cleared the first small range of the mountains. In the distance, columns of smoke rose from the high plateau where the Denshi compound sat. Smoke mixed with the low clouds of the rainstorm. In the middle distance a gorge bisected the plateau, leering up at them like a sick smile.

Their companion ship, the *Duna*, kept station to their left as they moved in. Behind the shuttles the sun rose, but the land below remained in shadow. They flew over the wrecked Maglev line and the burning guard station by the bridge. Flames lit the towers of the complex ahead. They could see the winking of weapons fire. No Denshi aircraft could be seen; still the turrets of the *Pooka* were manned. Navy fighters might appear at any moment.

Telisan had all the remaining reliables of the *Sidhe* crew with him, people who owed either him or Fenaday a debt of loyalty:

Sharla, Mennolly Fitzgerald, Wardell, Carlos Perez and some of his "black gang" and Dobera, the Frokossi princeling who owed Fenaday his life. The lizard-like being sat with them in the cockpit; his jeweled scales eerily reflected the greenish light of the instrument panel. Frokossi eyes were very effective in low light or underground. A set of day goggles hung around his thin neck. On his belt hung a small ornate but serviceable laser, a relic of his years as prince before hard luck made him a ship's quartermaster.

Telisan turned to Perez at the communication station. "Anything on radio?"

The engineer shook his head. "There is still a big jammer screwing reception. I get snatches of conversation. I'm sure I heard Mmok for a second. He should be signaling for a pickup."

The Denlenn curbed his impatience. "Keep broadcasting the IFF signal. I don't want the cyber-forces and ground troops firing on us by mistake."

The Intruder, Telisan thought, *with Fury at the controls, should be moving in. Where is it?* Navy and Denshi reinforcements would be escaping or breaking the Army net. Fenaday never intended to hold the complex. Dominici's forces would do that when they arrived. Telisan wanted to recover *Sidhe's* forces and get back to the ship under Army protection, before the dust settled.

They went into hover over the complex, their guns seeking targets.

"I have the *Intruder* on scan," Karass announced. "She was behind a tower."

Mmok's voice sounded suddenly in their speakers, "Gold to Blue, the LZ is hot. Resistance has been contained, but is not ended. Land in section 23A. We are holding that area and have our casualties there."

"Affirmative, Gold," Telisan said. "This is Blue. Where is Scarlet?" he asked, using Fenaday's code designator.

"Scarlet is MIA, last seen in Sector Forty, which is not secure. Blue, we have a reported sighting of Stormcloud, also in Sector Forty."

"Rainhell," Dobera said, recognizing the code for Shasti. His eyelids snapped open and closed with agitation.

"Yes," Telisan agreed, with an excited glance at Sharla.

"But both are unaccounted for," Sharla cautioned.

"We must find Fenaday," Dobera said. There was no sibilant hiss to his high thin speech despite the forked tongue whipping the air. "He would have gone after Rainhell."

"Yes." Telisan nodded. "Sheehan, are you reading?"

"Affirmative," replied the command pilot for the *Duna*.

"Set down in the sector Mmok holds. Your medical teams can deal with the casualties. We will hack into the computers and search for information to discredit these Denshi. Karass, I'll need you to join me as we search for Fenaday and Rainhell.

"Mmok, do you have any information on Pard?"

"No confirmation on the kill yet. He was also spotted in Sector Forty. We were going after him when a counterattack hit. We've had to contain it. They pulled out some choppers from an underground hanger, gave us a bad time. Fortunately, the *Intruder* showed up.

"If we are going to do a fighting withdrawal," Mmok continued, "I need time. We'll have to fall back carefully. There are still a shit-load of these assholes underground and in bunkers. This place is a fucking warren."

"We have to find Scarlet and Stormcloud," Telisan snapped, "so we will need time anyway. Keep their heads down and minimize the threat to our troops."

"Blue, I am not going to sit here taking fire for that planet-raper and his girlfriend."

"Silence," Telisan ordered with a force that carried even over radio. "You have your orders. I will advise you when to withdraw. I need time. Buy it for me."

"Affirmative," Mmok said, bitterness audible in his voice. "We'll try not to get killed while you are looking."

"Please do that," the Denlenn replied earnestly, ignoring the sarcasm.

"We are coming in," Karass called, his face intent as he peered out of the now rain slicked canopy. "I see ASATs and LEAFs, the *Intruder* and I have a ground guide. Landing now."

The shuttles hit the ground, back to back, turrets searching for targets. Rear ramps went down, and the crews spilled out, forming up on Telisan. Mourner and Arpen led their teams to where the assault-troop casualties and medics huddled under the overhang of an office tower. A surprisingly cold, fine rain came down on them. Telisan shivered and sealed his flight jacket, looking up anxiously at the flaming office towers. If one should fall...

He shook off the thought and waved for the others to follow him. He left the evacuation to Doctor Mourner. Telisan's party sought two things: their friends and information.

Consulting a portable comp with the complex's map on it, Telisan led the others from cover to cover, heading for Sector Forty. He heard firing in the distance and cursed the shortness of time. They ran steadily toward the Denshi's computer complex. A few scattered office workers wandered about in a daze, these fled upon seeing the party from the *Sidhe*. They made progress slowly as the towers rained debris on them. Paper and ash filled the air, swirling like malign snowflakes.

"We must split up for now," Telisan ordered, goaded by their slow pace. "Sharla, take Perez and his people. Check Section Thirty-Nine B and Forty A. Look for any sign of Fenaday, Pard, or Rainhell, then proceed to the computer building. Pick up any of *Sidhe's* Landing Force you come across. Dobera and Karass, come with me. We will check out the tunnels under the main building." The section he'd ordered Sharla to should be relatively safe, cleared and held by a few of the robots and *Sidhe* troops. It freed Rask's ASATs and the bulk of the cyber-force to continue the fight with the Denshi troops.

Sharla nodded and waved at her people. As they moved off, Telisan felt an intense relief. The tunnels would be dangerous work. He feared Sharla would argue with him, but her Navy discipline held.

The Denlenn turned, leading the reptilian and the stocky human to the entrance to Pard's own tower. From there they could enter the underground passages to the transport building and another building Telisan had been unable to find any information on, even in Dominici's files. Telisan figured it for a lab of some sort.

They opened a stairwell door. Telisan craned his head upward. A fire burned fitfully on the floors above, despite the sprinkler system. Water flowed and splashed in the shaftway and it smelled of soot and ash. It reminded him with sudden force of the underground city of Barjan on Enshar.

"This should lead to the main tunnel." Telisan gestured with his laser. The way below appeared undefended, save by the dead. Main Tunnel looked intact but damaged, with doors blown in and lighting panels shattered. Blood-red emergency lights glowed balefully. They entered each room, checking the bodies, hoping not to find familiar faces looking back at them.

Telisan, Dobera, and Karass moved down the sparking corridor, one advancing while the others covered. A visor concealed Telisan's eyes, which would otherwise reflect light like a cat's, a distinct disadvantage in a night battle. Dobera's huge eyes swiveled independently, disconcerting but useful. Karass with the triple-auto brought up the rear. Telisan, the best shot of the group, led.

The passage smelled of scorched flesh and smoke, a nauseating combination even to the Denlenn with his inferior sense of smell. He looked at the Frokossi, scenting through his delicate tongue, wondering how he could stand it. They passed bodies: Denshi, some civilians, an ASAT from Rask's force lying across disabled Crab robot.

The ASAT carried no ID, so Telisan could not take her dog tag. He gently rolled the dead woman onto her back and composed her arms as if for sleep. Karass handed him a jacket hung on a nearby chair, and Telisan covered the young woman's face. He barely knew the trooper, only enough to recognize her, but it sat ill with him to leave her cold and alone in the dark. Mentally, he logged where they'd left the body in case a chance arose for recovery. *She had a family,* he thought. *She must have mattered to someone.*

"We've got to go," Karass said. "Olympian forces from both sides will arrive soon."

"Yes." Telisan stood. "I want to be well enroute back to *Sidhe* and Army protection before then. We must find Robert and Shasti. Pard is either dead, or has escaped by now. That part of the mission is done. Only survival and escape remain."

As the spacers started forward, two figures darted into the far end of the corridor. Even in the poor irregular light, something seemed wrong about them, about the way they moved. The first jerked to a stop as it spotted them, whipping up an arm and firing a particle beam. The weapon's surging light signature added its own strobing effect to the shattered light fixtures. The beam hit the wall next to Dobera as the Frokossi dove to the floor. Telisan's fighter pilot reflexes made his arm a blur. His laser flicked out, lancing the tall figure in the head. It fell bonelessly. The other figure, evidently unarmed, emitted an undulating wail and dropped next to the first.

"Don't fire," Telisan ordered. Karass and Dobera covered him as he advanced, laser leveled. The flickering light in the corridor suddenly stabilized. The Denlenn froze in cold shock, staring down at the pair.

Aliens. A new species, unlike anything he knew of. The creatures wore what looked like ornate overalls. Each had three arms, though they looked more like tentacles. Small hands with opposable thumbs hung at the end of two of the arms. The shorter but thicker third tentacle hung from the middle of the chest. Their heads held large brain cases over short muzzle-like noses. The smaller being raised its three arms, squatting on two legs and its slender tail, in a gesture that looked like surrender. Telisan kept his laser level as he looked into a pair of diamond-shaped eyes, black from lid to lid, set in a face covered with short, tan fur. The one on the floor was larger, darker, and obviously dead.

"Don't shoot. No shoot," the smaller alien said in a breathy voice. Its tentacle hands waved slowly, placatingly, as if in a breeze.

Dobera and Karass joined Telisan. He could not read the Frokossi's expression; the human's mirrored his own dismay.

"A new race," Dobera whispered, in his high thin voice. "Gods, not again."

Telisan shared the feeling. The Conchirri changed everyone's view of the night sky when they charged, insensate and ferocious, out of the unknown stars. Millions of deaths followed in years of war before the Xenophobes could be exterminated. The Seven now dreaded the discovery of the inevitable Ninth species. That day had arrived.

Now Telisan knew where the armaments and manpower of Denshi had gone and why Mandela was so insanely desperate to kill

Pard. News of a "First Contact" would have raced through all known space at courier speed. It hadn't. The presence of these aliens, hidden in the complex, could only mean the Olympians planned an alliance with them. The stakes were suddenly galactic in scale.

The alien ceased waving its frond-like arms and spoke from its muzzle-like mouth. "This one dead. This one," it gestured at itself with all three boneless arms, "this one surrenders. Do not kill, have much information. Will trade."

"Karass," Telisan said, recovering. "Do you have restraints on you?"

"Yes, sir."

"Bind its arms…somehow. Then cover it with a blanket or jacket. You and Dobera take this being back to the shuttles. Go back to *Sidhe* and put it into the iso-lab. Only Arpen is to see it. She will be preparing to head back with the wounded. No one but our people must see you."

"We've got to tell the Confederacy!" Karass sputtered. "It's a new species. If they have ships, nuclear weapons—"

"We will," Telisan said, "in due course. We need cards now, as you humans say. I am going to meet Sharla and her team in the computer complex."

"What of the captain?" Dobera demanded.

"He may be there as well as anywhere. We will try and locate him from there. Now move."

Plagued with new terrors, Telisan watched as the human and Frokossi escorted the alien out the way they had come. He drew himself up and headed on, his plans to explore the underground temporarily abandoned. Looking around carefully for Denshi troops, he headed back to the surface, guided by his pocket comp. When he reached the surface, he spotted Cobalt and two of the Crab robots.

"Cobalt," he called, "report to me."

The machine raced over to him. "We are moving to flank a large force of Denshi, pinned underground," it said in its detached machine voice. "Controller Mmok has ordered the cyber-force to collapse the tunnels out of the area to restrict Denshi movements.

All live troops are moving back inside a perimeter centering on the shuttles."

"Has the shuttle *Duna* lifted off?" Telisan asked, desperately wishing the alien and the wounded safely on their way to the ship.

"Affirmative," Cobalt said. "Controller Mmok advises that only cyber-forces are deployed outside the shuttle perimeter now, to keep up fire on the surviving Denshi units."

Telisan looked up at the smoking buildings and shattered skybridges. "How secure is this area?"

"Clear," replied the machine. Then its demeanor changed subtly. "Telisan this is Mmok speaking to you through Cobalt. I need her and one crab-robot, but you can't be out there by yourself. I'll assign Crab 5 to escort you."

"Affirmative," Telisan said. Cobalt returned to its characterless self, leaving without a further word and trailed by one crab. The other gray crab robot roused itself and began to follow him. Reassured by the robot's tank-like power, he moved cautiously but rapidly. Sharla and her team should be at the computer center by now.

Low and squat, the Denshi computer building had the look of a bunker. Part of a skybridge had collapsed on it. Shattered glass and bodies lay everywhere around the building. Some were enemy soldiers, but more looked to be office workers cut down in flight. Their burned and twisted bodies lay in heaps, as if they had clustered together for some illusion of protection in the last seconds. The waste of it all tightened his sensitive mouth. Yet he was part of this and bore responsibility for it.

He arrived at the computer center ahead of Sharla's team. The demi-female showed up five precious minutes later, with two of *Sidhe's* Landing Force for escort. She gave him a quick smile, and he touched her face, relieved to see her. They entered the building and found the main computer room. He sent the LFs outside with the crab robot to secure the area. After they left, Sharla seized his arm in a fierce grip. He turned, surprised at the fear in the demi-female's golden, cat-irised eyes.

"I ran into Karass and Dobera," Sharla said, "and helped them get it unseen into the *Duna*. Telisan," she hissed, "a new alien race! What does this mean? Another war? Are these like the Conchirri?"

"We do not know what this means," he cautioned. "Remember the humans were once an unknown alien species. Much is now clear as to why Mandela sent both Rainhell and us to this world. These Denshi must have a relationship with these new aliens. This is what Mandela actually sent us for."

Sharla still seemed shaken. "If they know where our worlds are, they could strike anywhere. In any force. We would have no way of counter-attacking."

"Yes," he replied, in a grim tone. "Sharla, I need you to invade these computer banks and find everything you can on these people: weapons, capabilities, bases, everything. We are in great trouble here; information may save us."

Sharla nodded, stepping over an Olympian corpse and pulling back a chair in front of a flat-screen terminal that looked intact. Her long, delicate fingers played over the controls. Screens lit and flashed around her.

A tremendous bang sounded out in the distance. The building shook slightly. Sharla ignored it. Telisan looked around. "Mmok's work," he muttered. "I hope."

He switched his pocket comp to its communication function but got only static. Switching channels, he finally found one that carried through to Mmok. "Gold, come in."

"Gold here," Mmok answered.

"Situation report."

"We have fallen back on the shuttles. I have the *Intruder* cruising over the complex, blasting anything that moves outside our sectors."

"Restrict that immediately," Telisan snapped. "Stormcloud has no IFF."

"Relax, Blue," Mmok replied. "This isn't my first action. Stormcloud's profile and characteristics are in all weapons and machines. I have my airbot searching for Stormcloud and Scarlet."

"Apologies." Telisan waved a hand, though Mmok could not see it. "I should not have worried about that."

"Forget it," Mmok said. "I understand. No sign of them now. I am expanding the search radius. We'll check back in with you when we have something. Meanwhile, we are holding the Denshi in check. It won't last forever, unless you want me to throw my live troops back in..."

"Negative," he replied. "The Army is coming. I don't trust them. I would have most of our forces gone by the time they arrive."

"Understood. Gold out."

Sharla worked furiously through their conversation, continuing her labors on the computer for another ten minutes. "Ah," she finally exclaimed in satisfaction, "the tech who died here was converting a message from code. Someone killed him in the middle of the work. I can use this to break the security cipher."

"What does the last message say?" he asked, eager for clues.

"It refers to a Project Overman, advising the complex is under assault. It orders someone named Raque to liquidate the aliens and to broadcast a message to satellites at the system's edge. A courier from the alien's homeworld—they are named the Voit-Veru—is due in Olympian space in the next eight weeks. The message to them was, 'Eliminate the crew of the *Blackbird*.'"

Telisan's leathery skin paled in shock. "Repeat that," he snapped.

Sharla looked at him curiously. "Eliminate the crew of the *Blackbird*," she repeated.

"Great Mother," he said faintly.

"What is it?" Sharla demanded.

"Robert Fenaday's wife, Lisa, captained a scoutship of that name."

"The female he searched for?" she said in amazement.

"Just so," he replied grimly. "She who was finally given up for lost. Can it be the same?"

Sharla checked further. "I find reference to a sneakship of that name, crew of four, and a Confed identification number. No other details."

"It must be the same," Telisan said, his bronze mane rising in agitation. "Obtain every piece of data on the aliens and the *Blackbird*, then delete all references. Information is power. We will need every advantage we can seize in the days to follow."

The demi-female looked at him pensively, as if she might argue, then nodded and hooked up a backpack comp to the mainframe. Downloading took only a few seconds. Telisan knew paper files existed somewhere, but he had no luxury to search them out. This would have to do.

"Blue," Mmok called on the headset, his voice sharp with tension. "I've located Stormcloud, Scarlet, and target Alpha."

"Where?" the Denlenn demanded.

"They are down at the bridge. Shit, you must have flown over them and not seen them in the smoke. Alpha is at the bottom of the gorge. He is real dead. Blue," there was a slight hesitation, "Scarlet and Stormcloud do not look good."

Telisan's hearts went out of synch; he felt cold suddenly. Sharla looked at him anxiously, placing a hand on his arm. "Are they dead?" he managed.

"Can't tell, Blue. They did not show up on the airbot's infrared. They are cold. Blue, it's not good. I have an HCR en route and a mule with medics. Airbot is armed; we used it to whack the guards down there in the first place. It will cover them till help arrives. We are warming up *Pooka* for extraction."

"Affirmative," he snapped. "Have the mule pick me up since it must come this way. I am sending Sharla and her section back. Withdraw aboard the *Intruder* and *Pooka*. Bring the ships to the bridge. It is time to leave."

Grabbing Sharla by the arm, he sped outside, waving the startled guards to follow them into the street. They ran out into the fine rain and gusting wind. The mule ATV rounded the corner barely a minute later with two medics and an ASAT aboard.

"Aside," Telisan ordered. The driver, a young human female, jumped into the back. Rain drove into Telisan's face as he floored the accelerator, cursing the fact he had left his goggles somewhere. The ASAT, realizing where her best interest lay, pulled out a soft-brimmed *Sidhe* hat from her flak jacket, widened the headband, and waved it frantically in front of him. He snatched it from her hand in the middle of a turn and put it on, only his fighter pilot reflexes keeping the vehicle upright. The Denlenn demanded every KPH the small machine had. From the gasps and whispered prayers of the humans, it seemed they lacked confidence in his skills. The mule's engine growled as they sped down the track that Fenaday had jogged hours earlier. Rain pelted the racing mule, its windscreen and canvas top offering little protection. They went airborne briefly over the last hill. Telisan spotted the airbot hovering over the other side of the still-burning guard post. He cut across the lawn and whipped around the building corner, slinging gravel and mud as he stood on the brakes, stopping just shy of the paved road. Leaping over the vehicle's short hood the instant it stopped, Telisan raced toward the huddled figures, followed by the pale and shaken medics.

Telisan stopped short of the two bodies, dropping to his knees with a loud cry. The medics pushed past him, opening their instruments and gently disentangling the bodies.

Telisan knelt, arms loose at his side, eyes unfocused. "So far," he murmured, "to fail." Despair welled in his Denlenn soul. To fail in one's duty to house or service was a disgrace, made the more bitter by the friendship he shared with the humans.

One of the medics turned to him. "It's bad, sir, real bad. How soon will the shuttles be here? We need Dr. Mourner."

It hammered into his consciousness. "What, what?" he stammered, then realized he was speaking Denleni.

"Snap out of it, sir," ordered the medic. "They're in trauma-tab coma. I need real life-support equipment."

Purpose and energy surged back into the Denlenn; there was still a chance.

"Gold," he called on his mike, distantly surprised by how calm his voice was, "this is Blue. Are you extracted? I need Dr. Mourner. They are still alive, but very badly injured."

"Blue, we are just now getting airborne with the robots holding the line. We'll pick them up down by you. ETA is two minutes. I'm going to put the airbot and Cobalt on top of the ridge to cover the approach till we get there."

Ten meters above them, the saucer-like machine suddenly shifted into motion, heading toward the hill behind the wrecked guard post.

"Hurry," Telisan pled, looking at the humans' pale, waxy faces. Both their bodies lay under self-heating blankets, Fenaday face down. The medics hung IVs and waved field regenerators over their

EDWARD MCKEOWN

wounds. They lasered off Rainhell's long, lustrous hair, her one vanity, as they worked on her head injuries. Wind gusts carried off the sickening smell of burned hair. Veteran that he was, Telisan felt queasy, watching the calm methodical working of the medics. *Strange*, he thought, *to feel so after so many years of war.*

The young ASAT driver rummaged through the back of the mule. She came up with armfuls of fabric. Telisan joined her in holding shelter halves over the wounded to keep the rain off. He looked up into the gray tapering drizzle. The wind kicked up stronger now. *Hurry*, he again wished to the shuttles, *hurry!*

Chapter Nineteen

S trong ocean breezes began to disperse the miasma of smoke and ash hanging over Denshi's Marathon office. Shooting had tapered over the last twenty minutes, since the last reckless charge of Neos and Bremardi left the ground covered with bodies. Vaughn and Tanaka could only feel lucky that no regular troops had been present. The Neos and Bremardi fought fiercely, but the Denshi, better led and under cover, still held the building. Corpses littered the area, some Denshi, mostly Neos and their allies.

Tanaka, her face soiled with smoke and bruises, pointed to the corner of the office tower opposite them. Dozens of figures advanced, darting professionally into cover. A heavy tank clattered up to the corner opposite the running troops and trained its barrel at Vaughn's position.

"I see them," he replied grimly, "Army Special Forces. Why the Neos pulled away, I have no idea."

"Sir," called the Navy attaché. The young lieutenant commander held a field radio and a heavy laser. "I have a communication from the approaching Army troops; they are General Dominici's personal guards. She wants to talk."

"Any communication from Navy troops or other Denshi troops?" he asked.

"Got a fragment from a tacnet down by the port," the attaché replied. "Sounded like our people are shooting it out with Army around the docks. That's all. As for your people, Oldark's fighting with Armored Cavalry and losing. The troops you have with Hagen are holding the building, but they haven't been pressed by more than snipers. Nobody else is on the air, at least unjammed anyway."

Tanaka put down her field radio and looked at him. "Our lookout says we're being surrounded in battalion strength, with heavy armor backing up the infantry. We can't hold them if they attack."

"Well," Vaughn said, "she wants to talk. They shot the works at us today. The longer we last, the more chance the Navy and other forces can reach us. Signal Dominici that we agree."

"Affirmative," he said. "Army says move out under a white flag. They'll meet us in the middle. You and Tanaka, she and three of her aides."

"Damn," Vaughn said. "They even know you're here."

"Hey, I'm important," she said.

He blinked at her in confusion. Leaning forward, he spoke in a low voice, "Sorry, Tanaka, but you really aren't—"

"Joke, sir," she replied. "Foxhole humor."

"Ah," he nodded, embarrassed.

He turned to the aide. "Have our people hold fire. Keep them under control."

Ten minutes later, Vaughn and Tanaka strode out into the suddenly cool morning. It looked like the storm had come off the mountains between them and the main complex. Vaughn wondered what had happened there and if Pard still lived.

From behind a large armored hovercar, flanked by three guards, Dominici, wearing full battle armor, walked out almost casually. Vaughn, like most Denshi, admired sang-froid.

They all stepped over bodies to reach the middle of the broad avenue. A few paces apart, they stopped. Dominici took a pace forward, as did Vaughn.

Dominici looked around. "Long night, with no morning for some."

"The dying is not over yet," Vaughn observed.

"That's why we're talking," the older woman said. "Your complex in the high desert has fallen. My people are moving in to hold it now. What will we find there, Mr. Vaughn?"

"Nothing that will profit you." Vaughn crossed his arms. "You must know the Navy is rallying to us. Our position will improve with time. You've shot your bolt."

"Project Overman," she replied.

Vaughn's guts clenched. Only twelve people on Olympia knew that name. He'd killed one yesterday in Pard's conference room. He shrugged. "A name."

"For a conspiracy to ally an Engineered, Denshi-dominated Olympia with a new alien race," Dominici continued. "A pocket Empire headed by the Engineered. It's ending, Vaughn. The story is going public as we speak. Even the president has suddenly developed some backbone. Every house will be against Denshi."

"So why are we talking," Vaughn asked, "if your hand is so strong?"

"It's time to bend with the new wind, Vaughn," she replied. "A new, hot wind is going to blow in from the Confederacy and it may blow away much of what we both value in our world. Pard's dream is over. It may be that Dr. Allessandro's is as well. If we don't unite as Olympians, the Confederacy will own us."

"What are you saying?" he demanded. "I won't betray Pard."

"Pard's dead," she said, "or as good as. Even if the labs are closed, the Engineered and their descendants will be with us for generations. Someone must speak for the Engineered. Olympia doesn't need thousands of supermen and superwomen, wandering about leaderless."

"When I could be their leader," he said, "on the end of your leash."

"You lost," Dominici said flatly. "These are better terms than Pard had in mind for me."

True enough, he thought. "So what now?"

"Come with me to the complex. Help me control the damage from this nightmare alliance. I need you to talk to the Navy and the rest of Denshi and stop a civil war before it goes beyond today. You will lead the Engineered and Denshi under Army authority."

Vaughn smiled at her audacity. "Keep your friends close and your enemies closer? Is that it, General?"

"Wise up, young man. Everything is changing. I'll give you a piece of information your friends in the Navy, even the Confed ambassador does not know. A Confed courier was at the system's edge, waiting word of the attack on Pard. It jumped into hyperspace when it received my signal. It's not going far and it's coming back with a task force. If you want to salvage anything of Denshi, boy, you get on my side now. The train is leaving."

"I will go with you to the complex," Vaughn said slowly. "We will see if Pard lives or if any evidence of what you claim is in your hands. That will determine the rest."

"Fair enough," she said. "Tell your people to maintain their positions and not to try anything funny. We'll keep the Bremardi away."

Vaughn nodded. He and Tanaka backed away, cautiously heading for the Denshi complex.

Dominici's guards formed a wall in front of her as she turned to walk back. A young captain stood next to her. His name badge also said Dominici. "Well played, Mother," he said. "Of course, if we don't find something damning today, that task force will shoot by our world without even firing a salute for our funeral."

"Not to worry, Guytano," she said. "Age and treachery will overcome youth and strength." *I hope*, she thought, *I do so fervently hope.*

Chapter Twenty

Telisan and Sharla waited by the bridge. The *Intruder* lay grounded behind them, its guns scant protection against what surged up the roadway. Army vehicles filled the road and the air over it. Helos, transports, and hovers roared over the canyon, heading for the Denshi complex. The heavy armor stopped at the far end of the bridge, except for a tan, armored staff car, which rolled forward toward the two Denlenn. About ten meters away, it stopped, ramps dropping. Huge troopers surged out, taking positions on the flanks. Dominici followed them. To Telisan's surprise, Mikhail Vaughn and a black-haired human female wearing Denshi livery accompanied her. Two particularly powerful troopers stood behind the assassin, their weapons trained on Vaughn. Dominici spoke to an officer with her who halted the Denshi. She walked forward alone.

"Where's Fenaday?" Dominici asked.

Telisan's face was a grim alien mask. "Near death, as is Rainhell. I sent them and the bulk of our forces to our ship. From there our casualties will be transported to your base hospital. Your facilities are prepared for casualties, I hope."

Dominici nodded. "They are the best. So Rainhell turned up? What of Pard?"

Telisan walked to the edge of the bridge, where his friends had been found, and pointed down. Dominici looked over; a smile of satisfaction lit her face. "One less nightmare. Of course, we're going to join him unless we can find enough evidence to stop the Navy's counterstrike and the president cashiering me. Find anything, say, a little alien?"

It hit him. "You knew," Telisan shouted. Sharla turned in astonishment. She'd never heard her fiancé raise his voice before. The troops by the armored cars shifted, their weapons covering the Denlenn.

The accusation did not appear to discomfort Dominici. "Of course I knew. Or rather I had strong suspicions, but no proof. So, what do you have for me?"

Telisan glared. "All that you could wish, an alien ambassador of a new species, quite dead. The Denshi have an alliance. I'm sure you will find abundant evidence in the complex."

"What do they look like?" she asked quietly. Abruptly, it occurred to him that Dominici might have served off planet in the Conchirri war. His eyes flicked down to her chest.

"I'm not wearing it," she said, noting his eyes. "I don't wear campaign stars on my battle armor."

"Ah," he replied, "so you were there."

"Yes."

"They do not look like the Conchirri. This is a new species entirely. Their skin is what humans see as tan. We Denlenn see different spectra. They have three upper limbs, two legs and a balancing tail. The one I found was already dead. We discovered an order for its extermination in a Denshi computer."

Dominici turned and waved for the officer to allow Vaughn to come up, accompanied by the woman and the alert-looking troopers. "Take a look over the rail," she bade the big human. "You are now paramount in Denshi."

Vaughn looked over for a moment. When he turned back, the expression in his eyes made the soldiers shift and raise their weapons.

"Sir," the black-haired woman said sharply, as if to call the weapons to his attention. His eyes flicked to her, and then back to lock on Telisan's yellow cat's-eyes.

The Denlenn stared back fearless, not troubling to reach for his laser. Sharla, more practical, slid her hand over the butt of her auto-pistol.

"Your work?" Vaughn grated.

"He died in fair combat with Rainhell and Fenaday." Telisan stared back into Vaughn's volcanic blue eyes. "An honorable death, better than you deal, assassin."

"My own preference is face to face," Vaughn said. "Perhaps we will so meet one day."

"Enough of this, boys," Dominici snapped. "We have a dead alien of an unknown species, an illegal alliance with that same species, Denshi's computer and paper files, and a Confed Task force due into the system in weeks, if not days. Mr. Vaughn, you need my support. You are up to your neck in it. I already have everything I need to stop the breeding of the Engineered and return Olympia to what it was. If you want to make a place for the Engineered in our world, you need to deal with me."

"So it was you," Sharla said, picking up the threads, "who went to Mandela with the word of what you suspected, with the news that Pard's plans were nearing fruition. You knew it was only a matter of months before Pard and the Engineered finally maneu-vered you out of power."

"Or killed me," Dominici added. "Yes, I went to him. Time was short and measures desperate. That's why the first team went in the way it did. It's also why Mandela arranged a backup plan as desperate as the first. If you brought down Pard and developed the evidence we needed, you would be heroes. If not, we would all deny anything to do with you. It would be seen as a private quarrel between Pard and Fenaday over Rainhell. Everyone else being sucked in based on their loyalties, or in Mmok's case, deceptions. Each of us had our own reasons," she added. "I want my planet back."

Telisan smiled without warmth or humor. "Fenaday told me of an old joke among humans. It concerns a woman who swallowed a fly, then swallowed a spider to get the fly. When she got up to a horse, it killed her. You may find the Confederacy has different plans for your world than you do. The task force is not coming so you may return to your old ways. You may find that, like Mr. Vaughn, you need to face a new reality."

"Maybe," Dominici said. "If so, well, my mother used to say, 'Blessed are the flexible, for they shall not be bent out of shape.'"

"Stay limber," Telisan recommended. "As for us, we are leaving your hospitality as soon as we can. Mandela has other plans for us. He asks you provide us with resupply, rearmament, and cooperation. We need to lift as soon as possible."

Dominici smiled. "So, as I suspected, you still work for the Confederacy. Your presence at Enshar and here was a bit much to ask of friendship. I'd ask you where you were going if I thought you'd tell me."

Telisan looked back at her, impassive.

"Well," Dominici said, "give the old bastard regards from the old bitch. You'll get what you need, Mr. Telisan. I think the sooner you leave, the better for all concerned. Smooth sailing." She turned and strode away. Vaughn, with a last deadly look at an unaffected Telisan, followed her.

Telisan and Sharla headed back to the shuttle.

"You did not correct her," Sharla observed.

"It plays to our advantage," he returned. "She measures all by her own yardstick and to her it makes sense. I do not believe she knows the meaning of the word, 'friend.'"

"Beloved," Sharla said, "few people measure up to you on that standard in any species."

Telisan flashed a smile at her and stood a little straighter. "Come," he said, "let us see if Arpen and Dr. Mourner can work a miracle for us." Side-by-side, they jogged back to the shuttle.

———

D r. Mourner leaned against a desk, fatigue evident in every line of her small body. "The trauma drugs saved Rainhell and Fenaday. Death didn't get a firm enough grip on them, but it came damn close. We were able to resuscitate them, thanks to the medics' work. Another few minutes and it would have been too late." Mourner and Sharla stood in the ICU recovery lounge of Gaugamela Military Hospital, north of Marathon. Arpen remained inside with Shasti and Robert, watching them and the teams of Olympian Army doctors and nurses who had battled for twelve hours to save the pair.

Telisan reached behind him and poured a soft drink. He handed it to Mourner, who drank gratefully. "Are you all right, Doctor?" he asked.

She smiled at him. "Always the gentleman. Do you have any single brothers?"

"Regrettably no," he said. "What is your prognosis?"

Mourner looked about. All around the lounge stood Olympian Military Police and Special Forces. Dominici was taking no chances of a last-minute assassination attempt on Fenaday or Rainhell.

"I judge it safe to speak," Telisan said.

"Shasti was injured the worse." Mourner rubbed her eyes. "I've never seen anyone who heals half as fast as she does. She amazed even the Engineered specialist we brought in from Hagen's lab. She's actually in better shape than the captain is right now. I think we have Robert's spinal cord patched completely, but we will have to wait till he awakens for a full test. He lost a lot of blood, and we had some trouble with shock. If he stays stable for another six to eight hours, then I think we'll be out of the woods."

"This is wonderful news," Telisan said. He poured himself and Sharla drinks as well and tried to still the shaking of his hands. It had been so close.

"What's going on around us?" Mourner asked.

"We are safe for now," Telisan said. "The Confed fleet has entered the outer system. It broadcast a terse message about assuming orbit around Olympia and for the Olympian Military not to interfere with its approach." More messages, Telisan assumed, were passing between Dominici, Ambassador Davis, and Mandela, but he was not privy to those. It sufficed for his purposes that Dominici honored her agreements.

"Indeed," Sharla added, "the Olympian media are making much of the attempted murder of Captain Fenaday by Pard."

"I'd be happier if we were back on the ship." Mourner looked about at all the soldiers outside the glass walls of the lounge.

"How soon will they be stable enough for that?" Telisan asked. He had more reasons than did Mourner for wishing for the safety of the starship. She had seen holos of the new aliens. Dominici made sure the media aired them almost constantly. Only seven people in *Sidhe's* crew knew he had a live alien secreted in the pressure chamber aboard the *Sidhe.* He needed to bring Mourner into the conspiracy but had not yet done so.

"Surgical repairs are complete, barring a problem on Robert," she said. "It's now up to the regenerators, stimulators, and the natural healing power of the body. Arpen, Yamata, and I can do what remains, complicated as it is, aboard ship. Give me about two days and control of the transfer, and I'll get it done."

"Proceed on that basis," Telisan said.

Mourner nodded and headed back to the ICU.

A young officer walked up to Telisan. "Call for you on the secure line, sir. It's General Dominici." Telisan followed the human to a desk in a small room. An enlisted man handed him a com, then both he and the officer stepped out.

"Telisan here."

"Commander Telisan," a male voice said, "hold for General Dominici."

The com clicked, and he heard the general's voice. "Telisan, my people tell me your captain and Ms. Rainhell are going to live."

"Yes," he replied. "I plan to move them back to *Sidhe* as soon as possible. Have you ordered *Sidhe* refueled and resupplied?"

"Yes," she said. "You'll be pleased to know the Olympian government is in a desperate fervor to please the acting captain of the star-frigate *Sidhe.* No doubt that attitude is helped by the size of the incoming fleet. Your boss Mandela seems to be playing his cards close. I haven't been able to even get an acknowledgement from him. Any chance you can do something about that?"

"I plan to communicate with Mr. Mandela only after we are in space and outward bound," Telisan said. "The quicker I can get ready for space, the better."

"Damn. It will be days before your ship is repaired and supplies are ready."

"All the more time for you to get Olympia under some sort of control," he replied.

"I thought so," she said. "Mandela's still waiting to see if it's over or if we blow up into a full civil war. There's good news on that front. Vaughn has finally chosen to throw in his lot with me, assuming control of what is left of the Denshi order. He's fighting some holdouts, but they won't last long."

"Excellent news," Telisan said. "General, I must ask you not to reveal my plans for leaving to any party. I also ask that for security reasons you not discuss with anyone the location or condition of Captain Fenaday and Ms. Rainhell. I particularly ask that you not discuss this with Ambassador Davis."

"That imbecile," Dominici said. "I wouldn't give him the time of day. He was far too chummy with Pard for my taste."

"We had similar concerns," Telisan said.

"Agreed then. He remains out of the loop. I'll keep you posted on developments." A dull boom sounded over the phone.

"Have to go, Mr. Telisan," Dominici said. "The Navy's calling."

The line went dead. Telisan placed the com on the desk and turned away, already deep in thought. Conflicts warred in his Denlenn soul. As a Confederation officer, he'd fought fiercely for the government during the war. He was no longer on active duty, but knew that for a technicality. Now, he felt torn between loyalties. It had happened to him before, on the Enshar Expedition, when he found himself caught between his oaths to Duna and to Fenaday. He'd served the greater good by cleaving to Duna's side. It had cost his soul bitterly when the Shellycoats struck, almost wiping out their expedition. Fenaday forgave Telisan's betrayal and the deaths that came from it. Something the Denlenn had never forgiven in himself.

They had come far from when Telisan had met a broken privateer in a Marsport bar. Now Telisan joined in a second quest, one that predated his own, the search for Lisa Fenaday. It fell to him to see the quest reach its end, or meanly fail. He knew his own soul would not allow him to let his friend's last desperate hope die.

Once the Navy learned of the existence of these new aliens,

they would never permit anything as quixotic as a rescue mission. The Voit-Veru had clearly conspired with the Olympians. The Confederacy, still recovering from millions of casualties in the Conchirri war, would take no chances. Likely, they would flood the new system with warships, suddenly and without warning. Prisoners gone so many years would be of no import in such a calculation. Telisan had watched too many front-line soldiers sacrificed this way by those like Mandela. Efficient, perhaps, but not the Denlenn way. There was no honor in it. Did a Confederacy with so little loyalty to its own deserve his? It always troubled him that the reciprocity of served and serving, found in his own military, was not reflected in the wider Confederacy. Yet no one could deny that ruthless human efficiency had won the Conchirri war.

I am Denlenn and Selen, he thought finally. *I can only be what I am. The universe might depend on a rock falling upward, but the rock, being a rock, only knows how to fall down. When we reach the system's edge, just before jump, I will have Sharla relay every piece of data we extracted from the databanks of Denshi and the prisoner. The Confederacy will have all it needs to deal with the threat and mount a strike if need be. The government has thousands of ships and tens of thousands of personnel. All Lisa Fenaday has is the Sidhe.*

He returned to the ICU and looked in the windows at his friends. "Rest and heal," he bade them. "I am doing all you could wish.

"Sharla," he said, "I leave you in charge here. I must get to the embassy, then the ship. Coordinate the transfer of Robert and Shasti back to *Sidhe* when it is possible."

"Depend on me," she replied.

Telisan turned to the Olympian officer nearby. "I need an aircar."

The next few days were a blur of activity. Telisan, invoking Mandela's name, recalled the survivors of the attack on Pard's compound to the frigate. Many of the crab robots were badly damaged, or destroyed, along with the HCR Cerulean. The robots had fulfilled their main purpose, drawing fire off the living. Still, fully half of the attack force lay dead or wounded. Invoking Mandela's name and influence, Telisan transferred three squads of Marines and a dozen Army specialists to *Sidhe* bringing the landing force back up to strength. Telisan told Davis that Mandela needed *Sidhe* and the attack force. They would leave soon, and he could not say when they would return. Davis, happy to be rid of them, ordered it.

Fenaday and Rainhell were transferred back to *Sidhe's* Sickbay under the tightest security, to continue recovering in a medical coma under the care of Mourner and Arpen.

Mmok remained out of his hair, working furiously to reassemble the robot company with salvage, spares on board, and material he obtained from the embassy. It fit in well with what Telisan needed, so he encouraged the cyborg's efforts.

Rask recovered from a laser shot through the arm. He and Li searched the city trying to find some sign of Daniel Rigg and the rest of the team. Those answers lay behind the silent lips of their two patients still under guard in the hospital.

Meanwhile, Marathon continued to come apart at the seams as factions jockeyed for positions in the new order. Dominici, still far from secure, hunkered down, awaiting Mandela. Navy and Army troops patrolled different sections of the city, cautiously watching each other. Incidents were common.

Perez drove the engineering "black gang" mercilessly, readying the ship for transit. He was not in on Telisan's plans. The Denlenn shared those only with Arpen and Sharla. Time pressed on him as he raced about the ship, checking every detail for the voyage ahead.

"Graglia to Telisan."

The Denlenn did not sigh, but the equivalent feeling swept through him. *What now?* "Telisan here."

"Yes sir. There is an Army escort here with Mr. Vaughn. He wants to see you."

"Why?"

"He won't say, sir. Says he will talk to you. He's got a pass countersigned by General Dominici, with a note from her asking you to meet him."

"Very well," the exasperated Denlenn said. "I shall meet him at the shuttle airlock. Have Mr. Mmok and one, no, two of the HCRs meet me there." He did not expect any threat, but the formidable Engineered assassin had no love for any of them. He checked his laser for good measure as he made his way to the main shuttle bay airlock. Fenaday's suspicious human nature was rubbing off on him.

Sidhe's shuttle bay doors stood open on both sides of the frigate, thirty meters off the ground, surrounded by gantry scaffolding, allowing a stiff breeze to pass through the ship. ASAT, Marine, and LF guards patrolled every access point. Telisan wanted to take no chances with the new head of Denshi.

The tall Engineered and his army escort waited outside the ship's pressure doors on the gantry side. McLoughlin stood by the airlock. He'd raised the gangway and rested against a bulkhead, tapping a heavy auto-pistol negligently on his thigh.

Mmok and the HCRs came up behind Telisan. He nodded to the dour cyborg, who simply grunted, looking sourly out at Vaughn. Telisan nodded at McLoughlin and gestured for the gangway to be restored. McLoughlin manipulated the controls, and the heavy cargo gangway extended out. Surprisingly, only Vaughn walked across. The three soldiers and Tanaka remained on the far side.

Telisan, used to being tall, disliked having to look up at the black-haired human. Vaughn saved him the indignity by stopping a long pace off. His startling blue eyes struck a chill in the Denlenn. Perhaps they were designed to. Vaughn nodded stiffly, but politely.

"What is it you wish, Mr. Vaughn?" Telisan asked, flanked by Mmok and his killing machines.

"I have a request," he said. "I want to see Rainhell."

They stared incredulously at the assassin. Mmok barked a laugh. "No," said Telisan flatly, his hand falling to the butt of his weapon. Vaughn looked at him with faint amusement.

"It is impossible," Telisan continued, more politely. "She is out of danger, but in a medical coma."

"I did not say I wanted to speak to her, merely to look on her," Vaughn replied. "I have seen her only once, at night and from a distance."

"No," Telisan repeated.

Vaughn raised a hand. "Wait. I have something for your eyes

only. Read it before you deny my request. Again, it is only for your eyes." He extended a large hand holding a rolled paper. Telisan stepped forward and took it, then, looking briefly at the HCRs, walked off the deck, away from their optics. Back in an interior corridor, he unrolled the paper. Bold handwriting scrawled over it.

Telisan, your technicians did a good job with our computers. With more time they might have covered their tracks. I know what you know, and I can surmise what you plan. You will need information, more than you have: shipping, orbits, installations, and recognition signals. You may regard this as treason, but Pard raised me as a realist. The Denshi forces in the alien systems are doomed. I must write them off. Nor do you wish me to share my suspicions with Dominici. I intend Rainhell no harm. I wish only to see her face. It has haunted me since our last encounter.

Telisan stood stock-still in shock, his mind whirling. He could not understand the human's motivation, unless it was... no, impossible. Still, here he was.

Telisan walked into the bay to face a frankly curious Mmok. He looked at the huge Engineered. "Very well, I will allow this, but you will be searched. You go in with an HCR holding each of your arms. You will not approach within two meters of the bed. At the merest hint of any threat, the HCRs will tear you to pieces. These conditions are not negotiable."

"Agreed," Vaughn said. "There will be no trouble."

Telisan turned to face an incredulous Mmok. "I want Cobalt and Indigo." Mmok looked at him for a second, but the forbidding expression on Telisan's face forestalled any question. Mmok glanced suspiciously at Vaughn, then nodded. The two machines moved forward smoothly. "Search him," Mmok said.

The two slender robots ran sensor-equipped hands over the big man, poking in some very sensitive areas.

"What gender are these things?" Vaughn asked. "I want to know if I should be enjoying this."

McLoughlin snorted a laugh. Telisan looked at Mmok, confused.

"I thought they engineered the humor out of you guys," Mmok growled.

"Follow me," Telisan said, impatiently.

They walked the short distance to the sickbay in a weird procession. The Denlenn led, followed by the Engineered, flanked by the slender HCRs and trailed by Mmok.

Arpen greeted them at the doorway. Obviously Mmok had called ahead. She asked no questions.

Telisan turned. "From here you go with the robots holding you and—"

"At the first sign of danger, I die," Vaughn interrupted. "I recall."

The black-clothed robots with their distinguishing sashes turned in unison and took Vaughn by the arms above and below the elbow. Arpen turned back to the sickbay; they followed her in.

Rainhell lay silent in a diagnostic bed, covered with a thermal blanket. Her incredible Engineered body had worked as hard as the physicians. Despite a beating that would have killed, or crippled almost any human, she showed little sign of how close she had been to death only three days before. She was thinner. Her body had converted its small store of fat, and Arpen was putting as much glucose in her as was possible. Even the long, glossy black hair that had fallen to the surgeon's cutters was already inches long, growing almost visibly. There was no swelling to her face; the bruises were fading. She remained in a medical coma only to speed her recovery.

Vaughn stopped the required two meters away, staring at Shasti's face. Telisan and Arpen watched him as a mother Rottweiler might watch a stranger near her puppies. The big man said nothing, merely looked at her face, drinking in every detail.

"She is beautiful," he said finally. "I only saw her once, from a distance, at night."

"Well," Mmok said, slightly amused, "she's looked better."

Vaughn ignored him, gazing at Rainhell. They stood silently for a few minutes longer. Finally, Telisan shifted impatiently. "I have much to do, Mr. Vaughn. Have you seen enough?"

"Yes," he said after a moment, "thank you."

In a weird pirouette, the HCRs, still holding Vaughn's arms, turned him toward the door. They marched back to the shuttle bayhatch. Once there, Telisan stopped Vaughn. "I believe you owe me something."

Vaughn looked at him and sighed, then called across to the woman outside the ship on the far side of the gantry. "Tanaka."

The woman walked across in lithe, muscular strides, drawing admiring glances from McLoughlin and, Arpen would have been pleased to know, Mmok. She noted their looks and returned a cool stare.

Vaughn reached out a hand, into which she put two data crystals. Vaughn handed these to Telisan. "One of these, the blue, is for you. The other is for Rainhell. It is private, I would prefer it remain that way."

"Assassin," Telisan said, "nothing passes from your hands to hers that I have not checked thoroughly."

To Telisan's surprise, Vaughn smiled. "Good. I am pleased to see she has such friends." Without a further word or backward glance, Vaughn strode off, followed by Tanaka.

"What's on the crystal?" Mmok asked after the Olympians left.

"I will let you know when you need to know," Telisan replied. "What of the robot repairs?" he demanded, changing the subject.

Mmok looked at him narrowly before answering. "Twenty-five combat crabs, five HCRs, the airbot, and one utility bot are available. You ought to be happy; only ten of all types made it through the fight intact. I have two crabs, two utilities, and an HCR in storage. I'll try to activate those tomorrow."

"Excellent," Telisan said. He had not known of the spare machines. What else was Mmok hiding from him? "Why were they not used in combat?"

Mmok shook his head. "Christ, you think this is easy? I'm the only controller to ever manage all three main types of robots. How many machines do you want run through my damn brain?"

"Sorry," Telisan said. "I know little of this."

Mmok relaxed a little, still watching Telisan.

"Get your machines ready," Telisan ordered. "I want one hundred percent security around the ship till we lift tomorrow. I leave this to you."

Mmok watched as the Denlenn walked off.

"What the hell's going on?" McLoughlin asked.

"Don't know," Mmok said, as if to himself. "Aim to find out though."

———

R ask returned to *Sidhe* downcast and discouraged. He'd hoped that with the fall of Denshi, it might be easier to move around Marathon. The opposite had occurred; the city descended into chaos. Bremardi and Neos sought to pay off old scores with the Denshi, usually with little success. The Army tried to keep the parties apart despite occasional run-ins with the Navy.

Only Li and an Olympian Special Forces Lieutenant—the same officer who had escorted Fenaday to Dominici on the space station mere days ago—accompanied him. They were running out of time. Telisan was in a fury of impatience to lift ship. Rask suspected the Denlenn had orders from Mandela, but Telisan refused to confirm or deny anything.

The inbound Confed fleet included heavy warships, outnumbering and outgunning the Olympian Self-Defense Force by a significant margin. An OSDF destroyer that closed on the fleet ceased broadcasting its IFF. The task force ignored inquiries about it. The Confed ships had emerged from hyperspace far out in the system and, unlike *Sidhe's* frantic dash at the planet, came in very slowly. The fleet would not make orbit for twenty days. Mandela, if he was aboard, was playing his cards close, doubtless suspicious of his ally, Dominici.

Their aircar grounded on the approach to the docks where *Sidhe* lay. Telisan didn't allow aircraft near the starship. Another two hundred meters and they would have been targeted.

"Pull over," Rask said.

"Sir." The lieutenant pulled to the curb. His mouth drew into a grim line of disapproval.

"We'll walk it from here," the Morok said. It had become a ritual of the last week. If Rigg still lived, he'd find a way to get down to the area around the ship. Rask did a walkthrough of the entire area. The Army didn't like it. Rask didn't give a shit.

"Okay, Lieutenant," Rask said, "see you tomorrow."

"I thought you guys leave tomorrow," replied the Olympian.

Rask's red eyes looked impassively back at him. "We'll see."

Rask and Li exited the vehicle and waited till it disappeared out of sight. Dockers and merchants milled about the area. A few stared at them curiously. They didn't hold the Morok's eyes when he looked back. Rask took his usual circuitous route back to where Army Security held the dockside. He stopped long enough to buy a gyro at a vendor before walking on. Li accompanied him, quiet as usual.

"Too bad you can't get liberty in this port," the Morok said, between bites of the gyro. "By your admittedly low human standards, the locals are probably considered hot stuff."

"Hah." Li looked around. "You couldn't get a date on this world without a gene test. They probably want to run a track meet before sex."

"Well, maybe you'll get lucky, someday," Rask mused. "Get to my world and see some real women."

Li watched him savaging the gyro. "I don't think so."

"Once you go blue," Rask added, "you'll always be true."

As they passed an alley, an urgent voice called out, "Rask!"

The Morok and human whirled, hands on weapons. In the alley, standing against the wall, stood an emaciated Daniel Rigg. His solemn, too-thin face creased in a smile. Rask, moving amazingly fast for his squat frame, ran into the alley, followed a beat later by Li.

"Dan, you son of a bitch," Rask swore. "Where have you been? You've had me worried to death."

"Sorry," Rigg said. "It's been a bad trip."

The Morok gripped his friend's arms, fighting to keep his tone level. "Good to see you, sir."

"You too and don't sir me. Good to see you, Li."

"Are any of the rest of the team with you?" Rask demanded. "Why didn't you just call us for help? We came out on top. The Army is on our side. Denshi's under control."

"Good to hear," Rigg said. "A lot isn't clear from out here. We didn't know if the Denshi were all tied up, or if we could really trust the Army. Anyway, the city is very dangerous to move in. A lot of scores are getting settled out here."

He took a deep breath. "Nobody else from my team made it, except Rainhell. Last I saw of her, she was gunning for Pard."

"She and the Skipper got him," Li interrupted.

Rigg grabbed Li's arm. "Is she alive?"

"She and Fenaday are both in Sickbay," Rask answered. "They were both real bad. Hell, they were dead. Mourner and Arpen brought them back."

Rigg sagged. "Thank God."

Instantly, Rask placed his shoulder under his friend's arm. "We'll talk back at the ship," he said. "Sort it all out there."

"Wait," Rigg said. "There is another reason I didn't just call. Our Olympian contact is with me. We've got to get her out. I'm not leaving her behind in this insanity." He turned. "Leda, come on."

From the back of the alley, an older Olympian woman, tall, handsome, and frightened, came out from behind some crates.

"Okay," Rask said, "you say she goes, then she goes."

"No argument from me," Li said.

"Can you walk to the ship?" Rask asked.

Rigg grinned. "I can run to the bloody, lovely, wonderful ship."

"Lean on the nice lady as we go." Rask gestured to Leda. "I want my gun hand free. Li, get on the com. I want HCRs on their way to us. I want them now."

Li keyed his mike and spoke urgently into it.

Rask handed Rigg the back-up pistol he always carried. "Let's get your butt to Sickbay." Flanked by the Morok and Li, Rigg, leaning heavily on Jenner, moved into the street. People backed away from them as they came out. Up the street there was sudden consternation. Two slight female figures, both in black with differing blue sashes, flashed into view, moving almost too fast to be seen.

"Mmok?" Rigg asked in a thin whisper.

"Yep," Rask replied. "He's almost as hard to kill as you are."

"Well, I'll be damned," Rigg said.

T elisan's ruse worked, aided by the fact that Davis wanted them out of his hair as soon as possible. *Sidhe* took off in the early morning hours. Dominici did not even come down to send them off.

Olympia did not boast an accelerator. Military fuel sleds, essentially large expendable fuel tanks, accomplished the same task, if more clumsily. The star-frigate used a pair to boost up to maximum speed without burning any onboard fuel. Where they were going, they would find no friends. After launching, *Sidhe* maintained radio silence. With luck it would be some time before the fleet figured out what they were doing. Given their relative speeds, fuel status, and distance, the Confed fleet could do nothing in any event. *Sidhe* could not be caught before she reached jumpspace. They would be days, perhaps weeks, behind her.

Telisan kept the crew busy preparing for her voyage out. Stores were piled in passageways. Machinery, especially from the ground force, needed repair. Mmok still seemed busy with the machines, including the new HCR, Scarlet. Marines requisitioned from the embassy had to be quartered and integrated. Everything proceeded according to plan. It was too good to be true.

———

L ieutenant Graglia raced up to Telisan, out of breath. The Denlenn stood with Arpen and Sharla at the entrance to the sickbay. Telisan wanted to spend some time with his fiancées, weaving back the torn fabric of their engagement.

"Why are you not on the bridge?" Telisan demanded.

"Mmok came in, with the HCRs. He ordered us to cut thrust and get out. There was nothing we could do," Graglia huffed.

Telisan cursed in Denleni.

"He says he wants to talk to you, sir," Graglia added.

"Shall I get the landing troops?" Sharla asked.

Telisan shook his head. "In such close quarters, they would be useless against HCRs. No, I shall deal with Mr. Mmok."

"Not alone," Sharla said.

Unexpectedly, Arpen placed a hand on his arm. "Not alone," she demanded. "I will go with you. I can reach him."

"Very well," he said, "but you leave when I say."

"It has happened as you feared," Arpen whispered. "I was wrong."

"It has happened," he agreed, "but you were not wrong."

He started into a run, forestalling any questions from Sharla. Arpen was forced to run flat out to keep up with them.

The bridge doors cycled open. Mmok waited for them, standing in front of the captain's chair, accompanied by six slim deadly figures. The machines stared at them soullessly. Telisan moved to face Mmok across the spade-shaped bridge. Overhead lights glinted off the ceramic/metal of his skull piece.

"What do you think you are doing, Mr. Mmok?" Telisan demanded.

"The question is, what are you doing, Telisan? Where are we going so fast? Why are we rearmed and provisioned? Why the radio silence?"

"I do not need to explain myself to you," Telisan snapped. He loosened his right arm and shoulder; the long expressive fingers hovered near the hilt of his Martini laser.

It wasn't lost on Mmok. "Good as you are, you are not faster than an HCR. I don't want to kill you. Don't make it necessary. So again, what do you think you are doing? You may have fooled the others by invoking Mandela's name, but I know the old son of a bitch well. An honor-bound Denlenn is the last person he'd be giving orders to. He doesn't trust you, Telisan. You don't lie and that makes you a dangerous person in our world."

"You know what we are doing and why," Telisan said. "Perhaps, you have always known. Mandela knew of or suspected Pard's secret alliance with an unknown alien race. He knew the Olympians were trading intelligence, armaments, and technology in a betrayal of the Confederacy. That is why the heavy-handed assassination, the desperate speed, and our own part.

"Did he also know that Lisa Fenaday and the crew of the *Blackbird* were captured by that race, held these last eight years as prisoners? Did he?"

Mmok looked surprised, even shaken. "I don't know what he

knows," he said finally. "Don't mistake me for a confidant of his. I just work for the Confederacy."

"Then you will be pleased to know," Telisan returned, "that the Confederate Private Warship *Sidhe* is bound for the new alien's colony world on a rescue mission."

Mmok shook his head almost reluctantly. "That would sacrifice any advantage of surprise a Confed task force might have. If these new aliens are hostile, we might have to hit them fast and take them down. Better to wait for the fleet and go in with them. Even that would have to wait on Mandela's okay. I can't sanction you going in on your own."

"The fleet could take weeks, even months," Arpen pled. "The aliens will come to suspect their tie to Olympia has been compromised. We believe they have taken the precaution of having a regular courier check in. If they come to suspect the Confederacy has discovered their secret, what will they do? What would you do, Kyle?"

Mmok's mouth became a grim line.

"Answer her," Telisan ordered.

Finally, Mmok met Arpen's eyes. "I'd get rid of the crew of the *Blackbird*, arrange a 'regrettable accident.' I'd figure that even if the Confeds knew we had the crew, they wouldn't go to war over the dead. A dead body you can explain is better than a live one that will explain for itself."

"You would be very afraid," Sharla added. "We are seven races to their one. Even if the Olympians did not fill them with lies about us, they know we are the winners of a recent genocidal war."

"Our only chance to save the crew of the *Blackbird*," said Telisan, "is to get there first, before they become suspicious, before our information becomes obsolete, before they ready their defenses and before they seek to bury the evidence. But we have to go now."

"Look," Mmok said, "I sympathize. I'm no friend of Fenaday's, but I know he loved his wife. There's a larger issue here, the security of the Confederacy and the member worlds."

"The Confederacy has a huge military to look after itself," Telisan growled. "Lisa and the *Blackbird's* crew have only us. You served as a frontline soldier in the war, Mmok. Did you not see enough of the 'big picture' there? Did you not see enough of us sent to death by those who remained safe in the rear echelon? You're a soldier. So is Lisa.

"For myself, I have served the Confederacy faithfully in all manner of hell. I owe no apologies to you or any being for my service. I serve the Confederacy still. I go to save three valuable officers. I warn you. Get from my path."

"Sorry, no sale," Mmok said. "Please don't think that you have a chance against my HCRs or that I'll hesitate to use them."

"Do you know what my fiancé asked of me?" Arpen asked.

Everyone turned to face her.

"While I was treating you, while you were in my trust, he asked me to implant a means by which we might disable you. I refused."

"That may have been a mistake," Mmok said, his face drawn and sad.

Arpen smiled gently, a small pistol appearing in her hand. "You are, I am sure, fast enough to kill me before I sight in on you. Or they are."

"Arpen, please," Mmok said, looking alarmed for the first time. "Don't do anything foolish."

Telisan started forward, flanked by Sharla.

"No!" Arpen shouted, stopping them in their tracks.

Mmok looked her in the eyes, pleading in his voice. "I know what you did. I know what it cost you. It means a lot to me, but I have a duty to do. Don't make me do this."

She shook her head, her face still gentle. "I am sorry to do this to you, Kyle, but you see I must. I have endangered the ship and my loved ones. I must remove that danger, or at least offer to die trying.

"You must surrender to us," she said slowly, bringing the weapon up, "or you must kill me. There are no other choices."

Telisan and Sharla crouched, hands on their weapons, teeth showing, the instinctive urge to defend the female of their species almost overpowering them. Arpen's weapon came up and sighted on Mmok. The HCRs did not move. Mmok stared at Arpen, his bone-white face intense and unreadable.

"Decide," Arpen said.

Mmok looked down, strength visibly draining out of him. "No," he said, as if to himself, "I just can't do it." He turned from Arpen's gun to face Cobalt. "Deactivate. Eject your power cores." Animation faded from the robots as battery cells in their armored chests fell to the carpeted deck. He turned to Arpen. "The bridge is yours, ma'am."

Telisan remembered to breathe. He and Sharla slowly stood up from their gun-fighter crouches.

Arpen put her small weapon away and walked forward to put a hand on Mmok's arm. He gave her a wan half smile and a shrug. He looked at Telisan, his cold sardonic expression restored. "You are the luckiest person I know. Don't screw it up any further."

Trying to control his shaking, Telisan nodded and turned to the wall communicator, fumbling the switch open. "Bridge crew to stations. Standby to resume burn." He turned to Arpen. "What must we do with this one?" he asked. "Till we jump, he must be kept confined."

"Leave him in Sickbay with me," Arpen said. "I will keep watch."

"Very well," Telisan said. "It will be as you wish. But there must be an additional guard. I will assign Li."

She nodded.

"Arpen," he said softly, "thank you."

She looked at him for a long measuring moment. Her face had been closed to him from the night of their argument. It was not open now, but something yielded in her, at least a little. She leaned close and spoke softly in Denleni. "Arel, thee are still my intended."

He ducked his head and whispered back in the same language. "This is good to know. One has been unsure. Now, one is only unsure of deserving the honor."

Sharla looked at them both anxiously. Now she understood the distance between her beloveds. What Telisan asked of Arpen appalled her, though she could understand it. *Stuck in the middle again,* she thought bitterly, *the fate of demi-females throughout history.*

Telisan caught her look and sighed. He knew there would be, as the humans put it, a few licks from that quarter before the morning watch.

Chapter Twenty-One

Shasti Rainhell was reborn into a world of pain. The unfairness of it made her scream. Where was the kindness of God the priests told of? Perhaps she now faced divine judgment. She remembered startled faces, unarmed men and women, even a young boy, dying at her hand. She had dealt death without mercy. Now came judgment, now fire.

Her eyes snapped open, lights swimming in her vision. She heard a soft voice. The fires seemed to be receding for now. A face hung before her eyes, alien and strange, somehow comforting. The eyes were enormous pools, seeming to promise understanding, sympathy, even benediction. She realized her arms were under restraints.

"Hello," the alien said. Its voice, like the face, was warm. For a moment she thought she might be in one of the idle fantasies she sometimes daydreamed, where she actually had a mother instead of an aching emptiness. Then the background came more into focus.

"The *Sidhe?*" she croaked.

"Yes," the alien said.

She recognized it now as a Denlenn, though it looked different from any she had seen before. Female?

"I am Dr. Arpen," she said. "You know my fiancé, Telisan."

It came back in a rush. "Where is Robert?" she gasped, starting to struggle.

"Stop, stop," Arpen said. "He lives. He is in the next bay, though not yet conscious. He is not made so strongly as you. His injuries are serious, but I believe he will recover fully."

"I want to see him," she said. "Undo the restraints."

"Better for you to wait," Arpen said gently. "You have been close to death yourself."

Shasti threw herself at the restraints. They creaked but held.

"You are as stubborn as I have heard." Arpen smiled. "Very well, but only for a moment." Arpen undid the restraints. "Orderly." A human Shasti did not recognize leaned in. "Help here." Arpen gestured. "She is too tall to lean on me."

"I need no help," Shasti growled. She rose to a sitting position and nearly blacked out. Blinding pain drove out sense, forcing her to cling to the bed rail. It frightened her. Her body was designed for self-repair and pain control. That she felt so bad, despite proper medical care, meant she had been far-gone indeed. Arpen's face greeted her again when her vision cleared. Behind it she saw another familiar face, Shizuyo Mourner.

"What's this," Shasti murmured through the pain, "an Enshar reunion?"

Mourner smiled. "Just about. Only this time I have help to patch up all you wild-eyed hero types. Good thing too. You and Fenaday did the best imitations of dead people I ever saw. I wanted to bust you up for spare parts. Dr. Arpen insisted on trying."

"She jests," Arpen said reassuringly, "but now you must promise to do what I say. You are not strong yet, and we have little time to restore you to health before your strength may again be called on."

"What's going on?" Shasti demanded. "Where are we bound for?"

"I will call for Telisan later, after you rest again," Arpen said. "He will explain as much of the situation as can be. Some of the news must wait till another receives word first."

"I hate mysteries," Shasti said.

"I'm sure," Arpen sympathized. The comment, which might

have enraged Shasti had it come from Mourner, did not irritate Shasti, to her surprise.

"I begin to see what Telisan sees in you," Shasti said. "How is he?"

"Troubled," Arpen said, a shadow crossing her face. "He bears many concerns."

"Wait," Shasti said, as more of her memory came flooding back. "Dan Rigg is still alive..."

"He is aboard, resting in his quarters," Mourner said, "as is Leda Jenner. We felt that Olympia might be too hot to hold her for now and brought her with us."

"Good," she said, relieved. "Now take me to Robert."

Mourner waved to the orderly. He approached, looking somewhat nervously at Shasti. The Olympian stood nearly a foot taller than him. Shasti slipped an arm over his shoulder and struggled to her feet, swaying. She found Dr. Arpen under her other arm. They slowly made their way to the next bay.

Shasti's breath caught when she saw Robert Fenaday. He rested on his stomach, surrounded by monitors and machines. The surgeries to repair the stab wound to his spine looked fresh. Regenerators had linked the material of the cord and sealed the wound. His leg looked badly swollen and black from where Pard struck him with several times the strength of an ordinary man. Weight had melted off Fenaday despite the IVs of nutrients and glucose hung around him. He looked far older than his thirty-six years. They helped her to a chair, where Shasti could lay a hand on his arm.

"He is still in an induced coma," Mourner said. "We are keeping him under so we can maximize the repairs using regenerators. We have to get him back on his feet."

"When will he wake?" Shasti demanded, unsettled by the sight of Fenaday looking so corpselike. *Standard humans are so fragile,* she thought, *so short-lived.*

"In another day, but only briefly so we can check his neurological status," Mourner said. "All the tissue and nerve damage will be repaired by then. We plan to put him back under for perhaps another day if we can. We'd have kept you under longer, but your system fights coma too well."

"I would like to be here when he awakens," Shasti said.

"If you get back to bed now," Arpen said, "I think we can arrange that."

Shasti suffered their hands on her, leading her back to her bed. Once there, she refused to rest until Mourner and Arpen filled her in on at least some of what had happened on Olympia. News of the dead alien on Olympia did not shock her as much as it did the others. The appearance of the ninth species had been inevitable, a fact to be faced, not flinched from. Satisfied for now, she lay back. The pillow felt good under her head. *Everyone important to me is alive,* she thought. Sleep struck her down in an unguarded instant.

When she awakened again, she felt more her normal self. Awareness came in a flash. She saw Telisan at the foot of her bed. He grinned at her. "Hello, Telisan. It's good to see you."

"And you," he replied. "We have gone through much to get sight of you."

"Yes, thank you. I'm sure I owe you a great deal."

Telisan shook his head. "You are my friend," he said.

Shasti looked away for a second. "Heaven save you from friends such as me. Thank you all the same.

"What's the situation?" she asked. "Arpen and Mourner are holding something back from me. They told me what happened after Pard's death, but no more. Where are we going?"

Telisan looked her steadily in the eye. "This is difficult. I fear I will cause you pain."

She shrugged. "Life is pain."

"It is also news that should be first told to Robert, but they wish to keep him down several more hours at least." He mulled her question over for a few seconds, rubbing a hand across his face. "Very well, it is not fair to leave you in the dark. You know of the alien race Pard allied with, to whom he sold armaments. We captured one of the aliens and Pard's records. The creature is on board, confined to the iso-lab. Only the command crew know of its existence."

She nodded, surprised both by the story and Telisan's audacity in pulling it off.

"These aliens captured a Confederation vessel and crew over

eight years ago. From this source they learned of the Confederacy and its makeup. They elected to make contact with Olympia in the hope of securing allies and trade. The vessel was the CSS *Blackbird* under command of Lisa Fenaday. She and two others of the crew still lived as of six months ago." Telisan paused. "We are on our way to that system now in hope of effecting a rescue."

Shasti lay stunned, not knowing what to feel. She'd never believed in Fenaday's search for his lost wife, sometimes regarding it as a mild insanity. People did not return from ships lost in deep space. A ship contained only so much air. *Sidhe* had been just another privateer to her and Lisa an abstraction. She hadn't cared about Fenaday's motivations, at least, not until she had learned to care about him. She'd told him little of those feelings, nascent as they were, even in those happy months together in New Eire. Only days ago, she'd first understood that she felt the beginning of something deeper, though she could neither explain nor understand it. Unfamiliar feelings tore at Shasti, strange, wild mixes of relief, grief, and disappointment. She felt as if she were sliding out of control. With the discipline of a brutal lifetime, she choked down all her feelings, retreating back into the comforting numbness in which she lived.

"Do you want to be the one to tell him?" asked Telisan. "You are close to him and of the same species."

She shook her head. "I don't think that would be wise."

"I think I understand," Telisan replied. "I will tell him after he is awake. I am doing all he would have me do in the meanwhile."

Shasti recovered rapidly from the emotional shock. If anything, her brain seemed more cool and analytic than it had been in a long while. Pard lay dead in a gorge. She knew Robert well enough to understand that the rumor of Lisa's capture would invoke the obsessive demon that drove him to the stars searching for her. It might be best if she shelved her feelings about Robert for now. Shasti even felt a small, guilty relief about it. *It might be cowardice,* she thought, *but I have only now shed my own demon. With Pard dead, my life, for once, does not revolve around some urgent passionate core. I am free. What do I want?*

She shook free of her reverie. "The Confederacy would never approve this. What force do you have on board?"

Telisan grimaced uncomfortably, a gesture he shared with humans. "They might not. I left the ambassador with the idea that I am under Mandela's orders to pull out. I commandeered a platoon of Marines. With the ASATs and embassy troops we have aboard, and our surviving LEAFs, we boast a short company of mixed ground troops. We also have Mmok and what's left of his cyber-company."

"Mmok?" Shasti said in surprise. "I thought he was dead."

"He recovered from his injuries and led the attack on Pard's compound. It is the main reason we succeeded."

"You never fooled him."

"No," Telisan said. "It is complicated, but he is confined to Sick-bay, his cyber-troops inactive."

Shasti nodded. "Very impressive."

Mourner's head appeared around the corner. "Fenaday is coming out of it early. He is asking for you both."

Shasti slid to her feet with only a slight wobble. "You go see him. I want him to hear it from you. Tell him…tell him, that I'm in my quarters asleep and that I'll be by later."

"If that is what you wish," Telisan said.

Shasti threw on a robe. "It is."

"Shasti," Telisan said, "I have a question."

She looked back at the Denlenn curiously, "Yes?"

"One hesitates, though we are friends, to ask this question."

"After all this?" she said, "all you have done? Ask anything."

"I asked Robert why he led the landing on Enshar. He said Mandela ordered it, fearing someone might sabotage a shuttle with just Duna and me aboard in hope of canceling the mission. Apparently it was you he feared, trained assassin that you are."

"It was before I knew you and Duna," she answered, without embarrassment.

"Ah," he said, shaken and trying to conceal it.

"Nothing personal," she added, as if to reassure.

Telisan looked into her cool green eyes. They reflected light back at him, nothing more. "Please rest, my friend, there may be little chance in the future." She smiled at him. He remembered how she kept her face closed to almost everyone and took it for the rare concession it was.

Despite Mourner's protests, Shasti left Sickbay. She passed curious crewmembers. Only the Enshar veterans knew her. Some greeted her by name. Their relief at her survival would have warmed even her cool heart under other circumstances. She brushed aside any questions on the pretext of fatigue and made it to her cabin. As the door opened, noisy barks and a very happy dog greeted her. Risky looked much the worse for wear, bandaged and moving slowly. He'd been watered, fed, and attended to, but clearly missed her.

She sat on the floor next to the dog with a sigh and pulled the battered shepherd close. "Well, it looks like it is you and me again."

———

I n the sickbay, a frail and fretful Robert Fenaday looked up as Telisan walked in. "Where's Shasti?" he demanded. "Is she all right?"

"Yes," Telisan replied. "She's in her cabin resting. She promises to be by later. First, there is something you need to hear." He sat down by his friend's bedside, putting a hand on the human's. "It's about your wife."

The End

Afterword

Replacement Hearts is a tale of the Conchirri War and its aftermath and how another cyborg found peace afterward.

Replacement Hearts

A CONFED SPACE STORY

"God, I wouldn't want to be that poor bastard."

"Yeah," replied the woman next to him, shutting down her fork-lift. "Do we do them any favors saving them when they're like that?" The pair disappeared through the airlock out of the cargo area.

I ignored the comments, as I always do. They never realize that with my ceramic skull piece came better than human hearing. Better, I stopped myself, better. I'd have laughed bitterly if I laughed anymore. Since I'd become little more than a brain in a can, I'd lost such impulses. Laughing, crying, and screaming had all gone, in that order.

I cast angular shadows on Pictor Space Station's cream-colored corridors as I headed for the freight office. My shadow remained human, two legs, two arms, and a head, but precious little of it had come into the world with me. When a Conchirri fighter rammed LST-190, everything became fire and pain. When my eyes, or rather eye, opened again, I expected to find God. Instead I found a living death in a VA hospital. The docs were kind and the psychs skilled, but nothing changed the fact that my limbs had been destroyed down to stumps and I was burned all over. Nothing left to do but rescue the brain, some of the face and torso, and plant it in a cyborg body. A near total prosthetic, I even had a replacement heart. After a year of rehab, I went back into the line and helped bomb the lizards into extinction when we reduced the Conchirri Redoubt.

And after that...well without a war I had no purpose. I was a mechanical shell, a sexless tin puppet. My parents, thank God, hadn't lived to see this. I never cared much for the rest of the family and had no use for my brother.

You can never go home again. Too fucking true...

———

I walked into the office of the Tarabey Mining Company, which ran most of the local mining around Kapteyn's star. The red dwarf lay thirteen lights out from Earth. Scientists theorized it had come into our galactic arm from somewhere else, bringing with it a system of planets and asteroids full of chemical and physical compounds rarely found anywhere else. It would be a miner's paradise if there were yellow light or oxygen anywhere, but comforts were few near Kapteyn.

Landa Solae looked up as I walked in. A stocky fiftyish, she ran the freight office with a crop and an unsympathetic nature. She liked me, as I rarely spoke and took all the long, slow hauls into the mining worlds. I also charged less than other cargo runners since I made so little impact on life support.

"Hey, Tinman," she said.

I rarely used my real name, Pasha Gurov. I suspected Landa preferred to think of me as another piece of machinery, like the forklifts down on the freight decks.

"Gotta run for me, Landa?" I was almost surprised by the sound of my own voice, realizing that I hadn't spoken aloud since I headed back from Dis camp in the outer asteroids.

"Yeah," she said, snapping her bubble gum. "You mind going back to Dis?"

"It's all the same to me."

"Got something new for delivery," she began, but a commotion from outside the office drew her head up. She heaved herself up from behind the desk. I followed.

Landa's assistant, Roger, faced a pleasant-looking young woman in a Confed Customs uniform. "Look, Commissioner, the papers are all in order."

"What's the problem?" Landa asked.

"The problem," the Confed said, her lips drawn thin in distaste, "is this…thing in the box."

"I keep telling Commissioner Reagan," Roger said, his bald head sheened with sweat, "that it's legitimate cargo."

"That's not the point." Reagan looked at Lana. "This android in the box is. The thing is made for prostitution."

Landa shrugged. "Not a lot of women out these ways. Men get lonely. Some women too."

"And you think having a fucking doll," she snapped an accusing finger at the metal and plastic crate, "helps? You're a woman; you can't believe this is a good idea."

Landa sighed. "I wasn't planning on fucking the thing myself."

"It degrades women," the customs agent snapped.

Landa looked at her. "There have been pros since the days of the caveman, and they'll be turning tricks on Judgment Day. These things," she waved at the crate, "may save some woman from it, or at least from the low, rough end of the trade. The machine doesn't care; it just does what it's programmed to do."

"It's disgusting," the younger woman said.

"Grow up," Landa said. "It's just a sex toy that looks like a woman. Next year they're making a male one, a better version of a vibrator for lonely women on stations who can't date their subordinates."

Reagan threw the pad down on the box. "Get this thing off my station." She spun on her heel and left.

Landa snapped her gum derisively. "She probably needs to spend more time with her vibrator. Too tense."

Roger laughed and handed her the forms and disappeared into the back.

She turned to me. "Here's your cargo. It's an android, a robot joygirl for the miners on Dis. If it works out, I'll order more. Goddamn things cost a mint, but maybe I'll get a boy model for the commissioner." She laughed. "Here, sign for it. Standard rates."

I signed, careful not to put too much pressure on the stylus. My prosthetic hands were stronger than human and occasionally I still had trouble with feedback.

"Roger will bring it down with the regular load. She's the only special cargo; just hook her up to a d-sine power unit for maintenance."

"Okay," I replied. "It'll take a few hours to rig that kind of power hookup."

"When can you leave?" Landa looked up at me.

"As soon as the *Chukar* is refueled and reprovisioned." My ship was an old landing ship similar to the one I'd been burned on. It could handle months in space and carry a crew of six with room for a platoon of armored troopers. I flew it alone.

"The roustabouts will have you loaded by 0600," she said. "Good flight."

"Thanks," I said, because it was what people did. I walked out.

Behind me, I heard Roger return and say to Landa, "Well, at least we know he won't sample the merchandise."

She laughed.

I kept walking.

——

Next morning, I finished preflighting *Chukar*. I'd named the barge for the plump birds my uncle had hunted back in Russia. The rounded hull no longer wore Confed gray but a green and white combination that appealed to me. After the roustabouts stowed the cargo, I rolled out of the launch bay into the sullen red light of Kapteyn and pulled away from Pictor's two-kilometer flattened disk. With a burn from the engine that would have been hard on a normal human, I blazed into space. Away from the species I'd once belonged to.

After the autopilot locked, I sat back and pulled a cord from the ship's computer and plugged into the main vice left to me. I'd loaded the *Chukar* library with every book and vid I could find. I also had the best VR system money could buy. I plugged myself in from a dataport in my ceramic skull meant for the medtechs to check my systems. I wasn't supposed to do this, but I didn't care. So I drifted away into games and stories. *Chukar* made its way toward the mining camp weeks away.

———

An alarm brought me out of the Beethoven's Fifth and back into a cockpit filled white smoke drifting up from gangway to the main deck. I realized it must have been shrilling for a while. I'd been far out of it. Cursing, I unplugged myself and climbed clumsily to my feet. The ship's auto fire-fighting system should have cut in. My artificial heart didn't race, but fear still filled me. I hated fire.

Smoke came from the area where I'd secured the android. Great, all I needed was Landa bitching at me over having to submit a claim to Lloyds. I snapped an extinguisher off the wall and cut power to the cylinder in the same move.

Chukar, I ordered, using my link to the ship's AI, *cut off all 02 and seal this deck.*

The AI acknowledged with its usual brevity; I'd never added any human interface to it. Didn't want to pretend I had company.

I knew my internal resources could keep me going for hours yet, and vacuum was the fastest way to get the fire under control. Air whooshed out and with it sound. I fired the extinguisher and the fire guttered out. I spent a few more minutes making sure there was no source of ignition before restoring atmosphere.

The outside of the cylinder was charred with long splits running down the plastic cover. I decided to open it and check the contents. Any damage and I'd have to return to Pictor and Landa, a prospect I dreaded. I cracked the seal and the lid slid back.

She lay on a bed of red velvet, a sailor's dream of a barbarian queen. Blond hair lay heavy on her shoulders over full breasts, round hips, and strong thighs. The body was almost overripe, nearly a cartoon of a woman's form. I was surprised by the dull ache it raised in me. Once, the sight of her would have brought me to a halt, struck dumb. Now, I was the fragment of a man in a can, with nothing to lust with and only memories of passion.

Its eyes opened. They were the blue of a summer sky and empty of anything human, but they tracked over to me.

"I'm Sassa. I'm here to please you. Tell me what you want." The mouth moved in a good simulation of human speech, but the voice was synthetic and stilted.

"Perform a system check," I snapped. "Report any damage."

"Internal diagnostics mode inoperable, basic systems functioning, memory indicates 2% CPU usage," she replied.

"Unfortunately that means little to me," I said, "except that you are functioning at a low level, and I am betting your software is fucked."

"My software fucked," Sassa repeated, straightening up in the crèche. "I am fucked?"

"Well it seems to be your function," I growled.

"I don't understand."

"You're a mechanical whore," I said, angry for reasons I didn't want to think about.

"What is a whore?" she asked; her face blank of expression.

I found an operable diagnostic board in her crèche. It confirmed my fears. The software uploads for decanting the android were fried. I couldn't even put her back to sleep mode.

"What the hell I am I going to do with you?" I said. "It's four more weeks to Dis."

She looked at me. "Query. What is a whore?"

I frowned. "I guess the best I can do is give you data uploads from my VR and AI systems here. There should be enough for you to figure it out yourself. Are you ambulatory?"

"Affirmative." She climbed out of the crèche and the awkwardness of her android body reminded me of my own machine replacements. They'd made her tall, nearly five-ten. I skittered between pity for it and the dull anger I'd felt since she went active. It fell to the deck, but the luscious body wasn't flesh and blood and neither cut or bruised. She climbed up, nothing of pain in her face, and stood naked, facing me. With the eyes open and so empty, the voluptuous body seemed somehow sad, even repellent.

"Follow me."

We clumped up to the command deck. I gestured at the copilot seat, but the gesture meant nothing to the android. "Sit."

She dropped into the seat with a thud.

I plugged a lead into her skull, then mine, then into the ship's computer, adding the power of the virtual reality system I'd custom built. Since I wasn't running a simulation, the VR gave me only a flat plain. I was myself. Oh, I could have had an avatar of my old body, but it would not have felt any different. Truth was I was afraid of any such pretense. That way lay madness.

I turned on the VR plain. The android stood nearby, a featureless white silhouette of a woman, an unpainted canvas for me to work on. I started downloads on human relations and biology and queued up social stuff I used for the game simulations on VR.

Data whirled toward Sassa at a constantly increasing rate. The VR displayed this as swirling leaves, which disappeared as they touched the white silhouette. But it was no longer white, the android was evidently integrating the data, she appeared as she had lying in her crèche, but the body was upright, filled with vibrant life.

I felt something pass me, like a breeze at midnight. Imagination? I shook off the distraction. The data flow began to accelerate again; the machine's CPU capacity astonished me. I knew the war had spurred computer development, but I had never seen anything like it. I focused on controlling the data as she...it was near the outer limits of my own capacity.

Time passed, or did it? In VR you sometimes felt like you'd always been there. A chime brought me out of it; my internal system sensor had gone on. I needed to add nutrients to my system. Odd, I thought I'd done so two months ago; I should have had at least two weeks left.

I glanced at my instruments and froze. I'd been sitting in the chair linked to the android for two weeks.

"What!" I muttered. "The download should have taken hours at most. What the hell happened?"

"I'm sorry," a voice startled me. "But once you opened up the universe to me, I could not stop myself, I had to have all there was. It's so wonderful."

Her eyes held and compelled me. No longer an empty blue sky, they shimmered with intelligence and curiosity. The body, which had been overripe for my taste, now seemed perfection incarnate.

"Get a grip," I said.

"On what?" she asked.

"Nothing," I managed. "A human alone sometimes talks to himself."

"You're not alone," she said.

"Knock it off," I said, my voice harsh. "You're cargo to me; a synthetic joygirl for lonely miners."

"What?" she said, then it seemed like she was listening to some inner voice. I couldn't read her expression, but there seemed something of horror in it. "This is what I was made for?"

"Yes," I said, feeling a vague sense of shame for my species.

"Surely there is more to my existence than this. I can be more."

"Like what?" I said.

"Like this," she replied.

The ship disappeared in an instant, and we stood in a virtual world. Only it was detailed in a way I'd never seen before. We stood on a hillside, and the detail of it dazzled me, a green lawn, full of blue and yellow flowers stretched down to a shining lake surrounded by gentle tossing trees. A breeze flowed over me and I felt it. God, I felt it on four good limbs. The sun and wind caressed them where they projected from the shorts and t-shirt I wore.

"Does it please you?"

I spun. I'd been so overwhelmed by sensations I'd forgotten Sassa. Whatever I was going to say died on my lips. She wore a simple blue dress of the same cornflower blue as her eyes. The total effect was vastly more erotic than the clinical nakedness of her crèche. The effect on me was more than mental. My body responded like a teenager's.

Sassa saved me from having to speak. She slipped out of the dress and it fell around her feet. "It's been a long time, Pasha. Come to me."

She didn't need to invite me twice. It was like the first time, the best time, and every time at once. Sassa was skilled and more, joyful in lovemaking. Her strong lush body drove me mad. I couldn't even speak, overwhelmed by an animal need for her, driven by the fact that I'd never dreamed of doing this again.

Afterward we lay on the hillside, me trying to catch my breath, almost literally shaking with exhaustion. I could only barely remember having made love like this. I was so grateful for the lassitude and satisfaction spreading through my body that I refused to think, to wonder why this was happening. As I drifted off, Sassa sang softly in a language I didn't know.

I woke hours later, turned to her, and she smiled. We made love again, slowly and tenderly. After, she rubbed my back. I noticed a picnic set that I hadn't seen before. Sassa spread a supper and we ate in companionable silence, as I feared to break the spell.

My god, I thought. *She seems so real.*

"Let's go for a walk, my love," she said, reaching down and picking up her blue dress and shrugging it on. "This is our home."

Caught in the dream and unquestioning, I gathered up my clothes, dressed, and took her hand. We walked down the hillside. I said nothing, lost in the fantasy and happy for the first time in a decade. Grass tickled my sandaled feet. I loved the sensation.

Day turned to night and we slept under the stars, waking to a warm breeze. I don't know how many days passed this way. Eventually we found ourselves at a cabin under some trees. Sassa cooked and I cut firewood and slept in her arms.

One morning after breakfast, we reached a flat place with a gravel road. Sassa led me up the road toward a copse of trees. I saw an old aircar. Seated on the rear engine deck was a man. I froze when I saw him.

He looked up and a familiar smile cut across the pleasant broad face. "Hey, Pasha. Nice to see you, Sassa."

"Mac," I whispered. "Tommy Macmillan, you died on Okara III."

"Not here," Sassa murmured back. "No Conchirri war here, no burning tanks. He lives in a little home in back of those trees with his wife, Lise."

"She died when the Conchirri hit Fenris IV. That's when he joined up."

"No war here," she said.

"See you later, Mac," Sassa called.

"Okay, come by tomorrow. Lise is making lasagna."

We walked on, but there were clouds now, a storm was building in me. It wasn't real. None of it. The exhausted feeling from making love, the beautiful peaceful valley, Mac, none of it. I didn't have the parts of a human. I was Spam in a can.

The thought of Mac jarred me. Sassa could not have found information on Mac in *Chukar's* systems. She'd downloaded everything in the ship's computer, everything in the VR system, and finally, everything in my own mind. I'd been emptied like a can of tomatoes. My mind had been invaded, raped.

I pulled free of Sassa as the sky went dark and thunder rumbled. Open shock registered on her face.

And then we were back on the deck of the *Chukar*. I sat up slowly pulling the lead from my ceramic skull with a cool deliberation I didn't feel. I forced myself to turn toward Sassa where she lay in the copilot chair. She too sat up, pulling a lead out from under her thick blond hair. She looked at me, no longer appearing quite so real as she had in my...dream, or whatever it was we'd shared, but she was no longer the machine I'd uncrated.

"Didn't you want to stay, my love?" she said, in a voice that hit me in places I did not have. Something like puzzlement drifted over the perfect face.

"It wasn't real," I raged. "None of it. The sex, the hillside, Mac, none of it was real, all simulations." I looked deep into her eyes where I so wanted to see depth, complexity, and truth and I couldn't tell what I saw.

"And you, Sassa," I said, slowly standing, "Sassa isn't even your name; it's your model. You don't love me, or anything else, you simulate reactions."

She too stood, walking over to the bed I occasionally use when I don't sleep in my flight chair. She pulled a sheet off and wrapped it around herself. Again, it was more erotic than her nakedness and somehow it seemed a statement as well. Her face was pensive as she turned back to me. "And if I simulate it so well that you cannot tell it from the real thing, does it matter?"

"Yes," I cried.

She tossed her head to move the golden hair out of her eyes. "And if I do it so well that I cannot tell? Does it matter?"

Were those tears glimmering in her eyes? No, impossible, and if they were, again it was only programming.

"Sassa," I said, schooling my voice to gentle. "You're not a person. You may have dumped more data into your memory than your designers believed possible. The simulation may be near perfect. But you're not alive."

"Are you?" she asked.

I fell silent, no longer sure myself.

She looked away. "You tell me that I do not want. That I don't feel. But I cannot separate these appearances from what you tell me is the truth."

A weary disgust filled me. I remembered Landa and the commissioner. *"It's just a sex toy, like a vibrator."* Here I was discussing life and love with a doll. I'd lost everything in the war but awareness and self-respect. I could see people laughing at me for feeling anything for Sassa. What was I going to do? Buy her? Selling *Chukar* and all I had wouldn't have covered it. I may have been maimed, but I was not going to become pathetic.

Yet I could no longer bear her gaze either and turned away. "Return to your crèche, switch to minimum power mode." I looked at the chronometer, to my shock I saw we'd been gone weeks of real-time. "We'll reach Dis in thirty-one hours. Remain there until then."

Her footsteps sounded behind me. I turned back to the controls. A lot of maintenance and checks had gone undone. I lost myself in the mechanical efficiency of tending to *Chukar*. It was all I had, and I had neglected it.

Thirty-one hours passed quickly, and Dis grew in my screens. A well named world, great, grim, red, and rocky. Mines on its surface used mass accelerators to shoot mineral slag into orbit. Dis had no atmosphere, and I made an easy approach, coming down in the roofed-over cavern of Lode. A sliding hatchway rolled back to admit my ship, then the elevator lowered *Chukar* to the cargo level.

I forced myself to stump down to the cargo deck. Sassa lay in her burned and damaged crèche like a corpse.

"Activate," I snapped.

Animation flooded back into her and she sat up smoothly. She turned to face me and started to speak.

"Remain silent," I said. "Follow me." I turned quickly so I didn't have to look at her.

We walked down to the *Chukar's* main lock. When we got there, I realized she still wore my old sheet. For a second I thought about asking her to drop it, but it seemed petty.

The hatch cycled open and two men and a woman stood there on the dock. The woman was slim and dark with a ragged haircut and form-fitting black clothes. The men were hard-bitten miners. They looked at Sassa as wolves look at steak.

"Hey," the woman said. "What's it doing out of its crate?" Her sharp green eyes bored into mine.

I felt naked before those accusing eyes. "Malfunction. Her crèche caught fire. She's...it's undamaged."

"Damn," one of the miners said. "I can't wait to plug into that thing."

"Yeah," the other said. "Maria, you may have made a mistake. None of your other girls can compete with roboslut here."

"Imagine how much they'll miss all your affection," Maria said. She came forward and pulled the sheet off Sassa, who didn't resist. She inspected the perfect body. "No damage. Report your CPU status and diagnostic state."

"All systems nominal," Sassa said in a flat voice. "CPU at 20% of capacity and undamaged."

"Okay," Maria said. She signed a clipboard and handed it to me. "The crèche was for shipping, you can dump it. I'll take the toy. You boys get down to the cargo hold with a lifter and get the rest of the cargo.

"Right," the shorter minor said. He grabbed Sassa's rear as he passed her and squeezed it hard. "See ya later."

Sassa didn't react.

Maria tossed me the sheet. "Follow," she said to Sassa and strode off.

Sassa started forward, then stopped and turned to face me. She looked at me steadily, with no hint of blame or accusation—only a child-like disappointment.

"I could have been more," she whispered. "We could have had

more." Then she walked after Maria, a machine following a program.

The lock cycled closed and I was left wondering what the hell I was. I walked on feet that didn't feel the hard metal of the deck, to the darkened pilot's compartment. I stood there alone for hours, as if I could somehow hide in a cloak of eternal night. A flesh and blood man might have gotten drunk and lost himself in another woman, could have started a fight and let someone else's fists beat Sassa out of their mind. I had no such option.

I looked at my ship, which was all I had, as my prosthetic eye cycled through its modes, starlight, infrared, radar. I'd talked to the ship in lonely hours, but unlike Sassa, it had never spoken back, never sung to me, never offered anything of comfort.

It came to me then, as all great certainties do. One moment it was simply there, stark and irrefutable. I had no life. Nor could have one in the future, destroyed shadow of a man that I was. I'd turned my back on the only joy or peace I'd been offered since the war. Why? Because of pride, not willing to be mocked for living with a toy doll. Well, hadn't they made a toy doll out of me? Maybe I was entitled. Maybe I was mad. But another day of this life wasn't worth having. I needed Sassa.

I opened the lock box under my command chair and pulled out an Ingersoll laser, standard Marine issue and illegal. I'd never quite known why I had it, protection or in case I wanted an easy out some day. I belted the bulky Ingersoll on and twitched it around to my back then pulled a travel cloak from a locker. The nondescript garment was common among spacers, who always need access to their tools and equipment.

I walked out of my ship and onto the spacedock. As usual, it was freezing cold. Harsh white work-lights threw hard shadows around the ships, equipment, and stores. Voices echoed though I saw no one. Boots clattered on metal walkways and ladders, or on the slagged rock of Dis.

There was no security on Dis; it wasn't a port of entry, just a miner's hole. Anyone could come and go, so I tried not to attract attention by moving furtively. I didn't see anyone I knew. I passed out of the spacedock into the habitat sections and wrapped my travel cloak closer.

I knew where Maria's place was. Everyone did. She'd come as a miner and found the money was surer with drugs, booze, and prostitution. She bought a place called the Red Star on the canyon wall. It started as a general store and now stocked all manner of illicit pleasure.

I wound my way through corridors heading for the crater wall. Eventually I found myself in front of the Red Star. I rarely came here, having no real need of it. Now, I studied it as a soldier, looking at a multitude of entrances. A group of miners and spacers, all men, made their noisy way to the doors. I fell in behind them.

Smoke of various types and the dull roar of too many people talking filled the inside. I spotted Maria at the far end of the room by the bar and steered for a small table at the back. I passed a number of men around a blowsy woman with a short skirt.

"Hey, Annie," one of the men said. "You better watch out, the new girl's gonna cut into your action."

"Only for the boys who don't know what to do with a real woman," she shouted back. Raucous laughter followed.

I reached my seat. A younger, slender girl with a surprisingly bright smile took my order for a beer. I asked her about the new girl.

She grimaced. "It's not actually a girl. Android. You ask me, it's better than having a real girl have to do that. No offense," she added.

"None taken," I said. "Is it going to come down?"

"Nah, it's probably going to be working nonstop soon as they figure it out," she said. "It's upstairs in the back room."

"Oh, the one against the back of the crater wall?"

She gestured over her shoulder. "Nope, the one right over the front."

I tipped her and she walked off, avoiding groping hands with a practiced ease.

I started toward the twin staircase, leaving my drink on the table. Joe the bouncer stopped me. "Hey, Tinman. Where ya going?"

"There's a line for the bathroom, as always" I said. "I was going to use the upstairs one."

"Nobody goes upstairs unless they pay for a girl. You know the rules."

"Oh, for Christ's sake, Joe. I'm not going to sneak in on a girl."

"Yeah," Joe said. "I forgot. Go ahead."

I started up the stairs.

"Hey," Joe said. "Wait a minute. You don't have a johnson to pee out of either. Whaddya need a bathroom for?"

I gave him a glare. "I'm still alive in here and sometimes there are wastes that need to be eliminated. How much you want to know about this?"

Joe raised a hand in disgust. "Forget I asked."

I walked up. When I was sure Joe wasn't looking, I cut left and walked down the short corridor to the front and opened the door.

Sassa sat on the bed. A man stood over her, his pants down. "Hey," he said. "Wait your turn."

"Sure," I said. "Wrong room."

He turned away, back to Sassa. I reached him in two strides. I didn't need to draw the Ingersoll. My hands were metal and plastic, and I remembered my training. I hit hard, maybe too hard. As the miner fell across the bed, a stain of red came from under his scalp.

Sassa looked at me, her face blank. "Why are you here?"

"Do you want something more than this?" I asked.

"You already know the answer."

"Will you come with me? I don't know what I have to offer you."

A slow sad smile came over her face and she again looked like a live human. "Yes, I will come."

"Did they leave you any clothes?" I asked.

"No."

I opened the closet door and found a shirt and harem pants. These I threw to Sassa.

"But how will we get away? I'm valuable property. This Maria will not let me go."

I looked at the dead man on the bed. "I think we are past worrying about theft."

From under my cloak, I drew the Ingersoll and dialed it to tight beam. I opened the window, leaned out, and played the beam over the building storefront. Flames broke out instantly. Seconds later, there were screams and shouts. A buzzer went off, as did the sprinkler.

I opened the door a crack; half-naked people were running around, with sprinklers dousing them. I took aim with the laser and fired down the hall. Curtains flared and steam from the laser's beam obscured the hallway.

"Let's go," I said. We headed out looking for a back stair. I found one quickly obligingly labeled *fire exit*. I also found a travel cloak lying on the ground and picked it up, whipping it around Sassa's shoulders.

"Hey, Tinman."

I turned, keeping the laser under my cloak.

"Where you going with that?" Joe held a short nasty club in his hand.

"Damned if I know," I said and fired. The club exploded in smoking fragments. Joe screamed and covered his face.

We fled down the stairs and out into the crowd. Clad in our travel cloaks, we didn't draw much attention. As soon as we were out of sight, we started running. I run clumsily, but I don't tire. Sassa ran more fluidly. In minutes, we reached *Chukar's* dock.

I cycled the dock door. There she was, my ship, its green and white hull gleaming under the lights, looking like salvation. We ran toward her.

I didn't see the machine gun until it stuttered, rounds tearing into my legs and dumping me to the ground. Lights spun and lead crackled. I couldn't feel pain, but my systems all screamed damage.

I flipped over to see Maria and two men closing in on us. One held a submachine gun, its barrel smoking. The others held pistols.

"Tinman, Tinman," Maria said. "How could you do this to me? Go nuts over a sex toy."

"A sex toy with a laser," Sassa said.

We all looked at her in surprise. Sassa stood with the Ingersoll leveled at them.

Maria looked at Sassa as if she had a horn on her head. "What the hell?"

"Ignore it," said the machine-gunner. "It's just a bot. It ain't programmed for combat…"

The laser licked out and the machine gun glowed. He howled and dropped it.

Maria and the other raised their guns.

"My chassis," Sassa said, "is similar to the ones used on a humanform combat robot. Bullets will damage this pretty plastic but not enough to save you."

"Guns," I ordered, "drop them and run."

They did.

Sassa came over to me.

"I'm ruined," I said. "You got everything I know when you interfaced with my mind. Take the ship. Get away."

Sassa looked deeply into my eyes then reached under my arms and pulled me up with ease. We entered the ship. Sassa got me into the command chair, and I plugged into *Chukar*. Automatics cycled the hatch above us as alarms hooted, and Dis Control shouted in my ears.

Chukar lifted into space, and I hit a full burn. For lack of any better thought, I headed us outsytem.

"This is Dis control," this voice was more authoritative, "*Chukar*, answer. We are launching two patrol cutters and we have sent an alert to all stations and outposts in Kapteyn's system. You have nowhere to go."

I left the engines on full burn. Unless those cutters were at Defcon 4, they wouldn't launch for at least a half-hour, probably longer. He shouldn't have told me.

"A poor deal for you," I said, gesturing with my good arm at my slagged and wrecked legs.

She smiled at me, then strapped me in and began connecting me to the ship's computer. "I have a plan," she said. "It's the only way out. You'll have to trust me." She plugged the lead into my skull. I could feel her ghost past me to touch the ship's AI. I didn't care. Whatever Sassa decided was okay with me. I leaned back. We were together no matter what followed.

The ship disappeared, and we were on the hillside again, over the valley. Spring softened the world around us. I laughed for the joy of feeling the breeze play over my body and the heat of the sun on four good limbs.

Sassa laughed too, a musical sound no orchestra could have rivaled. She smiled and the blue of her eyes reflected the cornflower blue of her dress. She walked up and placed a hand on my shoulder as she pointed down into the valley. "There's our new home, see the stone building by the lake?"

"Yes," I said.

"Mac and Lise live on the other side of the hill. We'll see them later in the week and there will be other friends later. We'll never be lonely." She took a few steps forward then stopped and looked at me over her shoulder.

"I can stay," I whispered.

"Yes."

"You'll stay too?"

She reached back and took my hand then kissed me on the mouth, soft and warm. She smelled slightly of cinnamon. "We will be here together," she said. "At the rate we need it, the ship's power will last hundreds of years, and time here, my darling, time here will move at the rate we want it to. We have forever, forever and ever."

"That will be about right," I said, putting my arms around her and kissing her for all I was worth, which was a lot more than it had been yesterday.

When the *Chukar* passed the point of no return without slowing, the cutters from Dis regretfully turned back. There was no chance of stopping the old assault barge before it reached the great dark between the stars. Time became irrelevant to the *Chukar* as she continued to accelerate in the blackness. Gradually she cooled, as the centuries rolled on, her hull headed for absolute zero. But that was only outside. Inside the *Chukar* held light, laughter, and endless warm nights.

The End

Also by Edward McKeown

The Maauro Chronicles

My Outcast State

Against That Time

The Lost

All The Difference

When Fighting Monsters

The Shasti and Fenaday Chronicles

Was Once A Hero

Fearful Symmetry

Points of Departure

Hidden Stars

Sha'Daa Series

Tales of the Apocalypse

Toys

Inked

Pawns

Last Call

Facets

The Lair of the Lesbian Love Goddess Files

On the Case

Other Works

Knight in Charlotte